Praise for Meghan O'Brien

"Meghan O'Brien has given her readers some very steamy scenes in this fast-paced novel. *Thirteen Hours* is definitely a walk on the wild side, which may have you looking twice at those with whom you share an elevator."—*Just About Write*

"Boy, if there was ever fiction that a lesbian needs during a bed death rut or simply in need of some juicing up, *Thirteen Hours* by Meghan O'Brien is the book I'd recommend to my good friends....If you are looking for good ole American instant gratification, simple and not-at all-straight sexy lesbian eroticism, revel in the sexiness that is *Thirteen Hours*."—*Tilted World*

"In *The Three* by Meghan O'Brien, we are treated to first-rate storytelling that features scorching love scenes with three main characters....She hits her stride well in *The Three* with a well-paced plot that never slows. She excels at giving us an astounding tale that is tightly written and extremely sensual. I highly recommend this unique book."—*Just About Write*

By the Author

Infinite Loop

The Three

Thirteen Hours

Battle Scars

Wild

Visit us at www.boldstrokesbooks.com

WILD

by

Meghan O'Brien

2011

WILD
© 2011 By Meghan O'Brien. All Rights Reserved.

ISBN 13: 978-1-60282-227-6

This Trade Paperback Original Is Published By
Bold Strokes Books, Inc.
P.O. Box 249
Valley Falls, NY 12185

First Edition: June 2011

―――――――――――――――――――――――――――――――――――

Credits
Editor: Shelley Thrasher
Production Design: Stacia Seaman
Cover Design by Sheri (graphicartist2020@hotmail.com)

Acknowledgments

First and foremost, I want to thank Shelley Thrasher for another excellent editing experience. It's truly a pleasure to watch my first draft evolve with her guidance. Thanks, of course, to Radclyffe for being both an inspiration and a fantastic source of support. Also to the rest of the BSB crew, who work so hard to make us authors look good—thank you!

I also need to thank my friends Ty Justice, K.E. Lane, and Sandy Lowe for reading rough first drafts and offering feedback. Also, my sister Kathleen for being generally awesome (and because I always acknowledge Kathleen). Last but not least, thanks to my partner Angie for engineering quiet time for me to write—not always easy with a five-year-old in the house.

Dedication

To Angie, always.

CHAPTER ONE

Selene Rhodes hated the full moon. Not just what it did to her after the sun went down, but the way it hijacked her body during the long hours leading up to its appearance in the night sky. How it had her in its grip from the moment she woke up in the morning, skin too tight and nerve endings screaming. The sensations only intensified as the sun arced overhead, bringing not pain but pleasure so intense it nearly crippled her. By the time the escort arrived an hour before sunset, she was so aroused that even the simple brush of fabric against her arm threatened to usher her into mindless release, and that made an already difficult appointment absolutely unbearable. No matter how crazy the full moon made her, fucking wasn't an option, not even with a professional.

Tonight was particularly painful. Not only was it the perigee moon, the biggest one of the year, but she had to train a new escort for the first time in fourteen months. She was proud of the last girl for graduating from medical school, but this change in routine had Selene sick with worry. She had finally settled into some sort of rhythm and hated to start from scratch again, especially while battling horniness that would kill a weaker person.

And because the universe clearly hated her, the agency had sent a redhead. A gorgeous, curvy one who stood on Selene's porch oozing sex and looking like she knew a secret that would make Selene happy for the rest of her life. Selene suppressed a groan at the bolt of pleasure that shot straight down to her toes. Next time she definitely needed to request they send a blonde. This monthly ritual was hard enough as it was.

Gathering all her strength, Selene said, "You're late."

"I'm sorry. Traffic was a nightmare." The escort stepped inside Selene's house with a subtle glance around. "I'm Renee, by the way. Not sure if they told you who they were sending."

"It's nice to meet you, Renee." Selene stayed calm even as she eyed the wall clock. She didn't have much time to explain the routine, but what was done, was done. Now she had to focus on making it through this next part. "I hope you don't mind if we start immediately."

"Not at all." Renee searched Selene's face but betrayed no reaction other than attraction. She was very good at her job. "So you were one of Kelli's clients?"

"For over a year, yes. Really nice girl." Selene hoped she sounded polite and that it wasn't obvious she was struggling to put one foot in front of the other as she led Renee to her spare bedroom. "What did they tell you about this appointment?"

"Only that you like to be dominated. Tied up."

The smell of Renee's shampoo briefly chased away thoughts of the urgency of the situation. It would be so easy to push her up against the wall, to kiss her full lips and slide a hand under her skirt. To take her hard and fast while she still had time. She could smell that Renee wanted it, not just because she was being paid. Selene stopped in front of the guest room door and closed her eyes, exhaling.

Not an option.

"I think I'm going to enjoy tying you up, Selene." Renee's fingers trailed lightly down Selene's arm. "Very much."

Selene pulled away sharply, gritting her teeth as her pussy contracted and a weak orgasm rolled through her body. "Please don't—"

"Did you just…?" Renee's grin reached her eyes. "Wow."

Eager to put some distance between them, Selene opened the door to her guest room. Then she turned to gauge Renee's reaction to the large metal table bolted to the center of the floor. This was the part she hated, when the escort got her first notion that Selene wouldn't be her average client.

"Okay." Renee flashed a seductive smile. She was definitely a professional. No hesitation at all. "Why don't you tell me what you like?"

Selene untied the belt of her robe, letting it slip off her shoulders and fall to the ground. She picked up Renee's quiet inhalation at the sight of her nudity, then the quickening of Renee's heartbeat. Resisting Renee would be easier with her clothes on, but when Selene shifted tonight, she would become very large. The clothes would tear, which would lead to questions tomorrow morning. Naked, she would leave no evidence, nothing to indicate that she was anything other than a garden-variety fetishist.

"It's very simple." Without allowing her gaze to linger on the woman who obviously yearned to give her exactly what she craved, Selene hopped up to sit on the edge of the table. "I want you to secure me with the wrist and ankle cuffs, then tie me down with rope as tight as possible. Tighter than you think you should. Put the keys to the cuffs in your pocket when you're done. Then go home. You'll take my house key with you and lock up when you leave. In the morning you'll come back at eight o'clock and unlock my restraints."

"That's it?" Renee raised a perfectly sculpted eyebrow. "You don't want me to get you off?"

Even the words made Selene want to come. It had been years since she'd been with someone, and she burned to experience that closeness again. But she'd learned a hard lesson the last time she allowed herself to share such intimacy, one she never wanted to forget. Sex wasn't purely physical—at least not for Selene—and she refused to do anything that might cause her to form an attachment to a human. It could only end in heartbreak.

"No." Selene kept her tone as brisk as possible. "It's not about that for me." She pointed to a wad of bills and the house key she'd placed on the end of the table. "Half your fee up front, half when you release me in the morning."

Renee picked up the money. Her throat moved as she thumbed through the bills. "This is practically my entire fee right here."

"I'm willing to pay extra for discretion." Taking a deep breath, Selene lay back and raised her arms above her head. She placed her hands at the corners of the table, then spread her legs, lining her feet up with the ankle cuffs. "And for very, very tight rope."

Renee pocketed the money and the key. Her gaze ran down the length of Selene's body, then up until she met Selene's eyes. Licking her lips, Renee murmured, "You're wet."

That was an understatement. Selene's inner thighs were slick with arousal, and she could only imagine how she must look. "I take pleasure from the loss of control." Selene was so used to spouting the lie, it rolled off her tongue easily. But it still embarrassed her to tell it. "I like knowing I'm helpless in here, dependent on *you* to set me free."

"And what if I get hit by a bus?" Renee laughed, but Selene heard genuine concern behind the question. "Not that I have any plans to get killed tonight, but don't you worry about that?"

"I have an arrangement with your boss." Selene glanced at the door to the room, wishing she could see the evening sky. No windows in here, for her own safety. The sun had to be nearly down by now. They needed to hurry or Renee would get a hell of a lot more than she bargained for. "I'll call her tomorrow after you untie me. If I don't, she'll send someone to do it…and I imagine you'll lose your job."

Renee's eyes hardened slightly, but Selene didn't mean it as a threat. She paid for high-price escorts from a reputable service for a reason: She counted on their dependability and willingness to do what she required without asking questions. And she wanted to put Renee at ease, to convince her that she had no reason to fear leaving her helpless and alone. Renee had to follow her instructions to the letter, for everyone's sake.

"Please," Selene said quietly. "We need to hurry. Do you understand what I require?"

"Yeah." Renee grasped Selene's wrist and fit it inside the metal cuff attached to the corner of the table. This businesslike contact was no less potent than the previous seductive caress, and Selene had to grit her teeth not to react to the pleasure of warm fingers on her skin. "You really want the rope, too? Seems like these cuffs are more than enough to make sure you won't go anywhere."

"I need the rope. Yes." The cuffs alone might not hold her once the full moon rose and tore away the last of her humanity. She possessed a frightening strength on these nights, and tonight—with the perigee moon and the touch of a beautiful redhead lingering on her skin—she would no doubt be nearly impossible to contain. "As tight as you can, remember."

Renee secured the cuffs on her other wrist and her ankles in efficient silence. Then she picked up the rope and gave Selene a wary look. "Okay."

Selene concentrated on her breathing as Renee tentatively wrapped the rope around her upper body, lashing her to the table. "Perfect."

"Like this?" Renee tugged on the binds gently, then began to tie her first knot. "Is this tight enough?"

"Tighter." Renee was too tentative. The last girl hadn't been afraid to practically cut off her circulation, which was what she required. Renee was treating her like a porcelain doll that might break if handled too roughly. "I told you, tighter than you think you should."

Renee cinched the rope down slightly, but not nearly enough. "This will have to be good enough, Selene. I'm afraid you won't be able to breathe otherwise."

Selene shook her head forcefully. "No, that's not enough. You've got to do better."

"I'm sorry."

"I'm paying you for a service, Renee." Selene twisted her neck, watching as Renee tied the knot. "Please do as I ask."

"Listen, I don't care how much you pay me. And don't bother to threaten my job again, either. You're not the one who's liable if something happens to you. You want me to tie you down and leave you for hours, fine. But I'm going to make damn sure you won't suffocate while I'm gone."

Goddamn it. Renee didn't intend to listen to her, and it was far too late to call the agency to ask for a replacement. All Selene could do now was send Renee on her way as quickly as possible and hope for the best. "Fine. At least tie my legs, too. Okay?"

Renee clenched her jaw but did as she was told. She left the rope just as loose around Selene's lower body as it was on her chest, and Selene knew these restraints wouldn't hold her tonight. Not with the pull of the full moon this strong. Her stomach churned, both at what would inevitably happen and how much damage she would surely cause.

"There you are. All set." Renee looked Selene up and down, then sighed. "You're sure you don't want to just…" Her hand landed on Selene's forearm, tickling her bare skin and igniting a surge of lust so fierce it took Selene's breath away.

"No." Selene's voice came out harsher than she intended, but Renee was killing her. And the clock was ticking. "It's time for you to leave. I'll see you tomorrow. Eight o'clock."

Renee blinked and stepped away from the table. "Fine." She walked to the door, glancing back with a strange expression before stepping out of the room. "I'll be here."

Selene nodded, trying to conceal her tears of frustration. Whether she would also be here tomorrow morning was doubtful. She closed her eyes and listened for the sound of the front door. Only when she heard Renee leave the house did she allow her tears to fall.

She was so tired of this. Tired of relying on strangers who could never understand the stakes of the sex game she hired them to play. Tired of worrying that the ropes were too loose or that she would wrench the metal cuffs free from yet another solid steel table. Tired of being alone in the world with her terrible secret, of fearing that she might be capable of doing something truly monstrous.

Tired of the goddamn moon.

CHAPTER TWO

Selene startled awake, opening her eyes to stare at gray sky filtered through dark branches. A large rock dug into the bare skin of her back, and her whole naked body ached. Turning her head to the side, she exhaled shakily as she took in the grass and trees surrounding her. Two years without incident, and now here she was, waking up once again without any idea where she was or what she'd done the night before.

Stomach turning, Selene fought not to vomit. She closed her eyes and tried to filter through the meaningless jumble of memories that flitted through her mind. There was Renee, of course, and the loose rope. How scared she had been at the moment of transformation, and how quickly the fear dissipated as nature took over and conscious thought slipped away. But as for her night on the prowl, she had only flashes: the moon, dark city streets, and the trees her beast-self always sought out. She knew only that she was currently in Golden Gate Park, unless she had run very far indeed.

Selene steeled herself, then sat up, checking her body for evidence of the night's activities. Dirt and bits of leaves were stuck to her skin and in her hair, but she didn't detect any blood. At least not much. Selene studied a smear of crimson near her elbow. It was probably her own, though she couldn't find the source. That wasn't surprising—only a very recent wound would still be open. Along with the ability to shift form, Selene was capable of rapidly accelerated healing.

When her adoptive parents had found her the morning after her first uncontrolled shift, sleeping near the carcasses of the dead family sheep, Selene had been covered in blood. The sweet, pungent smell, so difficult to wash off her skin, stank like the end of childhood, like the severing of human ties. Since that day, her greatest fear was waking up with that scent in her nose again. That's what her whole routine was about, the charade she put on with call girls. She never wanted to harm another living thing. The absence of blood now, after a night out in the city, made her hope that her beast-self knew her human heart and had simply run free among the trees, hurting no one.

"Miss?"

Selene jolted at the sound of a deep male voice. Heart racing, she drew her knees to her chest, startled to see a dark-skinned man in a T-shirt and sweatpants standing on a walking path not fifteen feet away. Her senses were still heightened beyond normal, so he shouldn't have been able to surprise her like that.

The man held up his hands. "I'm sorry. I didn't mean to scare you. Are you okay?" He shifted his weight nervously, clearly uncertain about how to interact with a dirty, naked woman in public. Judging from the light sheen of sweat on his forehead, he was in the middle of a run. He kept his eyes locked on her face. "You look like you're in some trouble. May I help?"

"No, I'm fine." Selene grimaced at the foreign sound of her voice inside her head. It was always like this the morning after. She felt a strange disconnect with the body that had so recently betrayed her, not to mention the mind that withheld the details of what she'd just been through. "I'm okay."

"Do you...know where your clothes are?"

Selene exhaled, then shook her head. She knew exactly what the man thought had happened to her and realized that she wasn't likely to convince him otherwise. She didn't know what she would rather have him believe. "No. I'm not sure."

The man hesitated, then said, "I'm going to take off my shirt now. But I am *not* going to hurt you. I just want to give you something to wear, okay?"

Selene nodded, shamed by the kind gesture. Here this man thought she was a victim of assault, when in reality she'd been the baddest monster stalking the park last night. "Thank you."

Stepping closer, the man held out his shirt and scanned her body. He was obviously trying to be subtle, but she curled in on herself slightly. She couldn't imagine he would see anything that might give away her true nature, but the scrutiny made her feel vulnerable and unsettled.

"Do you know who did this to you?" The man dropped the shirt next to her, then backed away, averting his eyes as she pulled it over her head. He folded his arms over his bare chest, as though shielding her from the sight of his skin. "We need to call the police."

"No!" The ferocity of her refusal caught Selene off guard, so she wasn't surprised when the man flinched, too. While she appreciated his genuine concern, she certainly didn't want the police to start asking questions about why she had woken up naked in the park. "Please don't. I don't want to talk to the police."

"But they need to find the guy who…hurt you."

To get him to back off, she had to appeal to his obvious good nature. He clearly didn't want to upset her, so she let her emotion come to the front. Standing up, she tugged down the hem of his shirt, thankful that it covered the top of her thighs. "Please. After the night I just had…I just want to go home. I'll be fine there."

"But—"

"It's my decision." Selene played up the genuine guilt she felt at her deception, knowing he would interpret it as embarrassment or shame. "Please."

The man glanced helplessly up and down the path before nodding reluctantly. "Okay. It's your decision. But at least let me make sure you get there all right."

"That won't be necessary. Really."

He sighed and shook his head. Gripping the back of his neck, he asked, "You always this stubborn?"

"Most of the time." Selene smiled. It was ridiculous to try to convince him that she was okay, but she needed him to believe she could at least make her own way home. She didn't want him to know any more about her than he already did. It was bad enough that he'd seen her like this. "Listen, I live near the park. I promise I can get there myself, no problem."

The way he stared at her made Selene worry that he was growing suspicious of her behavior. After all, if she wasn't a victim of something terrible, if she really was all right, why would she be out here like this so early in the morning? But then his eyes softened and he dropped his hands to the waistband of his sweatpants. "Let me at least give you these."

Selene shook her head. She was lying to a man who would literally give her his pants. This was a new low. "No. That's okay."

"I've got running shorts on underneath." The man raised an eyebrow. "Look, you want me to let you go alone, I get it. But I can't in good conscience leave you to wander through the park without panties on. I just can't. So either take the sweats or allow me to walk you home. Your choice."

It wasn't worth arguing over. And the longer Selene stayed in the park, the greater the chance someone else would see her there. She had no idea what kind of devastation she'd left in her wake, and she didn't want to be connected in any way with whatever her beast-self had done.

"Okay," Selene said. "I'll wear them."

The man blinked. "Yeah?" At her nod, he slowly pulled them off.

Selene took them quickly, tugging them on, then cinching the waist tight. "I hate to take your clothes."

"I'll be fine. My car isn't far from here."

"Okay, then." Selene glanced behind her at a stand of trees. She had no idea where in the park she was at the moment, but she didn't want her Good Samaritan to know that. As soon as she was able to get her head on straight, she'd figure it out. "Thank you."

"You're welcome." The man laced his hands in front of his shorts, glancing away. "Take care of yourself, okay? Think about calling the police."

"I will." Selene hesitated, then said, "Is there some way I can return these clothes to you?"

"Don't worry about it. Just…what's your name?"

"Michelle." Selene hated to lie, but she couldn't let him know even that much about her identity.

"I'm Clarence. Just be safe. Okay, Michelle?"

Selene nodded. "Okay."

Clarence stared at her a moment more, then gestured to his left. "So I'll just be going…"

"Thank you. Again."

With a nod, Clarence jogged down the path. Selene exhaled as she watched him go. She appreciated the clothing—it would be harder to avoid drawing attention if she were naked. Worst-case scenario, she could have shifted into a dog or even a bird for the journey home. But it was better she didn't have to. Shifting right after the full moon took a lot out of her. And doing so in public, even when she sensed she was alone, meant risking exposure. She rarely shifted these days, too concerned about keeping her abilities a secret to enjoy using them.

Home. Selene winced and looked at the sky. The morning was gray and overcast, and she couldn't see the sun through the clouds to know what time it was. Had Renee already come back to her house to find her bonds broken, the room destroyed? She had to get back there quickly if it was possible Renee hadn't discovered the evidence yet. If she could meet Renee at the door and concoct some story to explain why she was out of her restraints, it would be far better than letting Renee see the destruction she'd left behind.

Selene ran onto the walking path and set off in the opposite direction of Clarence. She would be able to orient herself once she had the presence of mind to trust her senses, but in the meantime, she wanted to put some distance between them. Hopefully she'd be able to avoid seeing anyone else.

Only thirty feet down the path, Selene was hit by the sickening smell of fresh blood. It stopped her mid-step, and, for a moment, she felt like vomiting. That smell—she knew exactly what it meant. It was the same one that had covered her when she was sixteen and had slaughtered those sheep. That heady, pungent scent left no doubt that she'd killed again.

The thought sickened her. But she didn't know what it meant yet. Perhaps she'd torn open a squirrel as a meal—not acceptable, for sure, but not nearly as horrible as killing a human being. Selene scanned the trees and bushes surrounding her, but didn't see anything out of the ordinary. She stepped off the path, letting her nose lead her to the source of that terrifying scent.

She would have given anything not to follow this trail. But her feet moved of their own accord, even as she dreaded what she might find. She couldn't run away. She was most likely responsible for whatever was bleeding. If it was still alive, she couldn't just leave it to suffer.

As a human, Selene had senses much more acute than those of a normal person. She preferred tracking as a dog but could easily follow a scent trail even in her natural form, especially when she had such an overpowering odor to work with. Selene brought a hand to her nose as the smell strengthened, then skidded to a stop when she saw the body lying at the base of a large eucalyptus tree.

At first she saw only the blood. Not the age or gender of the corpse, or even the nature of the injuries. Just blood, soaking into the ground, smeared over every bit of skin visible. Selene gagged, then forced herself to take a breath and look closer. Maybe the person was still alive and needed help.

It was a woman. In her thirties, maybe, with dark skin and hair, possibly Latina. Definitely beyond help, she stared with sightless eyes up at the sky. Was the last thing they saw an inexplicably enormous creature, fierce and unrelenting, under the full moon?

Selene stumbled backward, losing her balance and falling on her ass. Numb, she simply sat where she landed. For all these years this had been her greatest fear. If killing a couple of sheep had made her a monster, she had no idea what she was now. A murderer. A demon. Selene covered her face with her hands and moaned quietly. Even as her beast-self, could she really have murdered this woman?

She didn't know enough about how an animal attack would look to say whether she was responsible. Multiple deep slices covered the woman's body, but it was hard for Selene to determine whether her teeth or her claws could have made them. The sheep had looked torn apart in a way this woman didn't, almost as though whatever killed her had used more precise instruments of death.

Who was she kidding? She stood with effort, weaving on shaky legs. What were the chances that someone else had killed this woman when Selene had woken up the morning after a full moon not even three hundred yards from her body? It seemed naïve to hope that she wasn't the culprit. Then again, with this much blood, why wasn't she covered in the stuff?

No matter what had really happened, she had to call the police. With that thought, her feet were already moving, walking her back to the path like she was on autopilot. Calling the police was the right thing to do. Turning herself in might also be right, but she wasn't ready to take that step yet. Not before she was absolutely certain of her own guilt. She'd spent too long in hiding to throw everything away only on probability, no matter how strong it was.

As Selene drew closer to the sound of early morning traffic, she finally recognized where she was. Maybe a half mile down the road from her house, which did indeed border Golden Gate Park—but on the other side. She sighed. This would be a long walk without shoes. It would be so much easier as a cat or, better yet, a bird.

Not having a watch, she could only guess how long it took her to hurry back to her house. It felt like hours but was probably only twenty minutes. She was out of breath when she reached her front door, but she was relieved to see it still in one piece, and locked.

Obviously she'd escaped from her spare room somehow, but not out the front. Thank the universe for small favors. Did her human concerns guide her beast-self? As much as she feared terrible destruction, those few times she did get loose she'd caused only minor damage. Almost as though her beast-self knew to be cautious.

Selene walked to the side of her house. A windowsill jammed at an awkward angle showed that she'd broken a pane and wrenched the window open. Taking a quick look around, she pulled over a garbage can and climbed up, boosting herself up and easing inside.

Now in her bathroom, she surveyed the minor mess—a towel lying on the floor, toothbrush and facial wash in the sink, knocked off the counter. She'd been in a hurry, but at least she hadn't trashed the place. She quickly tidied up, then walked to the spare room, steeling herself.

The wooden door was ripped off the hinges, no surprise. A steel door would have been better at keeping her in, but she couldn't afford that type of modification when paying San Francisco prices, especially when it probably wouldn't have held her, either. Her steel table was still bolted to the floor, but she had torn the cuffs from its surface and thrown them into a corner. The ineffectual rope lay scattered in pieces across the floor. One wall had a hole she'd need to patch.

"Damn it," Selene muttered. To her horror, tears welled in her eyes. Not for her table or door or window, but for the poor dead woman in the park, and for herself.

She gave herself exactly ten seconds to experience the full scope of her grief and self-pity, then forced the tears back. Sniffling, she walked to her closet and withdrew a wad of bills. The rest of Renee's payment. No matter how the evening had turned out, it wasn't Renee's fault. She hadn't understood the rules of the game they'd played, let alone the stakes. Selene was solely responsible for the breach.

She went to the kitchen and checked the clock—only six thirty. Renee wasn't due for another hour and a half. That gave Selene time to clean up a little, then do the thing that most weighed on her mind. She had to call the police. Not with a confession, not yet. With a tip. Once the police found the body and examined the crime scene, maybe they would allow the media to provide some details about what had happened, especially whether it was an animal attack. Maybe by then she would know how to move forward if she really had done the unthinkable.

If she made the call from the pay phone at the edge of the park, nobody would be able to trace it to her. She put on her shoes, propped the ruined door to her spare room against the splintered frame, and headed out.

CHAPTER THREE

When the man in the ski mask tore out of the brush to her left, Dr. Eve Thomas truly regretted not listening to her ex-girlfriend about the dangers of Golden Gate Park at sunrise. Jac had never liked Eve's early morning strolls when they were together, so Eve made them a daily ritual after they broke up. As the man intercepted her on the walking path, drawing back his fist with hatred in his eyes, Eve wished she hadn't felt the need to flaunt her newfound freedom. Even with pepper spray in her pocket, she was outmatched.

Eve was reaching for the canister when the man's fist crashed into her nose. The blow tore the glasses from her face, stealing her vision, but she didn't have time to panic before a second punch knocked her off her feet. Her world went into slow motion, up until the moment her back hit the pavement. Then everything sped up: The man grabbed a fistful of her hair and dragged her toward the trees, and Eve's one recurring thought was that Jac would be so upset about what would probably happen.

Once they were out of sight of the path, the man threw her onto the ground. Then he was on top of her, pressing the sharp edge of a knife to her throat. "Do I need to use this?"

Eve shook her head and swallowed. He had her arms pinned beneath his bulk, and she would never reach the pepper spray before he sliced her jugular. Her best bet for getting through this alive was to cooperate.

She waited for the inevitable assault to begin. But he stayed still, staring at her with piercing blue eyes that sent sick dread rushing through her. She yearned to turn her face away, but didn't want to move. Not with that cold blade against her neck. Forced to look back up at him, Eve studied what she could make out of his appearance, already thinking about the statement she would give the police if she survived. He was Caucasian, she could see that much. Taller than her, and heavier.

"I can do anything I want." His tone made it clear that he wasn't just talking about here and now, but in general. The way he looked at her, like she was less than an animal, made her certain that he wouldn't hesitate to end her life. "Understand?"

Eve's stomach turned over. "Take my purse. Please let me go." She doubted she could talk him out of whatever he had planned, but she couldn't think of anything else to do. If nothing else, she would buy some time, maybe give someone a chance to discover them and intervene. It had to be almost seven o'clock by now, so foot traffic was bound to increase. She just had to keep him talking.

"I don't want your goddamn purse." The knife left her neck and his free hand took its place. He dug his thumb into the center of her throat, restricting her breathing and sending bright pinpricks of agony to her brain. Just when her vision began to dim, the pressure eased and she gasped in relief. "I can do *anything*. Nobody will stop me."

Eyes burning, Eve whispered, "I have money. And an iPod."

"I don't want your iPod." The man blinked, then bent so close she could feel his breath through the black cotton mask. "I can fuck you. Kill you." He eased back, meeting her gaze again. "Make you cry."

Terror invaded the pit of Eve's stomach and squeezed painfully, loosening a wave of intense nausea. She'd never felt this before, this bone-deep fear: of pain, humiliation, maybe even her own end. She wanted to scream, but the fear held her back. Possibly no one would hear. And she would surely make him angry. The corners of his eyes crinkled. He looked pleased.

"Scared?" He dragged the knife over the center of her chest, snagging her shirt on its tip. Jerking the blade upward, he sliced through the thin material like it was nothing. Eve yelped, then whimpered when his hand shot up and caught her across the face. "Shut up."

Eve turned her head to the side and closed her eyes. Tears threatened to fall, but she refused to give him the satisfaction of seeing her cry. He grasped the front of her shirt and widened the tear he'd made with the knife. She waited for him to maul her breasts, then stiffened when instead the wicked edge of the blade traced a path from her cloth-covered nipple to the bare skin that rose above the cup of her bra.

The anticipation was the worst part. Imagining all the things he could do but not knowing which one would be her fate. He could strip her naked, rape her. Or maybe he got off on slow pain and would cut her instead. What if he skipped the pleasantries and just plunged the knife deep into her heart?

A scream rattled at the back of Eve's throat, the sound of pure, total terror, desperate to escape. Give it voice, and the man would probably just finish her quickly. Even that thought didn't quell her urge to call out. How else to deal with his looming menace, with her sudden, sick certainty of pain, then death?

"Look at me." The man drew the point of the knife over her clavicle, then placed the edge against her throat. "Open your eyes and look at me."

She did.

"This is easy for me." He ran the knife down between her breasts. His hand was steady, but a trace of uncertainty flickered in his eyes. "All I have to do is push the knife in and you're dead."

Eve's vision blurred as the tears she had been holding back came to the front. "Please don't."

The man froze on top of her, halting the motion of his knife. Eve held her breath, waiting to feel the sting of her skin being sliced open. To her surprise, he raised his head and looked at something just past Eve's line of sight. She yearned to see what had caught his attention, but stayed still, too scared to move.

A deep, rumbling growl cut through the noise of Eve's pulse pounding in her ears. Her attacker's eyes bulged, then she exhaled as he pulled his knife away from her chest. Another growl, like nothing Eve had ever heard, not up close, not in real life. Taking a deep breath, Eve craned her neck, then gasped at the animal standing not five feet away.

Without her glasses, she could make out only an indistinct gray beast, almost certainly a canid, but not a dog. It looked like a wolf, no matter how improbable that would be in the middle of San Francisco.

The beast snarled, drawing back its lips to reveal wicked teeth. Eve's heart pumped into overdrive. She had no idea how to react. A wolf was fierce, wild, and out of place in Golden Gate Park. In some ways it was just as dangerous as the masked man, yet its presence had stopped the assault.

"Keep still." The man shifted on top of her, clearly weighing his next move. "Don't provoke it."

The wolf stepped closer, its watchful eyes fixed on her attacker, challenging him. Eve held her breath, as frightened of being mauled as she was of getting raped and murdered. But the wolf never looked at her. It focused solely on the man in the ski mask, turning predator into prey.

With a vicious snarl, the wolf leapt onto the man, knocking him to the ground at Eve's side. As soon his weight left her body, she could breathe again. Brain finally engaged, she decided to run. She struggled to her feet as man and wolf wrestled for dominance beside her. Searing pain shot through her ankle as soon as she stepped down onto it. Panicking, she stumbled, then hit the ground hard.

Eve watched helplessly as the wolf drew back and sank its teeth into the man's arm. He yelped in incoherent rage, slashing out at the wolf. His knife sliced through the air in a frantic arc, but his aim was off and the wolf danced away unharmed.

The wolf took another step backward, almost as though giving the man a chance to escape. He took it. With a quick, angry noise, the man in the ski mask broke into a stumbling run, disappearing into the trees and out of Eve's range of vision. She squinted after him, then turned her attention to her new problem. The wolf.

To her surprise, it was sitting in front of her, staring at her with quiet intensity. Startled, she fumbled in her pocket and withdrew the canister of pepper spray. "Stay back." Her voice wavered, hardly a surprise when she was about to burst into tears. She raised her arm and aimed. "Go away!"

The wolf tilted its head, then trotted off as though obeying her command. Eve exhaled as it retreated. When she could no longer pick out the wolf's shape from among the trees, she finally dared to move. Slowly, this time, Eve struggled to her feet. Careful to keep weight off her ankle, she could finally stand unsupported, but pulling herself together was a far more difficult task.

Caught between logic and the primitive, emotional need to fall apart completely, she didn't know what to do next. She desperately wanted to run away from this place as fast as her injured ankle would carry her, but she had to find her purse with her cell phone inside so she could call for help. Without her glasses, she wouldn't be able to drive.

She decided to give herself one minute to find her purse. More than sixty seconds, to hell with it. She wasn't about to wait around so the man or the wolf could return.

Limping around the clearing, she conducted a frantic search before concluding that he must have taken it when he ran. That meant he had all her most important stuff: her wallet, her identification card for work, car keys, the contact list in her smartphone, even her spare tampon. Everything.

Eve fought back despair as she turned in the direction of the walking path. She couldn't think about it now. She had to keep moving, had to find help.

Taking slow, cautious steps through the brush, she tried not to stumble on unseen obstacles. She hadn't made it very far before the unmistakable sound of someone approaching made her break into a clumsy run, heart in her throat.

"Wait!"

Eve stopped immediately at the sound of a female voice. Turning, she saw a woman emerge from behind a tree to her left. At the sight of another person, someone who presumably didn't want to harm her, Eve put her hand on the trunk of a eucalyptus to steady her trembling legs.

"You look like you need some help." The woman stepped closer, holding up her hands as though pleading with Eve not to flee. "I won't hurt you."

Eve couldn't place the dark-haired woman's accent, but her low, soothing tone immediately lulled Eve into tentative safety. Swallowing, Eve said, "We have to get out of here. Before he comes back." Her voice sounded harsh to her own ears. She could only imagine how she must look, terrified, blood trickling down her face. "The man who attacked me."

The woman narrowed the distance between them. Quite beautiful, with worried green eyes, she offered Eve her hand. "Let's go, then."

Eve took the woman's hand, grateful for the warm, human connection. Though it loosened her control on her emotions, it also kept her tethered securely in the now. She was safe. "I lost my glasses when he punched me. I can't see without them."

"Then we'd better find them." The woman gave her fingers a gentle squeeze. "I'm Selene."

"Eve."

"Eve, where were you when he hit you?"

"On the path." She glanced over her shoulder as they emerged from the trees, half expecting to see him. "He came out of nowhere. I didn't have time to react."

"That must have been terrifying."

"I've never been so scared in my life." Eve's throat ached as she remembered being held down by the neck. "I thought he was going to kill me."

"But he didn't."

"No." Eve took a deep breath as they approached the path. "I know it sounds crazy, but a wolf…stopped him, chased him away."

"A wolf?" Selene didn't do a very good job of hiding her skepticism. "I didn't see anything like that. Just…you."

"It ran off before you found me. And it looked like a wolf, but I don't know. Maybe someone in the city is keeping one illegally."

"What matters is that you're safe." Selene tightened her fingers on Eve's as they approached the path, urging her to stop. "There they are." Selene knelt and picked up two objects. Rising, she held them out. One hand cradled Eve's damaged frames, the other, a single lens. "Looks like the lens popped out. We can fix that. The other one's scratched, so you'll need to have it replaced."

At the sight of her broken glasses, Eve heaved a sigh. Severely nearsighted since childhood, she'd grown up haunted by the fear of being unable to see. Becoming an adult hadn't eased that phobia. Simply knocking her glasses behind the nightstand in the morning could cause mild panic. Seeing them in pieces, especially after having just experienced excruciating vulnerability, was more than enough to shatter her control.

Eve's legs gave out, and she would have hit the ground if Selene's reflexes weren't lightning fast. At once, Selene held her in strong arms, supporting her as though she weighed nothing.

"Shh," Selene murmured, cradling her. "It's all right, I've got you. He can't hurt you now."

"We should go." Even though she meant it, Eve buried her face in Selene's neck and returned the embrace. The coldly rational part of her brain, the one she was used to relying on, recoiled in horror at the way she sought comfort from a stranger. But her lizard brain, still reeling from the threat of brutal slaughter, needed Selene like her lungs needed air. "He could come back."

"He won't," Selene murmured. Her hand stroked Eve's hair. "It's okay. Give yourself a minute. Then we can walk."

Eve allowed herself exactly five more seconds of her meltdown, then stepped back and wiped away her tears. "I'm parked on Thirtieth Avenue, not too far from here. If you could help me to my car…"

"Can you drive without your glasses?"

"No." Eve's lip trembled when she remembered that she didn't have her car keys anyway. "And I think he took my purse. So I guess I'm not going anywhere. Maybe you have a cell phone I could use?"

Selene fingered a lock of Eve's hair, tucking it behind her ear. "Come to my apartment. You can use my phone, and I'll do what I can to repair your glasses."

"Thank you," Eve said. She wasn't about to refuse the offer. Already her mind raced with things she needed to do: call Jac, order new car keys, cancel her credit cards, change the lock on her apartment. Amazing how five minutes in the park had upset the ordered balance of her life. "I'd like to clean up my face, too."

"Of course." Selene placed a gentle hand on Eve's arm. "May I lead you?"

Eve nodded and hooked her arm into Selene's. Gritting her teeth, she tried to match Selene's slow pace, determined not to show her pain. "Thank you, Selene. Really."

"You would do the same for me." Selene glanced at her and smiled. "I can tell."

Eve surprised herself by returning the smile. "Let's hope I never have to."

Selene led them to the edge of the park, where Eve was both relieved and embarrassed to see the moderate traffic on Fulton Street. Though the presence of so many people reassured her, she faltered as a powerful wave of self-consciousness rolled over her. She used one hand to pull the two halves of her shirt closed, covering the bra she only now realized was showing.

"It's okay," Selene said, pulling her closer. Eve felt a surge of unexpected strength from the contact and leaned into Selene hoping for more. "My place is just a block away."

Nodding, Eve held her head as high as she could as they walked down the sidewalk. The few people they passed stared at her in concern, but nobody said anything. Eve was almost glad not to be wearing her glasses, so she wouldn't have to see the questions in their eyes.

"Here we are." Stopping in front of a light blue house, Selene jogged up the short flight of steps and pushed open the front door. "Home sweet home."

"Do you usually leave your door unlocked?" Eve walked inside carefully, wishing she still had Selene at her side. "If nothing else, I hope you'll reconsider that after this morning."

Selene gave a nervous nod. "I had only just stepped out for a moment. Or that was the plan, anyway."

Eve limped out of the foyer into a hallway and glanced around. Selene strode past her, to a room with a door propped within its open entryway. She seemed embarrassed by the state of her apartment, and Eve inhaled sharply as a pang of shame hit her squarely in the stomach. The emotion was so intense it seemed almost foreign, as though it had been forced upon her.

It disoriented her so completely that for a moment she didn't know herself. Was this post-attack Eve, full of volatile emotion, lacking rationality? She hoped not. She normally clung to her sense of order and reason, her controlled emotions, so she could excel at her job. Studying dead people to help catch their killers was hardly a career for someone who couldn't detach.

"Excuse the mess." Selene placed the door in the frame, blocking Eve's view of the room. "I'm in the middle of some home repairs."

Eve managed an uneasy shrug. "I hate to intrude."

"Not at all." Selene walked to the door across the hall and pushed it open. "Here's the bathroom. Take your time." She moved aside as Eve approached. "I'll go get you a shirt and be right back."

"Thank you." Eve paused in the doorway, not particularly wanting to be separated from Selene. It was silly, but her presence made Eve feel less afraid. She was nervous what would happen once Selene was out of sight. "You're a lifesaver. Literally."

Selene's face reddened. "All I did was walk you home."

"It's more than that." Eve paused, unsure how to describe what Selene was doing for her. Though she didn't normally believe in such things, she felt an instant connection to Selene and was sure it was the only thing allowing her to function right now. "I don't know what I would've done if you hadn't found me."

Selene hesitated, then touched Eve's hand gently. "I'm glad I did."

Warm arousal, a welcome stranger that Eve hadn't heard from in months, inexplicably rushed through her and set her heart pounding. Hand shaking, she drew away from Selene and backed into the bathroom. "Me, too."

"I'll be right back." To Eve's relief, Selene betrayed no sign that she'd recognized Eve's reaction for what it was. "You'll be okay?"

Eve nodded, then shut the bathroom door. Alone inside, she fell back against the wall and closed her eyes. That was totally unlike her. She usually didn't feel instant attraction, especially after what she'd just been through. What was it about Selene that inspired such uncharacteristic behavior?

Whatever it was, Eve hoped she could make it out of Selene's apartment without making a fool of herself. Straightening, she walked stiffly to the sink and steeled herself for her first look in the mirror. Determined to assess the damage as unemotionally as possible, she still had to stifle a gasp at the sight of her face.

A small, bloody cut marred her forehead, and the skin around her eye was swollen and angry red. By tomorrow she'd have an ugly shiner. A trail of dried blood from her nose painted her upper lip reddish brown. Bits of leaves and twigs were tangled in her hair. None of that even hinted at the damage she felt inside. She wouldn't take any more early morning walks in Golden Gate Park.

Suppressing the urge to fall into self-pity, she turned on the faucet and began to gingerly scrub away the dirt and blood. Taming her hair was a bigger challenge, but she did her best. It would be easier to put on a brave face about going to work if she didn't look like she'd just been on the losing end of a brawl. And she was definitely still going, just as soon as she picked up a new pair of glasses. She had to perform an autopsy this morning, not to mention the mountain of case-related paperwork waiting for her.

Going to work was about more than just a sense of duty, of course. In a perfect world she'd run home and lick her wounds, happy not to face anyone. Given that they had an open homicide case, Jac would almost certainly come in to the medical examiner's office today. Eve couldn't imagine seeing her like this. But in a perfect world, the man who'd attacked her wouldn't have her driver's license and the keys to her apartment. She couldn't even think about going home until she called a locksmith.

It wasn't entirely about fear of being in her apartment, though. Eve needed to go perform that autopsy to prove that she hadn't lost the essence of who she was, that the man in the park hadn't stolen it from her. She needed to reassure herself that she could still handle violence and death in her professional life even after her terrifying personal encounter with it. That he could have damaged her in that way hurt far more than any physical wound he had inflicted. Her work was her life.

A knock on the door startled her so badly she gasped out loud.

Heart racing, she gripped the sides of the sink and exhaled. Calm down, she chanted in time with her breathing. Just calm down.

"It's only me, Eve. I have your glasses and a shirt." The sound of Selene's apologetic voice instantly soothed her nerves. "I didn't mean to scare you."

Checking herself in the mirror one last time, Eve opened the bathroom door. "Not your fault."

Selene stood awkwardly with Eve's glasses in one hand and a green shirt in the other. "I thought you'd probably want your glasses as soon as I could get them to you."

"You were right." Eve took them from Selene, gratitude overwhelming her. Regaining her vision was the first step to returning to herself. Being able to see would ground her. "Thank you so much."

"The frames are a little bent, and one of the lenses has a bad scratch. But it's better than nothing, I'm sure." Selene shifted her weight anxiously. "You clean up really well, by the way."

Eve pushed back another strange twinge of arousal as she settled her glasses on her nose. Then she lost the battle with her hormones completely. Blurry, Selene had been beautiful. In sharp focus, she was stunning. Eve had seen her brand of dark, exotic beauty only in magazines, and even then, it had been nowhere as extraordinary as what was now standing right in front of her.

Unable to speak, Eve fumbled with the front of her shirt, pulling it closed. Her attraction to Selene made her feel powerfully self-conscious, almost silly. After not having been enough to keep Jac interested, entertaining the notion of being with a woman who looked like Selene was positively delusional.

"I hope I didn't embarrass you," Selene said quietly.

Eve shook her head, not trusting herself to speak.

"Can I get you anything else?"

Eve shook her head again. "I'll return your shirt as soon as I can. I promise."

"No worries." Selene arched an eyebrow. "I have more."

Incredibly, Selene's good humor put Eve at ease. She loosened her grip on her torn shirt and took the one Selene offered. "I'll still return it."

"I'd like that."

Eve swallowed. If she didn't know better, she'd think Selene was flirting. But that wasn't possible, was it? "If it's all right, I'll just leave my shirt in your trash. I…don't want it anymore."

"Of course. I get it." Selene's gaze wandered down to Eve's chest, but before Eve could feel bashful, Selene's eyes widened. "He cut you."

Eve looked down, allowing the two sides of her shirt to gap open. For the first time she saw what had caught Selene's attention: a small slice along the curve of her breast where it rose above the cup of her bra. A thin line of blood had been raised, the cut so small and shallow she hadn't even noticed him make it. Feeling as though she had a rock in her throat, Eve struggled to breathe. "Oh."

"I should have been there sooner." The guilt in Selene's voice was palpable, far out of proportion with any reasonable sense of responsibility. "I wish I'd known sooner."

"You can't blame yourself," Eve said. For some reason, this one minor injury shook her more than all the other cuts and bruises combined. "I was the idiot who decided to walk alone in Golden Gate Park at sunrise."

Selene pulled Eve into a tight hug that should have made her claustrophobic. For the second time that morning, her body was trapped against a stranger's. But discomfort was the last thing she felt about the subtle, luscious joy of being in Selene's arms.

"You're not an idiot. What happened wasn't your fault." Selene placed her hand against the center of Eve's back. "He shouldn't have done that."

It was true. It was exactly what Eve would tell the victim of a violent crime, regardless of the circumstances. But that didn't make it any easier to believe. "I know better than to blame myself. I've helped investigate dozens of homicides, and not once did I ever think someone deserved to be victimized. It's different when it's me, I guess."

Selene pulled back from their embrace. "You work for the police?"

Eve wasn't entirely surprised to see a slight reticence in Selene's eyes. Women rarely met her choice of profession with enthusiasm. "I'm a forensic pathologist for the medical examiner's office. I deal with a lot of murders and accidental deaths." She stopped there, not about to tell Selene about her minor celebrity within the forensic world, the result of having helped identify one of the most twisted serial killers San Francisco had ever seen. That tidbit would almost certainly alienate her from a woman she wanted to get to know.

"That's fascinating," Selene said. She appeared interested, but Eve could feel her unease. "Do you enjoy your work?"

"I do." Blushing, Eve stepped backward into the bathroom. "I should change. And if I could use your phone to call the office and let them know I'll be late…"

"You're going to work?" Selene searched her eyes. "Maybe you should go home and get some rest."

Eve shook her head. "I can't. He has my purse, my keys…" At Selene's look of alarm, Eve said, "I'll call a locksmith from the office. And I'll tell the police what happened. It'll be fine." She wasn't sure she believed that, but saying it helped. Worry remained etched across Selene's face.

"I…have an appointment in about a half hour. Or else I'd offer to let you stay here—"

"Oh, no." Eve laughed nervously. It was clear the offer was sincere, but Eve couldn't help feeling that she should leave. Whatever drew her to Selene was like a drug, and she already worried about the withdrawal. Eve didn't want to depend on Selene for comfort, because she would be left with no resources of her own when Selene was inevitably gone. "I need to get to work. Corpses to examine, paperwork to fill out."

Selene nodded politely, and a sick feeling of disgust flared in Eve, then quickly vanished. Another foreign, fleeting emotion, so unlike anything Eve had ever felt before. It was enough to make her feel crazy and, even worse, illogical.

"Will you call me tonight and let me know that you're okay?" Selene handed her a cell phone. "That's all I ask."

Eve's face heated as she took the phone. "Sure."

"You calling a cab?" Selene looked down at her feet. "I wish I could give you a ride, but with my appointment—"

"You've done more than enough for me," Eve said. Tentatively, she placed her hand on Selene's arm. The simple touch sent desire shooting through her body to pool between her legs. Shocked, she pulled back. "Really. Thank you. A cab is a good idea."

Selene lifted her gaze and stared, then stepped back. "I'll let you change. And make your call."

Shaken by the way her body and thoughts no longer seemed under her control, Eve nodded and quickly shut the bathroom door. She tossed Selene's shirt on the counter, then shrugged out of her torn top. Taking a deep breath, she looked into the mirror. The pathetic sight of herself, scared and half-naked and bleeding, made her finally break down and cry.

CHAPTER FOUR

Heart racing, Selene turned from the bathroom and tried to ignore the pain, sorrow, and lingering desire emanating from behind the closed door. She had always been sensitive to human emotion, but never had she experienced such a deep empathetic connection with anyone. Not even her first love, Carla. Something about Eve literally called to Selene, a force that had almost certainly spared Eve from a terrible fate.

Selene had first received a powerful wave of fear. She'd just hung up the pay phone after leaving an anonymous tip about the body in the park, and the transmission had knocked her back a step when terror seized her gut. For a moment she'd worried she was finally losing it. The years of keeping secrets, of worrying about what her beast-self was capable of doing, were crashing down around her. Right in the midst of a moon-hangover. In public. As she tried to catch her breath against the rising panic, she concentrated on staying in control and in human form. Strong emotion had once triggered her to shift, a terrifying moment she never wanted to repeat.

Then her perception of the fear had changed. Though Selene experienced it with every bit of her self, she wasn't the source. The source, she realized, was back in Golden Gate Park. And Selene had to go to her. She had no choice.

As she had sprinted into the park, tracking that fear with an accuracy she never doubted, she realized if someone had discovered that dead body, that might cause her to feel this intense terror. However, it should have ignited a brief flare-up, not the sustained, soul-wrenching horror that rolled through her in waves. It was, however, possible that the woman she'd murdered had been found. Maybe it wasn't a good idea to run in to help.

The possibility hadn't stopped her. She needed to find the source of the fear. Nothing else mattered. Knowing she was drawing close, she had slowed long enough to study her surroundings. Finding nobody within eyesight, she'd shed her clothing and, still moving, shifted into a wolf. It was her go-to shape and would hopefully be intimidating enough to repel a threat. Not knowing what she would find, she wanted to stack the deck in her favor.

As soon as Selene had seen that man on top of Eve, using a viciously sharp-looking knife to toy with her, she had known that shifting was the right choice. She had broken her cardinal rule without thinking, but as Eve's relief at the interruption hit her square in the chest, Selene had no regrets. Well, except that Eve was almost as afraid of her wolf as she had been of the attacker.

Now that she had a quiet moment in the safety of her apartment, Selene reviewed her fight with the man. He had been afraid of the wolf, too. She could smell it on him. Though his fear was strong, his anger about being interrupted was far more potent. Selene didn't want to imagine what plans she'd ruined.

Selene hadn't wanted to let Eve's attacker go but had craved to chase him, to make him pay somehow. But Eve's turbulent emotional state held her back. The woman she had saved, the one who had called her, was on the verge of falling apart. So Selene had slunk into the trees, found her clothing, and dressed so she could run back and care for Eve as a human being.

Now she wondered if that had been the right choice.

Eve was dangerous, no doubt about it. Not only because she was beautiful, the first woman in years to whom Selene couldn't control her attraction, but also because of her profession. She was practically a cop and would probably be the one who examined the dead woman from the park, maybe as soon as later today. Dissecting Selene's handiwork, she would try to puzzle out how an animal *that* size had found its way into Golden Gate Park.

Selene shuddered. More than being found out, she hated to imagine Eve seeing her as just another killer. She'd known the woman for only twenty traumatic minutes, but already she cared about what Eve would think.

This was exactly why she'd given up sex: too much emotional attachment. But with Eve, sex wasn't necessary. Selene already felt strangely attached.

Selene turned around at the sound of the bathroom door opening.

Eve stood there wearing her shirt and glasses, doing a very good impression of someone who wasn't holding on by a very thin thread. Selene put on a friendly expression and tried to be calm. She sensed that their empathetic link was a two-way street, which had to feel strange to someone not accustomed to the supernatural. Deciding it was probably in her best interest to control her emotions, in case Eve dwelt too long on the notion that Selene was somehow different from other women, Selene centered herself.

Taking a deep breath, she said, "Feeling better?"

"Much." Eve closed the distance between them and handed Selene her cell phone. "The cab will be here in about five minutes."

Relief flooded Selene, then guilt. She was relieved that Eve would be gone before Renee returned to pick up the other half of her money and guilty that she had to worry about that potentially awkward moment at all.

Eve winced. "I…I need to sit down."

"Of course." Selene led her to the couch and perched on the arm, torn between staying close and keeping a safe distance. This confirmed Selene's suspicion. Eve didn't just transmit emotion, she received it and was tuned in to Selene. From Eve's perplexed expression, Selene guessed that Eve had no idea what was happening. That was for the best. Selene redoubled her efforts to stay neutral.

"You said you were planning to file a police report?" Selene marveled at the way Eve kept her face stoic even as she broadcast a wave of shame. "Is that correct?"

"I don't think I'll have much of a choice." Eve looked away. "My ex is a detective. Jac would never let me get away with not reporting this."

"Well, Jac's right." Selene spoke in what she hoped was a reassuring voice. She recalled Eve's fear when she talked about her attacker having her purse. Selene didn't like that fact, either. "It'll be okay. They'll find him."

Eve shook her head and shrugged as though it was a nice notion, but unlikely. She was probably right. "Well, I hope so. Unfortunately, I'm not sure they'll have much to go on from me. Chances are they'll have to wait until he tries again. Hopefully the next woman is as lucky as I am."

Selene's jaw tightened as she flashed on what she might have found had she arrived at the scene only moments later. "Yes, let's hope."

"I'm glad you heard me." Eve raised her eyes and met Selene's gaze shyly. "I was so afraid to make him angry, I didn't think I'd called out loud enough to attract any attention. It's a miracle you were so close."

Selene hadn't been close at all. It had taken her a full three minutes of sprinting before she reached Eve. But she nodded anyway. "I'm glad I decided to take a walk this morning."

"I can't say the same. But I am glad I met you." Eve looked surprised as the words left her mouth, and Selene felt her embarrassment like a knife to the gut.

"Me, too." The cell phone buzzed in Selene's hand and she picked it up without breaking eye contact. After a moment she hung up. "Your cab is outside."

Eve nodded. "Well…thank you again."

"Of course." Selene resisted the urge to gather Eve into another embrace. As unnerving as it was to sense Eve's mood so acutely, nothing had ever felt so right as holding Eve in her arms. "You be safe."

"I will." Eve walked to the front door, then paused with her hand on the knob. "Maybe I'll see you again?"

It wouldn't be wise, but Selene wanted nothing more than to say yes. Forcing a casual smile, she said, "Maybe."

Eve's happiness washed over Selene, and she didn't have to try so hard to keep smiling. "All right, then. Good-bye."

Selene stood at the open front door and watched Eve walk to the cab. She didn't allow herself to feel the disappointment of knowing that seeing Eve again wasn't a good idea, or worry for Eve's safety. It wasn't fair to burden Eve with any of the turmoil that churned in her stomach. As the cab driver pulled away from the curb, Eve gave her one last wave good-bye, which Selene returned politely. Once Eve was out of sight, she withdrew into her house and shut the door.

Selene missed her already.

CHAPTER FIVE

He shouldn't have hit her.

That was Kevin's first mistake. When he had come up with the Plan, the idea had been to leave the park immediately after he made the kill. Get away fast, don't hang around to looky-loo. And certainly don't end up in the background of any crime-scene photographs. Killers got caught like that, and he refused to let anyone stop him. That's what the game was about: telling the world, but especially Dr. Eve Thomas, that he could do whatever he wanted, to whomever he wanted.

All he had to do was stick to the Plan. Be logical. Stay calm.

Today, on his first kill, he had completely and utterly failed. As Kevin had stood over his offering and stripped off the bloody sweatshirt and gloves he would burn before he went home, a dark desire took hold. Dr. Eve Thomas would begin her morning walk in a mere half hour. The kill zone was far enough from her usual route that he could hang around that area of the park another thirty minutes, if only to catch a glimpse.

He had told himself that's all he wanted. A glimpse.

He had burned to see Eve stroll through the park unaware of what had just occurred, having no idea that he was watching from behind a tree. Would she be frightened later when she realized her proximity to the time and place of the crime? Angry? More determined to catch him?

The thought turned him on. To leave Eve the body of a woman who could have just as easily been the good doctor herself, having met a terrible fate so close to where she walked every morning, was a masterstroke. A grand gesture from a killer who wouldn't let science or psychology outsmart him. Kevin loved grand gestures. It was probably the one part of his Plan that was flawed. But what was the point of showing the world you could do whatever you wanted if you didn't want to do anything big?

And what was the point of challenging somebody if you were afraid to get near them?

That thought had made him deviate from the Plan. He could do whatever he wanted, and what he had wanted then was to see Eve one last time before their game really began. During the weeks he spent learning her routine, he had watched her from a distance, fascinated. They had a connection now. And he wanted to experience it one last time before she became his adversary.

At first he told himself he just wanted a quick look to satisfy his curiosity. To take a mental snapshot, something to remember later. No big deal, certainly nothing that would jeopardize their game.

That had been the new Plan until the moment she walked into view.

Instead of satisfaction, he felt rage. Arousal. Excitement.

She thought she was so clever. Why? Because she'd helped catch a serial killer? Charles Dunning had been an amateur, an embarrassment. He was sloppy, and that's why she'd discovered his patterns.

Not like Kevin. Nobody would stop him, especially not Dr. Eve Thomas.

He didn't remember consciously deciding to attack her. One moment he was crouched behind the tree, then the next he was pulling on his ski mask and running to intercept her. When he drew back his fist and punched her in the face, he genuinely shocked himself. That hadn't been in the Plan, and yet there he was, improvising.

Back in his apartment, Kevin winced and touched his arm where the wolf's teeth had punctured the skin. Improvising. That was exactly the kind of idiot move that would get him caught. Precisely the type of misstep he always criticized guys like Charles Dunning for making.

Yet seeing the fear in her eyes had thrilled him. It was the most delicious emotion he had ever witnessed. Certainly the best he had ever caused. Not only was she a worthy adversary, but no one had ever given him such pure, succulent terror before.

Already he wanted to experience it again.

That was a problem. Though he'd been angry about the wolf at first, now that he was home safely, he wondered if the interruption had been a sign that he had gone too far, that he was straying from his meticulously crafted plans. Maybe the universe was trying to protect him from his own impulses and keep him on the right path.

How else to explain something so bizarre as a goddamn wolf in Golden Gate Park?

It was too late to change what he'd done. Now he could only wait and see how his actions would affect the Plan. He'd grabbed her purse as he fled the scene, not because he needed anything inside it, but because he hoped she might dismiss her assault as a simple mugging. Realistically, he knew that threatening to fuck her and make her cry had probably negated any step he could have taken to make his motive look like robbery. Stealing her purse served a dual purpose, though: Not only might it introduce doubt about his motives, but it would also shake her up even further. Frighten her.

Kevin liked that idea a lot.

To be safe, he'd dumped it in a garbage can at the edge of the park. No way would he hang on to it. He didn't keep trophies. On a day when he had broken so many rules, he remained steadfast about the stupidity of trophies. If the cops discovered evidence in your home, you'd practically confessed. Kevin didn't want to find notoriety as a captured serial killer. He preferred an air of mystique, like the Zodiac Killer.

Kevin sighed and picked up the book on his coffee table. *Listening to the Dead: Forensic Science and the Serial Murders of Charles Dunning.* By Dr. Eve Thomas. He flipped to the first page, ready to give it yet another read.

The book was his bible, his blueprint. It was his secret weapon in the battle to outsmart Eve Thomas.

And, he hoped, it would help him forget about how much he'd enjoyed tracing his blade over her bare skin, how badly he wanted to do it again.

She was his opponent, not his victim.

At least not yet.

Chapter Six

Eve knew she was in trouble the moment she walked into the morgue. Detective Jacqueline Battle was peering over Dr. Wayne Black's shoulder as he examined a fresh corpse, a bad habit she had that always made Wayne nervous. Jac glanced up as Eve entered the room, eyes going from concerned to angry in a millisecond. Instantly Jac rushed to her side.

"What happened?" Before Eve could react, Jac cupped her face between her hands. Eve looked away as Jac examined her injuries, trying to ignore how comforting she found the touch of familiar brown fingers. "Wayne said you were running late. He did *not* tell me about this."

"That's because he didn't know," Wayne said from behind Jac. He pushed aside the magnifier he'd been looking through and stepped to Jac's side, genuine compassion in his eyes. "Did this happen in Golden Gate Park?"

When Eve called in she'd told Wayne only that she was running late and would be in before noon. He hadn't questioned her further, but clearly he regretted that omission now. Eve willed herself to appear far calmer than she felt. "I'm fine—"

"Fine?" Jac dropped her hand to Eve's chin, gently turning her face so their eyes met. "This is *not* fine. Who did this to you?"

"A man attacked me in the park this morning."

"*Attacked* you?" The panic and heartbreak in Jac's eyes hit Eve square in the stomach, a visceral reminder of the love she used to see there every day. "What did he do?"

Blushing, Eve stepped back and adjusted her glasses. She read the unspoken question in Jac's eyes and shook her head. "Not that."

"So it was a robbery?"

"He did take my purse," Eve said, trying to ignore the look of alarm Jac failed to suppress. "But I don't know if that was his motive."

"What do you mean?"

"He…" Eve struggled to revisit those terrifying moments. "He threatened me with a knife when he had me down on the ground. He acted like he was getting off on my fear."

Jac swallowed and the color seemed to drain from her face. "Wayne was just examining a body we found in Golden Gate Park this morning. It looks like she was slashed to death with a knife."

For the second time that day, time seemed to slow to a turtle's pace around Eve. She put her hand out, hoping to find something to rest against before her legs stopped working. Jac came to her side and led her to the counter that held her forensic tools. Eve stared at her favorite retractor and forced herself to calm down. That didn't necessarily mean anything. The victim's murder and her own attack could easily be isolated events. It was truly within the realm of possibility, Occam's razor be damned.

"It might not be the same guy." Jac's voice had gone from scolding to reassuring. She'd always been good at knowing when not to push. "But we'll definitely want a statement from you. It might help."

"Of course," Eve said. Taking a deep breath, she straightened and stepped away from the counter. She approached the examination table quickly, not allowing herself to falter at the sight of the dead woman's violent wounds. Multiple cuts and stabs across the torso and face, signifying a no doubt terrifying and painful last few moments. Two vicious slashes to the neck, most likely the actual cause of death.

It could have been her on that table. Could Wayne and Jac have brought themselves to examine her mutilated corpse?

Jac touched her back. "Maybe you should take the rest of the day off. Nobody would blame you."

Eve shrugged away from Jac's hand. "Don't be ridiculous. I'm fine."

Jac grasped her elbow and walked her to the corner of the room, out of Wayne's earshot. To Eve's relief, he stepped back to the corpse and continued his examination. At least one of them could proceed as normal.

"Eve, I won't pretend there isn't a chance that your attacker is also our killer. After what you went through this morning…" Jac's chin trembled and she instantly tightened her jaw. "You need to take care of yourself. Looking at that woman's body won't help you right now."

"Sure it will." Work always helped. Eve just needed to distance the victim from her own experience, even if they'd met the same man in the park earlier. "I have to do something, Jac. I can't go home yet."

Jac nodded reluctantly. Then she said, "How did you get away?"

Eve cursed her fair skin when she felt her cheeks flush. She knew her story was slightly incredible and didn't want to look anything but confident as she told it. "A wolf."

"Excuse me?"

"I don't know. My glasses were broken, but it looked like a wolf. Maybe it was a dog. Anyway, it attacked the guy and knocked him away from me. Then it bit his arm and the guy ran away."

Jac swallowed, looking as though she might be sick. "That's… lucky."

"I know." Eve shuddered at her memory of the man's weight on top of her. "I don't know what I would have done if he hadn't shown up."

"Personally, I hope it was a dog." Jac grimaced. "Easier for animal control to deal with."

"It could have been, I guess." Eve touched her temple, wincing at the tenderness. "That would make more sense."

"I'm not saying you're wrong. Even in that situation, I'm sure you'd know the difference between a wolf and a dog."

"Maybe it was a malamute. Or a wolf hybrid."

"You think whatever it was could have killed our victim?"

Eve shook her head. "No, she was stabbed. With a knife."

"I figured," Jac said. "But I thought it wouldn't hurt to ask."

"Besides, this wolf was…" Eve paused, unsure how to explain the way the wolf had only seemed interested in scaring away her attacker. "It wasn't aggressive. At least not to me. It jumped on the guy who was hurting me, then left as soon as I was safe."

Jac stared intently at Eve's face, probably trying to decide if her story was credible or trauma-induced. It was a cop look, one Eve had seen many times. "Why didn't you call me? I would have come and picked you up. Taken you to get new glasses."

She'd considered phoning Jac for only a moment. Then she'd decided that it was a slippery slope back into Jac's arms, and it was better not to fall into old habits. "I'm not your responsibility anymore. Remember?"

Pain flashed through Jac's eyes, and Eve couldn't decide how that made her feel. The petty, mean-spirited part of her was happy. After all,

Jac had hurt her worse than anyone ever had. But the part of her that still loved Jac recoiled at her impulsive words. No matter how badly Jac had screwed up their romantic relationship, she'd always been there for Eve as a friend.

"I'm sorry," Eve said. "A woman at the park helped me get cleaned up and let me use her phone. I figured I would talk to you once I got to work."

Jac folded her arms over her chest, looking small and sad. "You know, even though we aren't together anymore, I do still care about you. Deeply. I want to be there for you when you need me, Eve."

Eve bit back the first comment that came to mind. *I needed you last year when you were cheating on me. I needed you to need me, and you didn't.* Instead she said, "I appreciate that."

"When are you going to talk to the police?"

"I thought I just did."

Jac brushed the back of her fingers over Eve's cheek. "To give an official statement, I mean."

"Soon, I guess. Maybe you could come with me."

Jac's throat tightened and her eyes filled with emotion. "Of course."

"Thank you." Eve turned away quickly. She was too fragile to deal with all that Jac was leaving unspoken. "You're a good friend."

She didn't know what to make of their friendship these days. When they first broke up, things between them had been chilly at best. Eve was embarrassed and angry about Jac's betrayal, and guilt made Jac short-tempered and difficult to be around. Having to continue to see one another professionally had been a real challenge, and more than once Eve had questioned whether staying in San Francisco was good for her own mental health. But about six months ago, Eve woke up one morning ready to let things go. Shortly after that, Jac's attitude had changed as well.

Their conversations had become less formal, and their interactions had become warm again. Now it almost seemed as though some of the old love had returned to Jac's eyes. Eve tried her best not to see it. She'd forgiven Jac, but she refused to be lured back by the same charm that Jac had wielded to seduce other women while they were together.

"Eve—"

"Let me just take another look at the victim before we go. Okay?" Eve walked to the examination table, nodding curtly at Wayne's sympathetic look. He straightened, all business. That was the great thing about him. He understood that work was therapy for her, and he always allowed her to get lost in it. "What have we got, Dr. Black?"

"Victim is in her early thirties, Latina. She's been dead about six hours. Multiple stab wounds and shallow slices, double-edged blade." He tilted his head and studied her face. "It appears she died from the slashes on her throat, though there is evidence of petechiae on the face and eyelids."

Eve assessed the pinpoint hemorrhages that marred the woman's tan skin, then glanced at what remained of her throat to confirm bruising. "So she was strangled as well as stabbed."

"Yes." Wayne hesitated, then said, "The killer was on top of her when he asphyxiated her. Two hands around her neck."

Eve touched her own throat where her attacker had dug his thumbs in, restricting her breathing. She had a terrifying flash of memory: being unable to breathe, thinking she was about to die. Jac gently rubbed her lower back, pulling Eve into the present. Eve dropped her hand and took a deep breath.

"We didn't find any identification on the body," Jac said. "We don't know who she is. Her body was left in a heavily wooded area of the park, very secluded. I doubt we would have found her already if it hadn't been for the phone tip."

Eve moved away from Jac, pretending to study the stab wounds. She tried to remember the knife her attacker had used to nick her breast, but knew she wouldn't be able to determine if it had been the murder weapon. The details were just too fuzzy. "Someone reported the body?"

"A woman." Jac walked around to the other side of the table so she could meet Eve's gaze. "She didn't leave her name. Said she was taking her morning jog when she found the body."

Hearing Jac's skepticism, Eve said, "You don't believe her?"

"That's an awfully secluded jogging route for a woman to take at six thirty in the morning. She's either lying or foolish beyond belief."

Eve stiffened. Jac wasn't directly rebuking her for choosing to walk in Golden Gate Park alone, but her voice held a definite undertone of judgment. Grateful for the reminder that Jac wasn't her knight in shining armor, Eve turned to Wayne. "Any evidence of sexual assault?"

He shook his head. "No. She was found naked, but with no bodily fluids or evidence of penetration."

"Okay." Eve walked to the counter to pick up her purse, then remembered she no longer had it. Feeling naked, she tugged at the hem of her borrowed shirt and took a moment to collect herself. "Start gathering hair and fiber evidence. I'm leaving to go talk to the police, and I'll be back as soon as I can." Looking to Jac, she said, "Let's get this part over with."

Nodding, Jac tentatively approached her. "Eve, what I said before, about the tipster—"

"Don't worry about it, Detective Battle." Eve put on her best neutral expression, ignoring the way Jac winced at the formality. "I understand."

Jac let her walk out the lab door without comment, but as soon as they were in the hallway, she grabbed Eve's arm and tugged her to a stop. Shaken by the unexpected contact, Eve pulled away sharply.

Jac held her hands up and took a step backward. "I'm sorry."

"No, I'm sorry." Eve exhaled. She had to get a grip. If she wanted Jac to believe she was okay, she had to act the part. "I'm still a little shaken up."

"Understandably." Jac gave her a contrite grimace, ducking her head. "I meant that I'm sorry if I upset you in there. I know we used to argue about your walks, but I don't want you to think—"

"I don't."

"It wasn't your fault, Eve. And I'm glad you're okay. It never once crossed my mind to say I told you so or anything shitty like that." Jac tugged on an unruly sprig of her kinky hair, a nervous gesture Eve knew well. "I promise."

Though Jac's promises had ceased to mean very much months ago, Eve took her hand and squeezed gently. She let go after a single beat. "Thank you."

"You should stay at my place tonight." Clearly reading her reaction, Jac said, "I'll sleep on the couch. Totally innocent. I just… don't think you should be alone."

Warmed by the offer, and more tempted than she wanted to admit, Eve shook her head. "Thanks, but I'm fine. Really."

"Are you sure?"

Stay strong. She increasingly found herself repeating this mantra around Jac. Stay strong, and whatever you do, don't say yes. "I'm sure. If I need anything, I'll call you."

"Okay." Jac frowned. "But I don't like it."

"Noted." Shoving aside her conflicted feelings for the moment, Eve gestured down the hallway. "Shall we go to the station?"

To her relief, Jac turned and led the way.

CHAPTER SEVEN

Selene couldn't concentrate. She saved the changes she'd made to the corporate logo she was designing and shut down Photoshop, then her computer. Her deadline was in three days, but she wasn't in the mood to keep pretending that she might make progress. Right now, work was the last thing on her mind. Refusing to give her a moment's peace, images of the body in the park filled her thoughts, along with worry about the odd look Renee had given her that morning when she returned to find Selene untied and waiting with the rest of her payment at the front door. But most of all, thoughts of Eve distracted Selene.

True to her word, Eve had called Selene at eight o'clock the night before to check in. Terrified to let things escalate between them, Selene had let the call go to voice mail. And she'd regretted it every minute since. For fifteen years now she'd believed she just wasn't meant to be with anyone, but Eve was undeniably different. They had a connection, and Selene was almost positive it went both ways. Would it be possible for Eve to accept Selene for who she was, or did she represent yet another heartbreak?

She couldn't know without allowing Eve into her life. And that was the one thing she wasn't sure she could do.

Trying not to think about how badly she wanted to return Eve's call, Selene wondered instead about the man in the ski mask. What had he wanted? Judging from the way he hadn't attempted to remove any clothing past tearing Eve's shirt, it seemed unlikely that he had intended to rape her. If he had, Selene would have expected him to be actively working toward that goal when she came upon them. But he'd been focused on tracing his knife over Eve's chest, watching her face. Clearly Eve's fear aroused him.

Though he'd taken Eve's purse, he probably hadn't intended to rob her, either. The time he had obviously spent with her on the ground suggested that his interest had been Eve, not her bag. He had reminded Selene of a predator on the hunt, and she couldn't help but worry that his ultimate goal had been murder.

Maybe she hadn't killed the woman in the park. What if Eve's attacker had?

The thought brought sick, momentary relief, then worry. As much as she didn't want to believe she was capable of murdering someone, if that man was responsible for the dead woman, a killer had targeted Eve. And he knew where she lived.

Selene pushed back from her desk and stood up. More than twenty-four hours had passed since the attack, but the weather had been typical San Francisco: cool and damp. Surely his scent would still be there. Doing nothing wasn't an option, so she walked to her window and opened it slightly. Then she stepped away from the curtains to undress.

If she were smart, she'd try to forget about Eve and move on with her life. Especially if she *hadn't* murdered that poor woman in the park. She could still slip back into the shadows unnoticed, call to the police notwithstanding. She had already broken her rules once for Eve, shifting into wolf form in public. If she wanted to keep her secret, she needed to not make a habit of it. Simply having anything more to do with Eve would violate her ultimate rule: Relationships lead to heartache and pain, so avoid them at all costs, romantic ones in particular.

A relationship with Eve would quickly turn romantic. The connection between them was intense, and that force would surely pull them together physically. Selene wouldn't have the strength to resist it. Eve wouldn't realize that she should.

Then what? How would Selene explain to Eve why she always disappeared the day before a full moon, only to return the day after? A lover would want to know such things. That was why Selene never let herself get involved.

But Selene was already involved—whether she liked it or not. Even now, she could feel the faintest hum of Eve's emotion at the edge of her consciousness. She tried not to tune into it, didn't want Eve inside her head, but the transmission was persistent. It was also faint, which made Selene want to focus in even more to make sure Eve was all right.

"Damn it." Selene pulled off her panties and tossed them on the couch with the rest of her clothing. She glanced at the window, steeling her nerves before breaking another rule. "What are you doing to me, Eve?"

She wanted to see if she could follow the man's trail through Golden Gate Park after he left the scene of the attack. She didn't have a plan. Chances were she would follow his scent to the edge of the park only to lose it on the street or at a BART station, but she had to try. Even if she managed to never contact Eve again, Selene wanted to do everything she could to protect her. This was the only place she knew to start.

Taking a deep breath, Selene shifted into a sparrow. Nothing flashy. Leaving her apartment as a bird seemed easiest, as the open window would allow her to come and go undetected. Once in the park, she would find a secluded area and shift into a dog to do her tracking. To be honest, that shift couldn't come soon enough. She didn't like to fly.

Still, as she soared out the window and over the street, a powerful rush of exhilaration hit her. She spent so much time hating the baggage of her ability—that one night a month when she lost control of it altogether—that she rarely allowed herself to enjoy the wondrous, innocuous things she could do. Being able to experience nature as something other than human had its perks. Pity it came at such a cost.

She quickly located the spot where Eve had been attacked and, with a quick look around, swooped down to land at the trunk of a large eucalyptus tree. Having seen nobody within eyesight, she immediately shifted into a familiar shape: a hound, with the best nose possible at her disposal. She lowered her head to the ground and sniffed.

Just as she'd suspected, the man's scent still hung heavy in the damp shade of the trees. She took a good whiff and her lips curled instinctively, then she bared her teeth in a growl. The fur on her back rose and sent a shiver through her body. If evil had a smell, this was it.

Selene let her nose lead her through the trees near where she'd rescued Eve. She'd watched the man stumble away in the direction the scent was taking her, so she was on the right track. The odor remained strong long past the spot the man had disappeared from Selene's view, winding through the trees toward the opposite edge of the park. She trotted along after it, only needing to slow down and really start paying attention when she reached a sidewalk at the edge of the park.

The trail led her to a metal garbage can at the corner of the block. The man's scent was all over it, along with something else. The faint, sweet smell of Eve. Selene jumped up on the can, placing her front paws on the opening and taking a good whiff. As a human, she would have found the smell of garbage putrid. But as a dog, well, she understood the appeal. On sensory overload, she had to take a few long sniffs to sort out the dizzying array of odors.

She definitely detected a hint of Eve. Her purse. But she also picked up the obvious: The garbage can had been emptied sometime recently, so Eve's purse was already gone. Only a trace of its smell remained, as well as the intense odor of discarded Starbucks coffee.

Selene stepped back and let her paws hit the pavement. All she could do now was follow the trail until it disappeared. If she was lucky, the guy had walked home. She had no idea what she would tell the police if she actually found him, but she would think of something. She had to do whatever she could to protect Eve.

Selene followed the trail to Ninth Avenue, where it disappeared at the Muni stop on the N Judah line. She wasn't surprised. Public transit was a popular mode of travel in the city. Unfortunately, it rendered his trail completely useless. She had no way of knowing which car he'd entered, at which stop he disembarked, or even if he'd transferred to BART at some point.

In other words, she was out of luck.

"Here, girl."

Selene turned her head and saw an older woman standing in the open doorway of a taquería, bent low with her hand outstretched. She clicked her tongue when Selene looked up at her, and Selene sighed internally. This was definitely the drawback of being a dog. Everyone wanted to rescue her.

"It's okay, puppy. Are you lost?"

Selene turned and darted back in the direction of the park. The woman was calling after her, but she didn't turn around. She certainly didn't need anyone to take her to the shelter or, worse, have a well-meaning animal lover adopt her.

Running back into the park, she waited until she was deep among the trees before she returned to bird form. As she flew back to her apartment, she wondered what to do next. She had little hope of actually finding Eve's purse or the man who took it. It interested her that he had thrown her purse away so quickly, but she didn't know what that meant. And she couldn't tell Eve any of what she'd found, for fear of sounding absolutely insane.

So that left her with nothing to do, except try to forget about the woman who haunted her waking life, who even now sent unknowing transmissions to her, like a siren's song.

Selene was used to denying herself things she wanted. She hoped she had the strength to be content to watch over Eve from afar. That would have to be enough.

CHAPTER EIGHT

Three days after her attack in Golden Gate Park, Eve was frustrated by the lack of progress they'd made on their murder victim. They knew her name was Yasmin Mandujano and that she had been single, but they had very little to go on as far as identifying her killer.

The body had been free of any significant hair or fibers. The lack of physical evidence collected at the scene suggested a killer who was careful, even meticulous. Definitely not an amateur. Despite the amount of blood present around the body, he hadn't left a trail. With the exception of poor, broken Yasmin, he didn't leave them a goddamn thing. As far as the police and the medical examiner's office were concerned, someone had stabbed Yasmin eighteen times with a knife, all but two of the wounds too superficial to have actually killed her, then vanished.

Unfortunately, Eve couldn't shake her growing certainty that he had walked almost a mile away to punch her in the face and drag her into the trees. As much as she didn't want to subscribe to that theory, it had a certain logic. Yasmin's killer had restricted her breathing at some point, and he had obviously enjoyed using his knife to torment, not just kill. Just like her own attacker. Though Jac didn't say so, Eve could see that she had reached a similar conclusion. Her attacker and the murderer were almost certainly the same person.

Eve didn't know how to process that information. It brought her no closer to identifying the man, and it certainly left her worried about the implications. What kind of killer would attack two women in a public place within an hour, leaving a total bloody mess at the first scene, then manage to escape undetected? If he was the meticulous serial killer he appeared to be, Eve would have expected him to stop at one kill. If it had been a spree, she wouldn't have expected him to stop at all. Something wasn't right about the situation, but she couldn't put her finger on it. Nothing about what had happened made sense, least of all how a wolf had appeared in Golden Gate Park at exactly the right moment to save her.

Eve made a note in the victim's chart, then flipped it shut. They couldn't discover anything more on her body or at the scene, it seemed, so they now needed to give Ms. Mandujano's family the comfort of a proper burial. Eve needed to simply try to reassure herself that even if the murderer had attacked her, she was safe now. And chances were, he wouldn't risk coming back to finish what he'd started.

At least she hoped not.

"Hey."

Having let her guard down in the safety of the lab, Eve startled at Wayne's voice just behind her. She swiveled in her chair and pushed back with her feet, putting some distance between them. Wayne winced sympathetically.

"Don't." Eve was tired of the apologies, tired of feeling scared. Everyone had been tiptoeing around her, though she *had* given them several reasons to think it was necessary. She was jumpy, irritable, and, most of all, frighteningly out of control of her emotions. And she burned to regain that control with every cell in her body. "I'm fine. Just drifted away for a moment."

He nodded. "I have that report on the Williams case for you to review, when you have a chance." He offered her a folder, which she took with an admirably steady hand.

"Thank you." As much as Eve hated to admit it, she didn't want to be at work. While poring over the details of other people's deaths usually removed her from her own problems, it now reminded her of her own mortality. If not for a random twist of fate, she would be as dead as Yasmin Mandujano. "I'll get this back to you tomorrow morning."

Wayne reclined in his chair, watching curiously as she stood and put on her jacket. "Taking off early today?"

Eve tried to act nonchalant. "Yeah, I have a few errands to run."

"Not a problem. I'll hold down the fort." He hesitated, then touched her hand before she could move away. "You need anything from me, Dr. Thomas?"

Though their relationship was strictly professional, Eve also considered Wayne a friend. He wasn't the kind of guy to express his emotions easily, but Eve could see his concern. Acknowledging that she also wasn't very good at letting others in, Eve forced herself to drop her mask ever so slightly.

"Just keep doing what you're doing," Eve said. "It helps."

He tipped his head. "Yes, ma'am."

"I'll see you tomorrow, then."

"See you."

Eve limped out of the medical examiner's office building without a clue as to where she would go. The new lock had been installed on her apartment three days ago, but she still didn't feel comfortable going home. She wasn't afraid her attacker would come to her apartment, but she couldn't stand to be alone with her imagination.

Surrounded by the mundane artifacts of her newly single life, Eve had spent the past two evenings sitting on her couch imagining what could have happened. Though she had escaped with only minor cuts and bruises, she mentally felt the pain of rape, the agony of strong hands wrapped around her throat, the terror of her blood pouring out onto the dirt. When she had nothing to do but think, the scene replayed itself incessantly, each nightmare scenario more horrifying than the last. All of them were probable outcomes had that wolf not shown up.

As Eve walked into the parking lot, she pulled her spare car key from her spare purse and sighed. She wanted to feel safe again, to be the person she'd been before that man turned her life upside down. She wanted to be the woman who didn't think twice about walking alone in the park, but she wasn't that person anymore. And she hadn't felt secure since she left Selene's apartment.

Eve got into the driver's seat and started the car. She put her hand on the gearshift, then paused. Selene. The only thing that could pull her mind away from the assault was the memory of the beautiful woman from the park. Eve couldn't stop thinking about her. Not only her inexplicable attraction toward her, but also how being with Selene had made everything seem better.

True to her word, Eve had called Selene's cell phone after she got home the night of the attack. Disappointed to get Selene's voice mail, she'd left a brief message that she was all right and thanked Selene again for her kindness. Eve had hoped to get a call back, but wasn't shocked when it never came. Surely a woman like Selene led a full, busy life, with little time for socially awkward forensic pathologists.

Eve had told herself she should forget Selene and move on. But she'd also washed Selene's shirt and placed it in the trunk of her car, just in case. Every evening since then she thought about returning it, but until now, she hadn't been able to work up the courage. Selene hadn't called back. That meant she wasn't interested in seeing Eve again. And who could blame her? She was gorgeous, breathtaking. So Selene had been kind when Eve had needed help. What would she want with Eve now?

Probably nothing. But who was Eve to say? And she *had* promised to return Selene's shirt.

Perhaps this was the perfect first step to regaining control over her life. Eve would do something uncharacteristic and drop by Selene's place to thank her again. If nothing else, she owed Selene that, and maybe a chocolate cake.

Decision made, Eve pulled out of the lot and headed for Selene's apartment. It was possible she would make a complete fool of herself by showing up unannounced, but seeing Selene again felt important in a way she didn't understand. The pull toward Selene was even more powerful than her shyness around beautiful women.

In other words, it was damn overwhelming.

Here's to taking control, Eve thought, and didn't look back.

❖

The last thing Eve expected to see when Selene opened her front door was genuine, unabashed joy. Selene's happiness to see her was palpable, making Eve feel as though she was reuniting with an old friend instead of potentially disturbing a near stranger. Any doubts about dropping in on Selene instantly vanished.

"Eve." Selene took the pink bakery box out of Eve's hands and set it on a small table in the entryway, then held her by the shoulders and pulled her into a gentle embrace. "I'm so happy to see you again. How are you?"

Caught off guard, Eve surprised herself by returning Selene's hug easily. Because she usually didn't enjoy physical contact with anyone except the most intimate friends, she didn't understand why holding Selene would feel so comfortable. But it did. Despite the supple curves pressed against her body and the heady scent of Selene's dark hair, Eve didn't feel nervous. Instead she felt reconnected, at peace.

Nothing except work had ever taken her to such a balanced place. Shaken by her obvious attachment to Selene after having spent only about twenty-five minutes with her, Eve drew away. "I'm sorry to drop in on you, but I wanted to return your shirt—"

"I told you to keep it." Selene stepped out of their embrace but kept her hands on Eve's shoulders.

But I wanted to see you. Eve's face heated as she struggled to explain how she couldn't stay away. "I brought cake."

Selene grinned slowly. "That's an excellent reason to drop by."

"I hope you like chocolate." Eve gestured at the pink box. "It's from the bakery down the street."

"Chocolate is my kryptonite," Selene said. She picked up the box and indicated that Eve should follow her inside. "Let's go have a piece."

Selene led Eve deeper into her apartment, and this time Eve had the presence of mind to look around. Framed photographs, mostly nature shots, many of them spectacular, covered the walls. In the corner of the front room sat a massive desk covered in computer and camera equipment, leading Eve to assume that the photographs surrounding them were probably Selene's work. She saw no pictures of people, no hint of family or friends.

"You're a photographer?" Eve said, pausing to examine a photo of a large gray wolf. It didn't look exactly like the one she'd seen in the park, but its piercing stare sent shivers rolling down Eve's spine. "This is an amazing shot."

"Thanks. I like taking pictures, but I'm not sure I'd call myself a photographer." Selene paused with her hand on the kitchen door. "Professionally I do graphic design. Photography is just a hobby."

"These are excellent. As good as anything I've seen in *National Geographic*. Have you ever tried to make it your profession?"

"I've thought about it," Selene said. "But it would mean a lot of travel, and I enjoy staying close to home."

Nodding, Eve followed Selene through the kitchen door. The place was spotless, with a faint antiseptic scent that reminded Eve of her lab. Jac had always been the consummate slob, so to discover such tidy perfection aroused Eve more than she would ever admit out loud. She walked to the bar and took a seat on a tall stool, watching as Selene opened the pink box.

"Oh, yes. This was a *very* good reason to drop by." Selene pulled a large knife from the block on the counter and cut into the cake, her face the picture of sinful pleasure. "Thank you."

Eve realized she was staring with her mouth agape. With effort, she tore her attention away from what she decided was the most blatant display of unconscious sexuality she'd ever witnessed. "It's the least I could do."

Selene moved a large slice of cake onto a plate, then plucked two forks from the drawer next to the sink. "Do you mind sharing?"

Eve shook her head, struck dumb by how very much the idea appealed to her. Dimly she thought about how uncharacteristic this situation was for her, everything from pursuing a woman to sharing a dessert, but that didn't make it feel any less natural. Nothing had ever been easier. "That sounds perfect."

Selene brought the plate to the counter and set it between them, then handed Eve a fork. "So how are you doing? Really?"

Eve waited for Selene to take the first bite before spearing a small piece for herself. "I'm fine. Honestly."

Searching Eve's face as she chewed, Selene said, "You're not wearing your glasses today."

"Oh." Eve touched the bridge of her nose. "What happened in the park has finally inspired me to try contact lenses. I'm still getting used to them."

"I like being able to see your eyes. I didn't realize they were so blue."

Her face burning, Eve said, "Thank you."

Selene used her fork to point at the cake. "That's delicious."

"Yes, it is." Eve took another bite. She'd never eaten anything so incredible. Almost as though being with Selene made everything taste better. "You may have to wrestle me for the last bite."

Selene gave her a smoky look that whetted Eve's appetite for something more decadent than chocolate. "Oh, I could take you."

Eve's pussy clenched and she gasped slightly, dropping her gaze to stare at her fork. Since when did she engage in flirtatious banter and inspire double entendres? She had never been comfortable expressing herself sexually, and the ease with which Selene aroused her was startling. Eve took another bite so she wouldn't have to answer.

"Tell me the truth," Selene said quietly. "Because I know you're not just *fine* after what happened. Are you?"

"I'm...worried." Eve exhaled, almost relieved to have Selene call her out on the subject. She was glad that Wayne was mostly leaving it alone, and she hadn't wanted to depend too much on Jac by admitting how badly the attack had shaken her, but Eve appreciated the opportunity to talk it through with someone. Even though they had just met, Eve sensed Selene was the perfect confidante. "Physically I'm feeling better, but emotionally…I can't stop thinking about what happened."

"That's to be expected. Are you sleeping?"

"Enough," Eve said, though that wasn't entirely true. For the past few nights, sleep hadn't come easily, and more than once nightmares had torn her out of slumber. "It's getting easier."

"Did you have your locks changed?"

"I did." Eve took another bite of cake, surprised she still had her appetite. "Nothing else has happened, really. As far as I know, the guy's long gone."

"But you're still worried. Why?"

"The police found a body in the park the morning I was attacked."

"I know," Selene said, and Eve's stomach twisted with a surge of fear, though she didn't understand why. Despite their topic of conversation, she felt safer than she had in days. Incredibly, she sensed that she was picking up on Selene's disquiet. "I read about it in the paper. A woman, right?"

"Yes." Eve watched Selene's face, trying to decide how she knew that Selene was afraid. Selene didn't show any outward signs of emotional turmoil, but somehow Eve felt it just the same. "I don't want to upset you."

"No," Selene murmured, visibly relaxing. "It's just…unnerving. So close to my house and all."

"Of course."

"The newspaper didn't say much. Only that it looked like a homicide."

Eve set down her fork and Selene did the same. "She was murdered at least an hour before I was attacked. The police received an anonymous tip that led them to her body."

Selene stared down at their plate, studying the last of the cake. "What do they think happened?"

"I examined the body," Eve said, matter-of-factly. It was hard to talk about Yasmin Mandujano. Retreating into the cold, hard facts would allow her to keep her voice steady. "Someone stabbed her. Strangled her, too, but that's not what killed her."

"You told me there was a wolf in the park that morning. Is it possible—"

"No. I almost wish that were the case. Whoever killed that woman was definitely an animal, but also very much a human being."

Selene picked up her fork and took another tentative bite, watching Eve's eyes. "You think the man who murdered that woman is the same one who hurt you."

"It's a definite possibility." Trying to act more nonchalant than she felt, Eve speared another bite of their disappearing cake. It couldn't be healthy, how much better the rich dessert made her feel. "It's hard to say. He didn't leave much evidence behind."

"So what now?" Selene touched Eve's arm. "How do you catch him?"

"Maybe we get lucky," Eve said. She met Selene's gaze and instantly fell into her green eyes. Unless she was mistaken, her attraction wasn't one-sided. And suddenly the attack was the last thing on her mind. "Otherwise we wait for him to kill again."

"He won't come after you," Selene said with conviction. But Eve could feel a palpable sliver of doubt running through Selene's words. "He would be foolish to try anything now that you've alerted the police."

"I hope you're right." Eve hesitated, then gave in to impulse and covered Selene's hand with her own. The touch was electric. "If you don't mind, I really don't want to think about it right now."

"Of course." Selene glanced down at Eve's hand and exhaled. "I'm sorry I didn't return your call. I was so glad to hear from you, but I…wasn't sure what to say."

Staggered to hear anxiety in Selene's voice, Eve tried to imagine where it was coming from. When had she ever made a woman nervous? "I hope I didn't throw you, just showing up like this."

Selene regarded Eve with a warmth that left no doubt that dropping in had been the right thing to do. "Only in the very best way."

"Good." Eve set down her fork, ready to cede the final bite to Selene. "This isn't typical behavior for me. Being social. I'm not convinced I've got what it takes to be successful at it."

"You're brilliant at being social." Selene impaled the remaining chunk of cake and moved her fork close to Eve's lips. "Now have the last bite."

The idea of having Selene feed her was almost painfully sexy. Eve bit her lip and hesitated, unsure whether to accept Selene's offer or deflect it with humor. Nothing about Selene's intense stare suggested that Eve was misreading the unmistakable heat between them. Though Eve normally became shy when a woman even hinted at seduction, whatever drew her to Selene also emboldened her to play along.

Leaning forward, Eve carefully took the cake between her teeth, then pulled back. She chewed slowly, never breaking eye contact. Desire flared in Selene's eyes, making it difficult for Eve to swallow. As soon as she could form words, Eve whispered, "Please tell me you feel this, too."

"I feel this, too."

Before she could second-guess the impulse, Eve captured Selene's mouth in a firm kiss. More shocking than her own impetuous action was the passion with which Selene responded. Selene tangled her hands in Eve's hair and kissed back eagerly, letting out a groan of pure, carnal pleasure.

Everything about the kiss felt right. Their mouths fit together perfectly, and Eve felt none of the hesitation or uncertainty she usually experienced with a new lover. It was as though they had done this a thousand times—no first-kiss jitters for them—and yet it was also the most thrilling moment of Eve's life. Fierce, gnawing arousal bloomed in her stomach, followed by a jolt of what felt a lot like love. The intensity of the sensation Selene stirred inside Eve sparked a flicker of terror that she was indeed losing her mind.

Selene broke away from the kiss as though burned. "I'm so sorry, Eve. Forgive me. I didn't mean to frighten you."

Eve's head spun from the sudden change in mood. Everything had been so wonderful, but somehow her split second of doubt threatened to ruin the moment. She hadn't even been aware that she'd betrayed her anxiety. "You didn't."

"I shouldn't have done that." Selene touched Eve's cheek gently. Clearly stricken, she looked as though she might cry. "Your face hasn't even healed yet. That was totally inappropriate, after what you've been through."

Selene's self-flagellation hurt Eve's heart. She grabbed Selene's hand and squeezed. "Hey. *I* kissed *you*. Remember?"

"Yes, well." Selene blushed and studied their hands. "I shouldn't have gotten carried away. It just felt so—"

"Right."

"Yeah." Selene raised her face, searching Eve's eyes. "But it frightened you."

"For a moment." Reluctant to put her strange feelings into words, Eve murmured, "I surprised myself, that's all."

"Being attracted to a woman?"

Eve laughed nervously. "No, I've always been attracted to women. I've just never been so forward about it." Or so instantly, inexplicably infatuated.

"Me either."

"I wouldn't have pegged you as being particularly shy," Eve said. She sat back onto the stool, putting some distance between them. "You're very beautiful. You must have men and women throwing themselves at you all the time."

Selene rolled her eyes and picked up the empty cake plate. Carrying it to the sink, she waited until her back was to Eve before she spoke. "I don't have a very active social life. To say the least."

Eve picked up a hint of sadness in Selene's voice. "By choice, surely."

"Yes," Selene said. "By choice." She turned and leaned against the counter, folding her arms under her breasts. Her unreadable expression set Eve's heart thumping. "But there's something about you."

Eve didn't understand how she could feel so strongly about someone she barely knew. From the tone of Selene's voice, she sensed the confusion was mutual. "I know."

Selene came around the bar and took Eve's hand. "Let's go talk in the living room."

Eve allowed Selene to lead her to the front room, reeling from the turn things had taken. She didn't know what she'd expected from this visit, but it certainly hadn't been this. She hadn't kissed a woman since the breakup with Jac, let alone entertained the idea of a new relationship. She'd planned to focus on work for a good long while and worry about women later. Much later.

Meeting Selene had thrown all that out the window. Now Eve wanted only to feel Selene's naked skin against hers.

Selene shivered, releasing her hand and gesturing at the couch. "Sit." Her voice had dropped to a bare whisper. "Please."

Eve took a seat at one end, both relieved and disappointed when Selene sat at the other. Unsure what to say, Eve mustered what hopefully came off as a casual smile. "I hope I didn't make things awkward."

"No." Selene laced her fingers on her lap and straightened. "Not at all."

Eve could feel Selene's discomfort and shifted closer, wanting nothing more than to hold her. The idea that she could make a woman like Selene nervous was hilarious, but Selene's anxiety was definitely real. The last of Eve's fear dissipated with her desire to comfort Selene.

"I'm sure you're right." Eve touched her throat, an unconscious gesture she had noticed happened every time she thought of her attack. "This is probably a strange time for me to have these feelings. But that doesn't change the fact that I'm having them."

"And what are those feelings?" Selene's voice had dropped to a near whisper. She exuded a curious combination of hope and trepidation. "Exactly?"

Unable to believe she was admitting it out loud, Eve said, "I want you."

Selene licked her lips, sending toe-curling arousal through Eve's body. "I want you, too."

"Not just tonight."

Fear flickered in Selene's eyes. "I've…never done that before."

"Date?" It occurred to Eve that under normal circumstances, such obvious ambivalence would make her newfound courage wither and die. But she couldn't imagine anything dissuading her from pursuing Selene. Eve didn't simply want Selene. She *needed* her, needed her so desperately that instead of apprehension, all she could feel was delicious anticipation. Whatever this was felt so right that Eve had no doubt it would change her life for the better. "Dating can be fun. You should try it."

Selene's laughter warmed Eve and steadied her resolve. Shaking her head, Selene said, "I don't think I'd be good for you." Despite her expression of humor, Selene's tone turned deadly sober. "Seriously, Eve. If you were smart, you'd stand up and leave right now."

A twinge of apprehension curled in the pit of Eve's stomach. After Jac, Eve was terrified to trust someone wholly again, only to have that trust broken. No matter how right Selene felt, hadn't Jac also felt right? Eve had thought they were happy until the moment she discovered Jac was cheating. More than anything, her failed relationship with Jac had taught her that nothing was certain, not even when you believed it with everything inside you.

Selene seemed to recognize that her warning had hit the mark, but instead of looking relieved, she radiated sadness. Regret. "I'd never hurt you on purpose. I just—"

"This scares you." No matter how unnerving Selene's attempt to caution her away was, Eve sensed that pure worry motivated it. She also knew that Selene meant what she said about not hurting her. All her misgivings faded, bringing desire back to the front. "It scares me, too. But not enough to make me walk out the door." Eve shrugged. "Sorry."

"Well, I don't want to be scared." Now Selene shifted closer and, after a brief hesitation, rested her hand on Eve's. "I'm very drawn to you, Eve. Unbelievably so."

Too embarrassed to admit just how powerfully she felt the connection between them, Eve nodded. "Maybe if we kissed again, we'd realize that all this being-afraid stuff is kind of silly."

Selene's mouth twitched, then eased into a smile that made Eve's stomach flutter pleasantly. "It's a theory, at least."

"Well, I am a scientist." Pushing aside any lingering doubt, Eve closed the distance between them, pausing when her lips were mere inches from Selene's. "Testing theories is sort of my thing."

"Mine, too." Selene initiated their second kiss with a throaty moan that threatened to bring Eve to orgasm the instant their mouths met.

Once again, lust and love surged through Eve's veins, ratcheting her desire to new, unknown heights. Sex with Jac had been good, at least for her, but it had never come close to what Selene made her feel with a simple kiss. All the inhibitions that forever held her back had vanished, and for the first time in her life, Eve wanted nothing more than to physically lose herself in someone else. Usually she faced the prospect of sex with more than a little worry, but not now, not with Selene. She wanted to take Selene—and be taken by her—so badly she could hardly breathe.

Selene tightened her hands on Eve's shoulders and pulled away. "Perhaps we should take things slow—"

"If you need to take it slow, we can go slow." Eve punctuated her words with wet, hungry kisses across Selene's throat. She would respect Selene's wishes, she really would, but she didn't know how to stop until Selene absolutely commanded her to. "I usually take things slow. But—" Eve scraped her teeth over Selene's earlobe, delighting in the shiver the bold move elicited. "My new theory is that slow is overrated."

"So overrated." Having apparently decided to stop fighting what was happening between them, Selene pressed Eve back on the couch, settling on top of her. Eve spread her legs on instinct and Selene eased into the space between them. Then Selene placed a hand on either side of Eve's face and stared down into her eyes. "You'll tell me if this is too much, right?"

Eve ran her fingers through Selene's hair. She knew exactly what Selene was hinting at. The weight of Selene's body on hers could evoke memories of the man in the park, but it didn't. Not even close. "I'm not thinking about him."

For the first time since the attack happened, it was far from Eve's mind. Much more immediate was the slick wetness between her legs, the tight ache of her erect nipples. Selene's touch kept her firmly in the moment, safe from harm, and Eve wanted more.

Selene's entire body relaxed. She kissed Eve slowly, as though they had eons to explore, as though Eve wasn't about to explode. Selene rubbed her thumbs over Eve's cheeks, touching her so tenderly, so lovingly, soothing Eve's fierce need and replacing it with the calm desire to make this contact last. It was their first time together, hopefully the first of many, and Eve wanted to savor it. She looped her arms around Selene's neck and moaned quietly, but loud enough for Selene to hear. It was a shock to hear herself make noise like that, but also a turn-on.

Jac used to tease her about being silent in bed, and Eve had always felt powerfully self-conscious about giving voice to her pleasure. But not now. Just one more way her feelings for Selene confounded everything she thought she knew about herself.

Eve placed her hands on Selene's chest, pushing gently. When Selene broke away, Eve murmured, "Do you have a bed somewhere?"

"I do." Selene nipped at Eve's lower lip. "You sure that's what you want?"

"Take me there and I'll show you *exactly* what I want."

CHAPTER NINE

Selene hadn't touched a woman's body in fifteen years, so when she pushed her hands under Eve's shirt and cupped the heavy weight of Eve's breasts in her palms, it took everything she had not to come. Being with Eve made her feel like a clumsy sixteen-year-old, and it was no wonder. Selene had been a teenager the last time she'd made love to someone, in what felt like another lifetime. She had only vague memories of being with Carla—mostly that the other girl had been just as young and innocent as she was, with a slim body that only hinted at the womanly fullness of Eve's curves. Everything about being with Eve was different.

Particularly because Selene knew the stakes this time around. By opening her heart to Eve, she risked the possibility of a loss so acute she didn't know how she would survive it. But Selene hardly had a choice. No matter how she tried to resist Eve, she couldn't. Their bond was too strong. Selene had moved past *want* to *need*, and not even the possibility of heartbreak would stop her from claiming what was hers.

Selene broke their kiss and gulped in much-needed air. Eve stared up at her from under heavy lids, running her hands over Selene's sides.

"You feel so good." Eve placed her hands on top of Selene's, encouraging her to gently squeeze her breasts. "I've never been so turned on."

Face heating, Selene pushed her thumbs under the edge of Eve's bra and stroked her erect nipples. "Me, too."

"We're not moving too fast, are we?" Eve frowned as though something unpleasant had just occurred to her. "I don't mean to push you."

Selene shook her head and moved her hands from beneath Eve's shirt, backing off so that Eve could prop herself up on her elbows. "I want this," Selene murmured. "Want you. Desperately. I just…I meant it when I said I don't usually do this."

Understanding softened Eve's gaze. "It's been a while."

"That's an understatement." Unable to stay away, Selene caressed the soft skin of Eve's belly. "You're only my second lover. And the first one…she was a long time ago."

Eve radiated a strange mixture of sympathy, concern, and impossibly ardent arousal. "We can take this at whatever pace you need."

Selene ducked her head and closed her eyes, wishing she could explain to Eve that her fear went so much deeper than being uncertain about her sexual prowess. Making herself vulnerable with a human being went against every rule Selene had adopted for survival. She had arrived at a crossroads between a lonely life of safety and the chance for something more, and though she honestly felt no choice in the matter, she wasn't sure how to proceed.

Warm hands covered her own, prompting Selene to open her eyes and meet Eve's kind smile. "Why don't you let me lead?"

Selene nodded silently.

Biting her lip, Eve pulled her shirt over her head, allowing Selene to see the white cotton bra she had felt under her hands only moments ago. Eve reached behind her back and unhooked her bra, watching Selene's eyes with a slow-spreading smirk.

"I'm used to being the shy one," Eve said. She slipped her bra off her shoulders, revealing milky white breasts topped with pebbled pink nipples. Selene couldn't stop staring, even though she sensed she was making Eve a little nervous.

"I'm sorry." Selene dragged her gaze to Eve's face.

"Don't be." Eve straightened, projecting a wave of confidence that splashed over Selene and emboldened her as well. "I kind of like not being shy."

Drawing strength from Eve, Selene danced her fingertips over the slope of one breast, then used her other hand to cup its twin. "You're the most gorgeous thing I've ever seen." Disbelief radiated from Eve, and Selene shook her head to put a stop to the doubt. "I mean it, Eve. You're stunning. Incredible."

"Blushing," Eve added, and indeed, her fair skin had turned rosy. "Coming from you, well, that's amazing."

Selene knew that people generally found her attractive. Though she spent most of her time hiding from the world, when she did venture out she inevitably dealt with come-ons and compliments from more than a few people. Her features were pleasantly symmetrical, but Selene sensed another explanation for her universal appeal. Whatever imbued her with the power to shift form also seemed to grant her a certain energy to which people responded. But she inspired a shallow lust, more about sex than genuine interest. With Eve, the interest went deeper.

For the first time in her life, the universe was giving her a gift. A real one, something she hoped wasn't also a curse. Choosing to trust in how Eve made her feel rather than dwell on what might happen between them in the future, Selene let go.

Selene gently massaged Eve's bare breasts and kissed her throat. "Just bear with me if I'm a little rusty."

"You're perfect." Eve's fingers curled beneath the hem of Selene's T-shirt. "May I take this off?"

Selene raised her arms and allowed Eve to pull it over her head. Eve's nostrils flared at the discovery that she wasn't wearing a bra.

"I wasn't expecting company." Selene giggled, folding her arms over her breasts. Her girlish reaction surprised her. Two people had seen her naked a week ago during the full moon, but the circumstances were different now, and unlike Renee the escort and Clarence the jogger, Eve's opinion mattered. "You must think I'm ridiculous."

Eve gave her a salacious grin. "I told you. You're perfect."

Selene lowered her arms, shivering when Eve's eyes darkened with desire. Eve didn't even need to touch her to bring her satisfaction, not when Selene felt all of Eve's lust and pleasure. "Kiss me," Selene murmured, even as she rose on her knees to bring their mouths together again.

Eve placed her hands on Selene's throat and groaned. She scooted nearer until their upper bodies pressed together, so close Selene could feel Eve's heartbeat hammering against her chest. The sensation of Eve's breasts smashed against her own electrified Selene, igniting a hot curl of pleasure between her thighs. She swayed and her knees threatened to buckle, but Eve slid her hands down Selene's back to cup her buttocks, keeping her steady against Eve's strong body.

Instinct started to take over as desire overrode her adolescent nervousness. Selene reached between them and found the button on Eve's pants, thumbing it open and tugging down the zipper. Not quite bold enough to slide her hand inside to find what she most craved, she grabbed Eve's hips and squeezed, then slipped both hands into the back of her cotton panties. Eve's bottom fit perfectly in her palms, full and warm and so sensitive to the touch.

Selene closed her eyes and inhaled as Eve reacted to her caress. Every bit of pleasure Selene caused came back to her by way of Eve's visceral reaction, creating a feedback loop of sensation that threatened to undo Selene before she'd even begun.

Eve tore away from their kiss, exhaling shakily. "I think that bakery spiked our cake with a narcotic or something. Seriously. This is…weirdly incredible."

Selene laughed. "I feel the same. But I don't think we've been drugged."

Eve's eyes were heavy-lidded, her face totally relaxed. "Whatever it is, I like it."

Swallowing at Eve's seductive tone, Selene dropped her hands lower, brushing her fingertips ever closer to Eve's arousal. She didn't need to touch Eve to know she was soaking wet. She could smell her and wanted to howl.

Eve's hands found the button of Selene's jeans and worked it open. Lowering the zipper with one hand, Eve slid the other into Selene's panties and ran a finger along her slick labia. Selene cried out as her pussy contracted and waves of pleasure radiated throughout her body. She was used to reacting so strongly during the full moon, but never outside that time of the month. Stunned, Selene drew back and met Eve's eyes, wondering if she had felt it, too.

Trembling, Eve whispered, "You came."

"I'm sorry," Selene said. "It's just been so long and…"

Eve beamed, hitting Selene with a burst of genuine happiness that took her breath away. "I can't believe I just made you come like that."

Relieved that Eve wasn't questioning their amazing synchronicity, Selene nipped at Eve's lower lip with gentle teeth. "I guess that means you're perfect, too."

Eve wiggled her fingertips, gently playing with Selene's labia, and her thighs trembled as aftershocks tore through her. "Let me lick you," Eve whispered next to Selene's ear. She swirled her fingers in Selene's wetness. "I want to taste this."

That did it for Selene's knees. She half collapsed onto the bed, taking Eve with her. Eve took the change of position in stride, deftly removing her hand from Selene's panties so she could pull them down her legs with her jeans.

"I'm taking that as a yes until you tell me otherwise," Eve said. She tossed Selene's jeans over the side of the bed, then shed the rest of her own clothing, leaving them both bare. Selene's breath caught at the sight of Eve's naked skin and the triangle of dark hair between her thighs.

"Yes," Selene whispered. Eve drank her in with hungry eyes, stoking Selene's desire impossibly higher. "Definitely yes."

Still beaming, Eve pushed Selene's thighs apart and lay on her stomach in the space between them. She lifted Selene's leg over her shoulder, bringing her face close to Selene's pussy. Then she inhaled deeply, exuding a heady mix of hunger, anticipation, and shyness. It was getting harder to separate Eve's feelings from her own, and the resulting sensory overload made Selene's head spin.

The first touch of Eve's tongue against her labia set Selene on fire. She arched her back and gasped at the intensity of Eve's intimate kiss, knowing she wouldn't be able to stand very much of the white-hot bliss of Eve's mouth on her pussy. It was too much, and at the same time it could never be enough.

"Oh," Selene groaned. "Oh, *yes*."

Eve dove in deeper, moaning aloud as she sucked Selene's clit gently. She slid a finger along Selene's labia, then pushed inside her tight opening with deliberate care. Selene closed her eyes and concentrated on breathing, on not passing out. She'd never felt anything so extraordinary.

A throaty, languid moan burst from Eve, cutting Selene loose from the last bit of her control. The vibrations of Eve's own pleasure ushered Selene into climax, and she tipped back her head and gave voice to her soul-shattering release. Between her legs, Eve cried out and gripped Selene's thigh with her free hand as she quaked along with Selene.

As Selene came down from her climax, Eve drew back with a gasp. She collapsed with her face on Selene's inner thigh and trembled, breathing heavily. Selene tangled her fingers in Eve's hair and held her close.

"I came," Eve whispered. "I licked you and I *came*."

Selene closed her eyes, loving the wonder in Eve's voice, wishing she could help Eve understand what had just happened. But she couldn't explain that Eve had just made love to someone not quite human. Not without scaring her away.

Stroking Eve's hair, Selene murmured, "Think you could do it again?"

"What? Come?"

"Yes."

"I'm certainly not opposed to trying." Eve lifted her head, and Selene opened her eyes so she could catch her gaze. "That was amazing. *You* are amazing."

Selene gripped Eve's shoulders gently, pulling her up her body so they were face-to-face. Then she flipped Eve onto her back and nudged her thighs apart, taking her place between them. "*We* are amazing."

Eve cradled Selene's face in her hands. "You're right," she whispered. "We are."

Selene lowered her head and poured every ounce of her emotion into kissing Eve. They groaned simultaneously, twin sounds of pleasure that nearly brought Selene to orgasm again. She pressed her thigh against Eve's pussy, sliding over her wetness, and hummed when Eve inhaled sharply at the contact. Pulling away from Eve's mouth, Selene trailed kisses over her throat, then down to the tip of one perfect breast.

Eve's hands found Selene's head and held her close, encouraging her to lick and nibble, then tug with her teeth. As Selene stimulated Eve's nipple she could feel burning pleasure build in her own stomach, signaling yet another climax. Not wanting them to go off before she could taste Eve the way Eve had tasted her, Selene quickly kissed her way down Eve's stomach to the kinky hairs between her legs.

"I don't know if I can take that," Eve gasped, tugging at Selene's hair. "It feels too *fucking* good."

"You can," Selene said. She pushed Eve's thighs apart and gently kissed her labia. "You will."

Groaning, Eve tightened her fingers on Selene's scalp. Electric current seemed to shoot from Eve's hands, traveling down the length of Selene's body to the tips of her toes. Combined with the sweet flavor of Eve's juices, it was pure bliss. Selene kissed and sucked Eve's swollen folds, then her clit, until Eve stiffened and came with a hoarse shout. Selene held back the sound of her own orgasm as best she could, not sure she wanted Eve to know that pleasuring her had brought her to climax once again. But Eve couldn't possibly miss how Selene gasped and quivered as they lay there recovering.

"That was the best sex I've ever had," Eve murmured some time later, once her breathing slowed. "Our *first* time. The best of my life."

Selene's chest puffed with pride. She kissed her way up Eve's body, to her lips. Drawing back after long moments, Selene said, "You sure know how to make a girl feel good."

"So do you." Eve raised an eyebrow. Now that the sexual tension had eased slightly, her face seemed more relaxed. She was still bruised from the attack, and Selene frowned, feathering her fingers over the fading marks. Eve shook her head. "Let's not talk about it."

Nodding, Selene moved off Eve's body and lay at her side. She propped herself up on her elbow and gently caressed Eve's stomach with her fingertips. "Spend the night?"

Eve touched Selene's face. "Just try and get me to leave."

"You realize that I plan to ravish you many more times this evening, right?" Selene captured Eve's hand and kissed her fingers, pulling one into her mouth. Eve's eyes darkened. "I hope you're prepared."

"I hope *you* are," Eve said, in a voice that dripped with seduction. She blinked then giggled, turning red. "Not to bring up anything awkward, but I was with my ex for three years. It was never like this. *I* was never like this."

"Like what?" Selene tugged on a tendril of Eve's hair. "Beautiful? Sexy? Exciting?"

"Uh." Eve giggled again, averting her gaze. "All of the above, I guess."

"I don't believe it."

Covering her face with her hands, Eve looked beautiful with cheeks glowing deep pink. "No, it's true. I've always been all work and no play. Probably why I've never been able to keep a woman very long."

Selene slid her hand between Eve's legs, cupping her gently. "I don't think you'll have a problem keeping me."

Eve spread her thighs and dropped her hands to look Selene in the eyes. "I hope not. I could get used to you."

Selene heard and felt the undercurrent of love in Eve's voice, so strong it squeezed her heart painfully and didn't let go. Eve probably wouldn't feel that way if she knew what Selene really was, but the words filled her with joy anyway. No one had cared about her in a long time. She hadn't expected anyone to care again. Now that she had this chance with Eve, she vowed to do whatever it took not to screw it up.

Even if that meant hiding from the one person in the world she wanted to trust.

Scooting closer to Eve, Selene pushed a single finger inside her tight opening with excruciating slowness, then bent to kiss her again. Delighting in the taste of Eve's whimper on her lips, Selene pulled back just far enough to whisper, "I could get used to you, too."

CHAPTER TEN

When Selene woke up early the next morning, Eve was silently slipping out of bed. Glad to have caught her before she made her escape, Selene said, "Sneaking away?"

Jerking in surprise, Eve glanced over her shoulder. "No. Couldn't sleep, that's all. I didn't want to wake you with my tossing and turning, so I thought I'd make some coffee."

Not ready to lose the heat of Eve's naked body close to her own, Selene grabbed her arm and gently tugged her back under the covers. "Come here. Coffee can wait a few minutes."

"Yes, it can." Eve's eyes glittered in the low light as she stretched out on her side facing Selene. She hooked a leg around Selene's hip, bringing their lower bodies together with a contented whimper. "I'm going to be sore today."

"Me, too."

"You have no idea how badly I needed last night."

Tracing her tongue over Eve's lower lip, Selene whispered, "I think I have a pretty good idea, actually."

Eve giggled, moving forward to capture Selene's mouth in a deep kiss. When she pulled away, she murmured, "This is crazy."

Selene couldn't disagree—and Eve didn't know the half of it. A tiny kernel of panic took root in Selene's belly as she considered the ramifications of what they'd just done. She was bonded to Eve now. She could feel it to the depths of her being. And she still had no idea how she would manage a relationship with a human.

Eve kissed her again. "You okay?"

Shaking off her unease, Selene shifted her focus back to Eve. "Why couldn't you sleep?"

Immediately, a mask dropped over Eve's face. Though Selene

could clearly feel her distress at the question, Eve kept her expression neutral. "Just one of those nights, I guess." She gave Selene a grin that looked more like a grimace. "Too much sex?"

"That's not it." Selene brushed a lock of hair off Eve's face. "Tell me."

Rather than become frustrated at Selene's persistence, Eve relaxed all over. Selene could feel her rush of relief as though a dam had broken. "Bad dream."

"You should have woken me," Selene said. Pulling Eve into a warm embrace, she stroked her back and kissed her cheek. "You don't need to suffer alone."

Tensing slightly, Eve said, "We just met, Selene. I'm hesitant to admit just how much baggage I'm carrying."

"Nonsense." Selene didn't care how long they'd known one another. Considering how she felt after just one night, it might as well have been years. Besides, Eve's issues couldn't even begin to compare to Selene's dark secret. "I've got my own baggage, believe me. Yours couldn't possibly frighten me."

Snorting, Eve murmured, "Give me a chance."

Selene drew back and winked. "That's the plan."

Eve blushed, barely hiding her delight, and warm affection flowed from her like a fast-moving stream. Clearly Selene had said the right thing. "Where did you come from?" Eve's voice held a note of pure wonder.

Selene smiled but didn't answer. Frankly, she wasn't sure what to say, on so many levels. "Have you been having a lot of nightmares?"

"Some." Eve sat up in bed, pulling her knees to her chest. Sighing deeply, she wrapped her arms around her legs as though protecting herself. "I hate to admit it, but what happened has really shaken me up."

"I don't blame you." Selene drew a line down the length of Eve's spine with her fingertips. "Being attacked like that must be traumatic, to say the least. It's only natural that you'd still be dealing with it."

"I see a lot of sick, twisted stuff in my line of work," Eve said, relaxing into Selene's touch. "I have no illusions as far as what human beings are capable of doing to each other. When that man was on top of me, all I could see was all the murder victims I've examined over the years. Their wounds, their mottled gray skin, those empty, staring eyes. I could so easily imagine myself like that, on a steel table somewhere—"

"Hey." Sensing Eve's rising fear, Selene sat up and wrapped her arm around her shoulders, tugging her close. "You're safe now. I promise."

Blinking rapidly, Eve pressed the heels of her hands against her eyes. "I don't even want to walk outside anymore. One of my favorite things in the world, and…" She swallowed, turning her face away from Selene. "He took that away from me."

The sadness in Eve's voice tore at Selene's heart. "Not forever, darling."

Eve shook her head. "Just the thought of going on one of my morning walks…" She shivered violently, and Selene had to close her eyes against the wave of nausea Eve sent rolling over her. "I barely want to leave the house, especially early in the morning."

Selene took a deep breath, steadying her own emotions. Besides having to contend with Eve's residual fear, she struggled to keep her anger at bay. She hated seeing Eve in so much pain, and, more than anything, she wanted to find the man who had attacked her and hurt him. Taken aback by the fantasy violence that flashed through her mind at the thought of confronting Eve's attacker, Selene concentrated instead on projecting calm strength. Staying positive was the best way to bring Eve's tumultuous emotions under control.

"Tell you what," Selene said, patting Eve on the back. "We're going for a walk right now. This morning. Together."

Eve gave her a look of pure panic. "I don't think that's a good idea." She gestured out the window at the morning sky, just beginning to lighten. "It's still dark. I've got to go to work soon."

"The sun will be up in thirty minutes. When do you need to be at work?"

Hesitating only a moment, Eve said, "Eight o'clock."

Selene gave her a reassuring hug. "That gives us plenty of time for a short stroll. We won't go far."

Eve shook her head. "I vote for staying in and making love again."

Tempting as that was, Selene needed to help Eve overcome her lingering fears. Obviously Eve was an intelligent, logical, self-sufficient woman, and the introduction of unchecked fear into her ordered life had shaken her thoroughly. Even having known Eve only a short while, Selene couldn't stand to see her like this.

"Hey," Selene said, grabbing Eve's hand between her own. "You *can* do it. I promise. I'll be right next to you. We won't go anywhere near where it happened. We can stay at the edge of the park, if you want. If it's too intense, we'll turn right around."

"You're going to make me do this, aren't you?"

Worried about overstepping in a brand-new relationship, Selene shook her head. "Not if you really don't want to. But you'll be miserable until you face this fear head-on. And I very much want to be there to help you do that."

Eve's eyes shone with emotion. The jumble of love, affection, and surrender Selene could feel reassured her that she hadn't pushed too hard. "Okay. We'll take a walk."

"Good." Selene hopped out of bed, offering her hand to Eve. "Let's go have a quickie in the shower before we leave. There's a coffee shop a couple blocks away. We can get our morning fix there."

That promise brought genuine pleasure to Eve's face. She took Selene's hand, allowing herself to be hauled to her feet, then gathered into a tight hug. "I like the way you think."

❖

For the first block, Selene felt almost as though she was dragging Eve along against her will. Eve gripped her hand tight, staying close to Selene's side and darting her eyes around as though anticipating danger from all sides. Rank fear emanated from Eve's pores, nearly choking Selene with its intensity. It wasn't easy to stay relaxed in the face of such strong, instinctual dread, but it was the only way to ease Eve's worries. This was as frightened as she had seen Eve since the immediate aftermath of her attack.

As though reading her mind, Eve said, "I'm sorry. I'm being ridiculous."

Selene squeezed her hand, then wrapped an arm around her shoulders. "No, you're not."

"Logically, I know the chance of something bad happening is slim to none. But I can't stop flashing back to that moment when that man came running at me. It happened so fast, and I was totally unprepared."

"Focus on the fact that you're not alone this time." Selene raised Eve's hand to her mouth, kissing her knuckles gently. "I would *never* let anything happen to you. Seriously." It was a scary thought, but

Selene meant what she said. For years, staying hidden had been her only priority. But she had no doubt that if given the choice between shifting in front of Eve to save her or seeing her hurt, she'd expose herself in an instant.

That someone she'd just met could already mean so much to Selene unnerved her. Short of threat of death or physical harm, she never wanted Eve to know the truth. Undoubtedly such a revelation would end their relationship. Nobody wanted to be with a freak, especially not one who became a genuine monster under the light of the full moon.

"Are *you* okay?" Eve said, giving Selene a sidelong glance. She rubbed a thumb over Selene's knuckles. "Where did you just go?"

Selene forced a nonchalant shrug. "Nowhere. Just thinking about how much I like you."

The last trace of anxiety melted from Eve's face. "I like you, too."

"Good." Selene stopped in front of the coffee shop two and a half city blocks from her house. Bumping Eve with her shoulder, she said, "Look. We made it."

Eve looked behind them as though internally measuring the distance they had traveled. Then she scanned their immediate surroundings. At seven fifteen in the morning, the streets were active if still quiet. A jogger moved purposefully down the sidewalk across the street, and a pair of older women waited at the corner for the Walk sign to light. Selene watched Eve take in the normalcy of the situation, her breathing now calm and controlled.

"You've walked in this city hundreds of times, right?" Selene said quietly. "One time something bad happened. And maybe you don't walk alone anymore, not in the park. But this is still your city. He hasn't taken that away from you."

Nodding, Eve bit her lip and her nostrils flared. "You're right." She threw her arms around Selene, kissing her softly on the neck. "Thank you."

Selene returned the hug as her chest filled with so much love she felt like she would burst. Making Eve happy was the best thing she'd ever done. It stirred answering joy in her own heart, a feeling of hope and promise that had been missing from her life for far too long. Selene never wanted to lose that heavy fullness inside, this sensation of having her whole being entwined with another soul.

Eve drew back from their embrace with a tremulous chuckle. "Should we get some coffee?"

"Coffee sounds good." Shaken by the depth of her feeling for Eve, Selene jogged to the entrance and held open the door. "After you."

Selene stood silently at Eve's side as they waited through the short line and ordered their drinks. Eve drank her coffee black, which didn't surprise Selene. As Selene stood at the counter dumping sugar into her own coffee, Eve gave her an indulgent grin.

"You like the sweet stuff, huh?"

Selene chuckled. "Half the appeal of that cake last night was sharing it with you." She snapped the lid back on her coffee cup and took Eve's hand, walking them to the door. "But, yes, I love sweet stuff." As they stepped out onto the sidewalk, Selene bent close so nobody would overhear. "My favorite is your pussy."

Eve blushed fiercely, taking a sip of her coffee as she fought back a grin. "Wow."

Deciding to take advantage of Eve's distraction, Selene steered them in the direction of the crosswalk. "Let's walk back on the other side of the street." She could sense how much Eve loved Golden Gate Park and how upset she was to have it associated with fear and death, so Selene wanted to help her reclaim that part of her city, too. "Prettier view over there," she said, pointing at the tall eucalyptus trees that loomed over the sidewalk, signaling the edge of the park.

Eve tightened her fingers on Selene's. "Okay."

They crossed the street in silence, and Selene positioned herself closest to the trees as they began to stroll back. She could surely defend Eve if it came down to it, so she wasn't worried about their safety. But Eve would feel safer if she didn't have to worry about someone rushing at her from the brush, like last time.

"When I was a kid my father used to take us for picnics in Golden Gate Park," Eve said, staying close to Selene's side. "He loved Stow Lake. After we ate we'd take out a boat, him and me and my mom, and paddle around for hours. Talking and laughing, just being together as a family."

Feeling the bittersweet melancholy behind the memory, Selene put her arm around Eve and squeezed. "Do your parents still live in the area?"

"No, my father passed away when I was in high school. It was very sudden. My mother and I woke up one morning and found him dead on the bathroom floor. Healthy one day and gone the next. The autopsy revealed he'd died of a brain aneurysm." Eve's voice remained steady, but Selene could feel her sadness. "My mother was killed shortly after

I graduated from college, during a robbery at the gas station she used to frequent. According to witnesses, the guy with the gun panicked and started firing. She was just in the wrong place at the wrong time."

"I'm so sorry."

"Me, too." Eve cleared her throat and straightened her shoulders. "My father's death is actually what made me decide to become a forensic pathologist. The shock of having someone you love die, and not knowing why, is unimaginable. I like being able to answer those questions for people. And now, with the work I do for the police, I feel like I'm also honoring my mother's memory by helping catch and convict murderers. Not that answers *or* convictions make a loss like that hurt any less."

There was something so noble about how Eve had used her personal pain to drive her toward a career that helped ease the torment of others. Selene admired Eve's desire to give back almost as much as she envied the obvious bond she'd had with her parents. "You were very close with them, huh?"

"I was. They're probably the complete opposite from what you'd expect, as far as who would raise a pragmatist like me. Open-minded, spiritual, nature-loving—they lived in the Haight during the sixties, if that gives you any idea of the kind of people they were." Chuckling, Eve said, "When I was little they'd take me to the park and just want to mellow out with nature—and I'd keep tossing question after question at them. Why do leaves change color in the fall? Do birds fly at night? They never knew the answers, and I think they preferred it that way. To them the world was mysterious and magical, which was exactly what they loved about it. Me, I always wanted to know *why* and *how*."

The thought of a bespectacled, inquisitive child-Eve warmed Selene. "So you harshed their mellow?"

Eve burst into giggles that made Selene happy all over. "I guess so." She glanced into the park, and Selene felt her body relax slightly. "Even though I was always the coldly rational type, having parents like that was a gift. They taught me to appreciate nature and the universe on a purely emotional level. To recognize that even if there are things in the world nobody can explain, we should be grateful for those things, and for that mystery. I've only realized in the past few years just how much I value having that attitude. Keeps me more balanced than many of my colleagues."

"Sounds like you miss them a lot."

"Yeah." Eve waved a hand at the park. "Spending time in there makes me feel closer to them. It always felt safe, like a refuge. So this…is hard."

Selene completely understood the importance of refuge away from the noise of daily life. Moving from place to place, she always required being close to nature. Even when she was in human form, the sight and smell of trees and damp earth soothed her in a way nothing else did. Once a month, her beast-self was drawn so powerfully to nature that if she escaped, she would likely run miles to find it, if necessary.

Feeling a strange kinship with Eve, Selene murmured, "I never knew my birth parents. A couple in Italy adopted me when I was four years old. But I…lost them, too. When I was sixteen." She hoped Eve wouldn't ask for details, because she didn't want to lie. But she couldn't possibly tell Eve that her parents had disowned her after she murdered the family sheep. "It doesn't matter how long ago it happened. It still hurts, right?"

Eve nodded, rising on her tiptoes to kiss Selene's cheek. "Right."

A distinctive call cut through the quiet morning and Selene stopped, searching the branches above them until she spotted the source. "Eve, look." She pointed at the large bird perched on a tree just ahead of them. "A Cooper's hawk. Isn't she gorgeous?"

Eve squinted for a moment, then lit up. "I see her."

"Did you know that ninety percent of bird species are monogamous?" Selene noted the way Eve's mouth twitched and the obvious pleasure she seemed to derive from that fact. "Some birds mate only for a season, or even sequential seasons, but most Cooper's hawks mate for life."

"I like that," Eve said. "I wonder where her mate is."

Selene touched the small of Eve's back. "Maybe she hasn't found him yet. She's a juvenile."

"You know a lot about birds." Eve stood quietly at her side, watching the hawk as she cried out again. No longer anxious about being so close to the park, Eve seemed genuinely interested in Selene's dorky cache of wildlife knowledge. "Do you watch them?"

Shrugging, Selene said, "I just love wildlife, including birds."

"I should've guessed, from your photos." The hawk flew away suddenly, leaving them staring up at the empty tree. "We should probably keep moving," Eve said. "I have to leave for work soon."

Selene tried to suppress her disappointment at being separated, but knew she'd failed when Eve's eyes sparkled with sympathy. "I know what you're thinking," Eve said as she started them walking again. "Spending the day in bed would be better."

"Spending the day with *you* would be better." Selene rubbed her hand over Eve's side, delighting in her warmth. "When can I see you again?"

"How about tonight?"

Selene's mood soared. It should have scared her, so quickly going from a near hermit to being desperate for Eve's company, but right now she felt too good to dwell on the inevitable difficulties involved in having a relationship. Not to mention the danger of caring about someone who would surely be horrified by what she was. "That would be excellent."

"Yeah?"

"Yeah." The light at the corner turned and Selene led them across the street, back to her doorstep. "I can't wait."

"Me either." When they reached Selene's porch, Eve stopped Selene before she could unlock the door, initiating a deep, passionate kiss. After a few moments she broke away, panting heavily. "I had a great time, Selene. Thanks for that walk."

Eve wasn't making it easy to say good-bye. Gritting her teeth against the burning desire that pounded through her veins, Selene said, "You be safe today, okay?"

"I will."

Selene stepped away, eager for some breathing room. "Call me if you need anything. *Anything*."

The look Eve gave her was positively naughty. "What I need wouldn't be appropriate for a phone call at work."

Exhaling in a rush, Selene said, "Go to work before I pull you inside and have my way with you again."

Eve grinned, clearly pleased to be causing such a reaction. For a moment she looked as though she was thinking about accepting Selene's invitation, then she walked to her car with an extra sway in her step. "I get off between five and six. I'll be here by six thirty at the latest."

"I'll be waiting." By that, Selene meant counting the seconds. As she watched Eve get into her car and pull away from the curb, she drooped against her front door with a heavy sigh.

She was in so much trouble.

CHAPTER ELEVEN

Later at work, Eve was sore, exhausted, and happier than she had been in a long time. Maybe ever. She sat at her desk with the Golden Gate Park victim's file spread out around her, finalizing her forensic report with a grin on her face. Feeling this good made no sense at all when she had just spent the past hour staring at crime-scene photos of a woman who might have been murdered by the same man who had attacked her, but very little made sense these days. The past twenty-four hours with Selene had defied logic altogether, though that hadn't stopped Eve from enjoying every second of it.

"Knock, knock."

Eve glanced over her shoulder and waved at Jac, who stood just inside the lab door. "Hey, you."

"Hey, back." Jac raised an eyebrow as she stepped inside. "What's up?"

"Just putting the finishing touches on your forensic report," Eve said. She sounded chipper, didn't she? Jac would definitely pick up on that. Eve was never this cheerful, even in her best moods. "I'll have it to you in just a moment."

"Thanks," Jac said carefully. She approached Eve's desk and gave her a sidelong look. "But I meant what's up with the sunny disposition? You're…glowing."

Eve's face heated. Jac was a detective for a reason, so she couldn't try to hide her joy. "I had a good night, that's all." She glanced up at Jac. "Can't a girl be happy?"

"Of course." Jac studied her face, probably trying to decide if Eve's good night was actually what it sounded like. "You just haven't been lately. Not that I blame you, of course. With what happened in the park and everything…" Jac tilted her head. "Did you get *laid* last night?"

Clearing her throat, Eve made a big show of jotting a final note in Yasmin Mandujano's file. She refused to admit that she'd spent all of yesterday afternoon and last night making love to someone she'd just met. "Not that it's any of your business, but…I did have a date."

"You're kidding."

Eve frowned. The sheer disbelief in Jac's voice offended her. Was she really so socially awkward that Jac didn't think she could find someone who was interested? "Gee, thanks."

"No!" Jac shook her head, propping her hip on the desk next to Eve's hand. She was so close Eve could feel heat radiating from her. "That's not what I meant. It's just…after what you've just been through. I'm surprised."

"Well, don't be. Life goes on."

"Apparently it does." Jac folded her arms over her chest, clearly waiting for more. She'd have to ask. Eve wouldn't supply any more information than necessary. What she had shared with Selene was too precious to reduce to tedious gossip. And something about discussing Selene with her ex-girlfriend made Eve uncomfortable. Jac held out for almost thirty seconds before she said, "Who is she?"

"Just a woman."

"I figured," Jac said, smirking. "What else?"

"She's the one who helped me the other morning. In the park, after…you know. After."

"Huh." Craning her neck to meet Eve's eyes, Jac winked. "She have a name?"

"Selene," Eve answered shortly. She was about done playing along with the interrogation. Closing the file, she offered it to Jac. "She's very nice, we had a good time. End of story."

"Is it?" Jac took the file and tucked it beneath her arm without glancing at it. Obviously she found Eve's personal life more riveting than something so trivial as solving a murder. "You said she found you in the park that morning?"

Eve sighed. "I'm trying to decide why the police are suddenly questioning me about this."

"Because I care about you," Jac said. "And I want to know. What was this Selene doing in Golden Gate Park so early in the morning?"

"Same thing I was, I guess." Eve's mood was quickly deflating. "Jesus, Jac. Can't you just be glad that I'm happy and move on?"

Looking only mildly chagrined, Jac put a hand on Eve's shoulder and squeezed. "Nothing would please me more than to see you happy. You know that. I'm just—"

"A cop."

Jac chuckled. "Yes. And someone who loves you."

"Yeah, well…" Eve rolled her chair backward and stood, wanting to be at eye level with Jac. It made it easier to assert herself. "I appreciate that. But this is kind of a new thing, so I'd prefer to keep it to myself for a while."

"I get it," Jac said. "Sorry."

Now Jac appeared fully chagrined. Eve softened. "It's okay. I get it, too."

"Cool." Jac eased into a wide smile, the one that had always reduced Eve to jelly when they were together. "So, I actually intended to ask you if you wanted to join me for dinner tonight. I figured I could make your favorite. Chicken fajitas?"

"I go on a date and suddenly you want to cook dinner for me?" Eve chuckled to cover her uncertainty about Jac's motives. She hadn't been to Jac's place for dinner since the breakup. Her timing was suspicious, to say the least. "Is that what's happening here?"

"I was planning to ask you to dinner before I found out you went out with someone," Jac said. "You just laid that one on me, remember?"

"Why now? Broken up for almost a year and all of a sudden you want to get cozy again?"

Jac gave her a pained frown. "Look, I know we've had some rough times. But what happened to you in the park…it really got me thinking. About how much you mean to me. How lost I'd be if something happened to you." Reaching for her hand, Jac entangled their fingers and tugged Eve closer. "I'm just asking you to dinner, Eve. That's all. I want to spend time with you." Jac's brown eyes were wide and sincere, but they no longer drew Eve in. "Shit, we used to be best friends. And I know I screwed everything up, but…that doesn't mean I don't still need you in my life."

Anger flared in Eve's stomach, spreading through her body like wildfire, then burning out just as quickly. For months she'd struggled over their breakup, and *now* Jac wanted to rekindle something? She didn't believe for a second that Jac was only after friendship. The look in Jac's eyes was familiar. Eve hadn't seen it since they first became lovers, and it threw her for a loop. Now that she was finally over Jac, she was worth desiring again? For the thrill of the hunt?

"Actually, I've got another date tonight." Eve tried to sound casual, but knew she'd just dropped a bombshell. "But thanks anyway."

Jac blinked. "Really? Two nights in a row?" She wasn't even trying to hide her lack of enthusiasm. "Wow."

"I'm sure you've seen women two nights in a row," Eve said. "Maybe not the *same* woman, granted."

Jac tensed, then forcibly relaxed. "I don't expect you to believe me, but I have changed, Eve. I made a mistake. And I've learned my lesson." Stepping away from Eve, she pulled the case file from under her arm and tapped it on the desktop. "All I've got left to do now is prove it to you."

Wayne chose that moment to return from lunch. As he opened the lab door and hurried inside, not pausing even when he saw her and Jac locked in a meaningful stare, Eve was glad for his occasional social ineptitude. This wasn't the first time he'd saved her from a conversation she'd rather not have.

"Hello, peeps." Wayne flashed Eve an enthusiastic Spock greeting gesture with his hand. "What are we talking about?"

"Nerdy science stuff," Jac said easily. "But I was just leaving."

"Perfect." Wayne pointed at his microscope on the counter. "Because I have something you've *got* to check out, Dr. Thomas. The biggest maggots you've ever seen. Dug them out of some necrotic flesh."

"Okay." Jac exhaled and put a hand on her stomach. "Things just got a little *too* real for me in here." Waving at Eve, she rushed to the door. "I'll see you later, Eve." Glancing at Wayne, she said, "You... well, thanks for that."

"Bye." He waved cheerily until Jac shut the door behind her. Then he rolled his eyes, glancing at Eve. "I hope I didn't misread that you wanted her gone."

Eve laughed. "So you don't really have giant maggots for me?"

"Unfortunately, no," he said. "I do have some necrotic flesh, though."

Eve patted him on the back. "You're a good friend, Dr. Black. Truly."

Wayne ducked his head, obviously pleased by the praise. "Yeah, well. Us geeks have to stick together. Right?"

"That *is* in the handbook. At least the last time I checked." Eve went back to her desk and sat down. Now that Jac was gone, she was determined to recapture the good mood Selene had given her. At the thought of her, Eve's tummy fluttered pleasantly, and she stared dreamily at the wall.

"You almost ready for our eleven o'clock autopsy?" Wayne said, not bothering to hide his excitement. He probably enjoyed the hands-on portion of his job a little too much, but Eve understood. It was better than paperwork.

"I am." For the first time since the attack, she faced the prospect of confronting a dead human being with scientific curiosity instead of mild dread. Selene had given her that gift, a return to normalcy. And she'd also given Eve something so much better than normal. Something decidedly *not* normal: the possibility of soul-twisting, reason-defying, head-over-heels love.

Eve hoped she could offer Selene something even a fraction as compelling in return. At least she had the whole evening to try.

After her second all-night lovemaking session in as many days, Eve sat at her kitchen table watching the sunrise through the window and wondering how she had gotten so lucky. Dressed in only a loose-collared button-up shirt and black panties, Selene stood at the stove with a spatula in hand, every inch of her sex personified. Eve couldn't stop sneaking peeks at Selene's bare legs, remembering how they'd felt wrapped around her only thirty minutes earlier. She was tired, hungry, even sore, but above all, she was gloriously content.

"Do you know that I've had more sex in the past forty-eight hours than the entire rest of my life?" Selene glanced over her shoulder, taking her eyes off their pancakes for the first time since she'd poured them. "Seriously. It's fantastic."

Humming, Eve tilted her head and gazed longingly at the very tops of Selene's muscular thighs. Eve wouldn't believe such an incredible statement from most women as beautiful as Selene. But she knew Selene was wholly sincere. "We agree, then. The sex is *fantastic*."

"The sex is just the tip of the iceberg." Selene transferred a pancake from the skillet to a plate, then set her spatula on the counter. She sauntered over to Eve's chair, hips rolling in the most sensuous display of movement Eve had ever seen. "*You* are fantastic." Kneeling beside Eve's chair, Selene gave her a slow, wet kiss. "And I think I'm falling for you."

Eve's heart thudded. Not because she didn't feel the same way, not even because she hadn't already guessed how Selene felt. If she'd been uncertain yesterday at work, the past eighteen hours had erased all doubt. She was just reacting to the simple shock of hearing the words spoken aloud and, more than that, believing them.

"Me, too," Eve whispered, closing the distance between them to steal another kiss. She thumbed open the top two buttons of Selene's shirt and slipped her hand inside. She grazed Selene's erect nipple, and suddenly pancakes were the last things on her mind.

"We can reheat them," Selene said, once again on exactly the same wavelength. They always seemed to be in synch, which made being together easy in a way it had never been with Jac.

Eve moaned into their kisses. "We're going to kill ourselves. Starvation, dehydration…where will it end?"

"Satisfaction." Selene hissed as Eve pinched her nipple. "A small price to pay, I think. For this."

Eve opened her mouth to answer, but stopped when someone knocked on her door. Pulling back from Selene, she was instantly wary. She hadn't buzzed anyone in. Nobody ever visited her so early. For the first time since their walk to the coffee shop the other morning, Eve felt afraid of the man from the park. It wasn't logical that he would knock, but that didn't stop her flight instinct from kicking in.

Selene seemed to pick up on her unease. "Not expecting anyone?"

"No." Eve stood and forced herself to walk to the door. "Definitely not." Someone probably just had the wrong apartment. She put her eye to the peephole, shocked, relieved, and a little angry to see Jac. Opening the door slightly, Eve stepped into the hallway and frowned. "What are you doing here?"

"Good morning to you, too, darling." Jac held up a familiar blue box. "Bagels. Cream cheese. What do you say?"

"I say I've already got breakfast plans," Eve said, even as Jac was edging past her into the apartment. "Hey!"

Jac stopped only a few steps inside her living room. Feeling as though her worlds were colliding, Eve turned and swallowed at the sight of Jac and Selene sizing one another up.

Selene smiled warmly. "Hello," she said, crossing the room and offering her hand. "I'm Selene."

"Jac." Taking Selene's hand, Jac raised an eyebrow and unsubtly scanned Selene's bare legs. "I apologize. I didn't realize Eve had company."

"It's quite all right," Selene said. "Would you like to stay for pancakes?"

Trying to hide her alarm, Eve grabbed Jac's arm and tugged her toward the door. "Actually, Jac has to leave."

Jac shrugged away from Eve's hand. "That's a fascinating accent, Selene. Unusual. Where are you from?"

Though Selene's friendly expression never faltered, Eve sensed her discomfort. "I was born in Italy, but I've lived many different places. Mostly in Europe. I've been in the States for three years now."

"Europe," Jac said softly. "Ah."

Eve recognized Jac's tone. She thought she was on to something, though Eve had no idea what that might be. All she knew was that Jac was turning an excellent morning into something unbearably awkward. "Really, Jac. You should go."

"Well, it was nice meeting you." Jac gave Selene a wide, charming grin every bit as fake as the sentiment. "You two enjoy your breakfast."

"Nice meeting you, too, Jac."

Jac raised an eyebrow. "I'm Eve's ex, by the way."

"Yes, I got that," Selene murmured. "Sorry you have to run."

Unable to stand any more, Eve dug her fingernails into Jac's arm and dragged her to the door. Opening it, she pushed her into the hallway, then shut the door behind them. "What the hell are you doing?" Eve said once she was certain Selene couldn't hear.

"Damn, girl." Jac pulled her arm away, rubbing at the faint marks. "You're surprisingly grumpy for someone who obviously had another very good night."

"My night is none of your business," Eve said in a tight voice. "It stopped being your business the moment you chose to fuck other women."

Irritation flashed over Jac's face. "Look, I don't know how many times I can apologize, or tell you I've changed. But this, right now, has nothing to do with that. I had no idea you'd have company. I just wanted to bring you bagels. As your friend."

Eve forced herself to calm down. She really didn't want to fight with Jac. The adrenaline from her surge of fear at the sound of Jac knocking had fueled her anger, and now she just wanted to let it go. Move on. "I appreciate the gesture, Jac. But I told you I had a date last night."

"Second date?" Jac gentled her voice. "I don't care what I said in the lab yesterday, I didn't honestly expect her to be serving you breakfast."

"Yes, well…" Eve cleared her throat, knowing how out of character this all was for her. It was no wonder Jac was surprised. It had taken them three months to transition from friendship to intimacy. The idea of Eve sleeping with a woman so quickly would seem inconceivable. Before two days ago, it had been. "She's special."

"I could see that." Still holding the box of bagels, Jac leaned against the wall, striking what she probably hoped was a casual pose. "Beautiful, isn't she?"

Something about Jac's tone rankled Eve. "She is."

"So what do you know about her? Really?"

"Excuse me?" Eve folded her arms over her chest. "Are you actually pretending that our relationship is any of your business?"

"Your *relationship*?" Jac shook her head. "Oh, Eve."

"Don't," Eve said coldly. Condescension was the last straw. "You want to be my friend, Jac? You're on very thin ice right now."

Jac's eyes softened. "I'm sorry, Evie. I understand how this must seem. You start seeing this woman and all of a sudden here I am."

"Here you are," Eve said. "Yeah, that pretty much sums it up."

"Honestly…" Jac glanced at the apartment door, then moved close. "Something's off about her. I can't quite put my finger on it, but…really, what's her background?"

Eve stiffened. She might have known Selene for less than a week, been her lover for only forty-eight hours, but in that time she'd learned everything she needed to know about Selene. Maybe not the intimate details of her life, but the important stuff. Selene was a good person, and when Eve was with her, she was part of something greater than herself.

Above all else, Selene made her happy.

"Leave." Eve put her hand on her doorknob. "How dare you?"

"I'm not trying to be an asshole. I'm trying to be your friend."

"You want to be my friend? Go away. Let me finish my goddamn pancakes with the woman who's made me feel better about myself in the past two days than you *ever* did." Feeling terrible for enjoying the pain Jac wasn't able to hide at that statement, Eve focused on the ugly hallway carpet and wished for her peaceful morning back. "Just let me have this, okay? Please."

"Okay," Jac said. She took a step backward, looking stricken. "I just don't want you to get hurt."

Eve didn't know whether to laugh or cry. "Not every woman's going to hurt me, Jac. Not like you did."

Blinking rapidly, Jac turned and headed for the staircase. Eve watched her go, already regretting what she'd said. As much as she hated Jac's jealousy, she actually didn't doubt that Jac still cared for her very much. And that at least some of her concern did come from a place of love. But their time together was over, and that had been Jac's choice. Disrupting the order of things just as Eve had found Selene seemed unnecessarily cruel.

Eve exhaled, then opened her apartment door and walked back inside. Selene sat at the kitchen table with her legs crossed, staring at the door. When she saw Eve, Selene immediately stood, worry etched across her face.

"She upset you," Selene said. "Are you okay?"

Eve crossed the room and fell into Selene's arms. "I'm so sorry."

"Why?"

"For Jac."

Chuckling, Selene nuzzled Eve's neck. "Darling, she was fine. She just cares about you, no?"

"Barging in here, questioning you about your accent. Acting suspicious." Eve frowned even as she consoled herself by running her hands over Selene's curves. "She's such a *cop*."

Selene went still. "Suspicious of what?"

"Probably why such a hot woman's interested in me." Eve shrugged to hide the uncertainty Jac had caused. "I don't know. All of a sudden she's jealous or something."

Selene tightened her arms around Eve's middle, but said nothing. Sighing, Eve drew back and met Selene's eyes.

"I realize how this must seem. But things are settled between Jac and me, I promise. At least as far as I'm concerned." Hating the vague discomfort on Selene's face, Eve vowed not to let Jac pull anything like this again. She would never forgive Jac if she managed to scare Selene away. "I'm not interested in whatever game she's playing."

"I'm not worried about that," Selene said softly, and despite the lingering unease Eve could feel emanating from her, Eve believed her. "I just don't like knowing that she's upset you."

"I've spent the past year getting over a lot of hurt that she caused." As much as Eve hated to talk about Jac with Selene, she deserved to know what she was getting into. Clearly their history would creep into her relationship with Selene whether she wanted it to or not. "She cheated on me. A lot, I think. I know I was never exactly what she wanted in bed, so…" Eve blushed and stared down at the floor. "She made me feel like I wasn't enough for her, but now that I find someone who seems to want what I have to offer…"

"She's jealous."

"I guess so." Eve didn't know what to make of Jac's behavior. Did Jac really want her back? Or did she just not want to see her move on? "It's pissing me off."

"Sounds like she realizes she was a fool to break your heart." Selene touched Eve's cheek with the back of her hand. "Though I can't say I'm sorry she blew her chance."

Eve frowned. "I hate this. The last thing I wanted was to expose you to ex-girlfriend drama. At least this early on." Wincing at what her hasty words implied, Eve said, "Not to be presumptuous. About the lifespan of this thing, I mean."

Selene's obvious pleasure at her words drew Eve in, made her feel surrounded by love. "You're not being presumptuous. And as far as ex drama…I'm a big girl. I can handle it." Her lips found Eve's neck again. "Nothing will scare me away from you. I promise."

Eve tilted her head, giving Selene better access. "This is making me feel better," she murmured. "You're so good at that. Making everything better."

"Among other things?" Selene drew back, eyes sparkling. Her hands found Eve's hips and she walked Eve backward until her legs hit the couch. Tugging at Eve's pajama pants, Selene slipped a hand inside and cupped her between the legs. "Or do you need a reminder?"

"A reminder would be good."

And just like that, Jac was forgotten.

CHAPTER TWELVE

It had been two weeks since Kevin touched Dr. Eve Thomas.

Two weeks since he held her down on the ground and pressed his thumbs into her throat. Made her beg and quiver, reduced her to a pathetic shadow of the competent professional she pretended to be. It had been fourteen days exactly, and Kevin wanted to do it again.

But this time he yearned to take it further. To smack her in the face until she cried. Cut her. Maybe even work up the nerve to rape her. Not because he got off on that kind of thing, but because he knew it would frighten her.

And, Christ, how her fear fed him like nothing ever had.

He had planned to taunt Eve Thomas, not torment her. Confound her, not confront her. But now that Kevin had glimpsed another possibility for their game, the idea consumed him. For so long he'd told himself he would come up with a brilliant plan, then stick to it no matter what. That was the way not to get caught. That was his way.

After five minutes alone with Eve Thomas, Kevin didn't know if that was how he wanted to do things anymore. Where was the fun in being too afraid to improvise? Too rigid to seize an opportunity when it presented itself?

It wouldn't be enough to outsmart Dr. Eve Thomas. Not for him, not anymore. He wanted to destroy her. To be the last thing she saw before she died, the monster she feared until that day. He wanted her, full stop, because she was quite simply the strongest, most competent woman he'd ever encountered. And yet *he* could reduce her to a quivering mass of flesh.

What could be more exhilarating?

So he would change his Plan. Nothing held him to it, really. Nothing except his own expectations.

No matter what, he wouldn't kill her yet. The anticipation was too delicious. Once he killed her it would be over. He would have to come up with a new game. And at the moment, he couldn't think of another adversary he'd rather defeat. So he'd keep this going as long as he could. First he would kill another woman for her to examine, but then maybe he'd pay the good forensic pathologist a visit.

Touch her again.

Leave her afraid.

He wanted to destroy her mentally so she would never be able to defeat him with her science, the cold logic with which she had taken down Charles Dunning. Just because he didn't follow the original Plan, just because it served his basest desires, he wouldn't be sloppy. Wouldn't make the wrong move.

He could do whatever the fuck he wanted. And what he craved most in the world, even more than being untouchable, was to terrify the living hell out of Eve Thomas.

So he would.

CHAPTER THIRTEEN

When Selene's phone rang at five thirty on a Thursday evening just a little over halfway through the lunar cycle, she knew immediately that she was in trouble. It was Eve, and these phone calls had become a daily ritual. Selene's stomach flip-flopped happily that Eve was finished at work and they would be together soon. But worry niggled at the back of her mind, the ever-present awareness that soon a night would come they couldn't spend together—up to three nights, if Selene really wanted to play it safe. Even if she wasn't forced to shift the day before and after the full moon, its pull usually affected her for a solid seventy-two hours. Eve would surely notice that she was hornier than usual.

Coming up with an excuse to be away from Eve for even one night would be hard enough. Especially when being with Eve had become the best part of her life. Selene simply didn't want to be apart.

Picking up the phone, she said, "Hey, sweetheart."

"I've been thinking about you all day."

Selene warmed at the happiness that shone through in Eve's voice. "I've been thinking about you, too. Only every second."

"Good answer." From the slight hiss of background noise, Selene could tell that Eve was calling from her car. "Want to hang out with me tonight?"

"We should just agree that we don't need to pretend I might say no." Heart soaring at the thought of being together again, Selene took a steadying breath to tamp down her excitement. Eve made it very hard to play cool. "Of course I want to hang out. Always. This minute."

Eve laughed. "Have you ever been to the Castro Theater? They play older movies."

"No." Selene couldn't remember the last time she'd gone to a movie theater. She'd been a teenager, certainly, before her first forced transformation. Once she'd gone into hiding, being in a crowded room surrounded by other people didn't appeal to her. But now that she was with Eve, doing something as painfully normal as going to the movies intoxicated her. "What's playing?"

"*Ladyhawke*. Have you seen it?"

"I haven't."

"It's one of my favorites. It has everything…fantasy, romance, humor. The tragedy of star-crossed lovers, kept apart by a curse."

Eve's excitement made Selene's decision for her. "Sounds great."

"Yeah?"

"I'd love to go on a date with you."

Chuckling, Eve said, "I guess this is like a date, huh? Our first real one."

"You mean where we go out and do something fun first, *then* come home and have sex?" Selene was confident where their evening would end—in bed. "I'm up for it if you are."

"I'll even buy you dinner."

Selene snorted. "Well, then I guess I'll *have* to put out."

"Damn right," Eve said. "Listen, I'm about five minutes from your place. If you can get ready quickly, we could grab something to eat right now. That should give us just enough time to make the movie."

Unable to believe this was her life now, Selene shook her head as she struggled against face-splitting joy. "That sounds perfect. I'll just throw on my shoes and meet you outside."

"Awesome." She could hear Eve's anticipation in her voice. "See you soon."

"Bye." Selene hung up and sighed deeply. Things were going so well with Eve that she hated to rock the boat. With a week and a half left until the next full moon, she had to figure out how to juggle a girlfriend and her transition for the first time. It definitely put a damper on the thrill of dating, but Selene wouldn't let it bring her down tonight.

Not when she was about to go out and have fun like a normal person.

"A movie," Selene murmured. "Look at me."

❖

Spilling out of the theater onto the crowded Castro sidewalk hours later, Selene could hardly believe what she'd just watched. Leave it to

Eve to pick a movie that so closely hinted at Selene's dual nature. As it turned out, *Ladyhawke* was a fantasy movie about a pair of lovers who were kept apart because of a curse—by day she was transformed into a hawk, and by night he shifted into a wolf. Consequently they could never be together as human beings—at least not until the end of the film.

"Are you okay?" Eve asked as they walked down the street toward the car.

Selene choked out an embarrassed laugh. Not one to get emotional over films easily, she had tears pouring down her face by the time the lovers got to be together. The idea that happy endings might be possible even in the most impossible of circumstances definitely stirred her and made her own situation that much more painful.

Because real life wasn't a movie. And though the thought of a fictional character who turned into a hawk or a wolf enchanted Eve, Selene doubted she would be so understanding about her own girlfriend being able to shift into either at will. Even less so about the fact that once a month Selene turned into a monster who couldn't remember her nocturnal activities the next day.

"It must be that time of the month," Selene lied. "I'm just a little emotional."

"I think it's sweet." Eve clasped Selene's hand, tangling their fingers together as they strolled down the sidewalk. "It's a beautiful story, isn't it?"

"Yes." Hesitating, Selene tried to decide if she wanted to offer an explanation as to why the movie had touched her so much. Eve seemed content to chalk it up to hormones and good storytelling, and that was probably best. But despite her need to maintain secrecy, Selene craved a deeper connection with Eve. She wanted Eve to understand her as much as possible, even if Selene could never tell her a lot. "It's just so sad. Not having any control over your life and your body, to the point that you can't enjoy the love you've managed to find with another person…" Aware that she was on the verge of tearing up again, Selene forced a sheepish chuckle. "I'm just glad they were able to be together in the end."

"Me, too."

Exhaling shakily, Selene swiped at her eyes with her free hand. "I'm not usually this sappy." She gave Eve a sidelong glance. "Must be a consequence of all these new feelings you've inspired."

Eve blushed, stopping them in front of her car. "I like it."

"That's a relief." Selene wrapped her arms around Eve and held her tight. After enduring two hours of tortured longing and shape-shifting that cut too close to reality, she was ready to take Eve home and lose herself in physical pleasure. "What do you say we go back to my place and you cheer me up?"

Drawing away, Eve dropped a light kiss on the tip of Selene's nose. "I could definitely do that."

"I know you can." It had nothing to do with sex and everything to do with the way Eve made Selene feel. Like she was worth loving. Like they could somehow be normal together, even if Selene couldn't quite figure out how she might make that work.

Soon Selene would need to find an excuse to keep Eve away during her next transformation. And the one after that. And the one after that. It wouldn't be easy, but she needed to do it.

Real life wasn't a movie, and Selene had no idea whether a happy ending was even possible for her relationship with Eve. But she had to try to make one happen.

CHAPTER FOURTEEN

Lying had never come naturally to Selene.

Until she was sixteen years old, she hadn't wanted or needed to cultivate the skill. She loved her adoptive parents and was generally a good kid. But the night of her first, uncontrolled shift—when she'd killed those sheep—lying suddenly became necessary for survival. That night she lost everything important to her: her home, her adoptive parents, her girlfriend. Her innocence. She gained the keen awareness that even those people who professed to love her would never accept her true nature, so in order to stay alive, she had to learn to hide in plain sight.

That meant becoming a master of deception.

Fifteen years of practice had made Selene very good at living in the shadows. She maintained relationships with escort services, did contract graphic-design work for numerous employers, and kept an apartment in one of the bigger cities in the United States without letting anyone know who or what she really was. For a child who had once been unable to sell even the most reasonable half-truth, as an adult Selene excelled at keeping secrets and misleading people.

She didn't enjoy telling lies. It still made her nervous, not to mention guilty. Although she was good at hiding that emotional turmoil from most people, she wouldn't be able to hide from Eve.

How could she lie to a woman who felt what she felt? A woman who'd already captured her heart, who'd shown her what it was like to feel loved? Not only would lying be difficult, but also Selene just plain didn't want to do it. She knew how Eve felt about dishonesty— how broken trust had been the crux of her problems with Jac—and she dreaded the thought of starting down that road with the woman who'd quickly become as essential as the air she breathed.

Even so, she had just a week until the next full moon. That meant she was rapidly running out of time to come up with a good story for why she wouldn't be around that night. She had to work on staying calm when she told that lie. She had to believe it. Otherwise Eve would sense her dishonesty just as surely as she sensed everything else Selene felt.

Hating herself, Selene hung up from her call to the escort service she'd been using for the past year and a half. She'd just arranged for a new girl, someone who could tie knots to her satisfaction. Escaping as her beast-self wasn't an option this time, not when she wasn't sure who or what she might seek out in her most primal form now that she'd found a mate.

Selene sensed Eve a moment before she heard a knock at her front door. Excited to see Eve despite her anxiety, she struck a casual pose as she answered. "I was just thinking about you."

Eve beamed. "Good things, I hope."

Her bright mood washed over Selene, lifting her spirits. "Always."

"You okay?" Eve tilted her head as she stepped inside. "You seem…unsettled."

"No, I'm great." Selene pulled Eve into her arms. Their connection flared deep in her chest, soothing her worries and refocusing her on what was important. This woman. She had to do whatever it took to keep Eve, and if that meant lying, then so be it.

"You sure?" Eve put a hand on the back of Selene's head and held her close, turning her face so their foreheads touched. "Because it's like I can feel things, you know. It sounds ridiculous, but with you…I don't know. I guess you're easy to read." Giggling shyly, Eve said, "I feel things."

Selene put every ounce of her concentration into not reacting to Eve's confession. She knew that they had an empathetic bond, but Eve didn't. Scientist that she was, Eve most likely wouldn't even believe in such a concept. And yet here Eve was, skirting the edge of articulating what it was between them that made their chemistry so explosive.

"I was just missing you," Selene said quietly. She forgot any notion of trying to sell Eve a story about the night of the full moon. Eve's intuition of her feelings spooked her, and she didn't want to risk their newly formed bond. Not yet, anyway. "I'm feeling much better now."

"Good." Eve giggled when Selene's hands found her ass, caressing her gently. "Should we eat dinner? We could order pizza."

"I can think of something I'd rather eat," Selene whispered into Eve's ear. She felt the immediate impact of her words as a tightening in her abdomen, then a surge of lust that seemed to flow directly from Eve's hands to Selene's brain.

"Since when did you get so naughty?"

"You're a bad influence." Selene nipped at Eve's throat. "You've totally corrupted me."

"Apparently so." Eve threw her head back and hissed when Selene slipped her hand down the front of her pants, into her panties, fingers instinctively finding wet heat, then pushing between her folds. "I can live with that."

"Trust me, I'm *not* complaining." Selene worked a single finger inside Eve, delighting in the tight warmth of her pussy. She loved the way Eve clamped down around her, the way her fingers dug into Selene's shoulders like she was desperate to get closer. "How about we go to the bedroom now and worry about dinner later?"

Eve nibbled at her ear with sharp teeth. "You talked me into it."

Selene knew it was wrong to distract herself from the necessary task by initiating sex, but the seduction wasn't a purely cunning move. Making love was better than lying to the woman she adored, certainly, but Selene simply couldn't stop herself from taking Eve physically, over and over. The emotional pull between them was so intense that the only way to ease the sweet agony was through sexual release. Even that only offered a temporary reprieve from the desperate craving for Eve that constantly thrummed through Selene's veins.

Lying could wait. Tonight she'd enjoy Eve while she still had the chance.

❖

Sometime in the middle of the night, Eve's cell phone rang. Groaning, she opened her eyes and reached for the glowing, vibrating object, hoping like hell that she wasn't being called to examine a body. After hours of strenuous physical activity with Selene, the thought of dragging her ass out of bed and to a crime scene was spectacularly unappealing. Usually the late-night calls went to Wayne, who valued a good corpse much more highly than sleep.

Eve glanced at the display. She didn't recognize the number. Picking up, she mumbled, "Hello?"

Silence.

"Hello?" Eve said again. She pulled the phone away from her ear to check that the caller hadn't hung up. When she saw that the connection was still active, she brought the phone to her ear and listened. She heard the faintest trace of street noise, then a beep that signaled that the caller had disconnected. "Nice."

"Everything okay?" Selene murmured. A strong arm curled around Eve's waist, tugging her closer. "What time is it?"

Eve glanced at the phone's display. "A little after one in the morning."

Selene hummed in acknowledgment. Then she kissed Eve's throat, scraping her teeth over a pulse point. "Need any help getting back to sleep?"

Chuckling sleepily, Eve seriously considered another round before conceding defeat. "I'm not sure I'm physically capable right now."

"Good." Selene slid her hand between Eve's legs and cupped her gently. "Me either. No matter how badly I want to."

Eve closed her eyes and sighed. "You make me feel so sexy."

"Because you are."

That was the amazing thing about being with Selene. For the first time in her life, Eve believed in her own desirability. How could she not?

The ringing of Eve's cell phone tore her out of sleep once again. "Leave me alone," Eve mumbled. But she reached out and swiped her thumb across the screen to answer it anyway. "Hello?"

"I'm sorry to wake you," Jac said. "But I'm standing over a very fresh corpse that you need to know about."

Eve groaned. "Wayne isn't available?"

"No, Eve. *You* need to know about this one."

Jac's sober tone wrenched Eve fully awake. "Why?" Selene's hand landed on Eve's back. "What is it?"

"Female, approximately mid thirties, looks like multiple stab and slice wounds. Two bad ones on her neck, same pattern as the last victim. And I'm not exactly sure, but I think her eyelids show signs of…what is that called?"

"Petechiae," Eve murmured. "You're saying she was strangled, too?"

"Well, you're the expert, but—"

"So we're looking at the Golden Gate Park killer?" Eve glanced over as Selene sat up in bed, giving her a worried look that sent fear rolling through Eve's stomach.

"I think it's definitely a possibility." Jac cleared her throat. "There's something else."

"Just tell me."

"Well, I'm standing in an alley about a block from your apartment."

A cold sliver of dread pierced Eve's throat, making it hard to breathe. Immediately Selene's arm was around her, strong and warm and somehow able to sweep away her disquiet in a way that defied logic. Eve burrowed into Selene, greedy for the comfort. "I'll be right there."

Jac exhaled. "You want me to come to your place and walk you?"

"I'm not at my place."

Jac was silent for a moment, then said, "Then drive safe, okay?"

"Okay." Eve hung up and exhaled, dropping her face into her hands. Now she was not only exhausted, but also frightened, because it probably wasn't a coincidence. Same MO as the victim in the park, found only a block away from her apartment. Eve was a big believer in Occam's razor—the simplest explanation is most likely the correct one. And the most likely scenario here was that they were looking at a new victim of the same killer from Golden Gate Park—who almost certainly knew where Eve lived.

"He killed another one?" Voice choked with dread, Selene radiated unease.

"Sounds like it." Eve lit the display on her phone again to check the time. Four in the morning. The three hours of sleep she'd managed to get after the last phone call would have to be enough. "I'm sorry, I have to go."

"Where?" Selene tightened her arm around Eve. "Let me take you."

Eve tried to keep her face calm even as her guts churned. "She was dumped about a block from my place. And you should go back to sleep. I'll be fine." Eve hoped she sounded more confident than she felt. "Jac's there. The place will be swarming with cops, honestly. It'll be the safest spot in the city."

Selene threw back the comforter and stood, switching on the lamp on her nightstand. "No way. I'll drive you."

"I'll probably end up going straight in to the office afterward—"

"I can either wait for you there, then take you to work, or else you can call me to come back and pick you up when you're done." Selene grabbed Eve's hand, pulling her to her feet and into a tight hug in one swift motion. "But I'm *not* letting you go alone."

"Sweetheart—"

Selene drew back and met Eve's eyes. "You're scared. You can hide it all you want, but I know this has you freaked out. Please let me be with you. Let me protect you."

The thought amused Eve. Selene was many things, chief among them a source of comfort, but the idea of her gentle lover being able to offer physical protection was almost laughable. However, the determination in Selene's eyes told Eve that she'd die trying.

"Okay." Eve touched Selene's cheek, marveling at the way her fear dissipated as Selene accepted the caress. "Thank you."

Selene curled her hand around the back of Eve's neck, drawing her into a slow kiss. "I will *always* be here for you. I love you."

Eve's heart stuttered, then jolted into overdrive. Selene startled slightly, easing back to regard Eve with serious eyes. Now she looked terrified, as though she understood the enormous weight of her words and honestly had no idea how Eve would react.

Eve opened her mouth but nothing came out. No matter how perfect things had been between them, no matter how intense her feelings were, she had never imagined hearing Selene say those words so soon. With anyone else, she would have found them ridiculous. After all, how could someone fall in love in less than three weeks?

Improbable as it was, Eve had, too.

"It's too soon." Obviously embarrassed, Selene seemed to suddenly find her feet very interesting. "I'm sorry, it's too soon to talk like that. I just—"

Eve stopped Selene's mouth with her fingertips. "I love you, too."

Selene lifted her face, giving Eve an expression of pure joy that almost knocked her off her feet with its luminance. "Yeah?"

Five minutes ago Eve had been weak with fear. Now she returned Selene's smile easily. "Oh, yeah."

"Good." Selene gave her a quick kiss on the lips, then patted her bare bottom shyly. "Now get dressed."

CHAPTER FIFTEEN

By the time they reached the row of police vehicles parked near an alley not even a block from Eve's apartment, the euphoria of Selene's declaration of love had all but faded, leaving Eve unsettled about what this crime scene would bring. Though she'd seen some terrible things over the course of her career—especially while hunting the serial murderer Charles Dunning—Eve had never experienced trepidation like this when faced with the prospect of examining a body. Quite the opposite, in fact. Usually she felt a sense of purpose, even excitement that she might be able to help bring a killer to justice. Tonight all that gripped her was disquiet.

Why dump a body so close to her apartment, on a well-traveled residential street? Was it merely chance? Or had the killer done it on purpose? If he was the man who attacked her in the park, he had her wallet. That meant he knew where she lived. Was he sending a message? Threatening her? But if he wanted to hurt her, why not just come after her instead? Was it because she hadn't been home? If she hadn't been at Selene's place tonight, would Jac be standing over Eve's dead body now?

"Everything will be okay." Parking near the curb, Selene put a hand on Eve's knee. "You and Jac will catch this guy. I know it."

Eve nodded resolutely. "Hopefully before he kills another one." What she didn't say out loud was *Like me*.

"You don't know that this was the same guy." Selene was obviously reaching, desperate to assuage Eve's anxiety. "You don't know that he chose this location on purpose."

"You're right." Taking a deep breath, Eve exhaled, centering herself. "Time to go find out."

Selene stopped her with a hand on Eve's wrist. "Should I wait for you?"

Technically, Jac could drive her to work. But Eve liked the idea of having Selene close, especially when she suspected that this would be a difficult crime scene. "How about you give me a few minutes until I know what we're dealing with here. If it looks like it'll take a long time, I'll let you know."

"I can wait as long as it takes." Selene gave her a brave nod. "Don't worry about me."

Eve kissed Selene soundly, then she pulled back with a small, forced laugh. "Wish me luck."

"I'm pretty sure you don't need it, but good luck." Selene waved her away. "Go be a super-smart crime solver, will you?"

"Yes, ma'am." Eve opened the passenger door and stepped out, meeting Jac's gaze instantly. Jac stood on the sidewalk with her arms folded over her chest, a very unsubtle glare on her face. She shifted her focus to Selene and scowled harder. Irritated, Eve closed the car door and strode over to Jac with her shoulders thrown back, pretending to project confidence, at least. "Get up on the wrong side of the bed?"

Jac's sober expression didn't waver. "Selene. What a surprise."

"Get over it."

"You two spending every night together now?" Jac glanced over Eve's shoulder, shooting an icy-cold stare in the direction of Selene's car.

Stepping close to Jac, Eve lowered her voice so none of the cops around them would hear. "This is the last time I'm going to say this, so listen well. Back the hell off. You want to be my friend? I'll give you a tip. Treating Selene like some kind of animal who's pissing on your turf is *not* the way to do it."

"That's not my problem with her."

"Oh, really?" Eve folded her arms over her chest. "Enlighten me, then. What has Selene done to offend you, besides fucking me?"

Jac blinked rapidly, clearly taken aback by her crude language. "Christ, Eve."

Tired of Jac's jealous act, Eve pinched the bridge of her nose, wishing she still wore glasses so she could push them up. "Listen, it's early, I'm exhausted, and quite frankly I'm pretty damn freaked out about this murder. Can we just go see the body now?"

"Fine." With one last glance at Selene's car, Jac gestured for Eve to step into the alley where police personnel gathered around the still form of a woman who lay near a large metal Dumpster. "After you."

Taking a deep breath, Eve pushed away her lingering fear. She had a job to do. Above all else, she was a professional. Eve gave Jac a curt nod and led the way.

❖

Even through the car window, Selene could feel Jac's bile rolling over her, anger mixed with jealousy and sharp, stabbing regret. She couldn't sense Jac's feelings on a soul level like she could with Eve, but she didn't have to. The death glare said it all.

Selene understood all those emotions. She even expected them. Jac had thrown away an incredible woman, and now that Eve was moving on, she was realizing what an idiot she'd been to break Eve's heart. It didn't take an empath to figure that out. If Selene screwed things up with Eve, then saw her with someone new, she'd feel the same way.

What worried Selene about Jac was that her dislike didn't stop at simple jealousy. She was obviously suspicious, about what, Selene wasn't sure. The nature of Jac's suspicion hardly mattered—as long as she was motivated to study Selene for flaws, she might expose her. Being discovered was bad enough, but having a jealous cop find her out would mean the end of her life as she knew it.

Selene watched Eve and Jac walk into the alley, joining a throng of men and women who moved back and forth with purpose. Almost immediately she felt a surge of clenching horror from Eve, so powerful that Selene had to double over and hold her stomach to stop from vomiting. Whatever Eve had just seen, it was bad.

Nauseated, Selene rolled down the car window and took a deep breath. Instead of the fresh air she craved, she choked on the strong smell of fresh blood. The scent hung thick and pungent in the night, leaving no doubt that the victim had bled out. But unlike the last time Selene had smelled death, now she also discerned another scent in the air, one that froze her insides in fear.

It was him. The man who'd attacked Eve in Golden Gate Park.

Selene stuck her head out the window and drew in another whiff. Not because she doubted her sense of smell, but because she wanted to determine just how strongly the man's presence still lingered. On a damp morning like this, she would be able to detect his scent long after he left the scene. But if he was hanging around, she should also be able to pick him up.

These were the moments when Selene wished that she didn't have to hide her ability. If she could shift into a dog, she would be better able to track the killer. As a bird, she could survey the scene from above and possibly find him watching from afar. In human form, all she could do was sniff ineffectually to confirm something she'd never be able to tell anyone: that the man who attacked Eve had also killed this woman.

Unfortunately, Selene couldn't use her ability to sense his agenda—to know whether Eve was in danger or if his dumping site was simply a sick joke, or even an accidental coincidence. She knew only that although he had definitely been here, he wasn't anymore. He was probably far away, but Selene burned to try to track him.

"Damn it," Selene murmured, and glanced at the alleyway. It was far too risky to even consider abandoning the car and shifting. Not with this many people around, especially when one of them was Jac.

Another jolt of sharp agitation hit Selene in the gut and she closed her eyes again, certain she was about to start retching onto the street. Whatever Eve was going through, it wasn't good. Selene wished she could go to Eve and comfort her, using the steel will she'd summoned so many times in the past few weeks to soothe Eve's fears, but she knew she wasn't welcome at the crime scene.

She could only wait for Eve to come to her.

❖

Usually Eve was impervious to the smell of death. It was disgusting and repulsive, but after years in its presence, she'd developed immunity to its sickening presence. However, standing over a woman who looked not unlike her—a thirty-something brunette whose smashed eyeglasses lay on the ground in a pool of crimson—the oppressive odor of blood and gore had Eve swallowing convulsively in an effort not to contaminate the crime scene by throwing up on the ground.

"Are you okay?" Jac kept her voice low, ensuring that nobody overheard. Her hand found the small of Eve's back, and despite their confrontation just moments ago, Eve moved into the caress.

"I don't know," Eve said. "This is him. I feel it."

"It may very well be." Stroking her back lightly, Jac spoke in a trembling voice, betraying her nerves. "But we don't know what it means. This location."

"It means we have our work cut out for us." Eve tore her attention away from the woman's empty eyes, meeting Jac's concerned stare. "We've got to catch this guy. Now."

Nodding, Jac said, "I think the evidence collection team is just about done here. We should be able to move the body to your lab within the hour."

"Good." Eve tried not to think about having to stare at this woman's injuries under a bright light. It would be a messy, terrifying display, even in a clinical setting. She'd never been squeamish before. But the thought of coming face-to-face with this killer's work nauseated her. "Do we know who she is?"

"She had a cell phone on her. That's all." Jac's hand lingered on her back, telling Eve that she wasn't doing a very good job of hiding her emotions. "I'll come back to the lab with you and see what I can find on it."

No matter how frustrated she might be with Jac, Eve was glad for the company at the lab. An ID badge was required to get inside the building, but even that didn't make Eve feel entirely safe. Just as she was starting to really get past what had happened to her in Golden Gate Park, her old fears came back tenfold. What had been nervous speculation now appeared to be cold, hard fact. The man who'd attacked her was more than a simple thief or rapist. He was a psychopath.

Eve was truly lucky to be alive, and whatever had passed between them might not be over yet. Not if his choice of a kill site was any indication.

"Come on," Jac said quietly. "They're ready to load up the body."

"Who found her?" Eve walked out of the alley on rubbery legs, grateful for the opportunity to escape momentarily. "Or did you get another anonymous tip?"

Jac's eyes flicked over Eve's shoulder to Selene's car. "Couple of drunk guys walking home from the bar. One of them stopped to piss in the alley and practically tripped over the body."

"You questioned them?"

"As best as I could. They were stupid intoxicated." Jac shifted her focus back to Eve's face. "Look, Eve. You asked me what my problem was with Selene. I admit, at first I just wasn't thrilled about the idea of this mystery woman seducing you right when you're at your most vulnerable."

"I'm a big girl, Jac." But Eve could hear genuine concern in Jac's voice and kept the rebuke as gentle as possible. "I hope you realize that."

"After I met her at your place, though, something else bothered me."

Remembering Jac's words in the hallway of her apartment, Eve frowned. "Something 'off' about her, I think you said."

At least Jac had the good grace to look uncomfortable as she shifted her weight from one foot to the other. "Yeah. Well, anyway, so I thought a lot about it. I really asked myself—am I just being a selfish asshole? Jealous when I have absolutely no right to be?"

"Keep going." Eve wasn't sure whether this was leading to an apology, but there was a first time for everything.

"So then it came to me, and I listened again to the recording of the anonymous tipster who called in that first body in Golden Gate Park. The morning you were attacked." Jac swallowed. She looked like she knew this might set Eve off, but was determined to plunge ahead anyway. "It was her, Eve. I'm sorry. Selene's the anonymous tipster."

At first Eve didn't know how to react. It was a ridiculous accusation, certainly. Completely out of left field. And Eve didn't believe it for a minute. She *couldn't* believe it. Selene would have told her if she'd been the one to report the body. Wouldn't she?

"That's ridiculous," Eve said finally. "I wish you'd stop grasping at straws."

"Evie, she has a really distinctive accent. 'European,' I believe she said." Wearing an expression of honest-to-goodness regret, Jac seemed almost apologetic about having to deliver the news. "I'm not just saying this because I don't care much for her. I promise. It really was her."

"She would have told me," Eve said, but even as the words left her mouth, she wondered if that was true. If Selene had called in her discovery of the body, that had been before she and Eve knew one another. She'd done it anonymously for a reason and surely wouldn't have told a new acquaintance—especially one associated with law enforcement—about her activities that morning.

But what about in the days and weeks since? After all they'd shared? Eve was convinced that their bond, though new, went deep enough that Selene would have trusted her with that secret. In a crazy way, Eve felt like she would have sensed it.

Unless Selene was a very, very good liar.

The thought chilled Eve. Jac was a good liar. That was exactly why dishonesty was the one thing Eve couldn't abide in a relationship. Not even with someone who felt as right as Selene did.

"I wouldn't lie to you about this," Jac said softly. "I can play the tape for you."

"No." Eve's voice came out more forcefully than she intended. But she was angry with Jac for introducing doubt into a situation that had, until that point, brought Eve nothing but pure happiness. Selene was the best thing in her life right now. She was possibly the only thing holding her together in the face of this Golden Gate Park killer debacle. She couldn't allow Jac to destroy the trust between them, the way everything about their relationship felt both natural and intense beyond reason. It was far too valuable. "I don't want to hear it."

A shadow passed over Jac's face. "She might know something, Eve. Maybe she saw something, or maybe…maybe she's involved somehow."

Eve flinched, taken aback that Selene might have more information about her attacker than she was letting on. Selene knew how frightened Eve was and had offered nothing but support. She couldn't comprehend that Selene could be hiding something like that from her. Eve refused to believe it and hated Jac for even going there. Lowering her voice to an angry whisper, Eve said, "Fuck you. Fuck your tape. And fuck your suspicious bullshit."

"Eve—"

"No. I'm not listening to any more of this. I'm going to get in Selene's car and she's going to drive me to the lab. If you want to meet me there, fine. We can review the evidence together." Eve folded her arms over her stomach, needing the illusion of self-protection. Jac's insinuations had shaken her. "If not, then I'll see you later. But we're not talking about this again."

Irritation flashed in Jac's eyes. "I'll meet you there."

"Great." Eve turned and met Selene's concerned gaze, soothed momentarily as their connection sparked to life. "Thanks for calling me."

"I just want to catch this guy," Jac said to her back. "That's all. I know I was a jealous bitch the other morning when I showed up at your place, but that's not what this is about right now. It *was* her, Eve. If you don't want to listen to the recording, ask her. You don't believe me? Ask her. See what she says. But don't let your feelings for a woman you just met cloud your judgment. There's a killer out there, and I guarantee you he's not done yet. If there's a chance, *any* chance, that Selene knows something that could help us find him, isn't it worth pursuing?"

Tensing, Eve watched as Selene's expression hardened and her focus shifted to Jac. It had to be obvious to Selene that they were arguing. Did she have any idea what about? What if Jac was right? For all the times Jac had been dishonest within their relationship, Eve had never known her to be anything but honest and ethical when it came to her investigations. Even if she was insanely jealous of Selene, Jac wouldn't just pull this type of accusation out of the air.

"I'll think about it." Eve turned back to meet Jac's eyes. "But even if she did make the call, I don't believe for a second that she's involved. There's no way."

Jac's jaw tightened. "Just be careful. Okay?"

"Always." With a tired wave, Eve left Jac and walked to Selene's car. She opened the passenger door and slid into the seat, resting back against the headrest with a weary sigh. "Mind taking me to the lab now?"

"Of course not." Selene started the car, giving Eve a sidelong glance. "You okay?"

"That wasn't fun."

"I know." Selene's voice radiated sympathy, washing over Eve like a calming wave. "It was bad, wasn't it?"

"Yes." Eve caught Jac's eyes one last time as Selene pulled away from the curb, but glanced down quickly, not wanting Jac to see how unsettled their conversation had left her.

Back in the car with Selene, Eve was even less convinced that what Jac said could be true. How could Selene—her Selene—hide something of that magnitude? Knowing that Eve was frightened, knowing that the killer could be targeting her in some way, would Selene really remain silent about having played an integral role in discovering Yasmin Mandujano's body? It just wasn't possible.

Closing her eyes, Eve said, "It's the same killer. I don't have to get the body back to the lab to know for sure. It's definitely him."

"So what happens next?"

Eve sighed. "All I can do is hope he left us more to go on than he did with the first one. Bodily fluids, hair or fiber samples…anything. Otherwise, I just cross my fingers that a witness comes forward with something substantial this time."

If the pointed comment disturbed Selene, she didn't show it. "Looked like you and Jac had an argument. Was it because of me?"

Eve shook her head, pinching the bridge of her nose firmly. "It doesn't matter."

"It upset you. It does matter."

Selene had just given her the perfect opening to bring up the topic of Jac's anonymous tipster, but Eve didn't want to. Asking Selene was just taking Jac's bait, admitting that a part of her still found it difficult to trust anyone completely. Eve didn't want to feel that way with Selene, especially not because of something Jac had said. Jac was the one who'd made her so afraid of being lied to in the first place. To allow Jac to sow distrust within this new relationship was giving her far too much power over her future happiness.

"She's just jealous. Old news." Eve mustered what she hoped came across as an indifferent shrug. "She'll get over it."

"She'll have to." Selene's hand landed on Eve's thigh and squeezed gently. "I plan on sticking around for a while."

"You'd better." Eve stared out the car window at the darkened city streets. He could be anywhere right now. Watching her, even. Aware of her movements, the company she kept. Eve's throat tightened at the sudden thought that if a killer was targeting her, everyone she knew could also be in danger. Whipping around to stare at Selene, Eve tried to decide how to broach the subject without causing unnecessary alarm.

"I'll be fine, sweetheart." Selene gave her a sideways glance. "I promise."

Eve blinked, wondering for a moment if she'd been thinking aloud. But she hadn't. Selene just had a spooky way of sensing her thoughts. "Can you read my mind or something?"

Selene stiffened and Eve swore she could *feel* the shocked guilt that quickly passed across Selene's face. It was gone in an instant, leaving behind only an amused expression that made Eve wonder whether she was searching for signs of deceit where none existed. Had Jac succeeded in planting a seed of doubt that would only grow and tangle their relationship in constant mistrust?

"I could tell you were worried about something. Since you'd just said that I'd better stick around…well, I just assumed maybe you were worried about me." Selene's eyes darted away from the road for an instant to search Eve's face. "I wasn't sure if you were worried about me in regard to Jac or this Golden Gate Park killer, though." When Eve said nothing, Selene shrugged and looked back to the road. "Or maybe I'm just completely off the mark."

"You're never off the mark when it comes to me, Selene."

Frowning, Eve thought about just how true that was. She didn't actually believe that Selene was a mind reader—the scientific evidence for telepathy was sketchy at best—but it did seem that Selene was a highly empathetic individual. There was hardly anything sinister about that. "I *was* worried. If there's any chance the killer is targeting me, he could learn about my routine. That includes where I go, who I see."

"I'll be careful."

"Just…" Eve bit her lip, worried about Selene's ability to defend herself if something did happen. Not that Eve had been a powerhouse of self-defense. But the idea of Selene getting hurt because of her was heart-wrenching beyond anything she'd ever felt before. "Just be aware of your surroundings. If something looks suspicious, trust your gut. Okay? And call me."

Selene nodded easily. "I promise. I really will be okay."

Eve exhaled. She wished she could be so certain about her own safety.

CHAPTER SIXTEEN

When Selene dropped Eve off at nearly five thirty at the medical examiner's office, Jac was already waiting for her in front of the building. The sky had lightened to a foggy gray, but the morning was still dark enough that Eve was very glad she didn't have to walk inside alone. From the easy wave Jac gave her as she approached, Eve knew they were about to play the everything's-fine game and pretend they hadn't just argued at the crime scene.

That worked for Eve.

"How in the world did you beat me here?" Eve said lightly as she carded them into the building. "I saw you standing on the sidewalk as we pulled away."

"I drive like a cop." Jac chuckled lightly as they walked down the still-deserted hallway to Eve's lab. Their shoes squeaked on the tiled floor, so loud that Eve couldn't help searching every dark, empty doorway they passed for fear they were announcing their presence to some unseen enemy. "Remember?"

"We did go on some pretty wild rides together." Stopping in front of her lab, Eve willed her hand not to shake as she swiped her card through the reader, then opened the door. She stepped into her sanctuary with a sigh of relief. For whatever reason, she felt as safe in her lab as she did at home. Probably because, for a workaholic like her, the lab *was* her second home. "Is the body en route?"

"It is." Jac held up a zippered plastic evidence bag that contained a cell phone, and another smaller bag that contained the victim's jewelry. "I brought the rest of the evidence."

"That's all she had on her?" Eve sat at her desk, watching silently as Jac pulled over a chair to sit at her side. Regardless of their personal history and their current tension over Selene, she and Jac had always made a good team. She didn't know anybody she'd rather have by her side on this case, anybody she trusted more to help find this killer before he could hurt anyone else.

"That's it. No wallet or purse, unfortunately."

"He likes to take their purses," Eve said softly. He'd taken hers, hadn't he? "Maybe he keeps them as trophies."

"Or else he's just trying to slow down the identification process." Jac shrugged, pulling two latex gloves from a cardboard box on Eve's desk. She slipped them on and dumped the cell phone out of the bag. "At least he left the phone behind. Maybe we can find her name in here."

Eve watched Jac power on the phone and flip through menus with a flick of her thumb. What bothered Eve most about this murder was where it had happened. Not only the proximity to her apartment, but the open, public nature of the kill site. From her cursory examination of the body, she estimated that the murder had taken place between twelve thirty and one thirty in the morning. While her street certainly wasn't the most heavily traveled in San Francisco, it was close enough to a few popular bars that it attracted moderate foot traffic even in the middle of the week. That traffic wouldn't make it impossible to kill a woman in that alley without being detected, but taking the risk indicated a killer with real confidence.

Was that confidence earned or merely foolish?

Jac gasped sharply, eyes shooting up to meet Eve's in a way that turned Eve's stomach to stone. "That woman. Did you recognize her? Did you know her?"

Eve had stared at the woman's face long enough to know the answer without thinking. "No, of course not. Why?"

Biting down hard on her lip, Jac held the phone so Eve could read the on-screen text. It was the call log. The last recorded outgoing call was at the top of the list, made just after one o'clock in the morning.

To Eve's cell phone.

Eve felt the blood drain from her face, leaving her light-headed and dizzy. "Oh, my God."

"That's your number, right? I'm not crazy."

Eve flashed back to the first phone call that had woken her up at Selene's. No words, not even the sound of breathing. Just quiet street noise, then *beep*. "He called me. He didn't say anything and I just chalked it up to a wrong number, but..." Shivering, she imagined what the killer might have felt, listening to her sleepily fishing for a response. Totally ignorant of what he'd just done, apparently with her in mind. "This murder was about me, wasn't it?"

"I'm assigning a protective detail to stay with you twenty-four seven," Jac said, already dialing her own cell phone. "No arguments."

Eve shook her head, dazed by the enormity of the situation she could no longer deny. The man in the ski mask—the man from her nightmares—had called her tonight from a dead woman's cell phone. A woman he'd killed less than a block from Eve's apartment. Why? What did he find compelling enough about Eve to risk his anonymity? If he knew her cell phone number, that meant he'd definitely taken her purse. Which meant he knew she worked with the police—her purse contained the identification and credentials to prove it. By pursuing her, he was not only making it easy to link his crimes but also increasing his threat of exposure. Was his motivation simply that she'd escaped his grasp?

Was he that determined to maintain a perfect record of murder?

As she listened to Jac speak to her captain in a hushed tone, another, more sinister thought struck her. Maybe her attack hadn't been a matter of chance. All this time Eve had assumed that she'd been jumped due to pure dumb luck. Because she had been in the wrong place at the wrong time, unfortunate enough to take that particular running path on that particular morning. But what if that wasn't true?

What if he had intentionally targeted her? Perhaps this had always been about Eve, even before Yasmin Mandujano was stabbed to death in the predawn hours of that fateful morning. It wasn't too big a stretch to think that he had some kind of vendetta against her. Or, perhaps more likely, the man in the ski mask had created a challenge for himself.

After all, in criminal and forensic circles, Dr. Eve Thomas was something of a celebrity. Her book had spent eight weeks at the top of *The New York Times* best-seller list, and since Charles Dunning's arrest and the subsequent publication of her account of the role her science had played in his capture, she had enjoyed moderate attention in the mainstream media. The country loved a juicy serial-murder case, and when it had a happy ending, *CSI*-style, even better. What if this man had seen all that and decided to take Eve down a notch? Or even to make her a victim in his own string of sick killings? The ultimate trophy.

"Protection detail's all set. They're sending a couple of detectives over right away. I've asked them to keep a car on your apartment at all times and someone with you whenever you're out." Jac hesitated a moment, then made eye contact. "I know this will make dating a little…awkward. But please believe that's not why I'm doing it."

Eve nodded, too numb to worry about the impact Jac's surveillance might have on her relationship. "I know."

"And I'm getting you a gun. I want you to carry it concealed."

Eve winced. "I don't have a permit." And she hated guns.

"We'll take care of that. I insist, Eve. Carry a gun, at least until this is over."

Eve could hear from Jac's tone that she couldn't win this argument. Dropping her shoulders in resignation, she said, "Okay."

"Okay," Jac said quietly. She lifted a hand as though she might touch Eve's face, then dropped it to her side. "What are you thinking?"

Exhaling, Eve said, "I'm thinking that maybe this has always been about me."

"In what way?"

"These murders, my attack…maybe this guy is taunting me. Trying to prove something."

"But why?" Jac's throat tensed as a familiar, protective fire flared in her eyes. "Why come after you?"

"Maybe he didn't like my book." Eve managed a weak laugh. If she could find the humor in this, perhaps she wouldn't fall apart. It was a theory, at least. "Or he wants to be part of the sequel."

"You think this is about your work on the Dunning case?"

"I don't know. Possibly the attack *was* a coincidence, and he just doesn't like knowing that I'm 'the one who got away.'"

Jac shuddered. "If he does know who you are, if this *was* intentional, it's possible he's tried to make contact with you in the past. Do you keep fan letters and e-mail?"

One of the more interesting aspects of her newfound celebrity had been the outpouring of interest, gratitude, and just-plain-creepy messages from the general public. Eve had hundreds of e-mails that ranged from curious to flirtatious to downright disturbing. They all lived in a special folder in her e-mail account. "Yes, I keep them."

"I'd like copies, please." Eve knew Jac well enough to realize that she was desperately trying to maintain a calm façade. But the quaver in her voice betrayed inner turmoil. "Everything you can dig up."

"Of course." Eve dropped her head in her hands and groaned. "God, Jac. Why me?"

Jac put a gentle hand on her back, rubbing circles over her spine. "We'll catch him, Eve. I promise. He will *not* hurt you." In a soft, fierce voice, Jac murmured, "I won't let him."

Touched by the obvious love in Jac's voice, Eve turned and fell into the familiar embrace she found waiting for her. All of a sudden their arguments over Selene seemed trivial. The important thing was that Jac truly did have her back. Even if she hadn't been there for her as a romantic partner, Jac would always be her friend.

"Thank you," Eve mumbled into the shoulder of Jac's leather jacket. "And I'm sorry I said 'fuck you' before."

Jac squeezed her tighter. "Let's not talk about it right now."

Sniffing, Eve pulled back. "I've been telling myself it was over, what happened that morning. That I was safe. That's been the only thing keeping me going. The thought that it was over." That, and Selene. Not that she'd admit that to Jac. "I'm not sure I know what to do now. The idea that I could see him again—"

"Not on my watch." Jac opened her mouth to say something else, but the loud chime of the lab's doorbell cut her off. Eve's heart constricted, then stuttered into overdrive, her entire body tensing as her fight-or-flight instinct kicked in. Immediately Jac's warm hand covered hers. "I'm sure it's the techs delivering the body. I'll go get it."

Normally Eve would've jumped right up to help receive a new corpse, but she didn't trust her legs to support her. "Thanks."

Eve watched Jac cross the lab and peek out the window into the hallway, exhaling in relief when she immediately stepped back to open the door. Two familiar police technicians wheeled in a gurney and carefully transferred a black body bag to the steel table in the center of the room. Eve watched the process—something she'd witnessed hundreds of times before—with a sense of mounting dread.

She didn't know how she would bring herself to stare into that woman's lifeless eyes again. Not when she felt somehow responsible for her death. She'd faced the same evil this woman had stared down tonight and escaped—if only because of the freak appearance of a wolf in Golden Gate Park. She was alive and this woman wasn't.

Eve could have just as easily ended up on that steel slab. Even more horrifying than that thought was that she might wind up there yet.

Jac told both technicians good-bye, closing the lab door behind them. Then she turned to Eve and planted her hands on her hips, fire in her eyes. "All right. We gonna catch this motherfucker or not?"

Eve snorted at Jac's characteristic bluntness. "Yes."

"Then get up, evil genius, and work your forensic magic."

Eve knew perfectly well what Jac was trying to do—motivate her with flattery, banish her fear with a reminder of their purpose. And it worked. She could either live in terror of another encounter with the Golden Gate Park killer or she could take her fate into her own hands. She was Dr. Eve Thomas, for goodness sake. She'd helped catch one serial killer. Damn straight she could do it again.

Eve slapped her hands down on the surface of her desk and stood, shooting Jac a determined grin. "Let's do this."

"That's my girl."

Eve locked away her disquiet, forcing back every nonanalytical emotion so she could prepare the body for the autopsy. It was "the body" now, not a woman. Not someone who had been walking and talking mere hours ago, before being forced to stare into the same eyes that haunted Eve's nightmares. It was a body. An empty vessel. And, potentially, their key to tracking down the man who cut short its owner's life.

The examination felt very familiar. Multiple wounds, all made with the same type of knife used on Yasmin Mandujano. Similar patterning of shallow cuts and deeper slices, with two perfectly placed slashes across the throat that had caused her to bleed out. As Jac had indicated over the phone, the evidence of petechiae covering her face and eyelids confirmed that he had strangled this one, too.

"Do you think he asphyxiates them until they pass out, then cuts them, then asphyxiates them again when they wake up?" Eve tilted her head, considering the question objectively, trying not to remember the feeling of thumbs digging into her own vulnerable throat. "That could explain how he's able to kill them so brutally in such public places without anyone hearing."

"If that's true, he's one sick bastard." Jac grimaced. "Seems like a lot of effort to go through, especially in a scenario where time is limited and the threat of discovery is high."

Swallowing, Eve let herself remember the man who'd attacked her. His eyes, the cold certainty in his voice when he said he could do whatever he wanted. "He thinks he's invincible. That nobody can stop him."

Jac hesitated, then touched Eve's shoulder. "Is that what he told you?"

Eve stripped off her bloody gloves, crossing the room to toss them in the medical waste bin. "He gets off on fear. He *definitely* got off on my fear. Using that knife to toy with me. Cutting me—"

"He *cut* you?" Jac rounded the table as though Eve were bleeding right then and there. "You didn't tell me that."

Eve met Jac's eyes. "A nick. On my breast."

Jac's expression turned deadly. "I will fucking *kill* him."

"No, you won't." Eve picked up the evidence she'd collected from the body—fibers that could very well turn out to be insignificant, pubic-hair combings despite no indication of sexual assault, and scrapings from beneath the victim's trimmed fingernails. But if this was anything like the last body, none of it would lead them any closer to their killer. "You'll arrest him."

"Maybe I'll just hit him first." Touching Eve's cheek, Jac tightened her jaw. "A little."

Eve stepped away from her, needing the space. Protective Jac stirred feelings inside her that no longer had a place in her life. "Don't you dare do anything to jeopardize your safety *or* your career. Okay?"

Jac followed Eve to her desk, perching on the edge again. "I want to say something, but I don't want you to get angry with me."

Eve knew exactly where the conversation was going, but after the care and concern Jac had shown over the past hour or so, she didn't have the heart to shut her down. "I'll try to remain calm." She forced a neutral expression, hoping to put Jac at ease.

"Selene," Jac said, and held up a hand when Eve tensed. "I know she's important to you. And I trust your judgment. But that phone call—"

"You can't prove it was her. Can you?"

"It was her. I know it in my *gut*, Eve. For all my faults, I think you've always trusted my gut." Jac gave her a pleading look, and Eve could see that this truly wasn't simply about jealousy. Jac believed that Selene was their anonymous tipster. And Eve *had* always trusted Jac's gut. It usually seemed to be right.

"She could have a lot of reasons to want to remain anonymous." Eve tried to think of what might prevent Selene from telling her about something so important, but came up short. But she was certain Selene had reasons, legitimate ones. "It's not against the law to make an anonymous tip."

Jac stared into Eve's eyes. "Are you in love with her?" Eve opened her mouth to answer, but Jac looked away with a pained grimace. "Don't bother. Your face says it all."

"I can't explain how it is with Selene," Eve said. "But it's good, Jac. It's really good."

"Then ask her." Jac glanced at the exam table, then back at Eve. "Please."

Eve exhaled shakily. If Selene had discovered the body, Eve did want to know, and not only because it might help their investigation. That was a big secret to keep. Selene might have her reasons, but if Eve didn't ask, she could only guess what they might be. Eve was tired of relationships built on lies. She wouldn't have one again, not even for Selene.

"I will," Eve murmured. She wanted to know, didn't she? But how to do it without destroying what had so far been perfect in every way? "Just give me some time."

"Two bodies in less than a month," Jac said meaningfully. "Don't take too long."

Eve gave Jac a grudging nod. "I won't."

CHAPTER SEVENTEEN

Selene knew something was different the moment Eve answered her door the evening after the second murder. Eve's face softened at the sight of her, and Selene's entire body hummed as their connection flared to life, but Eve seemed almost reserved as they embraced. The stream of emotion that flowed from her directly into Selene was difficult to decipher, almost overwhelming in its complexity. Familiar love and desire were there, but new—and unsettling—feelings were in the mix.

Anxiety. Fear. Worst of all, uncertainty.

Those negative emotions seemed directed at her, an unexpected turn of events that jarred her into stunned stillness. She knew that Jac and Eve had argued about her that morning at the crime scene, but now she wondered what exactly Jac had said. Whatever it was, it had clearly gotten to Eve.

"Is everything all right?" Selene asked as she drew back from their embrace. Cautiously, she stepped into Eve's apartment and closed the door behind her. She had planned to tell Eve this evening that she wouldn't be around on the night of the full moon, so the last thing she needed was unspoken distrust between them. That would make lying even harder to pull off. "You seem upset."

"I am upset," Eve said, but gave her a brave smile. "Rough day at the lab."

"I'll bet. Anything I can do?"

Eve smiled wider, blushing. "Why don't we talk a little first?"

Relieved by Eve's reaction, Selene walked deeper into the apartment. Flirting was a good sign. If Eve was still flirting, Jac hadn't managed to completely poison her mind against her. At least not yet. After a moment of hesitation, she sat on Eve's couch. She needed to act casual, to push aside her nerves. If she wanted Eve to trust her, she had to project calm honesty. That was the only way to make Eve believe that she wasn't hiding anything.

Eve put her hands on her hips. "Want something to drink?"

Selene shook her head, patting the cushion next to her. "Sit down, sweetheart. Tell me about your day. About the woman from the alley."

Eve shook her head, then turned to walk into the kitchen. "Let me get a glass of wine first."

"Of course." Selene stood and followed Eve to the refrigerator, watching as she pulled out a bottle of chardonnay. She hoped Eve had been able to scientifically establish the fact that her own attacker was the same man who killed the woman in the alley. Selene had smelled it, of course, but could never tell Eve. "So it's the same guy, right? The one who killed the woman in Golden Gate Park?"

Sighing, Eve poured a generous glass of wine, then took a large sip. After another sip, she topped off her glass, then recorked the bottle, sticking it back into the fridge. "Without a doubt." Eve gestured for Selene to follow her back to the sitting room. "Same exact wounds. Same knack for creating the cleanest messy crime scene I've ever encountered." Eve sat and took another healthy drink, shivering after she swallowed. "And there was something else."

Selene sank onto the cushion beside Eve. Her gut churned as Eve struggled with whatever she intended to say next. "Tell me."

"Remember the phone call I got last night? The hang-up?"

Throat dry, Selene nodded. "Was it him?"

"He placed the call from the victim's cell phone—probably as he stood over her body. We found the entry in her call log." Eve hiccupped out a humorless laugh. "Pretty big clue that not only are my attacker and this killer one and the same, but he's clearly fixated on me for some reason." Another drink, more like a gulp than a sip. "Jac assigned a protective detail to watch my apartment. You probably walked past them on the way in."

"I didn't notice."

"Well, they're my new shadows, for the time being." Eve gave a weary chuckle. "Hope you don't mind having the cops watch you when you're with me."

Selene forced down her natural panic at the idea. Eve blinked, staring hard into Selene's face, and Selene worried that she hadn't hidden her reaction well enough. "Whatever keeps you safe, darling. That's all I care about."

"Is it?" Eve asked, then blushed and quickly stared into her wineglass.

"Of course." Selene frowned. She could feel that Eve was struggling with something, almost as though she wanted to ask Selene a question, and her heart thumped as she considered all the possibilities. Could Eve have found out about her abilities somehow? Was it the mind-reader thing from the other night? Or did Eve actually know she was a shape-shifter?

But how could she? Selene had been beyond careful not to shift at all since her brief foray into Golden Gate Park to track the killer shortly after Eve's attack, terrified that Eve or Jac would somehow find out. If that wasn't what Eve wanted to ask her about—if that wasn't the cause of Eve's obvious lapse in trust—then what was it?

Did she simply sense that Selene was keeping secrets?

"I love you, Eve." Selene took Eve's hand between her own, shocked by how cold and fragile her slim fingers felt. Drawing from deep within herself, Selene channeled every bit of love and devotion she felt for Eve into her touch, desperate to wrap Eve in the warmth of their bond. "Keeping you safe is more important than anything else."

Eve's eyes filled with tears and she blinked rapidly, setting down her wine to swipe at her face with a shaky hand. She left her other hand within Selene's grasp, curling her fingers around Selene's palm to give her a gentle squeeze. "I'm so scared, Selene." Breaking eye contact, she whispered, "And I love you, too."

Eve still wasn't saying something. She was holding back, too frightened to vocalize the lingering unease that still hung between them. Hating to see Eve so torn up, Selene took a deep breath and prayed she wasn't making a mistake by probing deeper. "What else is wrong, darling? Is there something you need to talk about?"

Fear shot from Eve to Selene like a stab in the gut. Eve jerked her head back and stared into Selene's eyes, desperately searching for... Selene didn't know. Selene lifted Eve's hand to her lips, forcing herself not to tremble, and kissed Eve's knuckles.

"You can tell me anything," Selene murmured. If Eve knew about her, Selene wouldn't deny it. After all, Eve had allowed her inside her apartment, so how disgusted could she be? "Don't be afraid."

Eve took a breath, then hesitated. After a moment she shook her head. "No, it's nothing. I'm just...shaken up."

Scooting closer, Selene pulled Eve into a loose embrace. She kissed her hair and stroked her back, sending as much positive, healing energy to Eve as she could muster. That meant suppressing her own anxiety about the lie she had yet to tell, about whatever Eve didn't feel comfortable saying. But Selene knew it was important. Though it felt slightly manipulative to influence Eve's mood when Eve was so clearly uncertain, Selene told herself that it was for her benefit. There was nothing wrong with wrapping Eve in love and desire right now, not when it would ease her obvious disquiet.

Eve exhaled, seeming to melt into their embrace. "This is what I needed." Fisting her hands in Selene's T-shirt, Eve buried her face in Selene's chest and inhaled deeply. "You always make me feel so good."

"I'm glad." Selene closed her eyes, not allowing herself to feel the guilt that tickled her subconscious. She wasn't abusing Eve's trust by making her feel better this way. She was just using their connection to both their advantage. "I try."

"I want to trust you."

Selene stiffened slightly at Eve's mumbled words, then forced herself to relax. The comment was probably more about Jac than Selene. She knew Eve had trust issues—which made keeping secrets doubly painful. "Of course you can trust me." Drawing back, she met Eve's gaze. "I will always do everything I can to protect you. And I will *never*, ever hurt you. Not if I can help it."

Eve stared deep into Selene's eyes. Her face relaxed as she shed the last of whatever had been bothering her. "I know you won't."

"Good." Selene kissed Eve's lips, then pulled back a few inches to watch her reaction. Success. Eve was no longer anxious, suspicious, or uneasy. She was full of love, and Selene's chest hurt at the intensity of having all that emotion directed toward her.

"I want you to take me to bed." Eve blushed as soon as the words came out of her mouth, but she didn't break eye contact. "I need you to make everything else go away, just for tonight."

"I can do that," Selene murmured. She stroked down Eve's arm, raising gooseflesh. "You've had a long day. Maybe we can just hold each other."

Eve shook her head. "No. I want you to fuck me."

Selene went still. She wanted Eve—she always wanted her—but for a moment the sudden change in mood paralyzed her. Five minutes ago Eve had been full of doubt, and now she eyed Selene with so much hunger it made thinking all but impossible. "You sure?"

"I need you inside me. I need…" Eve closed her eyes and exhaled shakily. "I *need* you."

Selene stood, then pulled Eve to her feet. They could talk later. Right now she needed to reassure Eve that no matter what else happened, she was the most important thing in Selene's life. She needed to make Eve believe that she was loyal and true, that despite the secrets Selene had to keep, nothing would ever stand in the way of them being together.

She needed to make Eve trust her again.

CHAPTER EIGHTEEN

Eve didn't know what to think about the drastic shift in her mood over the past twenty minutes. Before Selene came over, she was scared—of the strange turn the Golden Gate Park killer case had taken, of Jac's revelation that Selene might be the anonymous tipster, of the possibility that she had once again fallen in love with someone who could so easily mislead her. But more than being afraid, Eve had been determined. She had sworn to herself that she would ask Selene about the anonymous phone call straight up, to hell with the consequences. If Selene hadn't made the call, at worst Eve would embarrass herself for having lent any credence to Jac's suspicions. But if Selene was the tipster, Eve needed to know. Not only because Selene could have useful information without knowing it, but also for Eve's own peace of mind.

If Selene *had* discovered that body, she had been keeping a pretty big secret. And it needed to be brought out into the open if their relationship had any hope of surviving. After Jac, Eve couldn't deal with more lies. She just couldn't. She was willing to give Selene the benefit of the doubt that she had hidden the truth for good reason. What she couldn't do was look the other way.

But all that fear and determination had disappeared within Selene's embrace on the couch. The simple touch of Selene's hands, then her gentle kisses, had chased away every bit of Eve's negative emotion, leaving her filled with almost crippling desire. The only thing Eve felt now was a fierce urge to connect with Selene at the most primal level. She could find no logical reason for her wildly vacillating emotions, but she was beyond caring. She wanted to trust Selene—she *needed* to trust Selene—because, plain and simple, Selene made her happy. Beyond happy. Selene was everything to her, inexplicable as that was.

Now Eve was another kind of determined. Determined to reestablish their connection, to prove to herself that she trusted Selene implicitly. And the best way to do that was in bed. Before Selene, Eve had never been confident in her sexuality. She had never trusted anyone enough to truly let go and surrender her mind and body completely. But Selene made that easy.

That had to mean something. Didn't it?

Eve led Selene to her bedroom by the hand, nervous anticipation fluttering in her belly. Together only two weeks, they'd already had a lot of sex. Passionate sex, loving sex, laughing sex—even a little rough sex. Tonight would be something different. Something special. When they made love tonight, it would be to prove something about this relationship, about the trust Eve had in Selene, and about Eve's ability to give herself fully to another person.

She couldn't bear the thought that Jac had broken her forever, that the fear and distrust that relationship introduced into her life could seep into this thing with Selene and destroy it. Selene had never given Eve any reason not to trust her intentions. Whatever had happened that day in Golden Gate Park—whoever made that anonymous call—Eve believed in Selene. She trusted that their growing feelings were real. By taking Selene to bed right now, she was putting that trust into action.

Eve began to undress the instant she entered her bedroom, tugging her shirt over her head, then unbuttoning her jeans. Selene stopped just inside the doorway and watched with hooded eyes. Eve slowed down once she realized that she had an appreciative audience, walking backward until her thighs hit the mattress. Reaching behind her back, she unhooked her bra with seductive languor. The desire that flooded Selene's face as she bared her body stunned Eve. Nobody had ever made her feel so beautiful. Selene's obvious admiration gave her the courage to perform a playful striptease, something so outside her comfort zone she'd never even considered it before now.

Selene made her feel like anything was possible. Even trust.

Once she was naked, Eve beckoned Selene forward with a crooked finger. "You're overdressed."

"Just enjoying the view." Selene closed the distance between them, pulling off her shirt as she walked. "Trying to savor every moment of your little show."

"You liked that?" Bolstered by the overwhelming love in Selene's eyes, Eve ran her finger down the center of Selene's chest, between her breasts. Then she slipped a hand around Selene's back to thumb open the clasp of her bra, guiding it off her shoulders with an appreciative smirk.

"Loved it." Selene's hands landed on Eve's bare hips, gripping her gently while pulling her closer. "Do you have any idea how badly I want you right now?"

"No. Show me."

Selene gave her an almost feral growl. "With pleasure."

Eve glanced at her nightstand, the bottom drawer, with barely conscious thought. When she remembered what was in there, she blushed and her stomach tightened with nervous anticipation. She couldn't ask for that—could she? Did she even want it?

"Tell me," Selene murmured, moving forward to kiss Eve's neck. "What's in the drawer?"

Eve shivered at Selene's perceptive question. She didn't know why she'd looked there. Her unconscious mind had probably made the connection between what was inside and the question of trust. Yes, Eve wanted to prove just how real the safety Selene created for her was. But consciously Eve didn't know whether she wanted what her body was clearly excited about.

"Tell me, Eve." Selene slid her hands around to cup Eve's bottom, gripping her tight. Eve gasped and closed her eyes, shocked by how the rough touch affected her. Immediately she was soaking wet, thighs slick with arousal. Selene brought her mouth to Eve's ear and whispered, "Or do you want me to look for myself?"

Eve shivered. This was a completely new dynamic, forceful Selene, and Eve couldn't believe how it turned her on. She would never have predicted enjoying something like this so much. Part of her wanted Selene to make the discovery herself, to take control of the situation, to leave Eve without any choice but to surrender to her desires.

As though Selene knew exactly what Eve was thinking, she drew away from their embrace and yanked open the drawer. Eve's face flooded with heat at the sight of the leather harness and brand-new silicone dildo inside. Selene sucked in a noisy breath, then picked up each object in turn. Raising an eyebrow, Selene murmured, "You want me to fuck you with this?"

"I…" Eve closed her mouth, swallowing against her suddenly dry throat. "I've never done that before."

Selene held her gaze. "But you've wanted to."

"I bought those after the breakup." Eve blushed as she remembered the day she went online and placed her order. "Tired of feeling vanilla, I guess. But I never…there's never been an opportunity to use them."

"Vanilla?" Selene hefted the dildo in her hand. "Jac call you that?"

"She didn't have to."

"Well, I don't think you're vanilla." As Selene tossed the dildo onto the mattress, her eyes darkened. "I think you're a dirty girl who wants to be taken hard and fast with that big, thick cock. Am I right?"

Eve gasped at the heat that shot through her body at Selene's unexpected words. "I—"

Tipping her head, Selene gestured at her pants. "Unbutton me."

It was like Selene was tapping into thoughts and desires Eve could scarcely admit having, even to herself. And Eve was excited beyond belief. Every word from Selene, every movement, evoked undeniable arousal. Eve yearned to give up control completely, to trust Selene to guide her through an experience that would have been unimaginable even a month ago.

Eve's hands shook as she thumbed open the button of Selene's jeans. She tugged down the zipper, then hesitated, checking Selene's eyes. Somehow she knew she needed Selene's approval before moving any farther.

"Take them off." Selene seemed to be enjoying this new role just as much as Eve. Her expression had turned predatory. "Now."

Pushing Selene's jeans down over her hips, Eve took a chance and also hooked her thumbs in the waistband of her panties, baring Selene completely. She got on her knees in front of Selene, steadying her as she lifted Selene's feet out of her pants, leaving her gloriously nude. Eve stared up from her submissive position, waiting for her next instruction.

Selene set her feet apart, tangling a hand in Eve's hair. She pulled Eve forward roughly, until her nose and mouth were buried in the slick, swollen folds between Selene's thighs. "Suck me."

Eve poked out her tongue, eager for Selene's sweet taste in her mouth. Licking Selene was something she'd never tire of, and being ordered to do so while on her knees ratcheted her excitement to dizzying heights. Slipping between Selene's labia, Eve groaned at the thick liquid that immediately coated her lips and tongue. Selene's hand tightened in her hair, holding her in place.

"Yeah, you know how I like it." With her other hand, Selene stroked Eve's face gently. "Just like that, good girl."

Eve closed her eyes. Selene's murmured encouragement should have made her feel degraded somehow. She was being treated like a sex object, for God's sake. After years of being shy and reserved in bed, she should have been overwhelmed. But Selene was tapping into what she'd always wanted but never would have admitted. Eve would have died before handing control over to Jac like this, but with Selene…in her heart, Eve knew that she was important to Selene—her thoughts, her feelings, her desires. Selene would *never* hurt her on purpose. She believed that with everything inside her. After having her ability to trust completely shattered, Eve never imagined feeling it so strongly again.

The revelation that she could feel it, and *did* feel it, was startlingly arousing. That trust made her want to admit her deepest, darkest kinks, the things she fantasized about alone in the shower but could never have brought to a lover before Selene. She *did* trust Selene never to betray her, and there was no more powerful aphrodisiac in the world.

Selene's body tensed and she quaked as Eve drew out an orgasm with her mouth. Then Selene curled a hand around Eve's chin, forcing her away from the sweet juices she lapped up hungrily. "You do like this, don't you?" For a moment the commanding presence dropped away and only Selene, her tender lover, remained. "This is something you need." Her grip on Eve's chin tightened slightly. "Isn't it?"

"Yes," Eve whispered. Though it defied reason that in the same month a serial killer had torn away her control, she could feel safe enough to be her most vulnerable with a woman she had only just met, Eve didn't doubt this choice for an instant. "I need this."

Selene's eyes hardened even as her lips relaxed into an easy smirk. "Good. Because I'm going to give it to you." She grabbed Eve's upper arm, hauling her to her feet. "Get on the bed."

Eve crawled onto the mattress, grateful not to have to try to stand. Her legs felt boneless. Lying back against the headboard, she bit her lip as she watched Selene fasten the harness around her hips. She had fantasized about using these toys for a long time but always doubted she would ever actually do it. The idea of living out her secret fantasy with someone who made her feel safe was nearly enough to make her come without even being touched.

Selene tightened the straps on the harness, raising an eyebrow at her. "I can smell how much you want this."

Heat flooded Eve's cheeks, a curious mixture of embarrassment and excitement. She glanced down at the dildo that rested on the mattress beside her, then picked it up and investigated its length and girth with her hands. When it had arrived in the mail all those months ago, she'd opened the package and simply stared in shock. It was bigger than she'd pictured. Not *too* big, she suspected, but larger than anything a lover had ever given her. The thought of allowing someone to guide that phallus inside her body, to stretch her open around it, had made her uneasy. That meant really putting herself into someone else's hands, at her mercy, for what felt almost unbearably intimate. The potential for discomfort or humiliation seemed high, and Eve had simply never met a woman she trusted enough to be so vulnerable around.

Until now.

"Give it to me." Selene extended her hand, stopping inches from the dildo. "If you want that cock inside you, hand it to me right now."

Eve handed it over without meeting Selene's eyes. Silent subservience.

Selene's upper lip curled into a smirk, lending her a distinct air of danger. It did nothing to diminish Eve's trust, and everything to jack up the rush of endorphins their play sent through her body. Eve watched as Selene fit the dildo in the harness, then exhaled shyly when Selene used one slim hand to stroke it from base to tip.

"How do you want to take this?" Selene knelt on the side of the bed, devouring Eve's body with her eyes as she continued to caress the dildo. "Missionary position?" She met Eve's stare, tilting her head searchingly. "Do you want to ride my cock?" Her eyes flashed as though she'd read something on Eve's face. "Or get fucked on your hands and knees like the nasty girl we both know you are?"

Eve's mouth dropped open slightly as burning hunger twisted her insides. "I—"

"Get on your hands and knees." Selene's tone banished any thought of refusal. "Now, darling."

Blushing, Eve sat up, then turned to balance on her hands and knees. She could feel Selene move into position behind her and held her breath, uncertain what to expect. The gentle touch of Selene's hands on her bottom made her jerk in surprise, then she moaned loudly when those hands gripped her buttocks and pulled her open, exposing her scorching flesh to the chilly air.

"Let me see that wet pussy." She could feel Selene's breath as she brought her mouth next to Eve's labia, fiery hot and so very close. "I had no idea, Eve. None at all."

"No idea about what?" Eve whispered. Tensing, she nearly came when Selene's mouth suddenly covered her labia and her tongue snaked its way to circle Eve's swollen clit.

Selene pulled away with a quiet groan. "I had no idea you wanted to be taken this way."

"Me either." Eve dropped her forehead to the mattress, rocking back on her knees. She bumped Selene's mouth, but Selene pulled quickly away, wrenching a cry of disappointment from Eve's throat. "But I do."

"I can see that."

Selene's tongue was everywhere, exploring every fold, tracing her opening, then poking inside. Tightening her hands on Eve's buttocks, Selene held her open and spent long moments thrusting her stiff tongue in and out of Eve's pussy. Eve grabbed the headboard with both hands, hanging on tight. She had never been devoured like this. It made her feel wanton and decadent and like she was Selene's last meal. Eve's thighs quaked as her climax began to build.

Selene pulled away. "No, you're going to come on my cock, darling." As Eve gasped into her pillow, unable to believe that Selene had just *stopped* like that, she felt Selene straighten, then take one hand away from her bottom. A moment later the thick, silicone length of the dildo was sliding along her wetness, making her shudder in pleasure. "And not until I say so. Understand?"

Eve managed a noncommittal groan. "Please."

Selene smacked her sharply on the ass, then gave her a rough squeeze. "I mean it. You come without permission and I *promise* you'll be sorry."

Lifting her head, Eve nodded quickly. "Not until you say so. I understand."

"Good." And with that, Selene pushed the dildo forward, carefully working the thick head into Eve's opening. "Let's take this nice and slow."

Eve's forehead hit the pillow and her mouth dropped open as her body stretched to accommodate the thick length of Selene's cock. The sensation was incredible—she was so wet, so open and ready, that the penetration immediately soothed the crippling ache between her thighs. Selene filled her, firm and unyielding, until her belly was flush against Eve's ass. Both hands moved to Eve's hips, gripping her tight and keeping her impaled.

"You took that like a good girl, didn't you?" Selene's fingers squeezed her buttocks, then she drew one hand away to deliver a light slap. "You sure you've never done this before?"

Looking back over her shoulder, Eve met Selene's eyes, which softened instantly. "I'm sure."

Selene slid one hand up Eve's spine to settle on the back of her neck. "Thank you for giving this to me." She drew back her hips, then drove forward again. Then another thrust, faster and harder. "For giving me this sweet, tight pussy."

Eve cried out as Selene set a steady rhythm, filling then withdrawing, somehow hitting all the right spots deep inside. She buried her face in her pillow, muffling the loud moans Selene's deep strokes wrenched out of her. Selene's hands kneaded the tender skin of her bottom, the rough handling intensifying the sheer pleasure Eve got from Selene's skillful motion.

"Tell me you like it." Selene pulled her open, exposing her anus to the cool air. "Tell me how much you like being fucked."

"I love being fucked." Eve came up on her hands and arched her back, rocking to meet Selene's thrusts. "I've never felt anything so *goddamn* good."

Strong hands slid up her sides and around her chest to cradle her breasts. Selene tugged sharply on both nipples, then pinched the turgid flesh in time with the speed of her deep strokes. "You're mine. Aren't you?"

Stunned by the quiet intensity of the question, Eve glanced over her shoulder and returned Selene's heated gaze. The fierce, possessive look on Selene's face jolted Eve into sudden climax, and when Selene gritted her teeth and quaked with her own release, the contractions in Eve's pussy grew so violent that all she could do was collapse on her stomach and ride out the wave beneath Selene's solid, trembling form.

When she finally came down from her orgasm, either minutes or hours later, Selene kissed the edge of her ear and said again, in a growl that sent shivers through Eve's body, "Aren't you?"

It took Eve a moment to remember the question. "I'm yours."

"I never gave you permission to come." Selene nipped at her neck, grabbing her hands, then pinning them above Eve's head. "Didn't I warn you about that?"

"Yes." Eve had completely forgotten Selene's admonishment. Quite frankly, she couldn't wait to find out how Selene intended to make her sorry.

Scraping her sharp teeth over Eve's shoulder, Selene murmured,

"What kind of punishment do you think you deserve for such willful disobedience?"

"Whatever you feel is appropriate." Eve groaned as Selene pumped her hips against her bottom. She was going to be deliciously sore in the morning. "I deserve it."

Selene withdrew, then rolled Eve over, pushing her thighs apart and settling between them. She reached between their bodies and guided the dildo back into Eve while staring into her eyes. Eve whimpered, unsure how much more stimulation she could handle.

Kissing the corner of Eve's mouth, Selene murmured, "I'll be gentle."

Eve laced her fingers behind Selene's neck. "I trust you."

Selene deepened their kiss and just barely shifted her hips, pressing into Eve with excruciating slowness. Eve moaned into Selene's mouth, then again when Selene tore her lips away to whisper in Eve's ear, "I'm in love with you."

"Good." Eve bit her lip as Selene angled her hips just right, sinking deeper inside. She had no idea how a piece of silicone could make her feel so connected, but it almost seemed as though the toy was merely an extension of Selene's body, conveying all her ardent desire. "Because I'm in love with you, too."

"And I will do everything I can to protect you." Tracing her tongue over Eve's upper lip, Selene tightened her embrace. "I will do *anything* to keep you safe."

Selene's solemn words warmed her from the inside out, and Eve couldn't help but think of that anonymous tip. It seemed impossible that the same woman who spoke so passionately would keep a secret of that magnitude. No way Selene had made that call. No way.

Selene brought their mouths together again in a passionate kiss. She pumped her hips faster, but kept her strokes shallow and gentle. The friction of their pelvises rubbing together was more than enough to bring Eve to the brink again. Selene slid a hand down Eve's side, then curled beneath her bottom, tugging Eve's leg over her own hip. Then she growled, *"Mine,"* and Eve spasmed around her and cried out in release once again.

Dropping her head onto Eve's shoulder, Selene trembled and gasped like she'd forgotten how to breathe. Eve placed her hands on Selene's back and stroked calming circles up and down her spine. "Yours," Eve whispered. "Easy, darling. Take a deep breath."

Selene's body rose beneath Eve's fingers as she inhaled deeply. Snaking her hands beneath Eve's shoulders, she tugged Eve closer without withdrawing, still buried deep inside. Eve blinked in surprise when moisture fell upon her shoulder, craning her head to peer at Selene's face. Tears streamed from Selene's dark, searching eyes.

"What's wrong?" Eve could feel that although Selene's emotion was part joy, it had another level—sorrow, maybe. Or regret.

"Next Thursday night…" Selene lifted her head but didn't quite meet Eve's eyes. "I have to go out of town overnight. For a job. I should be back the next day, but…" Guilt tightened her features. "I can't be with you on Thursday."

A bitter stab of disappointment knocked the wind out of Eve. Shocked by the intensity of her reaction, she tried not to let it show. "I understand." Selene winced and dropped her forehead on Eve's shoulder again. Guiltily, Eve traced her fingertips down to the small of Selene's sweat-slicked back. "It's okay, Selene. Really. You have a life—and responsibilities—beyond me."

"I wish you could come with me," Selene mumbled. "But you can't." She drew back but seemed to have trouble meeting Eve's eyes. "If I could cancel, I would. I swear. But I don't have a choice."

Eve forced a casual chuckle, taken aback by the self-loathing in Selene's voice. Sure, it was unfortunate timing, but Selene had no reason to feel bad about fulfilling professional obligations. As a workaholic, Eve understood better than anyone. "Sweetheart, stop. It's okay, really. It's just one night." She mustered a light tone even she didn't really believe. "I'm a big girl. I'll be just fine."

Selene finally met her eyes. "I don't want you to be alone that night."

"Honestly, Selene—"

"No." Every bit as forceful as she had been during their sexual play, Selene made it clear that the topic wasn't up for discussion. "You can't stay by yourself. If I was away and something happened to you, I'd never forgive myself." Selene swallowed and looked away. "Never."

"I won't be alone. Jac has two detectives watching me at all times, remember?"

Selene scowled. "Even so, I'd feel better if you had someone inside with you. Or even if you stayed at a friend's place."

Eve touched Selene's jaw, forcing her eyes back to Eve's face. "Okay."

"Maybe you can stay at Jac's."

That was the last thing Eve had expected Selene to suggest. "Jac? I'm not sure that's a good idea."

Looking as though she was struggling to swallow a mouthful of bad food, Selene said, "She has a gun. She can take care of you."

"I have a gun, too." Jac had stopped by that afternoon with a concealed weapons permit and a handgun. Eve hoped she'd never actually have to use it.

"Please, darling. For me."

Eve's belly flipped at the very real fear she sensed behind Selene's concern. "I'll see what Jac says."

"Are you joking?" Selene kissed the tip of Eve's nose. "She's still in love with you. She'll agree. Probably jump at the chance to have you all to herself."

Face heating, Eve tried to interpret Selene's tone. "Does that bother you?"

"No. I trust you."

Eve tangled a hand in Selene's dark hair and pulled her down for another kiss. "May I see you on Friday when you get home?"

"Just try and keep me away."

❖

Selene lay awake for hours after Eve fell asleep, struggling with guilt so intense she worried it might seep into Eve's unconscious and darken her dreams. Their lovemaking earlier had left Selene shaken, humbled, and deeply, deeply ashamed. She had lied to the woman she loved. Worse, she had done so while still buried deep inside Eve after the most intense sex she suspected either of them had ever had. In a moment when she felt more connected to a human being than she had ever imagined possible.

She was a piece of shit.

The worst part was that she had no choice. For two weeks she had tried and failed to come up with other options, anything to avoid betraying Eve's trust. But the only way to be honest would be to tell Eve that she was a shape-shifter who transformed into something horrific once a month on the eve of the full moon. And that her solution to the problem of safety—her own as well as the rest of the city's—was to get naked and have a call girl tie her to a steel table.

Yeah, right. That would not only end their relationship, but could possibly get Selene committed. Or worse.

Truth was, Selene wished she *could* tell Eve and have her accept the truth. Eliminating the need for secrecy would only cement their already-strong relationship. Better than that, if Selene could tell Eve what she was, maybe they could use her ability to hunt down the Golden Gate Park killer. Selene had tools at her disposal that all the police investigations and forensic science in the world couldn't replicate. With the freedom to take advantage of her true nature, Selene could protect Eve properly.

Unfortunately Selene was a coward. No matter how intense their connection was, she just couldn't believe that Eve could handle the truth and accept her for what she was. Nobody else had, so why would a woman she'd known for a month—a woman of science—be any different?

She exhaled and put a hand on her stomach. She didn't want to throw up, but it was taking everything she had to keep her dinner down. Eve was her mate, the undeniable nucleus of her universe, and Selene's entire being burned with the need to protect what was hers. Knowing that Jac would have to do it instead, even for one night, was excruciating. She trusted Eve totally, but she hated the idea that Jac would take the opportunity to point out that Selene wasn't good enough. Again.

Particularly because Jac had a point.

Eve whimpered in her sleep, stirring uneasily beneath the comforter. With effort Selene quieted her thoughts and turned on her side to pull Eve into a warm embrace. Immediately Eve calmed down. Whether her troubled dreams stemmed from the threat to her life or Selene's own tortured thoughts, Selene didn't know. What she did know was that she needed to figure out how they could possibly have a real relationship without Selene needing to lie every month.

Something had to give. Lying wasn't a long-term strategy—it was a weak, cowardly way to buy some time. At some point, she would be forced to put their relationship to the test, to see if Eve truly was the one for her.

But not this month. Not yet.

CHAPTER NINETEEN

Selene was right—when Eve explained to Jac that she was going out of town and didn't want Eve to be alone, Jac couldn't have looked more pleased about being designated her bodyguard for the night. So pleased, in fact, that it took every bit of Eve's willpower to shove down the irritation she felt at Jac's failure to hide her smug glee. But she did, because she was glad for Jac's company. She didn't want to spend the night in her apartment wondering if the Golden Gate Park killer was lurking in the shadows.

When Jac mentioned cooking her dinner, Eve knew she would have to be on guard. Cooking was a wooing tactic for Jac, probably used successfully on far more women than Eve wanted to imagine. It had certainly worked on her, once upon a time. After turning down Jac's last dinner invitation, Eve knew that Jac saw this evening as a second chance.

Jac said dinner was at five thirty, which meant she'd decided to leave work early to prepare their meal. She didn't doubt that Jac wanted to make sure they were together well before dark, but she suspected that Jac was also just plain excited about finally getting Eve over to her place again. Still, Eve wouldn't complain about the early meal. She didn't particularly want to be out late anyway. Tonight was the full moon, and though Eve wasn't superstitious, she recognized that the lunar cycle sometimes played into the patterns of psychopaths. The first murder had been committed the night of the previous full moon.

Eve left the lab early and was at Jac's door ten minutes before she was due. She intended to spend the night discussing the case, so along with a bottle of wine, she carried a stack of forensic reports. Poring over case files would be the best use of their time together and would keep things professional, which was exactly where Eve wanted their relationship to stay.

Jac answered the door wearing an apron and a brilliant smile. "Hey. Fajitas will be ready in about five minutes."

"Great." Awkwardly, Eve offered her the bottle cradled against her side. Bringing wine had seemed like the thing to do until the moment she smelled Jac's cologne and saw that Jac was wearing the purple shirt that had always turned Eve on when they were together. Apparently Jac had decided to be blatant about being in full seduction mode. Alcohol really didn't need to be introduced into the mix, but it was a bit late for that now. "I brought the forensic reports on our two victims. I figured we'd comb through them to see what we've missed."

Jac ushered Eve inside. "Of course. But let's eat first, have a glass of wine. Unwind a little." She looked Eve up and down, then kissed her cheek. "You look lovely."

Eve stiffened. "This isn't a date, Jac."

"I know that." Glancing at the bottle's label, Jac whistled. "My favorite."

"It's a thank-you for giving up your evening to babysit me." Eve followed Jac to the kitchen. She stood at the counter as Jac set the wine down, then checked her sizzling skillet of peppers and onions. "I hate knowing I messed up your plans."

Jac shook her head. "No plans. There's no place I'd rather be. And no one I'd rather be with."

Sometimes Jac was wholly exasperating. Nine months ago Eve would have taken this about-face differently. Not that she would have necessarily forgiven Jac, because her betrayal had cut so deep, but at least then it would have vindicated her belief that they really had been in love. It would have proved that she hadn't been crazy to believe their relationship was working right up until the moment she discovered Jac in bed with another woman. But coming as it did now, after Selene had entered the picture, Eve just felt like Jac was desperate to reclaim something Selene had rightfully won. And that made her angry.

All she could do was keep things friendly and courteous, and dissuade Jac from crossing the line Eve had clearly asked her to maintain. "Smells delicious."

"I haven't made them in a while." Jac shrugged as she stirred. "I've missed having my most appreciative audience around."

Eve forced a noncommittal hum, picking up a case file and flipping it open. "You know, I've been thinking about the lack of hair and fiber evidence at the scenes. What if—"

Jac raised her wooden spoon into the air. "I mean it. No talking shop until after dinner. Then you can knock yourself out."

"Fine." Eve tossed the file on the counter and sighed. Then she walked to the bottle of wine and snatched it up. "Where's your corkscrew?"

"Drawer next to the sink."

Eve found it and removed the cork from the bottle, filling two wineglasses halfway. She set one next to Jac, then stepped away, out of reach. Leaning against the door frame, she took a sip and watched Jac finish her masterpiece. Her fajitas really were the stuff of legend. In the past, Eve had considered them an aphrodisiac, and Jac knew it.

"So how are things with Selene?" Mouth frozen in insincere cheer, Jac managed to keep her voice light. "Still head over heels?"

"Don't," Eve murmured. "Please."

"What?" Jac tried to sound innocent, but Eve knew better. "I'm just trying to make conversation. Be friendly." She didn't meet Eve's eyes as she poured the vegetables onto a platter. "You ask her about that anonymous phone call yet?"

"She doesn't know anything, Jac."

"Is that what she said?"

Eve took another sip of wine. Truthfully, she had no idea why she hadn't questioned Selene. She'd been ready to do so the night of their intensely passionate lovemaking, but every time Selene touched her, Eve lost all desire to rock the boat. Partially because she couldn't bear the thought of finding out that Selene had been keeping secrets, but also because her gut told her that Selene would never betray her. She had all but given up on her gut after Jac and hated to imagine it might fail her again.

There was no way to make Jac understand without sounding naïve. "Jac—"

"I'm just asking. Did she tell you she didn't know anything?"

Coming over tonight had probably been a mistake. But walking out and going home—or even to a hotel—wasn't particularly appealing. And it would mean breaking her promise to Selene. Eve had sworn she would stay with Jac until Selene returned, no matter how awkward the situation might be. "She didn't have to. Believe me, if Selene knew anything that might help us catch the guy, she'd tell me. I know she would."

"Because she loves you?" Eve could hear the resentment in Jac's tone.

"Yes," Eve said simply. "Think what you will about Selene, but our feelings for one another are real. I don't know how to explain it to you. It's surprised me as much as anyone. But there it is. You have to trust me."

"It isn't you I don't trust."

"I know." Eve didn't bother to disguise her irritation, hopeful that Jac would back down if she sensed that her show of jealousy was about to ruin her perfectly choreographed evening. "Let's drop it now, okay?"

"Okay." Jac handed her the platter of fajitas and the bottle of wine. "Would you carry these to the table? I'll be right behind you."

"Sure." Grateful to escape the confined space of the kitchen, Eve heard her stomach growl at the incredible sight of the meal Jac had prepared. For all her faults, Jac really knew how to express love through her food. And judging by the spread in front of her, Jac was full of love tonight.

Jac sat next to Eve at the table, gesturing at the tortilla holder in the center. "Don't be shy. Dig in."

"Thank you." Eve spared Jac a genuine expression of gratitude as she filled her plate. "I'm starving."

"Good, because I probably went a bit overboard. I hope you're ready to take home some leftovers."

"Always."

Jac ate in silence, dragging her gaze over Eve's body without visibly reacting. When she spoke a moment later, her voice came out husky. "You're really looking good, Eve. I mean it. I'm guessing it's being in love, but you look different than I've ever seen you. So... *vibrant*. Alive."

"Ironic, considering I'm marked for death." As much as she tried not to let her mind go there, fear had become Eve's constant companion. Even more so when she wasn't in Selene's calming presence. But she didn't doubt that Jac was right—being in love and sexually confident for the first time in her life, Eve felt like a new woman. Despite the terror this stalker had brought into her life, she felt freer than ever. She wasn't surprised that Jac could see it, too. "Thank you, though. Besides the obsessed-psychopath thing, I'm doing well."

"Clearly." Jac stared at her with an intensity that quickened Eve's heartbeat. "I'm not going to let anything happen to you, you know. So as far as being marked for death, forget about it. This is some scary shit, for sure, but it'll end well. And soon."

"I know." Eve managed to sound braver than she felt. At the moment they had an almost total lack of physical evidence, no solid witnesses, and not even a weak lead. Still, Jac would do everything possible to catch the guy. "Doesn't stop me from worrying, though."

"I get it. But just know that I can't live without you. I refuse to. That bastard will *not* hurt you again." Suddenly sober, Jac spoke in an intense tone that sent a shiver through Eve. Regardless of her feelings for Selene, Eve wasn't immune to Jac's desire. Cheater or no, Jac had once been the center of her world. Hearing genuine love in her voice still made Eve's heart beat faster. "Hurting you was the worst thing I ever did. I'll spend every day of my life atoning, if that's what it takes."

Eve swallowed a mouthful of food, then set down her fajita. "Jac—"

"Maybe it's unfair of me to say these things now that you're with Selene." Jac took a large sip of wine, as though bolstering her courage. "I made some terrible mistakes, I know, but you can't deny that we still have something special. Something that could be fixed, if you'd forgive me."

"I do forgive you," Eve said. "But forgiving you isn't the same as wanting to be with you."

Hurt flashed across Jac's face, but she hid it quickly. "I deserve that. I know I do." She took another long sip, then set down her glass with an easy chuckle. "But I can be persistent, and patient."

"I wish you wouldn't."

Jac looked as though she was trying to decide whether to say something more, but simply cleared her throat. "Ready for dessert?"

Stuffed from the fajitas, Eve doubted she had room for more. "Seriously?"

"Chocolate mousse."

Oh, that was low. Eve scowled at Jac. "Bringing out the big guns, are you?"

Jac grinned cheekily. "What, you like chocolate mousse?"

"Hmmph." Eve stood and started gathering their dirty dishes. "You know I do."

Grabbing her own handful of dishes, Jac followed Eve to the kitchen. "I know a *lot* of things about you. Very important things."

Eve couldn't deny that was true. "Then you should know that

you're not getting me into bed tonight, no matter how much you turn on the charm." She scraped the remnants of her dinner into the garbage, then set her plate in the sink. "You should also know—"

Before she could tell Jac that it would take more than chocolate mousse to get her to cheat on Selene, Jac turned her around and pushed her against the counter, crushing their mouths together in a hungry kiss. Stunned, Eve grabbed onto Jac's biceps, intending to push her away. But she hesitated, the safe familiarity of Jac's mouth on hers overwhelming her. Dimly aware that kissing back made her refusals not only weak but also empty, Eve couldn't help but briefly sample Jac's mouth before turning her face to the side with a gasp.

"I said no." Eve's legs seemed to melt beneath her. "Stop."

Immediately Jac backed off. "I'm sorry."

"Goddamn it, Jac." Eve touched her lips with her fingertips, unable to believe what had just happened. She hadn't meant to hesitate before pulling away and hoped Jac hadn't noticed. "I don't think I was unclear. This—us—isn't going to happen. I'm not coming back to you. You had your chance and you blew it. It's time to accept that and move on. I have—and it wasn't easy. Don't make it even harder now."

"I'm not trying to hurt you." Jac walked backward, folding her arms over her chest. She couldn't quite meet Eve's eyes. "And you're right, that was out of line. I'm sorry. I just…I know you're in love with her. I know that. This isn't about being jealous. It's about really and truly realizing what I did to you, what I lost, and wanting desperately to believe that I might get another chance."

"You're not getting another chance," Eve whispered. "Especially because you're making me not want to be around you."

Jac clenched her jaw. "Do you want to go listen to the recording of our Golden Gate Park murder tip? Let's do that right now. I've got it on my laptop."

Heart pounding, Eve tightened her fists at her sides. "And what do you think that'll accomplish? I'm going to hear a voice that sounds like Selene and decide to fall into bed with you?"

"No. But at least you'll have all the necessary information before you start making choices."

"I have all the information that I need, to know I don't want to be with you anymore." Eve edged around Jac, escaping the kitchen on shaky legs. "And you're really making me regret coming over here tonight."

"Come on, Eve. It's not like you have a choice." Jac didn't even bother to hide her frustration as she followed Eve back into the living room. "If Selene and I don't agree on anything else, it's that you will not be alone while that monster is still out there."

Whirling to face Jac, Eve fought not to raise her voice. On the heels of that kiss, hearing Jac invoke Selene's name bordered on offensive. "I doubt this is what Selene had in mind."

"Probably not."

"So I'm a captive audience, then? Is that it?" Eve's throat tightened at the memory of Jac crushing their mouths and bodies together. "You think you can ambush me?"

"I just want to protect you. That includes making sure you know the truth about the woman you've fallen in love with. Even if it hurts your feelings." Jac puffed up her chest, challenging. "You can't tell me that kiss was entirely unwelcome. I know there's some part of you that isn't sure about Selene, that misses me."

"I'm *not* a cheater," Eve said coldly. "You took me by surprise. But I would *never* do to Selene what you did to me." The thought made Eve tremble. She could think of nothing worse than betraying Selene's trust like Jac had once betrayed hers. That Jac was the one who put her in this position enraged Eve. "And I don't care what you *or* Selene say. I do have a choice about being here, and I'm choosing to leave. Right now."

Alarm flashed in Jac's eyes. "No. You're right, I shouldn't have said that. That was unfair. I promise to drop it for the rest of the night. But you're not going anywhere."

"Goddamn you, Jac." Eve walked to the door, grabbing her coat from the hook in the entryway. "Yes, I am. I'm going outside to tell my friends from the department that I'm getting a hotel room tonight. I have no doubt they'll keep me perfectly safe without hitting on me." She buttoned her coat with trembling hands. "I don't need you. Not to protect me, or to tell me whom I should date. I don't even need you as a friend, if you're going to put me in the awkward position of having to constantly push you away."

Jac grabbed Eve's wrist, stopping her from turning the doorknob. "I said I was sorry. Please don't go."

Eve shivered under Jac's touch. Guilt turned her stomach at the memory of kissing back, even for an instant. She couldn't stay with Jac tonight. She couldn't even imagine waiting until tomorrow to confess what happened to Selene. Selene was probably already on her way out of town, but if she hadn't left yet, Eve had to go see her. To clear her conscience. To reassure herself that she hadn't just royally screwed things up.

Eve yanked her wrist away and opened the door. "Thanks for dinner, Jac. I'll see you later." She hurried out of the apartment, rushing down the hallway before Jac could try to convince her to stay.

She had to see Selene—and apologize.

CHAPTER TWENTY

Selene gritted her teeth as she walked to her front door, waves of pleasure rippling through her body from the simple friction of her silk robe brushing her naked skin. She hadn't expected the new escort to arrive for another fifteen minutes, but was thrilled by her punctuality. This month's impending transformation was already more intense than the last, even without the perigee moon, and Selene knew it had everything to do with Eve.

Consumed by Eve's lingering scent on the furniture around her, by the memory of the last time she touched Eve's skin, Selene could think of nothing but her desire to fuck Eve hard and fast, to make her scream out shuddering release. More than once today she had orgasmed simply by thinking of what she would do to Eve if they were together. It was probably better for Eve they weren't.

Now that she had a mate, the sexual frenzy the moon sparked within Selene burned so hot it left her barely able to hold on to conscious thought. She had no idea how she would restrain herself if Eve were near. As it was, it would surely take everything she had to explain her ritual to the new girl—even more not to seem like a complete lunatic while doing so. Selene hoped the escort's early arrival boded well for her ability to follow instructions and tie rope tighter than her predecessor.

Selene opened the door, then went very still. For a few breathless moments she hoped she was seeing things, that her sex-clouded mind was tricking her into imagining Eve standing there on her porch looking delicious enough to devour.

"Oh, good. I thought you would have already left." Eve's eyes shone with emotion even as she flitted her gaze over the length of Selene's body. "Were you about to take a shower?"

Bracing a hand against the door frame, Selene gritted her teeth and tried to hold herself together. Answering the door in a robe had to seem strange when Eve believed she should be on her way out of town already. The least she could do was try to act normal.

Working against her was not only the maddening influence of the moon but also the knowledge that her escort was due to arrive any moment. Selene struggled to focus on the task at hand—it was absolutely necessary to make Eve leave before she got caught in a lie. But her body didn't want Eve to go. The satisfaction she craved was right in front of her, staring at her with troubled eyes. Selene felt a myriad of emotions pouring off Eve, chief among them guilt. Dimly, Selene wondered what could have happened to bring Eve here when she knew Selene wasn't supposed to be home.

"I was just getting ready to go." Cursing the breathiness of her voice, Selene tried to affect a casual air. "What are you doing here? You're supposed to be at Jac's."

"I couldn't stay." The guilt that flowed from Eve intensified, but instead of dampening Selene's arousal, it only inflamed her more. Right now every bit of Eve's emotion served as kindling for the fire of her lust, stoking the flames to dangerous heights. "She kissed me, Selene. I didn't want her to and I told her nothing could happen between us, but…" Swallowing, Eve could no longer seem to meet her eyes. "I know you wanted me to stay with her tonight, but I can't. And I'm so sorry to just drop in like this when you're on your way out of town. I needed to tell you what happened…and apologize."

Selene exhaled through her nose. Her heart pumped alarmingly hard, every beat thrumming in her pussy and making it more and more difficult to function. The idea that Jac would touch *her* Eve unleashed a flood of jealous need, stretching her control to the breaking point. The easiest way to make Eve leave would probably be to accuse her of cheating and send her away, but Selene couldn't do that. Not even to protect her secret. With effort, Selene bared her teeth in a tense smile.

"No need to apologize, darling. I trust you. Is there somewhere else you can go tonight?" Selene concentrated on moderating her breathing, trying to ignore the scent of Jac she now picked up on Eve's skin. The visceral reminder of Jac's transgression made it all but impossible to resist pulling Eve inside and staking her claim. "I hate to turn you away, but I'm already running late…"

"Of course," Eve murmured, face falling. "I'm sorry to have

bothered you. I probably shouldn't have come—" She turned slightly and her shirt pulled tight across her breasts, snapping the last thread of Selene's control.

Growling, Selene caught Eve's arm in a forceful grasp and pulled her forward, inside the house, then slammed her up against the wall next to the door. She attacked Eve's mouth with vicious passion, crushing their lips together in a hard kiss. Eve gasped beneath her, then clutched at Selene's shoulders, giving off a jolt of shocked pleasure that made Selene climax violently against her. Tearing her mouth away, Selene turned her face to the side and closed her eyes without retreating.

"You're *mine*," Selene choked out. She buried her face in Eve's hair and inhaled deeply, quaking as an aftershock rolled through her body. Rather than sate her need, each orgasm only cranked it up higher. "But you need to go, Eve. Right now."

Eve curled a hand around the back of Selene's neck, holding her close. She couldn't have moved even if she'd wanted to, pinned in place by Selene's heavy bulk. But it didn't seem like getting away was on her agenda. "If you've got five minutes, we could say good-bye properly."

Too weak to resist, Selene shivered. The smell of Eve's wetness saturated the air between them, wiping every bit of rational thought from Selene's mind. The longer she let Eve stay, the greater the chance of getting caught. But her body simply wouldn't obey her mind. She couldn't send Eve away when every cell of her being screamed with the need to take her.

"Goddamn it," Selene groaned. She reached between their bodies and yanked open the button on Eve's pants, tearing down her zipper, then plunging her hand into the front of Eve's panties. She found silky hairs, then slick folds with her fingers, too desperate to sink into Eve's tight opening to bother with being gentle.

"Selene—" Eve squeezed her shoulders and cried out when Selene thrust up inside her. "Oh, fuck."

"Am I hurting you?" Selene gasped. She hoped like hell that she wasn't because she didn't know how to stop.

"No." Eve set her feet apart and clung to Selene like her life depended on it. "Fuck me, baby. Take me."

The front door stood open beside them, and though nobody could see them from the street, Selene knew anyone passing by would hear the sounds of their frenzied joining. Stunned that Eve would allow such an exhibition, the thought of Eve that far beyond self-consciousness only made Selene hungry for more. Harder. Faster. She drove her fingers into Eve over and over again, as deeply as they would go in this awkward position, and used her thumb to rub harsh circles over Eve's swollen clit. When Eve stiffened beneath her, right on the edge of orgasm, Selene bent to Eve's neck and bit down roughly, sucking the tender flesh into her mouth hard enough to leave a mark.

Selene's eyes were tightly closed, but she saw Eve's release as a fiery burst of yellow light behind her eyelids. Her pleasure exploded into Selene's body, triggering an orgasm in Selene that seemed to send Eve tumbling over again just as her first climax subsided. Every orgasm Eve endured touched off another in Selene, no less intense than the one before, and every time Selene came Eve tipped her head back to start the process again. Selene had no idea how long they stood there holding one another up as they rode out their feedback loop of pleasure, but the only thing that brought Selene down was the sound of a throat clearing beside them.

Full moon or not, Selene sobered in an instant. Her call girl had arrived.

❖

Eve didn't know what hit her. One moment she was standing on Selene's porch thinking she shouldn't have dropped in, then suddenly Selene had her crushed against the wall inside the apartment—next to the *open* door—taking her hard and fast, making her love every second of it. Like a woman possessed, Selene seemed to be acting out of sheer passion, and Eve doubted she realized just how rough her hands were, how sharp her teeth. Every bit of pain Selene inflicted instantly turned into white-hot pleasure. There wasn't one moment during their frenzied coupling when Eve didn't want exactly what Selene was giving her.

Just as quickly as Selene exploded into frantic need, she froze with what felt like silent fear. Yanked out of their incredible mutual orgasm by Selene's wild-eyed look of terrified guilt, Eve struggled to catch her breath even as she contracted weakly around the fingers still buried deep inside her pussy. When Selene's attention shifted to the door beside them, Eve turned her head and noticed a beautiful blonde standing not three feet away.

"Oh." Eve grabbed Selene's arm and tugged, mortified that the woman had no doubt witnessed the conclusion of their mindless fucking. Selene pulled her fingers from Eve quickly, without a trace of tenderness. Wincing, Eve buttoned her pants with shaking hands as Selene stared at the blonde as though she were seeing a ghost.

"I'm sorry to interrupt," the stranger said lightly. "I'm here for my seven o'clock with Selene?"

The stricken look on Selene's face sent hot, gut-wrenching pain shooting through Eve. She wore an expression of pure, panicked shame—of disbelief at knowing she had just been caught. Jac had once given her the same look after Eve caught her going down on another woman in their bed. Eve shifted her attention from Selene to the blonde in the doorway, trying to understand what this meant.

"She's Selene," Eve said thickly, pointing at her lover.

Selene opened then closed her mouth. Her eyes were unfocused and Eve suddenly realized just how out of it she seemed. When Selene had first answered the door, Eve had sensed something was off, but chalked it up to simple confusion over the fact that she wasn't where Selene had expected her to be. Now she realized that Selene had probably been anxious about her visit because she knew the blonde was due for their appointment.

So who was she? And why had Selene pulled Eve inside for a quickie if she was expecting someone she clearly didn't want her to meet?

"I'm sorry." The blonde shifted uncomfortably, looking between Eve and Selene like she suddenly realized just how volatile this situation could become. "Is this a bad time?"

Eve waited to hear what Selene would say. Alarm flashed across Selene's face. "No. Not a bad time. Why don't you wait for me in the living room?" She shifted her attention back to Eve. "I'll walk you to your car."

When Selene reached for her arm, Eve jerked away sharply. "No, I think you owe me an explanation."

Glancing at the blonde, Selene gestured toward the living room with a visibly shaking hand. "It's just in there."

"Great." The blonde chanced one last apologetic look at Eve. "Sorry."

Eve had never wanted to punch someone so badly in her life. She glared at the blonde's back as she walked inside, only returning her focus to Selene when the woman disappeared from view. "You're not really going out of town. Are you?"

Sweat dripped from Selene's forehead and her breathing emerged in heaving gasps. "Eve, you need to leave. I can explain later."

Selene might as well have plunged a knife into her chest. It couldn't have hurt nearly as bad. "I don't want you to explain later." Pushing away from the wall, Eve limped out the front door. Until that moment she didn't realize how sore her pussy was. Tears stung her eyes and she gritted her teeth in an effort not to react. Not because of the pain, but because what should have been the reminder of wild, uninhibited lovemaking now felt like the aftermath of a lie. "You don't need to explain. It's written all over your face."

Selene followed her out the door. "I *did* hurt you." She grabbed Eve's wrist, and even that simple touch ignited fierce need and longing within her that left her infuriated. With a connection like theirs, why did Selene need to screw someone else? Selene let out a strangled groan and instantly pulled back her hand as though she'd been burned. "Wait."

Disgusted, Eve whirled around and put out a hand to stop Selene from touching her again. "I thought you wanted me to go."

Tears streamed from Selene's eyes. "I do," she whispered, "but not for the reason you think."

"Not because you're going in there to fuck that woman?" Eve never thought Selene would do this to her. Not after everything they'd experienced together. Not when Eve had made herself more vulnerable with her than anyone. "Tell me why you *really* want me to leave, then."

Selene opened her mouth but no sound came out. Rivulets of sweat tracked down her face, and she couldn't seem to stand still. Eve sensed confusion in amongst the guilt and fear, and had a sudden, sickening thought.

"Are you on drugs?" Scanning Selene's face, Eve now saw that something was quite definitely not right. "Or sick?" She glanced over Selene's shoulder, inside her apartment. Was it possible the woman was there for some other reason? It sounded like they had an appointment. What if Selene was hiding a health problem, not sleeping with another woman? Determined not to let her history with Jac prevent her from giving Selene the benefit of the doubt, Eve forced herself to see the situation clearly. "Tell me what's going on, Selene. So I don't think the worst."

"I'm not having sex with her." Jaw clenched, Selene seemed

caught between desperation and reticence. "That's all I can tell you. I need you to trust me."

After Selene had lied about going out of town, Eve didn't know how to offer that level of blind trust. "How? How can I trust you when you lied to me, when I can see you're scared out of your mind and obviously full of guilt?"

"Because you know me. I'm not Jac."

Eve didn't know what to believe anymore. All of a sudden she wanted to ask about that anonymous phone tip just as badly as Jac wanted her to. "Did you report that body in Golden Gate Park to the police?"

Selene's face drained of color. "What?"

"Jac says it's you on the recording of that call. She wanted me to listen to it, but I refused to believe that you'd keep something like that from me." Folding her arms over her chest, Eve said, "But obviously I *don't* know you. At least not as well as I thought I did."

"Eve—"

"Did you make that call? Just tell me. The truth."

Selene looked up at the rapidly darkening sky, then stared at Eve with haunted eyes. "Yes."

Eve's insides turned to ice. Yesterday she would have sworn she understood Selene's heart. Now she didn't understand anything. "Who is that woman in your living room?"

Wincing, Selene brought a hand to her head and clenched her teeth. Eve watched warily, unsure how to interpret the histrionics. Nothing about what was happening made sense. How could she have been so wrong about someone? Eve had come to trust Selene more than she'd ever trusted anyone, at a time when her life was filled with fear and uncertainty. That didn't just happen without a reason. Did it?

Tears poured from Selene's eyes. Every word she said seemed torn out of her, as though she didn't want to let them go. "Get out of here, Eve. We're done for tonight. I'll call you tomorrow."

"Don't bother," Eve said, as surprised by the cold, angry words as Selene appeared to be. Ten minutes ago she'd thought Selene was the love of her life. Now she felt like she was looking at a stranger, one who cared more about keeping a secret than saving their relationship. "You're right. We're done."

Selene's face dissolved into anguish so painful that Eve felt it, too, deep in her chest. It hollowed her out, made it hard to breathe. She turned her back on Selene, but that didn't diminish her heartbreak.

"Be careful, Eve." Selene's voice cracked with emotion. "Please. Go back to Jac. Be safe tonight."

Eve didn't know where she'd go. She glanced across the street, where she saw the car with her protective detail parked. The detectives were watching the scene but turned their attention away quickly when Eve stared them down. How long would it take Jac to hear about this?

"Eve—"

"Good-bye, Selene." Each step away from Selene took effort. But as Eve walked the ache in her chest diminished slightly, so she picked up her pace until she was nearly jogging to her car. Once she got to the driver's side door she threw it open and dove inside, starting the engine and pulling into the street as quickly as she could.

She didn't know where she was going. She just had to get away.

CHAPTER TWENTY-ONE

Selene staggered back into her house after Eve sped off, forcing her mind to the task at hand. She could fall apart about what had just happened later. Right now she had a call girl to instruct, and time was running out. The transformation was itching at her skin. Another forty-five minutes and she would be completely out of her mind from the moon. If the blonde didn't leave before then, Selene would have even more to worry about than breaking Eve's heart.

The blonde stood up as Selene stumbled into the living room. She looked Selene up and down with uneasy eyes. "Are you all right?"

"I'm fine." Selene gritted her teeth and gestured toward her guest room. "Shall we?"

Clearly uncertain what to think of her, the escort offered her hand. "I'm Dani."

Bracing herself for the inevitable, Selene shook Dani's hand, suppressing a groan at her body's reaction to the tactile stimulation. "Lovely to meet you." She withdrew quickly. "We need to hurry. I'm on a schedule and we're already running late."

Dani followed her into the guest room. Like her predecessor, she didn't react visibly to the steel table bolted to the floor. Her eyes were glued to Selene's face. "I'm sorry if I caused any trouble between you and your friend back there. If you'd like to reschedule, I completely understand."

"That won't be necessary." Selene tugged on the belt of her robe, pushing the flimsy garment off her shoulders and onto the ground. "Listen, what I need is very simple, but it's important you do exactly as I tell you."

It took every ounce of Selene's concentration to get through her bullshit speech about how she liked to be lashed to a table so tight she could barely breathe. Because she liked feeling powerless. Right. She felt powerless every day, and she was sick and tired of it.

Dani listened carefully to every word, never betraying any reaction at all, then tied her as tight as anyone had ever dared. By the time Selene was immobilized on the table, she could no longer speak. Mixed in with all the lust and power she felt just shy of her shift was the terrible memory of watching Eve limp away in tears.

Selene was glad Dani wasn't afraid to take things to the extreme. If Selene escaped tonight, her grieving, enraged beast-self could do anything, to anyone. One of her last coherent thoughts as Dani tied the final knot was that she would be sure to tip her well, and ask for her again.

"Eight o'clock tomorrow morning?" Dani walked to the guest room door, tossing the spare set of house keys in her hand. "I'll see you then, okay?"

Selene grunted in the affirmative. Speaking required too much effort, took more conscious thought than she could summon.

"You have a good night, Selene. I hope you get what you want out of this."

Selene waited until she heard her front door shut before she choked out the sobs that tore at her insides. What she wanted was already gone. Tipping back her head, she howled in pain.

It was going to be a long, dark night.

❖

Selene came awake with a strangled gasp. She tried to sit up, but the rope and steel around her limbs kept her prone on the steel table. Exhaling shakily, she let her head drop back. She'd made it through another transformation safe and secure. After a moment she lifted her head and surveyed the length of her body. The rope was frayed and nearly torn through in places. But it had held.

She'd forgotten how damn good it was to survive another full moon knowing she hadn't hurt anyone, herself included. But any relief she felt was short-lived. As she struggled to remember the events leading up to the loss of human consciousness, terrible, fragmented memories assaulted her. Opening the door to find Eve on her front porch. Fucking her hard, so hard she'd limped away in pain. The angry red bite imprint on Eve's neck where Selene had marked her. Worst of all, the betrayal in Eve's eyes when she realized Selene had never planned to leave town. When the call girl—whose name Selene couldn't remember—had arrived.

"Shit," Selene whispered brokenly. She craned her neck, glancing at the clock she had mounted near the door. The escort wasn't due back for another two hours, so she had plenty of time to relive every agonizing moment from the night before. In less than fifteen minutes, she guessed, she'd managed to destroy the one thing she held most dear.

It almost made her success at staying contained seem not to matter at all.

Selene closed her eyes. Though Eve's presence during her moon-frenzy had thrown her already-clouded mind into overdrive, she could still remember how good it felt when they climaxed together. How awful it was to watch Eve jump into her car and speed away. Tears poured down Selene's face, soaking her hair. She couldn't fix what had happened, not without telling Eve the truth. Even that was far from a foolproof plan—Eve would quite possibly freak out. Who wanted to hear that her girlfriend was a shape-shifter whose monthly cycle involved becoming a vicious beast with no human conscience?

By the time Selene heard the faint sound of her front door opening then closing, she thought she was all cried out. Her tears had run dry at least a half hour ago, partially because her eyes were too sore to keep producing them. Wishing she could fix her face before the escort opened the guest room door, Selene just took a deep breath and prepared to act as normal as a woman who liked getting tied to steel tables could possibly hope to seem.

The guest room door opened and an attractive blonde strolled inside. "Rise and shine, darling."

Selene mustered a weak nod. "Hey. Uh…"

"Dani." She gave Selene a sunny grin, immediately going to work untying the ropes. "Well, you seem like you're feeling better today."

Selene could only imagine how she must have seemed to Dani last night. Between the moon and her encounter with Eve, Selene had no doubt that she'd come across as either sick or crazy. Maybe both. "Yes, thank you."

"Still pretty broken up about what happened with your friend, though." Dani met her eyes cautiously before returning her attention to the restraints. "If I'm overstepping, feel free to tell me."

Selene considered telling Dani to mind her own business for only an instant before discarding the notion. She paid good money for these escorts without asking for much at all—a sympathetic ear actually didn't sound half-bad right now. "She wasn't supposed to know about you."

"Yeah, I gathered that." Dani freed one of Selene's wrists. "I'm sorry."

"Not your fault." As soon as Dani released her other wrist, Selene sat up and rubbed her hands together, getting her blood moving again. "I should never have invited her inside. I knew you'd be here any minute." She couldn't possibly explain what a slave to the moon she'd been, how she could have had such an incredible lapse in judgment. So she just shrugged. "I made a mistake."

Dani glanced up as she untied Selene's ankle. "She your girlfriend?"

"*Was* my girlfriend." Selene's chest ached from the finality of the statement, but she didn't doubt it was true. "Yeah."

"It's over?"

Selene's chin trembled. Apparently she hadn't run out of tears to spill, after all. "I think so, yeah."

"Well, that's a shame." Dani raised an eyebrow. "Because I'm pretty sure I interrupted some of the hottest sex I've ever seen."

Selene nodded, then dissolved into a fresh round of sobs. Mortified that she was breaking down in front of a stranger, she covered her eyes with her hands and willed herself to pull it together. She'd known from the start that this would happen someday. Lying to Eve every month would never have worked, but that didn't lessen her heartache. If anything, it made it worse.

"Hey." The restraint around Selene's other ankle opened, then Dani's arms were around her naked, shivering body, gathering her into a warm embrace. "I didn't mean to make you cry."

Every instinct Selene had screamed at her to pull away, to send Dani home and keep any further details of her personal life to herself, just as she'd always done. Not that her instincts were always correct, clearly. Selene really wanted to cuddle into Dani and let her try to ease the gut-churning pain of knowing she'd destroyed the love of her life.

"I screwed up." Selene's shoulders shook, and Dani squeezed her even tighter. "She was the one. She was *it*. And I…I lied to her. She thought she knew who I was—I *told* her she knew who I was—but I've been lying to her this whole time."

Dani stroked Selene's hair as though comforting a weeping child. "May I ask you a question?"

Selene had nothing left to lose. "Sure."

"You like being tied up, right? Feeling out of control?" Dani drew back and searched Selene's face. "Does she know that?"

Selene wished it were as easy as having the courage to share unusual sexual tastes. "No."

"You don't think she'd accept you?"

"No, I'm pretty sure she wouldn't." Embarrassed, Selene eased out of Dani's arms and crossed the room to slip on her robe. "It's more complicated than it seems."

"I'm sure it is." Dani sat on the edge of the table, staring at her thoughtfully. "But if she really is the one, don't you think she'd accept you no matter what? I mean, I hate to break it to you, but you're hardly the kinkiest freak I've ever met." Chuckling, Dani ran a hand over the edge of the table. "In fact, this is relatively tame. Hell, you're not even asking for sex. Just restraint."

Selene shook her head. She couldn't explain this without spilling her deepest secrets. If she couldn't tell Eve, she certainly wasn't telling Dani. "You just have to trust me on this. I don't think Eve would understand. If she knew about me—everything I've been hiding—she'd run away screaming."

"Kind of like she did last night?" Dani shrugged. "Look, you don't know me. God knows I don't have all the answers. But it doesn't make much sense from where I'm standing—lying to someone for fear of losing them, only to lose her anyway because of the lies. If you tell the truth, maybe she will leave you. I don't know. But maybe she won't. This way, you never even gave her a chance to prove you wrong."

It wasn't that simple, of course, but Dani's words tugged at Selene's gut. Would Eve have really exposed her if Selene had revealed her secret? Possibly, but somehow Selene couldn't imagine it. Would Eve have ended their relationship? Quite likely. But would Selene have felt any worse about it than she did right now? At least that way it would have been Eve making a choice instead of Selene violating her trust. If she truly loved Eve, she should have given her the opportunity to make that choice. Even at the risk of her own freedom.

Selene shook her head. "It's too late now."

"Is it?"

Exhausted from her difficult night, Selene didn't have the energy to even consider the possibility that their relationship could be salvaged. She couldn't decide whether to tell Eve the truth without thinking seriously about the matter and considering all the possible consequences. She would need to do that alone. Selene gestured for Dani to follow her into the living room. "Let me get you the rest of your payment."

Taking the hint, Dani didn't say anything until Selene withdrew a stack of bills and handed them over. Dani tucked the money into her pocket with a grateful nod. "You take care of yourself, okay?"

"I will. See you next month?"

Dani gave Selene a sad smile. "It's a date."

Selene walked her to the door and saw her off, keeping a stoic face. But the minute she closed the door she crumpled, totally and utterly lost. For years she'd been alone, never talking to anyone except her freelance clients and assorted call girls, yet she'd never felt as desolate then as she did now. Eve had given her a taste of something truly extraordinary, and now that it was gone, she felt as though her soul had been ripped from her body, leaving behind an empty shell.

All at once fear stabbed deep in Selene's gut. She had no idea where Eve had gone last night after leaving her place in tears. Back to Jac? Or had she returned home, alone and vulnerable? Selene closed her eyes and concentrated on reaching out with her mind, desperate to feel the gossamer pull of Eve's emotion that was usually within her grasp even when they were miles apart.

The good news was that she felt *something*, which had to mean that Eve was alive out there somewhere, hopefully safe from harm. Unfortunately, all Selene could read from her was pain, so thick and deep it threatened to choke Selene with its intensity. She couldn't determine what the source of that pain was. Selene suspected—hell, almost hoped—that it was because of her, not because she'd fallen prey to her stalker. But because Eve could be in trouble, Selene wouldn't be able to rest until she made sure Eve was physically unharmed.

Selene got her cell phone and typed in a text message. *I know you don't want to talk to me right now. Please let me know you're safe, okay?* Clicking Send, Selene held her breath, knowing that the sight of her name in Eve's in-box was sure to stir up some pretty intense feelings.

Crazily, Selene sensed the exact moment Eve read her message, less than a minute later. A pang of sorrow constricted her heart. Tears stung her sore eyes. A few heartbeats later, her phone beeped with an answer.

I'm safe.

Hands shaking, Selene typed out one last message, even though she knew it wouldn't be welcome. *I never wanted to hurt you. It's complicated and I wish I had the courage to explain. I love you.*

This time Selene felt Eve's reaction as a dim mixture of anger and grief. Trembling, she both anticipated and feared Eve's response.

One never came.

❖

Eve locked her phone, then slipped it into her desk drawer. Any feelings of obligation she had as far as communicating with Selene ended with her terse reassurance that she was safe. Beyond that, her life was no longer Selene's business. After a long night filled with tears, anger, and disbelief, Eve had come to work today determined to hold her head high and keep her dignity intact. So what that she'd been fooled again? She was a professional, respected in her field and responsible for helping catch a very bad man who'd killed many women. It would take a lot more than a woman she'd known only a month to destroy her—even if the idea of never being with Selene again left her bone-chillingly empty.

Wayne sat at the counter across the lab, eyes glued to a microscope. All morning he had studiously ignored the telltale signs that she was having a bad day, and Eve loved him for that. The thought of having to explain how two women who claimed to love her had put her through a night of hell—both of them acting in concert to break her heart—was more than she could bear. She just wanted to bury herself in work. She was due to testify in court at two o'clock and needed to brush up on the facts of that older case. Right now they had a newly delivered corpse to examine. As long as she kept her mind on her job, maybe she wouldn't have time to think about the fact that once she left the lab tonight, she wouldn't have anywhere to go.

Eve walked to the body bag that lay on the steel examination table in the center of her lab. A month ago work had been the most important thing in her life. It shouldn't be so difficult to refocus her passion on the one thing that had never broken her heart: science.

"Do you mind if I assist you?" Wayne said suddenly, seemingly distracted from his silent analysis of whatever sample he'd been examining. "I'd love to dig into a fresh corpse this morning."

Eve wrinkled her nose at his choice of words. "Of course, Dr. Black. I'd be happy to have a second pair of eyes."

Approaching the table with purpose, he met her gaze briefly. "How are you?"

"Just okay." She handed him the scalpel, more than willing to let him make the first cut. Lately she just didn't have the stomach for it. "I had a long night."

"But you're okay, at least?" Wayne glanced at her neck.

Self-conscious, Eve tried not to react to his frank examination. The red-purple bruise on her neck was impossible to miss. After checking into her hotel room the night before, she had gasped as soon as she walked into the bathroom and caught her reflection in the mirror. Selene's possessive mark stood out against her pale skin, an ugly reminder of the intensity of their final joining. Makeup couldn't cover it. That the love bite had been the result of unrestrained passion was obvious. In the aftermath of Selene's betrayal, it was also a mark of shame.

"I'm fine." Eve gave him a look that she hoped made clear that the subject was closed. "Now cut."

"Yes, ma'am." Wayne positioned the scalpel over the breastbone, readying for the first incision. Just as he sliced into the gray flesh, the lab doorbell chimed.

Instantly wary, Eve tensed and glanced back at the door. From this angle she couldn't see who rang. It would be just like Jac to push her luck instead of giving Eve space. "Go ahead. I'll see who that is." At Wayne's nod, she crossed to the lab door and peered out the window. As she'd feared, Jac stood in the hallway with a hangdog expression. Against her better judgment, Eve opened the door a crack. "What do you want?"

"Just to talk." Jac held up her hands in supplication. "I was an asshole last night. I know it. Please let me apologize."

Too exhausted for another emotional scene, Eve stepped into the hallway and shut the door behind her. She pointed Jac toward the exit with a shaking hand. "I can't do this right now. I just can't."

Jac's jaw tightened as she scanned the length of Eve's body. "Looks like you caught up with Selene last night. Is that hickey because you told her I kissed you?"

Even the sound of Selene's name brought a fresh wave of grief to Eve's heart. "I don't want to talk to you about this. Just go. Okay?" Chin trembling, Eve reached behind her for the door handle, fumbling in her desperation to escape. "Please."

Jac's whole body tensed. "No." She grabbed Eve's wrist, stopping her from leaving. "What's wrong? Tell me what happened."

Not wanting to admit that Jac had been right about Selene, Eve leveled an accusatory glare. "You know what's wrong."

"This isn't just about what I did." Jac's hand shot out and brushed a lock of hair off Eve's neck. Her eyes narrowed as she examined what Selene had left behind. "Something happened with Selene, didn't it?"

"Don't be ridiculous."

"You can be honest with me." Inspecting her face, Jac studied Eve with the same unflinching boldness she used on criminal suspects. "Detective Munoz called me last night. He told me he thought you and Selene might have had some kind of altercation. Please tell me what she did to you."

Incensed at the violation of her privacy, Eve jerked away from Jac's touch. "So the detectives are your spies, then? Is that it? Reporting my movements back to the boss?"

Softening slightly, Jac shook her head. "They were worried about you, Evie. All they told me was that you went to see your girlfriend, another woman showed up, and you and Selene argued on the porch. And it looked like maybe you'd been assaulted." Tightening her hand into a fist, Jac said, "I know you don't want anything to do with me, but I need to ask. Did Selene hurt you?"

"She didn't physically assault me." The answer was a cop-out and Eve had no doubt that Jac read the subtext loud and clear. But if Jac thought Eve intended to unload her emotional pain to the woman who'd constantly rooted for her relationship with Selene to fail, she could think again. "I'm not saying anything else about it, Jac. It's none of your business."

Jac's eyes shone with barely restrained contempt. "She's a goddamn idiot. Just like me. Both of us complete and total morons, to hurt someone like you."

Eve appreciated the sentiment, but from Jac it was too little too late. "Yeah, well. I must ask for it somehow, right?"

"No. We're just stupid."

"Guess I've got bad taste in women, then."

"Guess so." Jac swallowed. "The detective told me you stayed in a hotel last night. What are you planning to do tonight?"

The idea of another night in a hotel room, away from the familiarity of her space, was too much for Eve to handle. "I'm going home."

"I'd really rather you stay somewhere else. Until we get our killer off the street, at least."

With her life coming apart at the seams, only the thought of being surrounded by the home she'd made for herself brought Eve any comfort. Staying at a hotel indefinitely was not going to happen. She was too stubborn to let her stalker force her into any sadder a state than she was already in. "I'll be just fine. Your detectives will make sure of that."

"Street surveillance only goes so far," Jac said, sounding as though she'd anticipated this argument. "At least let me post them at your door."

"No." Let Jac's spies camp out in the hallway of her apartment building? Eve couldn't think of a more unappealing idea. "They can escort me inside, if that makes you feel better. I'll even let them sweep the apartment. But then they leave. I'll lock the door behind them."

Jac didn't bother to hide her irritation. "Why do you have to be so difficult? This is your life we're talking about. Someone's stalking you, someone who takes his time killing his victims in the middle of a densely populated city yet somehow never seems to attract any attention. Forget about your pride, forget that you've just been put through the wringer. You shouldn't be alone right now."

Snorting, Eve said, "That's exactly what I am, Jac. Alone. And I'm *fine* alone. I'm not going to be stupid about this. I know I need to be careful. We're doing all we can. I've got armed guards. I'll use them, within reason. And we'll catch this guy, hopefully before he can hurt anyone else." Careful not to take out all her anger with Selene on Jac, Eve modulated her tone, then said, "If something changes, I'll reconsider. But for the moment, he doesn't appear to be coming for me. I'm more worried about who he'll kill to send his next message than the possibility that he'll approach me directly. After all, if he's fixated on me—if this is all about taunting me—I'd say there's a good chance he wants me alive to see his work."

"For now, maybe."

"Maybe." Eve waved Jac away. "Listen, we'll talk about this later. I've got a cold one on the table and a lot of work to do. Why don't you go work on finding the guy? We do that and we won't have to worry about where I'm sleeping."

"I'll still worry about it." Jac's low tone conveyed her meaning loud and clear. Now that Selene had broken Eve's heart, Jac wasn't about to relinquish the idea of reconciliation. "But I do have a possible witness I'm planning to re-interview today. I'll let you know if I learn anything new."

"Thank you."

"And you let me know if anything happens, okay? Anything at all that seems out of the ordinary, no matter how mundane." Jac lifted a hand as though she might touch Eve's arm, then let it drop. "The barista even looks at you funny when you're standing in line at Starbucks, you let me know. Deal?"

"Fine."

Jac stepped backward but didn't turn away. "I really am sorry about last night. I never should have put you in that position, particularly because I know how you feel about infidelity."

"I appreciate that." Jac's sincere tone and genuine contriteness softened Eve's resolve not to let her off the hook so easily. In the aftermath of Selene's crushing betrayal, Jac's stupid seduction scene hardly merited Eve's continued anger. She just didn't have the energy to stay mad at both of them. "And I accept your apology."

"If you'll stay at my place, just until we catch this guy, I promise nothing like that will happen again."

Eve didn't entertain the thought for even a moment. "Good-bye, Jac. I'll talk to you later."

Sheepish, Jac said, "Can't blame me for trying, right?"

"I'm not so sure about that." Pushing open the lab door, Eve smirked to take the sting out of her words. "Go catch some bad guys."

"Will do." Jac watched as she retreated into the lab. As Eve closed the door behind her, Jac called after her, "Is Selene my anonymous tipster?"

Eve hesitated, debating how to answer. Technically there was nothing wrong about making an anonymous tip. Confirming Jac's suspicion was tantamount to giving her permission to harass Selene—Eve knew Jac well enough to be sure that she wouldn't back down, not where Eve was concerned—but at this point lying for Selene seemed ridiculous.

"Yes," Eve said quietly. "She reported the body."

"Do you think she knows anything she hasn't told us?"

Despite all the lies Selene had spouted over the past month, Eve still believed she wouldn't have held back vital, life-or-death information. Not when Eve's safety was at stake. "No. I don't think she knows anything."

"Good. But I may want to confirm that for myself."

Facing away from Jac, Eve closed her eyes. Grateful that Jac couldn't see the pain she knew was written all over her face, Eve took a deep breath and said, "Do whatever you want. It's not my concern anymore."

Jac was silent a moment. "I'm sorry, Eve."

"Me, too."

CHAPTER TWENTY-TWO

Kevin sat at a café table outside the local coffee shop around the corner from the courthouse, reading a magazine and trying to blend in. The dog he'd adopted from the shelter a week ago circled his feet, its leash secured around the leg of his chair. Kevin had never imagined owning a dog before, but he liked how having one made him seem both inconspicuous and non-threatening. It was a small mutt, not too cute as to draw a lot of attention, and it offered him the perfect excuse to walk the city streets as he studied Eve Thomas's routines.

She was due in court in forty-five minutes and would probably return to her lab after she gave her testimony. It was where she'd go tonight that interested him most. Lately she'd been spending a lot of time with the attractive dark-haired woman, but after their argument last night, her social patterns were probably about to change. Kevin had no idea where she slept after their fight—it had been too risky to follow her for long as she drove aimlessly through the streets after leaving her friend's place—but he planned to watch her apartment building tonight to see if she returned home.

The presence of her protection detail had complicated his plans, but he was adjusting. As soon as he spotted the same two guys parked in the street in front of her building three nights in a row, he knew that he needed to carefully choose his moments to interact with Eve. Though he yearned to get physical with her again, he had decided to hold back for now. Letting his obsession with Eve Thomas cloud his better judgment was the surest way to get caught.

He couldn't get caught. He was too goddamn smart. For all the trouble he went through to evade identification—to never take a trophy no matter how badly he desired one, to keep all his body hair shaved off lest he leave useful evidence, to keep bodily fluids to himself—Kevin wasn't about to throw his freedom away for a quick thrill.

He was ready to kill again, though. And this time, he wanted Eve to know before he completed the act so she could feel even worse after they discovered where he left the body.

The cops who watched her stuck with her throughout the day, so they wouldn't be guarding her apartment while she was in court. That would be the perfect opportunity to initiate the next phase of his Plan. Kevin couldn't think of a better place to leave his gift for her than on her doorstep. He hoped she decided to sleep at home tonight so she'd find it just when she thought she'd returned to a safe place. His cock stiffened at the thought of just how frightened she would be, knowing he'd stood at her apartment door only hours earlier, so close to invading her private sanctuary. Reminding her that she had nowhere to hide.

His dog—who didn't have a name, though the shelter had called it Nero—panted happily up at him as though sensing his excitement. Kevin stared back at it stone-faced. As good a prop as it was, he wasn't sure how long he'd bother to keep the animal. It was needy and messy, without any redeeming qualities except perhaps lending him some social legitimacy.

Though it was kind of cute.

Kevin lowered his hand and let the dog sniff it, then gave it a tentative scratch on the neck. The dog made a grumbling noise, licking his fingers appreciatively.

What would Eve think about a dead dog being delivered to her lab, wrapped up with a bow and a note that she could be next?

It was an option, at least, if the whole pet-ownership thing didn't work out.

CHAPTER TWENTY-THREE

The evening after the full moon, Selene struggled with what her next step should be. She was in for another intense time—the nights before and after the full moon didn't trigger a transformation, but the moon's intoxicating pull made it difficult for her to think clearly—yet she couldn't fathom not reaching out to Eve in some way.

The cynical part of Selene told her to just let their relationship go, to try to forget the fantasy of having a true life-partner. Eve had just been a diversion, albeit a magnificent one, but Selene couldn't get back what she'd lost. Telling Eve the truth about her nature was just asking for further heartbreak, and she couldn't sell any other lie. At least not without setting herself up for a greater fall when, inevitably, that story would crumble just like the going-out-of-town one had. Setting Eve up for a lifetime of lies and betrayal wasn't fair for either of them.

Not if she really loved Eve.

But Selene didn't know how to simply walk away. More than that, she refused to turn her back on Eve now. A maniac out there had attacked her once and would surely try again. In the meantime, he'd kill other innocent women in service of some sick game only he understood. Leaving Eve to face that threat alone wasn't an option. Jac could only protect her so much. Selene could do things that might possibly mean the difference between tracking down Eve's stalker and letting him hurt the most precious thing in Selene's life.

Even if Eve no longer belonged to her, Selene would never let that happen.

So at five o'clock in the evening, about an hour before she figured Eve might return home from work, Selene drove to Eve's apartment just in case she was stubborn enough to decide to spend the night there instead of staying elsewhere. Though they'd known each other only about a month, Selene sensed that in times of heartache, Eve relied on the comfort of the familiar. She had a bad feeling that Eve would insist on remaining in her apartment even though she was aware that her stalker knew where she lived.

The least Selene could do was help with security.

She scanned the cars parked along the street in front of Eve's apartment, trying to decide if any of them belonged to the detectives on her protective detail. She was pretty sure nobody was watching the apartment when she wasn't there, instead just keeping twenty-four-hour surveillance on Eve herself. Not what Selene would have chosen, though of course she had no idea what kind of budget and resource constraints Jac faced when creating the assignment. Honestly, had Jac been able to throw more manpower at the task, Selene had no doubt she would have. Jac clearly still cared for Eve deeply and genuinely wanted to keep her safe.

Now that Selene was out of the picture, Jac would probably think of all kinds of new ways to protect Eve. The fine hairs covering Selene's body stood on end at the very idea.

Keying the four-digit code Eve had taught her into the security panel—and breathing a sigh of relief when it still worked—Selene unlocked the door and slipped inside. She climbed the first flight of stairs, then stopped halfway up. Hackles rising, she caught a familiar, gut-churning scent lingering in the air.

Eve's stalker. He had been here, in this very stairwell, and not long ago.

Selene continued slowly, inhaling with focused intensity. Her human nose just couldn't tell her very much. She needed to shift into a dog. But that meant using her ability in an enclosed, populated space. Though she didn't sense anyone in the immediate vicinity, even entertaining the thought of pulling off a shift in Eve's apartment building ran counter to all her survival instincts. Yet what was the point of having this gift—she didn't often think of it as a gift, but if it might help her protect Eve, then that seemed like an appropriate word—if she never took advantage of it?

Pausing on the first-floor landing, she tried to decide what to do. She could hide her clothes in the stairwell and continue her investigation with a far more powerful nose. If the killer was still in the building, approaching him as a dog could very easily protect her own life.

Chances were he wouldn't perceive her as a threat unless she attacked him outright. But as a woman walking alone, she could very easily get herself into trouble if he found her before she found him.

Selene jogged to an isolated corner of the stairwell, tucked back behind a fire-exit door, and tore off her clothes simply because she couldn't do nothing when Eve might be in danger. If that man was in her apartment right now, she had to find out before Eve got home. If he wasn't, perhaps she could track him and discover his whereabouts.

The only challenge then would be to explain how she knew he was the man they sought without revealing her method for hunting him down.

Selene shifted into her trusty bloodhound form and put her nose on the ground, taking a deep whiff. The man's scent filled her nostrils, dark and pungent, and the fur on her back rose in response. She bared her teeth as she followed his trail up to Eve's third-floor apartment, dismayed when his odor only grew stronger. Trotting down Eve's hallway, Selene spotted an envelope propped against her doorway. She picked up speed, skidding to a stop over Eve's welcome mat, which smelled of rubber and wet leaves.

Lowering her nose to the envelope, she sniffed frantically. She blocked out all the other scents that floated around in her olfactory passages, most interested in the strangely familiar one that stood out among the rest. The man's smell permeated the manila envelope and its contents, but she detected something else. An earthy scent that Selene instantly recognized, but which seemed strangely out of place in this setting.

It smelled like shit. Literally.

Selene inhaled deeply, puzzled. The unmistakable odor certainly came from inside the envelope, so it wasn't merely a souvenir from the bottom of someone's shoe. Weird.

Lifting her head, she sniffed around the doorknob. Eve's scent was there but faint. She hadn't been here for a while. Selene guessed she hadn't returned home after their fight last night. She almost hoped she wouldn't come home tonight.

The man's scent wasn't on the door, which meant he hadn't touched it. Apparently breaking in hadn't been on his agenda. But how soon until he tried? Despite Eve's protective detail, he'd been able to leave something at her apartment door unnoticed. He could have just as easily broken in to lie in wait for her return.

Selene's ears twitched, pulled in the direction of the stairwell.

Her canine senses picked up the sound of the building door opening downstairs, then a male voice, and eventually the scent of two men and a woman. A woman whose unique smell Selene would know anywhere.

Eve was home.

Not wanting Eve to come home to a large bloodhound sitting on her doorstep, Selene quickly shifted into the least noticeable creature she could think of: a common fly. It was only the second time she'd tried this shape, and she still didn't like it. The reality of occupying so little physical space made her uneasy, as did the mechanics involved in using her wings and antennae. Emulating a mammal was so much easier than an insect or arachnid, probably because the basic physiology was relatively similar. Perhaps if she practiced more it would get easier, but Selene had always spent far more time cursing her ability than trying to master its intricacies.

Flying clumsily into the air, she perched on top of the door frame and waited for Eve and the men who accompanied her to appear. As far as she could tell, she had two choices. She could zoom over their heads back into the stairwell, throw on her clothes, and escape from the building undetected. Or she could stick around, a literal fly on the wall, and find out what was inside that envelope.

On second thought, that really wasn't much of a choice.

The man on Eve's left was talking when they stepped into view. "We'll do a quick sweep and be out of your hair in just a few minutes. You've got my cell number in your contact list, right?"

Eve sighed. She looked exhausted. "I do, Detective Munoz. Just like you have Detective Battle's number. If you know what I mean."

The dark-haired detective glanced over Eve's head at his partner, both of them sharing a sheepish grimace. "We're in charge of making sure nothing happens to you, Doc. What went down last night was definitely relevant to our assignment. Jac is in charge of that assignment, so we had to report back that your movements had become erratic. Especially after you refused to answer your cell phone when I called you first."

Clearly Eve's relationship with her protective detail had grown contentious. Selene hoped Eve realized that she needed them now more than ever. Crouching patiently on the edge of the door frame, Selene contended with the challenge of using human intellect to interpret what she saw and heard with her fly's senses. Though she kept her core intellect and personality despite the form her body took, Selene's sense of self was filtered through the strengths and frailties of whatever animal she mimicked. Just another reason that she didn't like shifting into insects. The way they experienced reality was too foreign not to clash with her human sensibilities.

Frankly, it drained her.

"Fair enough," Eve said, thawing slightly. "I'll answer my phone next time. Or, better yet, call you first. But please don't report my every movement to Jac, if you can help it. You know our history. It's just a little awkward."

The one she called Munoz nodded. "I get it. The important part is that you're safe."

Eve stopped abruptly in the hallway, staring at the envelope on her doorstep. Selene held her breath and waited for a reaction. Her heart ached at the fear that flashed across Eve's face as she struggled to speak. "We've got something."

The detective on Eve's right put an arm out, holding her back while Munoz hurried forward to crouch in front of the door. He pulled a pair of latex gloves from his pocket, then covered his mouth and nostrils with his hand as he peeked inside the envelope. Dropping his hand, he said, "Looks like a photograph. Maybe some kind of note."

Eve walked around the other detective's arm and joined Munoz at the door. Clearly struggling to maintain her composure, she bristled with fear and anger that nearly knocked Selene over with its intensity. "Let's get it inside and take a look."

Munoz looked over his shoulder at his partner. "All right, but you stay back. We'll go in first."

As Eve handed Munoz her keys, Selene took a deep breath, readying herself for a risky maneuver. If she wanted to see what was in that envelope, she'd need to launch herself off the door and follow the three of them inside Eve's apartment. The flying would require certain finesse, but Selene was most concerned about the possibility of getting swatted mid-flight. She'd need to do this quickly, attracting as little attention as possible.

When Munoz swung open the apartment door, Selene leapt from her perch and steered herself directly into Eve's apartment. The sharp turn, executed with a burst of speed, left Selene disoriented for a moment and she drunkenly buzzed too close to Munoz's head. He waved his hand absently, missing her by inches, but close enough to get her blood pumping. Taking a moment to orient herself in space, she shifted direction, then landed on the light fixture over Eve's dining room table, right above where they would probably empty the contents of the envelope to examine them.

The detectives entered the apartment first, guns drawn, and methodically searched every room. Selene stayed within sight of the doorway, watching Eve slump heavily against the wall and close her eyes. She was a jumble of emotions, and Selene couldn't help sending out a wave of healing energy, her typical shot of calm strength that had always soothed Eve's nerves. Eve's eyes snapped open and she inhaled sharply, looking around as though expecting to see a ghost.

Clearly Eve sensed her presence. Knowing it was reckless to use their connection when Eve couldn't understand the source, Selene pushed back her desire to comfort Eve, shutting off the flow of positive energy. Immediately Eve's shoulders sagged. Her hand drifted to her forehead and Selene could feel her rush of confusion. Hopefully Eve would simply write it off as misplaced grief, an unfortunate symptom of loss. She couldn't possibly guess the real reason their connection flared to life in a seemingly empty room.

"All clear," the unnamed detective called as they strolled back into the front room. "Come on in."

Eve closed and locked the door behind her. Now Selene was well and truly trapped, at least until the detectives left. "Do you have a spare pair of gloves, Detective Hunt?"

Munoz's partner withdrew a fresh pair of latex gloves from his pocket. "Sure thing, Doc."

Eve pulled on the gloves, then took the envelope from Detective Munoz. Opening the top, she spilled the contents out onto the table. It was an 8x10 black-and-white photograph of an attractive woman—similar in build and features to Eve. Someone had obviously altered the image, as the background was blurred, making it all but impossible to recognize where it was taken. The woman in the picture was clearly unaware that she was being photographed, half turned away from the camera, her head tipped back in laughter. Selene shivered at the candid nature of the photo and at the possibility that this woman might not yet know that she'd attracted the attention of a psychopath.

Picking up the photograph, Eve squinted at the handwritten words scrawled across the bottom of the image. "'I wonder if she'll be as scared as you,'" Eve read aloud. She turned the photograph over, scanned the back, then set it face-up on the table with a shaky exhalation.

"You think she's still alive?" Hunt asked.

"We have to assume she is." Eve picked up the print again, gingerly holding it by one corner. "Unfortunately I can't tell where this was shot. Or when."

"Me either," Munoz said. "Looks Photoshopped to me."

"Very likely." Setting down the photograph, Eve said, "Give me a few minutes, then we'll head to the department. I'll call Jac and have her meet us there."

Munoz nodded. "Yes, ma'am."

"Go ahead and wait in your car. I'll be ready in ten." At their immediate expressions of protest, Eve raised her hand to quiet them. "You've swept the apartment. Nobody's here. I've had a long day and I'd like to change clothes in private. So I'll be fine, gentlemen, if you don't mind."

Detective Munoz gave her a terse nod. "You'll answer your phone if we call, and call us if you need anything. Even if you just get a weird feeling."

"Of course." Eve sounded impatient.

"Let us know when you're ready to leave. We'll come to your door and get you." Hunt spoke to her in a no-nonsense tone. "The game has changed, Dr. Thomas. This guy has been to your place now. He's getting bolder. Jac wouldn't want us to let you out of our sight at all. She's running this operation, and your safety is more important to her than just about anything, so you'll just have to bear with us."

Munoz's voice softened. "We don't want anything to happen to you. This guy is a sick fucker, right?"

Eve nodded.

"Let us be overprotective, then. It's our job."

Relaxing slightly, Eve said, "I get it. And I appreciate you guys being overprotective in the car for the next fifteen minutes."

As the three of them walked toward the front door, Selene debated internally. She could leave with the detectives, which was probably the wise thing to do, or she could stick around inside Eve's just a little longer. She wasn't sure what she hoped to accomplish by staying. She just wasn't ready to say good-bye yet.

Closing the door, Eve engaged the lock and put on the chain. Then she sighed, pivoting to stare at the table with an expression of pure dread. "Goddamn it."

More than anything, Selene wanted to come out of hiding, shift back into human form, and hold Eve tight to reassure her that everything would be okay. For a moment the desire to do just that was so strong, Selene could hardly remember all the reasons why shifting back was a bad idea. Like giving Eve a heart attack, for one.

Below her, Eve shivered and closed her eyes. Selene could feel her struggling against a wave of emotion: pain, loss, and yawning grief. Her face contorted and a quiet sob burst from her lips, which she stifled by clapping her hand over her mouth. Eve's pain sliced into Selene, awakening a fresh wave of sorrow. Heart breaking, Selene left her hiding spot on the light fixture, flying down to land on the wall next to the dining room table. From this vantage point, she could see all of Eve's turmoil.

"Goddamn you, Selene," Eve whispered. Dismayed, Selene watched her touch the purple bruise on her neck with a shaking hand. "Get out of my head."

Startled, Selene didn't move. It was all too clear that her presence was only causing Eve torment. She should leave. No matter how badly she wanted to make sure Eve was safe, it wasn't right to stay. Eve didn't want her here. Their empathetic link no longer brought Eve comfort. After what had happened between them, any hint of that connection had to be confusing and traumatic for Eve, who no doubt wanted nothing more than to forget Selene had ever existed.

Exhaling, Eve dropped her hands to her sides and shook them out. Then she straightened her shoulders, walking briskly to her bedroom. She tugged her shirt over her head as she went, offering Selene a tantalizing view of her bare stomach and bra-encased breasts.

Now it was *definitely* wrong to stick around. Without hesitation, Selene launched herself across the room, flying for the front door as quickly as she could. She wasn't entirely sure how she would escape the apartment, but she sure as hell had to try, for Eve's sake as well as her own. It was excruciating to see the woman she loved in such distress, especially when she was the cause.

Selene landed on the floor mat just inside Eve's entryway, examining the narrow gap between the bottom of the door and the wooden floor. Although there seemed to be more than enough room for her to squeeze through, the thought of wedging her body into such a tight space nauseated her. She just couldn't shed her very human sense of caution that told her that squeezing into an opening an inch wide wasn't a good idea.

Unfortunately she had no choice. She needed to get away from

Eve, from the overwhelming evidence that she'd lost Eve forever. More important, she needed to follow the stalker's trail while it was still fresh. This might be her best opportunity to track him down.

Taking a deep breath, Selene cleared her mind of fear and crawled beneath the door frame. As predicted, she made it through with ease, though the sensation of the thick door hovering close to her head and the unyielding floor beneath her feet was enough to make her stop and gasp for air as soon as she emerged on the other side.

On the tail end of her panic, Selene felt her blood surge with exhilaration. Since meeting Eve, she had tested and stretched her abilities in ways she never could have anticipated. Protecting Eve was the best reason to embrace her nature and shift, and now that she was getting more comfortable with it, a part of her actually enjoyed experiencing the world from different perspectives. That her ability might actually give her an edge over normal people when it came to hunting Eve's stalker made her cherish it for the very first time in her life.

And damn, that felt good.

Quickly buzzing down the hall and around the corner, Selene landed on the carpet and swiveled, making sure nobody was watching. Then she gathered her strength and shifted back into bloodhound form. Each shift was more difficult than the last, and she would be exhausted when she got home tonight. She would come back for her clothes later, once she'd followed his trail.

Hopefully she'd have something to show for her effort. Either way, Selene was prepared to make protecting Eve her new full-time job. Eve's stalker was going down.

CHAPTER TWENTY-FOUR

When Eve arrived at the homicide division flanked by Detectives Munoz and Hunt, Jac was already at her desk. She jumped up as soon as she spotted Eve, worry etched across her face. "Are you all right?"

Embarrassed by Jac's obvious concern, Eve waved her off. "I'm fine. It's the woman in the picture he left for me that we need to worry about." Setting the envelope on Jac's desk, Eve waited as Jac rolled an extra office chair over so they could examine its contents together. "Unfortunately, I'm not sure he gave us much to work with."

"Let's take a look." Jac glanced at the detectives, who stood silently as though waiting to be addressed. "You guys want to take a break? Grab something to eat?"

Hunt nodded. "That'd be nice."

"You sure you don't need us?" Munoz asked, always the professional. Though Eve had given him a lot of grief, the man was clearly dedicated to his job—and Jac.

"We'll be fine." Jac gestured for Eve to sit and, once she had, dropped into the chair beside her. "Go ahead and relax. We'll dust for prints, see if we can come up with anything."

The detectives left them with muttered thanks, and Eve was glad to see them go. She knew they were just looking out for her, but she was really starting to feel like her life was no longer her own. In a perfect world she wouldn't have to spend the evening with Jac, either. She could soak in her bathtub and concentrate on not thinking about Selene.

Who was she kidding? That was clearly impossible. For almost the entire fifteen minutes she'd spent in her apartment earlier that evening, Selene's presence had lingered so strongly that Eve could have sworn she was in the next room. No matter how badly Eve wanted to write off Selene and move on—to not allow herself to grieve for a woman she'd known only a month—she was hopelessly, desperately sad that things had ended the way they had. Breaking up was bad enough, but not having seen it coming was even worse.

"You okay?" Jac murmured as she pulled on a pair of gloves. "I don't blame you for being shaken up, knowing this guy's been to your place and is actually leaving you presents now."

"It's not that." Eve cringed. That was probably ridiculous, wasn't it? What kind of person was she when her shitty love life upset her more than the thought that her stalker had just raised the stakes in his sick game? "I mean, it is. I'm upset, of course."

"About Selene, too." Jac shook the contents of the envelope onto the table, avoiding Eve's gaze. "You've had an awesomely bad past thirty-six hours. You deserve to fall apart a little, I think."

"I'm not falling apart." Eve pulled on her gloves. "I refuse to."

Jac gingerly picked up the photo of their potential victim. Eve watched Jac scan the note at the bottom—*I wonder if she'll be as scared as you*, Eve remembered, like she could forget—fascinated by the way Jac's jaw tensed in visceral anger. Jac glanced up, apparently checking Eve's reaction.

"I'm not convinced he hasn't given us anything to work with." Voice thick with anger, Jac nodded at the photo. "He's having too much fun with this. He thinks he's invincible, that he's just toying with you. He told you he could do whatever he wants and nobody could stop him. Right?"

"That's what he said." Eve let her gaze drift to the image of the woman who might very well be facing the same terror she'd endured even as they sat there looking at her photo. "He definitely wants to believe that he's unstoppable."

"So would he really resist the urge to give you some kind of puzzle to decipher?" Jac stared at the photo, first the front, then the back.

"He doesn't want to get caught. And so far he's been very smart. Why give us something to go on now?"

"Because he's controlling the scenario," Jac said, brows furrowing as she studied the back of the photo. "Leaving evidence on a body, well, that's just sloppy. But giving his adversary some kind of clue or challenge…" Flipping the photo around, Jac said, "What does that look like to you?"

Eve zeroed in on a thick, dark smudge on the lower corner of the paper. "I have no idea. Dirt."

Jac unzipped a bag that sat on the corner of her desk, taking out a shallow plastic dish and a metal instrument. "We should analyze it just in case."

"You really think this is a puzzle of some kind?"

"Well, I have to." Jac scraped a sample of the smudge onto a tiny blade and deposited it in the dish. Then she screwed on a clear plastic lid and set the evidence aside. "Better than the alternative, which is that all this will get us nowhere except feeling guilty when we find this girl dead."

"I already feel guilty," Eve said softly.

"Don't. He's involved you in his crimes, but you're not the reason he's killing. The psycho obviously gets off on the act of murder." Jac took out her fingerprint kit and diligently began dusting the envelope, though Eve suspected she knew it was a long shot that the guy would leave a usable print. "Whether or not he fixated on you, he'd be hurting people." Glancing up, she met Eve's eyes. "Trust me on that."

"I'm sure you're right." Of course she was. This man wouldn't be sitting at home watching football or playing with his kids instead of murdering women. But knowing he had apparently been killing with her in mind from the start was too much to take. "Doesn't make me feel any better."

"I know." Scowling, Jac examined the envelope. "Nothing."

"You didn't expect him to be *that* sloppy, did you?"

"Maybe I was hoping he wanted to get caught." Jac managed a tight smile. "He must, to mess with you."

Not knowing how to respond, Eve murmured, "Dust the photo. I'll cross my fingers."

Jac dusted in silence and Eve watched, grateful for the momentary lull in conversation. Her mind kept slipping away to thoughts of what Selene might be doing. Was she home alone? Or with another woman? Eve's stomach turned at the thought of Selene with someone else.

"I really thought this thing with Selene was for real." Eve hadn't meant to say anything out loud, especially not to Jac, but she couldn't keep this to herself anymore. She was angry and confused—not just at Selene, but also at Jac, all over again. Though she thought she'd forgiven Jac for her betrayal, this thing with Selene dredged up all her old resentments. Because she lacked the strength to confront Selene,

Jac made an ideal target for her rage. "I thought this time I'd found someone who wouldn't lie to me. Who understood that the one thing I want from a relationship is honesty."

Jac blinked, taking a deep breath then exhaling. In a low voice, she said, "You only knew her a month. That's not enough time to get a real read on someone."

"It didn't feel like only a month," Eve said quietly. She couldn't explain to Jac how she had felt connected to Selene from almost the first moment they met. How Selene had made her feel stronger, more beautiful, more confident and centered than she ever had. All that sounded illogical, silly—two things Eve prided herself on not being. "You know me, Jac. I don't trust easily. I'm not the type to fall for someone so quickly."

"I know you aren't." With a disgusted sigh, Jac packed up her fingerprint kit, having come up with nothing. "I was surprised you had."

"It just felt right." Eve bit her lip hard, looking away from Jac as she struggled to bring her emotion under control. "I'm an idiot."

"No, you're not." Stripping off her gloves, Jac collapsed back into her chair and folded her hands over her stomach. "I can give the photo to our tech guys, see if they can clean up the background and identify any landmarks. And we can get a handwriting analyst in here to help us construct a profile on this guy. Other than that…"

"Yeah." Eve picked up the photo, forcing herself to study the woman's face for the first time. Her obvious happiness was infectious, which only made Eve feel worse. "I'm not used to dealing with someone so careful, so meticulous. Charles Dunning wasn't like that."

"Not ultimately, no. But we spent a lot of restless nights hunting him down, too." Jac nudged Eve's ankle with the toe of her shoe. "We'll get this guy. Who knows, maybe the dirt from the photo will lead us somewhere."

"I hope so."

Jac cleared her throat. "And I hope you'll think again about staying at my place. Considering."

"Considering that I have a serial killer obsessed with me?" Mustering a brave chuckle, Eve shook her head. "That's hardly news, Jac. We already knew he was fixated on me, that he had my address and phone number. So, really, nothing has changed."

"Except now he's shown us how bold he can be. He went to your *apartment*. In broad daylight."

"He attacked me in Golden Gate Park, too, which seems even bolder, at least from my perspective." Though Jac obviously thought it foolish, Eve refused to cave to the temptation to flee. "Look, by staying right where I am, I've given him a specific target, a place where he may poke his head out again. It could be our best chance of nabbing him, really. If I retreat to a secure location, we may lose our only opportunity to draw him out."

Scowling, Jac said, "How did I know you'd come up with a semi-logical reason to be a stubborn ass?"

"I guess you just know me well."

"Guess so." Jac seemed pleased by that. "You eat dinner yet?"

"I haven't."

"Why don't you let me have something delivered? That is, if you don't mind hanging out here for a while."

Twenty-four hours ago, Eve would never have imagined having dinner with Jac again so soon. But she was hungry, she was shaken up, and she really didn't want to be alone. As determined as she was not to be chased away from her apartment, she couldn't quite imagine returning there yet. Especially not with the way it made her miss Selene so badly. Not that she would admit that out loud. "I don't mind hanging out."

"Cool. How does Chinese sound?"

"Delicious." Eve didn't let herself react to the familiarity of this scene. She and Jac had fallen in love over Chinese takeout when they worked the Charles Dunning case. In fact, Eve had been eating Kung Pao chicken from their favorite Chinese delivery place on the night she'd uncovered the evidence that cracked the case. As much as she didn't want to go back to that romantic place with Jac, sticking to what had worked for their investigations in the past probably wasn't a bad idea. "I'll have my usual."

"Figured." Jac didn't hide her pleasure.

"In the meantime, I'm going to call Wayne and ask him to start with this sample you collected." Eve lifted the evidence dish and peered at the meager specimen inside. Hopefully there was enough there to analyze. If it turned out to be nothing more than insignificant dirt, she would be extremely disappointed. "I'll make it his only priority. We should know within seventy-two hours."

"Okay. I'll make sure IT starts working on the photo analysis tonight." Jac picked up her desk phone but didn't dial. "Now that we've got a potential victim who may still be alive, this case just became the department's only priority. And on that note, I'm assigning round-the-clock surveillance on your apartment. No more of this leaving-presents-on-your-doorstep-without-anyone-knowing bullshit."

"Fair enough," Eve said. As much as she hated the loss of her privacy, her stalker's new gambit left her more than happy to be under constant watch. Their encounter in Golden Gate Park remained the single most terrifying experience of her life, and she had no desire to relive it. She had no problem stacking the deck in her favor.

"I plan to participate in at least some of that security detail," Jac said quietly. The caution on her face signaled that she expected Eve to argue. "It has nothing to do with spying on you. You won't even know I'm there. I'll just…feel better knowing you're okay."

It wouldn't be forever. And no matter how awkward it might be to have her cheating ex-girlfriend secretly shadow her, Eve didn't trust anyone more to watch her back. So with a determined nod, she said, "Sounds like a plan."

She could only hope it worked.

Chapter Twenty-five

After spending the entire night in a failed attempt to track Eve's stalker through the city streets, Selene was exhausted and frustrated to the point of tears. Though she'd been able to follow the man's scent from Eve's building to a corner several blocks away, once again his trail had suddenly disappeared. Now she was certain he either owned a car or traveled via taxi, but that brought her no closer to discovering his identity and keeping Eve safe. The hours she'd just wasted randomly wandering through various neighborhoods hoping to catch a whiff of his scent had gotten her nowhere. Unfortunately, it didn't seem likely that she'd find the guy by accident. For all Selene knew, he didn't even live in San Francisco.

That meant she needed to come up with a new strategy. Though she hadn't any idea what she planned to do when she found Eve's stalker, Selene had no choice but to try to hunt him down. The police weren't having any luck, and if she could do anything to help them, she planned to, even if it meant risking discovery.

Selene's best-case scenario would be to confront the guy during one of his attempts to get close to Eve. Then she could follow him as he fled and hopefully find out where he lived. To do that, she'd probably need to keep up a constant surveillance on Eve. The fact that Eve already had the police watching her meant that Selene would have to be creative in her attempts to provide a second level of security without being noticed.

Unfortunately, creativity would have to wait until after she'd had a nap. It had been a long, draining night and her brain wasn't cooperating. Right now she couldn't come up with a plan of attack if her life depended upon it.

As Selene pulled her car up to her apartment, bleary-eyed and ready to get some much-needed sleep, the sight of Detective Jac Battle standing on her front porch sent her gut into sour, twisting panic. Jac turned at the sound of the engine, nodding curtly as Selene pulled into her parking spot, then cut the ignition. Heart pounding, she prepared for what she was sure would be an unpleasant conversation with Eve's jealous ex-girlfriend. Without knowing whether Jac was there in an official capacity or simply as Eve's defender, Selene wasn't even sure what she should be nervous about.

Everything. Right now she was nervous about absolutely everything.

Taking a deep breath, Selene opened the car door and got out. She forced a polite smile and returned Jac's nod. "Hello."

"Good morning." Jac clasped her hands behind her back, studying Selene's face as she approached. Every inch the suspicious cop. "Long night?"

Selene didn't let herself react to Jac's subtle taunt. She had no idea what Eve had told Jac about what happened between them, but Selene wasn't about to rise to the bait. "Can I help you with something?"

"I hope so. I wanted to talk to you about that phone call you made last month. You know, the one where you reported finding a body in Golden Gate Park."

Selene kept her expression neutral and indicated that Jac should step aside so she could unlock the door. Jac did so with another curt nod. Inviting Jac into her sanctuary wasn't her first choice, but she refused to have this discussion on her front porch where anyone could overhear. She pushed open the door and strolled inside, gesturing for Jac to follow. "Would you like something to drink?"

"No, thanks." Jac stepped into her foyer, taking a none-too-subtle look around. "Nice place."

"Thank you." Selene led Jac to the living room and pointed her toward the couch. "Have a seat."

Returning her intense focus to Selene's face, Jac sat carefully at one end of the couch. "Sorry to drop by so early in the morning."

"It's okay." Selene sat at the other end of the couch, careful not to let her face or voice betray her anxiety. True, she had nothing to hide as far as knowing more about the murders than she let on. But so much of Selene's involvement in this case was tied up in her ability, so talking about any of it with Jac meant treading on dangerous ground. "This is an important case, I know. But the last time I checked, anonymous tips to the police weren't illegal."

"Not illegal, no." Jac gave her a slow once-over. "I'm not here to arrest you, Ms. Rhodes."

"Selene."

"Okay. I'm not here to arrest you, Selene. I just want to find out if you know anything that could help us find the man who's killing these women. For Eve's sake, given that he seems to be obsessed with dragging her into the middle of his psychosis."

Selene returned Jac's serious look, jaw so tense her face ached. "If I knew something that could help, I'd tell you. Believe me. The last thing I want is for Eve to get hurt."

Mouth twitching, Jac murmured, "That's not what I heard."

It took everything Selene had not to slap the smug look off Jac's face. "You've got a lot of nerve, you know. Seems to me you're the last person who should be passing judgment when it comes to hurting Eve."

"You're right, I made a mistake. A terrible mistake." Jac's eyes glittered with ugly satisfaction. "But I've learned from my mistakes. Quite frankly, I'm not entirely destroyed that you've gone down the same road I did. Not that I would wish Eve any more heartache, because she doesn't deserve it. But I'm glad she figured out you were no good for her now, before she got too attached."

"Are you here to talk about your ex-girlfriend, or did you want to discuss something in an official capacity?" Anger made it hard to get the words out. When Selene was this tired, it became difficult to control her emotions, and that was an extremely perilous state to be in. On a few occasions, though none within the past ten years, Selene had shifted against her will due to extreme emotional distress. That led her to try to stay calm at all times, but hearing Jac compare the two of them—and knowing that Jac saw their breakup as an opportunity to win Eve back—threatened to push Selene into dangerous territory.

"How did you manage to stumble upon that body so early in the morning?" Jac tilted her head, watching Selene's face. "She was dumped pretty far off the beaten path. Not someplace I'd imagine a beautiful woman to be exploring by herself at sunrise."

Shrugging, Selene said, "I was taking a walk. I decided to take a shortcut through the trees. I enjoy nature, and sometimes I want to pretend I'm not in the middle of one of the biggest cities in the country. So I detour off the beaten path."

"You don't worry about who might be lurking in the woods with you?"

"I have martial-arts training," Selene lied. In reality, she didn't often worry about her personal safety for two simple reasons. One, she didn't get out much. But more important, if push came to shove, Selene could shift into something that would terrify even the most vicious mugger or rapist. "I can take care of myself. I wasn't worried."

"I imagine you were pretty shaken up when you found the corpse, though." Jac gave her an expectant look. "Right?"

"Of course. Who wouldn't be?"

"So help me understand something. From what Eve has told me, it's clear that you called in the location of the body *before* you found her after the attack. So why did you go back into the park?"

Selene hesitated, trying to ignore the way Jac's mouth twitched in apparent delight at her momentary uncertainty. Briefly, Selene considered lying and telling Jac that she'd had to cut across the park to get home after making her call, but dismissed the idea at the realization that Jac might know exactly which pay phone she'd used. Although it would have been impossible for her to hear Eve's cries for help from that location, it was the only explanation she could offer. "I thought I heard something, so I went to check it out."

Jac raised an eyebrow. "Martial-arts training or not, I find it hard to believe that someone who'd just seen a murder victim minutes before would feel compelled to go chasing after a mysterious noise that led her anywhere near the scene."

"What I heard sounded like a woman screaming. Luckily I wasn't thinking about myself at that moment. When I found Eve, she was terrified, traumatized. I did the right thing, going back in there, no matter how shaken up I was."

Jac regarded her in silence for a long, uncomfortable minute. Then she said, "Eve is in serious danger, Selene. Right now I couldn't care less as far as what your actual involvement in this case might be. I know you didn't kill those women, okay? But if you have information about who did, if you saw *anything*—"

"I would tell you." Selene looked into Jac's eyes, willing her to see the sincerity in her words. "Nothing's more important to me than making sure Eve stays safe. If you don't believe anything else I say, please believe that. Look into my eyes and see that I'm telling the truth. Eve's safety means *everything* to me. I'll do whatever I can to protect her. I promise."

Though she didn't look particularly satisfied by Selene's words,

Jac's nod signaled that the interrogation was over. "On that note, I need to head back to work. Thank you for your time."

When Jac stood, Selene rose with her. "I really don't think Eve should be staying at her apartment right now. It isn't safe."

"Are you saying that because you know something? Or do you just want me to pass that along to Eve?" Jac might have decided to let her off the hook with the phone tip, but it was clear she didn't plan on making nice.

"Before, I was with her. Now she's alone. And he knows where she lives."

Concern momentarily softened Jac's face. "Don't worry. I can take care of Eve."

Selene couldn't read Jac well enough to decide whether that meant Eve planned to go back to her apartment or not. It wasn't important enough that she hear it from Jac to keep pushing, though. If necessary, Selene could follow Eve after she left work to find out where she was staying.

That sounded creepy. Selene didn't want to feel like just another stalker in Eve's life, but she'd do whatever it took to keep her safe. Just like Jac.

"If you remember anything you think might help our investigation, please give me a call." Jac handed her a business card. "I'm more than happy to be discreet. Unless it's a material fact in the case, I can keep whatever you tell me between the two of us." Smirking, Jac turned her back on Selene and walked to the front door. "No need to cause Eve any further pain."

As she trailed Jac to the door, Selene clung tight to her iron control, determined not to give her anger free rein until Jac was gone. But the cocky arrogance radiating from Jac forced Selene into defending herself, no matter how useless she knew it would be. "I didn't fool around on Eve, by the way. Whether or not anyone believes me, that's the truth. I'm not perfect, and I do have secrets, but I'd never have cheated on Eve. Not after how you destroyed her."

Jac whirled around, glaring at Selene. "Remind me, are you two on speaking terms at the moment? You really think you haven't destroyed her? You're no better than me. Not by a long shot. At least she's talking to me. Hell, she spent last night with me." Eyes narrowing, Jac said, "Yeah. *All* night."

Selene had no idea where Eve had gone, or what she'd done, after she went to the police station the night before. The last time Selene had seen Eve, she was lamenting their empathetic link and nursing a broken heart. Had she found comfort in Jac's arms? It didn't seem like something Eve would do.

But who could account for the actions of a broken heart?

Gritting her teeth so hard her jaw ached, Selene said, "I'll call you if I remember anything."

"Excellent." Jac's tone oozed condescension. "Have a wonderful morning, Selene."

"You, too." Selene shut the door hard as soon as Jac sauntered outside. There was no point in pretending she wasn't upset. She hadn't liked Jac from the start, but at least when Eve was on her side, dealing with her detective ex-girlfriend felt necessary. Now it was pointless torture. Worse than that, it reminded her of exactly why all the shifting and deception of the past month was so dangerous.

Using her ability increased her risk of being discovered. Until Eve, she'd never had a reason to take that risk. Eve's stalker was the best reason she could imagine, but the threats to her own safety were as real as they'd ever been. Jac was a visceral reminder of that simple fact.

But in the end, that didn't change a thing. Eve was in trouble and Selene was determined to keep her safe, regardless of the consequences.

CHAPTER TWENTY-SIX

It's feces."

Eve set down her pen, blinking, and looked up at Wayne towering over her desk. From the excitement on his face, she knew he was talking about the substance from the mysterious photograph left on her doorstep. She'd speculated about a number of different possibilities for the results of Wayne's analysis over the past couple of days, but she could honestly say that excrement wasn't one of them. "Seriously?"

"Oh, yes. Not human." He bounced on the balls of his feet, clearly thrilled by whatever he had to share. He always seemed to get the biggest charge out of the most disgusting things.

"Well, that's…gross. Do we think he planted it there on purpose, or did the killer's dog just decide to relieve itself on his masterpiece?"

"It's not canine, and I'd say he definitely left it there on purpose." Wayne paused, probably for dramatic effect, but Eve didn't take the bait and ask. Sighing, he said, "I find it very unlikely that our suspect managed to accidentally smear bison dung on his message."

Eve's awareness of time slowed even as her heartbeat thundered into overdrive. She knew where he was leading them. "Bison. He's sending us back to Golden Gate Park."

"That's a very reasonable assumption."

Bison had resided in the park since 1891, and the buffalo paddock in the western section was created in 1899 to house the growing herd. As a child, Eve had visited the paddock several times with her parents, and the incongruity of such giant, wild creatures living peacefully in the middle of one of the largest cities in California had always intrigued her. The presence of bison dung in that envelope was a message so obvious, Eve cursed that it had taken them so long to identify the substance.

"I'll call Jac. We need to canvass the area inside and around the paddock to see what we can find." Eve dreaded the possibility that they were looking for a body, but her gut told her that was exactly what they'd find. Unfortunately the photo analysis hadn't given them anything to go on, so they'd had to spend the time required to scientifically analyze the evidence. That the killer had apparently given them such a clear, distinct direction that they'd been so slow to recognize was frustrating, to say the least.

"Are you going with her to the scene?" Wayne asked. They didn't often join the police in the field, especially when a body hadn't surfaced yet. Still, Eve couldn't imagine staying behind in the lab for this one.

"I am." Eve picked up her desk phone. "I'll be back soon, hopefully."

"I'll cross my fingers that you *don't* bring a body with you."

"That's a change." Wayne wasn't cold-hearted, but his love for his work sometimes outweighed his sympathy for the people his cadavers had once been. Truthfully, it was probably part of the reason he was so good at his job. He never let emotion get in the way of logic and scientific fact.

"Tell me about it." Shifting uncomfortably, he looked almost painfully sincere as he said, "I know how you'll feel if we didn't find her in time. Just remember that it's not your fault, okay? Even if we are too late."

Eve gave him a weak nod. "I know. It's his fault."

If only it were that simple.

❖

They found the body only fifteen minutes into their search. With twelve men and women sweeping the area in and around the bison paddock, it didn't take long to discover the naked corpse of a female in her mid thirties stashed among the trees near the corner of Chain of Lakes and John F. Kennedy Drive. The killer had slaughtered her in an area that probably didn't get much foot traffic and was out of view of the well-traveled roads nearby, but was still near enough to civilization that Eve was struck once again by his sheer nerve.

Their victim appeared to have been dead for at least twelve hours. She had been killed in the spot where she lay. Their killer didn't seem to deal in transporting bodies. That meant he was confident enough in handling his victims that he apparently had no qualms about forcing them to accompany him to the locations where he took their lives.

He had clearly planned to kill this woman right here days before the actual murder, so Eve imagined that he'd grabbed her elsewhere, then driven her here. Somehow he'd managed to get her to this secluded spot without raising any major suspicions—if the lack of witnesses reporting unusual activity was any indication—then kill her without being discovered.

Though the bison paddock was hardly the most popular spot in Golden Gate Park, it was fairly well traveled. No doubt the killer had brought the victim here late at night.

I wonder if she'll be as scared as you. Eve imagined she must have been terrified.

A hand touched her shoulder and Eve jumped, tearing her gaze away from the bloody, stiff-limbed corpse at the base of a large tree to meet Jac's eyes. Wincing apologetically, Jac said, "Are you okay?"

Eve had no idea how to answer that question anymore. "This isn't what I wanted to find."

"Me either." Jac regarded the body carefully. "How long has she been dead?"

"I'd guess she died somewhere between midnight and three last night. He probably waited until the park was deserted before bringing her here." Eve pointed at the dried, tacky blood painting the dirt and vegetation beneath her body. "He killed her right here. And there's evidence of strangulation again—but I'm guessing that, like the others, she died from blood loss. The choking is just how he got his kicks before he put her down."

Grimly, Jac muttered, "I hate this guy."

"Agreed." Eve's cell phone chirped in her purse. Frowning, she pulled it out expecting to see the lab's number on the display. She couldn't think of anyone else who might be calling—especially now that she was single. Not recognizing the number, she let it go to voice mail. "We need to bag her up and get her back to the lab. If our guy's getting bold enough to leave us clues in envelopes, maybe he's decided to offer some evidence on his latest victim. You know, to test me."

Jac touched the small of Eve's back. "Let's hope so." She stepped forward and, gesturing at a detective who knelt on the ground taking photos of the body, said, "Let's document this scene quickly so we can get the corpse back to the lab."

"Yes, ma'am." The head of the crime scene investigation team crouched down next to the body, marking a piece of evidence with a yellow numbered tag. "We're on it."

Eve's cell phone rang again. Sighing, she raised her hand and glanced at the display. Same number. Frowning, Eve answered the call. "Hello?"

"Is this Dr. Eve Thomas?"

Something about the unfamiliar male voice set Eve's nerves on edge. Immediately she knew who was on the other end of the line. "May I ask who's calling?"

"*The* Dr. Eve Thomas?"

Eve swallowed. "Yes. Who is this?"

"Well, this is a thrill. I'm a big fan of your work."

Stumbling, Eve hurried over to Jac, gripping her arm tight. Jac opened her mouth to speak but took one look at her face and stopped. Jac mouthed, *Is that him?* At Eve's nod, Jac brought her head close to Eve's so she could listen.

The man chuckled. "You're hurting my feelings, Eve. Are you a fan of *my* work?"

"I'm looking at some of your work right now," Eve said, willing her voice not to shake. The more her stalker spoke, the clearer her memory of his words on the day of her attack became. His icy-blue eyes. The sensation of his body on top of hers, pinning her down. The sharp edge of his blade. Shivering, Eve said, "I wouldn't say I'm a *fan*, no."

Jac wrapped her arm around Eve's middle, tugging her close. Grateful for her warmth, Eve allowed Jac to hold her.

"Not a fan? Really?" He sounded genuinely disappointed. "Surely you have to appreciate how tidy I leave things. How conscientious I am of what it is scientists like you need to track down people like me."

"Are you killing these women to impress me? Because I can tell you right now, there are better ways."

He snorted. "Don't flatter yourself. No, I'm killing these women *here*, in your territory, because I want you to know that even if you were able to use your *science* to track down Charles Dunning, what you do is worthless when you have an adversary who has half a brain."

"And this half-brained adversary…is you?"

Dead silence met Eve's comment, and for a moment she worried that he had hung up or perhaps she'd dropped the call. Then he inhaled, clearly irritated, and spat, "Pity that science can be so inefficient, isn't it? You've had a veritable map to this location for days. Long before that lovely woman at your feet died. If only you'd been able to complete your analysis in a more timely fashion…well, who knows?"

Jac stiffened and stepped away from Eve slightly, sweeping the area around them intently. Though he spoke as though he could see them, Eve wasn't convinced. "You here right now? Maybe we should talk about this face-to-face."

"You didn't really enjoy our last face-to-face chat, though. Did you, Eve?"

A chill ran down Eve's spine. She stared at Jac's face, keeping herself grounded in the present. She was safe now. "Being assaulted and threatened isn't much fun, no."

"By the way, she *wasn't* as scared as you." His voice lowered, almost seductive in tone. "No woman has ever been as scared for me as you were, Eve. It was *delicious*."

Her face must have reflected the visceral disgust his words elicited, because Jac immediately returned close to her side. "So how does this end? You keep killing until I help the police identify you?"

"No. I keep killing until I decide you're next. Then I kill some more."

Jac opened her mouth as though she planned to interject, but Eve raised a hand to stop her. If they had even a small chance to get a concrete lead from this phone call, Eve was willing to play along even if it meant listening to sick threats. "Doesn't sound like there's much in this for me."

"I'm afraid not." He took a deep breath, then exhaled as though remembering some hazy pleasure. "Don't worry, though. I'm not done with you yet."

"No?"

"I hope we can spend some more time together soon. I miss seeing that fear in your eyes."

Eve tensed. This could be exactly what they needed to draw him out into the open. Hadn't she told Jac that she wanted to stay in her apartment for exactly that reason? But the idea that this man could get close to her again sent her into a cold sweat. "I'm willing to meet you at the police station. I'll even promise to listen to whatever you want to say—about me, about science."

He made a sound of displeasure. "I was thinking of something more intimate. Now tell me, Eve, what scares you more—being raped or being cut? Or maybe both, huh? I could fuck you, then carve my name into your face."

Willing her voice to remain steady, Eve said, "What name would you write?"

"Kev. But that won't help you find me."

Eve's phone beeped, signaling that he had disconnected. With a shaking hand, Eve checked the display to be sure. He was gone. Next to her, Jac was trembling.

"I'll fucking kill him first." Jac spoke in a low rumble, the intensity of her tone drawing a few odd looks from the detectives and technicians who had slowed in their documentation of the crime scene when it became clear that their suspect was on the phone.

Eve grabbed Jac's arm and pulled her away from the corpse, turning their backs to their colleagues. "No, you won't. If he comes for me, we'll grab him, then let the justice system deal with him."

Jac's chest rose and fell with the force of her deep, angry breathing. "Let me get the number from your phone. We'll try to track down the source of the call."

"Good luck. I have a feeling we won't find him that way."

"So what?" Jac snapped angrily, turning Eve's phone on and punching the number of her last incoming call into her own phone. "The only way to find him is to dangle you out there as bait?"

"Maybe."

Jac dialed his number and raised the phone to her ear. After a moment she cursed and hung up. "He turned it off."

"Are you surprised?"

"No. Just pissed off." Jac pocketed her phone and returned Eve's with a heavy sigh. "I can't remember ever feeling so powerless. No matter how many times I go over the evidence or the witness statements, I can't find a thing. Nothing to go on, except the fucking taunts he's dropping like bread crumbs. Meanwhile the body count keeps rising, and it's only a matter of time before the media catches on that we've got a serial murderer in the city. I'm desperate for a goddamn break, Eve. That's all I want—one goddamn break."

"We're going to get this guy, Jac. It's only a matter of time before he slips up." Eve squeezed Jac's elbow, speaking with a level of confidence she didn't really feel. "He may think he's invincible, but I sure as hell don't."

"Me either." Exhaling, Jac bumped Eve lightly with her shoulder. "We need to talk about your new security detail—constant surveillance of your building, officers on you at all times. And I want you to wear a device, a panic button."

"Okay." She might be stubborn, but she wasn't stupid. "Whatever you think's best."

That elicited genuine satisfaction from Jac. "I like the sound of that."

"Well, don't get used to it." Eve bumped Jac back. "I say such things only during emergency-serial-killer-stalker situations."

"Well, damn. I intend for this to be the last one of those we deal with."

"Me, too." Taking a deep breath, Eve shook off her lingering unease from the phone call. Now wasn't the time to let fear sweep her away. She refused to let Kev win. She'd beat him by doing what she did best. "Let's head back to the lab and prep for the autopsy. Maybe this time he made a mistake."

Jac gave a grim nod. "I'll cross my fingers."

CHAPTER TWENTY-SEVEN

A rmed with a brand-new knife, a lock-picking kit, and a handful of condoms tucked safely inside his backpack, Kevin leashed his dog and prepared for what he knew would be a challenging day. Going after Eve Thomas was a risk, no matter how good he was. At this point she had as much surveillance on her as the San Francisco Police Department could surely afford. It wasn't exactly FBI-level protection, but Kevin would have to be very careful if he wanted to get close to her without being caught.

He had set tonight's plan in motion the day he left his little present on her doorstep. Before he left Eve's apartment building he'd climbed the staircase to the top floor and located the roof-access door. Not surprisingly, it locked from the inside to prevent intruders from breaking into the building. As Kevin had hoped, Eve's old building had equally old security—a simple mechanical lock and no alarm. He'd gone home that day confident that his bump key would do the job and get him inside. No problem.

Tonight he'd find out.

It was probably only a matter of time before the SFPD called in the feds to assist on the case—in fact, Kevin was surprised they hadn't already—so this was as good a time as any to make his next move. Deep down, Kevin was confident he could slip past the layers of Eve's protective detail and catch her alone. The only thing that worried him about tonight's operation was that he might lose control and end their game before he was ready for it to be over.

Right now he told himself that all he wanted was more of Eve's fear—intoxicating as it was, the memory of her face and her shaking voice as she pleaded for her life had kept him going for weeks now. But it wasn't enough anymore.

The challenge would be holding himself back from just ending her life today. He had fantasized about it so many times now, lying in bed at night imagining the warm, red flow of her blood, the terror in her eyes when she realized her time was up. Fucking her tonight was more for her benefit than his. He didn't care much for sex but sensed that violating her in that way would crush her spirit. Carving his name in her face would be the real pleasure. It would take everything he had to keep the wounds superficial enough that she didn't bleed out.

When he started this thing, the point had been to be the killer Eve Thomas couldn't catch, the one who could outsmart both her and the police. That this whole thing had turned into an obsession with the woman herself was unsettling, but Kevin was long past trying to quell his desire to take things ever further.

Today was an important day. And he wouldn't fail.

CHAPTER TWENTY-EIGHT

Selene had never been so exhausted. After almost two weeks of near-constant surveillance of Eve's every move, she was running on only a few hours' sleep and questioning her sanity. Technically what she was doing felt like stalking, though her motives were more pure than simply wanting to stay close to Eve despite no longer being welcome in her life. Still, Selene had totally disrupted her schedule—leaving work projects undone and grabbing catnaps only when she was absolutely certain Eve was safe—all so that she could stay hidden in plain sight on the periphery of Eve's life: outside her apartment, at the morgue, everywhere she went.

Not wanting Eve to sense her presence, Selene had made it a point to stay far enough away not to trigger Eve's awareness while staying within range where she would be able to sense approaching danger. It wasn't that Selene didn't trust Jac's protective detail to do their jobs. Selene was just in a unique position to watch without being seen and, if necessary, to attack with incredible force. If Eve's stalker could possibly slip past the cops, Selene had to be there as a last line of defense. She wouldn't be able to live with herself if something happened to Eve and she could have stopped it.

Tonight, curled up as a large Rottweiler on the welcome mat in front of Eve's apartment door, Selene struggled to keep her eyes open. Falling asleep would be disastrous. She would almost certainly wake up naked and human, and if Eve found her like that she wouldn't be able to explain except tell the truth. Selene was working up the nerve to do just that. She missed Eve. If the truth could help smooth things over between them, maybe it was worth taking that risk. Keeping this secret wouldn't bring Eve back. After their miserable time apart, that was all Selene really cared about, even more than protecting herself from discovery.

Selene opened her mouth wide and yawned, letting out a whine that was louder than she would have liked. She laid her head on her paws and went still, blinking sleepily as she listened to the quiet sounds of the building at night—the hum of an air conditioner, the gentle flickering of the light at the end of the hallway. There was only silence from inside Eve's apartment, which didn't surprise Selene at two in the morning. Eve would be sound asleep by now. If she was able to sleep, that was. Every day Selene saw her, Eve looked increasingly weary. Whether she was exhausted or depressed, Selene wasn't sure.

If Eve was going through even half the pain Selene felt at their separation, it was probably some of both. As much as she hated to see Eve suffer, Selene took her obvious torment as a sign of hope. Clearly Eve's emotional turmoil didn't result from having a serial killer stalk her, as if that wasn't enough, but was due to the loss of their connection. Selene could only hope that if Eve missed her badly enough, maybe she wouldn't reject Selene if she knew the truth.

Exhaling, Selene closed her eyes for the space of two breaths before forcing them open again. She had to stay awake. She sat up and sniffed, shaking her head in an effort to chase away the urge to fall asleep. Mid-shake Selene froze, ears perking as she picked up an unusual scraping sound somewhere above her head. After so many long nights in Eve's hallway, she knew which noises to expect, and this one was definitely out of place.

She inhaled deeply, knowing her nose would pick up the scent of trouble if it was truly in their midst. Right now it was difficult to trust her instincts. It was entirely possible her sleep-deprived mind was playing tricks on her.

There. Selene lifted her nose and sniffed rapidly. There it was, the unmistakable scent of the man who was hunting Eve. Selene popped her ears up, rotating them as she strained to hear his approach. Ceiling lamps lighted the hallway so she would surely see him coming, unless he somehow managed to enter Eve's apartment another way—through a window, maybe, or the ventilation system.

His scent grew stronger. Standing close to Eve's door, Selene pressed her ear to the wood and listened for any sign that he was inside. Just as she began to panic, Selene heard the sound of soft footfalls approaching the end of Eve's hallway. It was him. Somehow he'd managed to get into the building, apparently without arousing suspicion, and now Selene was all that stood between a psychopath and the woman she loved.

Suddenly wide-awake, Selene bared her teeth in a silent snarl. She was ready for this, ready to kill this man if it came down to that, though she honestly hoped it wouldn't. She wasn't a murderer, even when her most animalistic urges drove her. Tonight her mission was to protect Eve and to assist the police in capturing this man so he could be punished.

He came around the corner so quietly that Selene wouldn't have heard him with human ears. He was pulling on a ski mask as he entered the hallway, so his face was covered by the time Selene had her first good look. Disappointed that she still didn't know what he looked like, Selene advanced a step and released the most menacing growl she could muster. The fur on her back stood on end, an unconscious physiological reaction to the threat the man presented.

The man stopped, clearly surprised to find a dog guarding Eve's door. Selene could see his mind working, and for a moment she wondered if he would just turn around and leave. Unfortunately, she had a feeling he was far too determined to let an aggressive dog stop him that easily.

Moving slowly, the man eased his backpack from his shoulders and unzipped it. The thought that he could have a gun flashed across Selene's mind and she raced toward him, hoping to attack before he could draw a weapon. When he pulled out a knife instead of the gun she had been expecting, she skidded to a stop. The closer she got, the better the chance he would slice her with his blade. Though she would heal quickly from most wounds, she wasn't invincible. Caution was important.

"That's right, pup. Back off."

Selene growled again. Beneath the sour smell of fear Selene could pick up the lingering scent of his excitement. His adrenaline was flowing, just like hers. Saliva dripped from her mouth, a primal response brought on by her urge to tear him apart. She knew it looked intimidating and so she played it up, snapping her jaw at him as she lunged forward then danced back.

"Goddamn it." The man grimaced, stumbling backward. He was obviously nervous, no doubt remembering the last time she'd sunk her teeth into him. Selene had no qualms about doing it again, and causing damage this time. "First a wolf, now this."

Pulling back her lips, Selene barked loudly. That would wake some people up. Maybe even get the cops in here. Clearly alarmed, the man came at her swinging his knife. Unprepared for the quickness of his reaction, Selene yelped when the edge of his blade sliced into her back. The wound was shallow and would heal before the night was over, but she drew back a few steps to get away. Then she barked again. She barked her fool head off.

"*Fuck.*" Leaving her with a murderous glare, the man took off running even as Selene heard a door open behind her.

Selene turned to see Eve poke her head out into the hallway, tentative and confused. Horrified that Eve would leave the safety of her apartment for even an instant, Selene growled and barked again, pleased when Eve disappeared inside quickly. Knowing that Eve would surely alert the police of the disturbance in the hallway, Selene ran in the direction the killer had gone, following his fresh trail with ease.

She ran up the stairs, until she got to a door that said Roof Access. The door was closed so Selene shifted into human form just long enough to turn the knob, then she changed into a bird as she threw herself outside. As tired as she was, every shift took enormous effort. But she was determined not to lose him this time. If she had to go through her entire wildlife repertoire to make sure she could follow him home, she would.

She needed to know where this fucker lived.

Flying high into the sky, Selene spotted the killer hurrying along the roof of the building next to Eve's. He hopped from that one to the adjacent building, making his way farther down the block. Eve's street was lined with buildings that stood so close together they practically touched, a San Francisco staple. It made sense that he would choose to use the crowded architecture to his advantage. The cops were watching the area at the street level, and only on Eve's block. No wonder he was able to get into her building undetected.

Selene followed him to the roof of the corner building, where he escaped inside via the roof-access door. Rather than follow him inside where she might get trapped, she swooped down to the street, taking note of the two doors from which he could emerge. She guessed he would take the side door since it couldn't be seen from Eve's street. Perching on a wire that powered the Muni electric trolley, she held her breath as she waited for him to appear. It occurred to her that there could be another way out of the building she wasn't able to see, but just as she started to worry that she'd lost him, the door opened and he stumbled outside.

The ski mask was gone. What struck Selene first about his appearance was his total lack of hair. His bald scalp shone in the moonlight, making him look sinister in a way that turned her blood to ice. She estimated he was in his mid thirties and guessed that the hair loss wasn't natural. Light stubble gave away his head as shaved.

Selene flapped her wings and took off from the wire, swooping low enough to stay close. She didn't want to risk losing him if he suddenly descended into an underground BART station. He adjusted his backpack, looked around, then pulled a baseball cap onto his head. He kept his steps deliberate and measured, as though he was merely taking a late-night stroll instead of escaping from the scene of an attempted crime.

The killer crossed the street at the corner, detouring into a small neighborhood park. Selene expected him to cut across to the other side, but instead he stopped at a play structure and bent down low. Shocked, Selene realized that he was untying a small dog that wagged its tail in excitement. He yanked hard on the leash, practically dragging the poor mutt back onto the sidewalk.

Clever. He'd walked into that park as a man who was out suspiciously late, conspicuous in a hat, wearing a backpack. And now he was leaving as a responsible pet owner who'd taken his dog out for a late-night potty break. Even if the cops drove by now, they wouldn't necessarily decide he looked out of place. The only thing out of the ordinary about him was the anger Selene could practically feel emanating from his large frame.

Unfortunately his dog bore the brunt of that rage. Every so often the man would pop the leash hard, seemingly for no other reason than to make the dog whimper in discomfort. Selene kept up her silent vigil overhead, worried for the little mutt. The man was obviously furious that his plans had been thwarted, by a fellow dog, no less.

Selene's mind raced as he turned down a residential street. She assumed he was parked somewhere nearby and worried about her ability to follow him once he got into a car. At this time of night, traffic would be light, and if he chose to speed away, she could have trouble keeping up.

At once an idea occurred to Selene, one so crazy she knew it had merit. If it worked, she would solve two problems at once: discovering where the killer lived and rescuing the man's unfortunate pup from what she imagined would be a gruesome fate once they got there. Without allowing herself to second-guess her instincts, she descended onto the sidewalk just behind the man and, when he didn't react to her presence, she shifted into the biggest, meanest dog she could imagine.

Sending out a silent apology to the little mutt she was about to terrorize, Selene took off running after the man and his dog with a low snarl. Immediately the little dog went on the defensive, yapping noisily as Selene closed in. The man watched her approach with wide eyes, as though he either didn't understand or didn't believe what he was seeing. Prepared to wrench the leash from his hand with her teeth, Selene was thrilled when he simply dropped it and the little dog tore off down the street. Selene gave chase, feeling simultaneously guilty and overjoyed at being able to give in to her natural urge to pursue.

As soon as she and the dog ran around a corner out of the man's sight, Selene forced herself to stop. Breathing heavily, she checked to make sure the street was still deserted, then ducked into a narrow alley to shift into yet another new form, that of the man's little dog. She trotted out quickly, worried that the man would reach his car before she could make her way back to him.

Her legs were shorter now so she had to run at top speed to catch up, but luckily she was able to close the distance between her and the killer without a problem. Her exhaustion returned swiftly as she circled in front of the man, whining to be picked up. She wore no leash and hoped the man would accept the idea that she'd slipped out of her collar during the altercation with the larger dog.

The man stared down at her, clearly surprised that his dog had returned. He glanced back over his shoulder, undoubtedly checking to see if the big dog was still in pursuit. The sidewalk was empty. Selene whined again and danced around, hoping he wouldn't just decide to abandon her here.

"Stupid mutt," he muttered, bending to roughly grab the scruff of her neck and lift her into his arms. "Thought you'd be dinner by now."

Selene pushed back the desire to vomit at the sensation of being carried beneath his arm, surrounded by his pungent scent. She stayed very still and didn't wiggle, afraid that his patience was worn too thin to allow him to put up with a difficult pet. She needed him to take her home, at the very least. Once she was there she'd figure out how to escape, making sure she could retrace her steps and lead Eve and the police to his door.

He carried her two more blocks before walking to the driver's-side door of a nondescript Toyota, using a fob to unlock the car, then practically tossing her into the passenger seat. He threw his backpack on top of her, unzipping the largest pocket to stuff his baseball cap inside. Then he started the car with a quiet curse.

"I should be fucking her right now." He threw the car into drive with an angry jerk of his wrist. "I should be *torturing* that bitch, but instead a goddamn *dog* ruins everything." As he pulled away from the curb, he pinned Selene with a murderous glare. "Stupid fucking dogs."

Selene avoided his gaze and sat very still, pretending to be a statue. She sensed that one wrong move would provoke violence, and her options for evading injury were limited inside a locked car. Hoping that he should be satisfied with ranting and raving, at least until they got home, Selene watched him from the corner of her eye as he ground his teeth together.

Angling her head so she could peer into his backpack, she spotted his knife and a foil packet that turned her stomach. From his words and the objects he carried, she had a good idea what he'd planned to do at Eve's apartment tonight. Her muscles weakened and she slumped against the back of the seat, overcome by intense gratitude that she'd been able to stop him.

The man spent the rest of the drive in silence. Selene watched out the window, paying attention to their route through the city. He appeared to be heading south, and when he got on 101, she realized that he was driving them out of the city. It was little wonder that she'd never been able to track him successfully in the past.

Slamming his hand against the steering wheel, the man roared, *"Fuck!"*

At that moment Selene comprehended just how precarious her situation was. She hadn't really thought at all before deciding to disguise herself as the killer's dog so she could go home with him. Trapped inside a car with a furious psychopath, she might be in real danger. Though Selene rarely feared for her personal safety, confident that her physical abilities would enable her to escape from serious harm, a very real sense of fear crept up her spine. She wanted to do two things before she made her escape—learn the killer's name and memorize his address. How she would convince Eve that the information was good was a problem for another time. Selene hoped she could find what she needed, then make her escape in one piece.

Only a few miles from the exit to the San Francisco International Airport, the man pulled off the highway and drove into the well-lit parking lot of an expensive-looking apartment complex. Without moving, Selene mentally prepared herself for what was about to happen. She hoped he'd carry her upstairs to his place, then put her down and let her explore. From the anger and adrenaline that obviously continued to surge through his veins, he might take out his desire to hurt something on her. She needed to be ready to react to whatever happened.

The man parked his car then pocketed his keys. He zipped his backpack, grabbing it as he opened the driver's door and got out. Selene waited in the passenger seat, unsure whether she should follow. He gestured impatiently.

"Come on, you fucker." As she scrambled onto the driver's seat he reached out and hauled her up by the scruff of her neck, shaking hard. "I've got plans for you."

Selene bared her teeth on instinct, shaken by the malice in his voice. She knew she was about to have to fight for her life and steeled her nerve. But she didn't shift yet, or attempt to run away. She needed to learn more so she had something solid to tell Eve.

He shook her again. "Don't you growl at me. I'm bigger. I'll win."

With effort Selene relaxed her mouth. If she pushed him into snapping her neck right here in the parking lot, everything she'd done tonight would be a waste. If he managed to kill her she would shift back into human form, she assumed, and with an inexplicable naked female corpse on his hands, who knew whether the man would retreat into hiding. She needed to flush him out so he could be captured, not send him running scared.

He carried her under his arm like she was an inanimate object, with absolutely no tenderness. Climbing the stairs to the third floor, he moved quietly. For a man of his height, which she would put at just over six feet tall, he was incredibly light on his feet. Clearly stealth was a real strength for him.

When they got to a door marked 12C, the man stopped and dug his keys out of his backpack. He unlocked the door and literally threw her into the darkness of his apartment. A hard object caught her across the hip and sent her tumbling to the ground. Whimpering in pain, Selene forced herself to stand and scamper behind the couch. She wanted to be out of sight before he turned on the lights. Perhaps that would also put her out of mind.

The overhead lamp came to life, illuminating the apartment. From behind the couch, Selene couldn't see much except worn brown carpeting and a couple of massive dust bunnies. She hunkered down and listened, hoping he would simply decide to go to bed. Best-case scenario, he'd give her some time alone to gather information so she could sneak out and fly home to Eve. If she could discover his name and address, it would be over. Eve would be safe.

Selene didn't move as he stomped heavily out of the room. The sound of his backpack hitting the ground startled her, and then a door slammed. A moment later she heard water running. That meant he was probably in the bathroom. This could be her chance to look for evidence.

Poking her head out from behind the couch, Selene took a tentative step away from safety. She scanned the room frantically as she searched for some clue as to what she should do next. She'd undertaken this mission with very little thought about the best way to get what she needed.

A banging noise came from a distant room, followed by an angry curse. The muffled, indistinct noise reassured Selene that he had indeed locked himself in another room. She spotted the corner of a magazine hanging over the edge of a coffee table and scurried over, eager to explore. There could be an address label on that magazine. If not, maybe she'd get lucky and find a stack of mail.

Too short to see what was on the surface, she hopped up and braced her paws against the edge of the table. The magazine had been discarded cover-down, obscuring any possible evidence of a subscription. Aware that she had very little time to act, Selene weighed her options. It would be far more difficult to conduct this search as a small terrier mix. She didn't have height, but, more important, she didn't have hands. Clearly she would need to move things around and really dig through this guy's belongings, fast, if she wanted to get something useful before he returned to the main room.

Taking a deep breath, Selene quickly shifted back into human form. Even without a canine's keen senses, she should be able to hear when he left the bathroom. As soon as that door opened, she'd simply shift. If necessary she'd try again later, after he'd gone to bed. Being discovered in his apartment—naked, no less—wasn't an option. She had no doubt he would know who she was, since he'd obviously been watching Eve. Even if she escaped unharmed, her presence would surely alert him to danger and send him running.

All too conscious that this opportunity was rapidly passing her by, Selene quickly turned over the magazine. No label. Probably purchased from a bookstore. She shouldn't be surprised—this was a man with a keen interest in staying off the grid. But that didn't mean there wouldn't be some other piece of evidence hidden in his apartment. It hardly seemed possible that anyone could completely divorce himself from modern society to the point where he didn't at least receive a utility bill, or something.

Selene raced around his apartment, quickly flipping through various papers stacked here and there. For some reason she'd expected him to keep a tidier home—too many serial-killer movies featuring meticulous psychopaths, Selene supposed—but in reality he had a dizzying array of books, journals, and loose papers stacked precariously on nearly every flat surface. He even had a copy of the book Eve had written, *Listening to the Dead*. Since it was dog-eared and worn, he had obviously read it over and over. It took tremendous willpower not to pick it up and destroy it, if only because she knew it fed his obsession. But he would surely miss it, and she didn't want to tip him off.

Spotting a small window above the kitchen sink, Selene took a break from her search and ran over to pry it open a few inches. Better to ensure she'd have a clear escape route later than leave that important detail to chance.

Finally Selene found exactly what she was after, an electric bill that he'd opened and cast aside on the kitchen counter. She picked it up with shaking hands, groaning when she saw that he'd reinserted the bill into the envelope the wrong way, making it impossible to see the address through the plastic window. That's when she realized how quiet the apartment suddenly was. The sound of running water had stopped.

Jerking her head around, she searched the hallway down which she assumed the man had gone. Empty. Surely she would have heard the bathroom door open if he'd emerged. That she hadn't meant that she might have just a bit more time. Nerves shot, she fumbled with the envelope, tearing the folded sheet of paper from inside and clumsily manipulating it until she could read the text.

A door opened somewhere beyond the empty hallway. Heavy footsteps approached. Selene searched numbers and letters that looked strangely like gibberish, desperate to locate the information she needed before she was forced to shift out of human form. Breathlessly, she spotted it just as she caught a glimpse of the man's shadow moving across the threshold of the room he was about to exit.

Kevin Pike. 106 South Third Street, Apartment 12C, Burlingame. Selene repeated it to herself even as she transformed into the poor little dog. Kevin Pike. 106 South Third Street. Apartment 12C. Burlingame.

Who knew if it was his real name or an alias? Selene wasn't sure it mattered. She had somewhere to lead the police. Soon Eve wouldn't have to live in fear.

"Dog." The man's voice cut through the silence of the apartment, sending her already-accelerated heartbeat into near arrest. He spoke with a light, singsong tone, but Selene easily read the malice within that single word. "Come out, come out. I've got something for you."

Selene cursed her impulsive decision to change back into his dog. Becoming an insect would have been better. Though that form was awkward to control, it worked well for staying hidden. Aware that her opportunity for escape was slipping away, Selene called up a mental image of a housefly and sent her body a silent command to mimic its form. Usually the transformation happened automatically. All she had to do was think it to make it so.

Usually, but not this time.

Horrified when her body refused to obey her mind, she skittered backward across the kitchen tile. Still trapped in a small dog's body, she could do little to protect herself. She could bite him, sure, but probably not hard enough to dissuade him from harming her. Certainly not hard enough to stop him. Her only real option for escape was to shift. Either because she was exhausted or the universe had decided to turn against her, she seemed to have run out of juice.

Selene closed her eyes and tried again. When she shifted, her body would tingle as though someone was passing a current through her bones, and sometimes her stomach would flip-flop in a way that wasn't entirely unpleasant. She'd discovered how to do it by accident when she was eight years old. Watching the family dog tear around their farm chasing butterflies looking like the happiest creature on earth, Selene only had to wish for that happiness to transform into a dog. Delighted, she'd spent nearly an hour playing with Daisy the border collie in a whole new way. From that day forward she knew how to shift, whether she wanted to or not. It had never failed her before.

Until now. No matter how badly she wanted to become a fly, her furry paws remained stubbornly planted on the cool kitchen floor.

Ironic that the ability she'd always yearned to lose would go away when she needed it most. Maybe the first time she'd ever truly needed it. She dashed under the kitchen table, buying herself perhaps only seconds more. She closed her eyes tight. Fly. A fly. She needed to be a fly.

"There you are." A foot caught her behind her bottom, sweeping her forward across the kitchen floor. Selene used the momentum to propel herself down the hallway into a dark bedroom. She crawled beneath the bed, heart thumping against the sour-smelling carpet. Trembling, she listened to Kevin Pike storm his way into the bedroom. "Let's see how fast you run when I pin you to the fucking door with this knife."

This wasn't how it was supposed to happen. Selene moved to the very center of the bed and curled into a tight ball, hoping he wouldn't be able to reach in and grab her. Getting caught would put Eve's safety in jeopardy. And the thought of never seeing Eve again was too painful to bear. Finally Selene had something to live for, just when she was closest to death.

With that thought in mind, she focused on an image of what she wanted to be. A housefly: red eyes, sponging mouth parts, translucent wings. Tiny. Capable of escaping the nightmare she was currently in.

A thrilling jolt of electricity shot down to the tips of her paws and her perception of the world changed. The carpet rushed up to meet her, the underside of the mattress suddenly far above her head. A dark shape appeared to her left, and a frighteningly large hand reached toward her.

Selene took off, zipping out from beneath the bed on the opposite side from where Kevin Pike crouched, searching for his dog. She flew to the ceiling, exhilarated by her narrow escape. Below her, Kevin grunted in frustration, banging his head against the bed frame with an angry curse. He fumbled with the lamp on his nightstand in an effort to turn it on. With the room dimly lit, he dropped back to the floor and searched under the bed.

"Where are you, little fucker?"

That was enough for Selene. She didn't want to stay inside his apartment one moment longer than necessary. She had what she needed. Kevin Pike. 106 South Third Street, Apartment 12C, Burlingame.

As she flew out the kitchen window, she heard a loud crash in the bedroom. She couldn't be sure, but she'd bet he was tearing the place apart looking for that poor little dog. Pleased with the knowledge that she'd saved one life tonight, Selene used her last bit of energy to shift into a bird and pointed back toward San Francisco, ready to save another.

CHAPTER TWENTY-NINE

Still in her pajamas at ten o'clock in the morning, Eve stretched out on her couch with a large bowl of cereal and an oversized spoon, ready for a long, pathetic Saturday at home. Going out was hardly worth the effort. She didn't want to do anything outside her own four walls badly enough to justify dragging San Francisco's finest along. Besides, in her apartment she didn't have to worry about watching her back. Out in the city streets, everything seemed ominous these days.

Picking up the remote, Eve clicked on the television just as her cell phone buzzed its way toward the edge of the coffee table. She sighed, muting the sound of the black-and-white movie playing onscreen. When she looked at the cell phone's display and saw Selene's number flashing, her stomach twisted. Two weeks had passed since their argument and this was the first time Selene had called. Their only communication had been the text message Selene sent the morning after, saying she loved Eve and wished she had the courage to explain. Eve had taken that as good-bye. Not having expected to hear from Selene again, she was torn about what to do.

Part of her wanted to ignore the call. If their relationship hadn't been important enough for Selene to fight for two weeks ago, Eve didn't know what Selene could possibly say to fix things now. But the bigger part of her, the part that desperately missed the way she felt when they were together, wanted to give Selene a chance to try.

Swallowing against the lump in her throat, Eve answered the phone. "Hello."

"Eve." At the sound of Selene's voice, so full of emotion, the lump grew bigger, nearly choking her. "Thank you for taking my call."

"What do you want?"

"I need to talk to you."

"Okay." Eve set down her bowl of cereal, no longer hungry. "Talk."

"Not on the phone. May I come over?"

Eve closed her eyes. She wanted Selene to do just that more than anything. But not this Selene—she yearned for the Selene she could trust, the one who could somehow make all her troubles melt away. Who shrank the world down to just the two of them, so connected in the safety of their little bubble that nothing else seemed to matter. Eve didn't have the energy to deal with Selene the liar, the coward who refused to take responsibility for her actions.

Eve shook her head. "I can't do this, Selene. I really can't. There's too much crazy in my life at the moment to deal with what happened between us. Maybe later. Just not right now."

A long, uncomfortable silence stretched out before Selene spoke. "I deserve that, I know. But I need to tell you something important about the man who's stalking you."

"What?"

"Let me come over and I'll explain—everything. I promise."

Shocked, Eve tried to imagine what information Selene could possibly have. Even knowing that Selene had called in the first victim's body to the police, never once had Eve truly believed that Selene knew more than she let on. It had seemed impossible that she could hold back, knowing Eve's safety was on the line.

Clearly she'd never really known Selene at all.

Wary, Eve said, "If you have information about the case, I can set up an interview for you with Detective Battle. You can tell Jac whatever you think we should know."

"No, I can't." Urgency permeated Selene's tone. "This is something I need to tell you. Then you can help me decide how, and what, to tell Jac."

"How about you talk to me with Jac present in the room?"

"Some of what I need to tell you, Jac can't know." As though aware of how much she was asking, Selene sighed deeply. When she spoke again, she sounded on the verge of tears. "Please trust me, Eve. You know I'd never hurt you. Right?"

Funny thing was, Eve did trust her, even if she didn't want to. "Okay. Why don't we meet somewhere for coffee?"

"I'd rather have some privacy. Either your place or mine."

Exhaling, Eve said, "You're not making this easy, Selene."

"I know. But some of what I have to tell you really needs to stay between you and me. It's…there's something I've never told anyone, about me. Something you need to know. I hope…I hope it helps you understand."

Eve couldn't ignore the earnestness in Selene's voice. She sounded resolute and passionate, crumbling Eve's determination to keep her distance. She told herself that didn't mean she was a fool. This was a woman she'd fallen for, hard, uncharacteristically quickly. There *had* been something real between them. Maybe there still was.

"I was planning to spend today on the couch," Eve said, "watching old movies. Come over whenever you want."

"Great. Thanks." Beneath Selene's relief, Eve sensed an undercurrent of fear. "I'll be over soon."

"I'll need to tell Jac and the others that you're coming," Eve said, before Selene could hang up. "So they'll let you through."

"Okay."

"I won't let Jac know you have new information. You and I can talk first. Then we'll decide what to tell her."

"That's all I ask." Selene exhaled shakily. "Thank you, Eve."

Eve hoped she hadn't just agreed to something she'd regret. She'd do anything for more information about her stalker, but she wasn't exactly ready to have her heart stomped on again. Whatever Selene needed to tell her, she hoped it was worth the risk. "You're welcome. I'll see you later."

Disconnecting their call, Eve took a deep breath before pulling up Jac's number and clicking the Send button. Jac answered on the second ring. "Everything okay?"

"Everything's fine," Eve said. "I wanted to make you aware that I have a visitor coming over this afternoon."

"Okay. Who?"

Eve hesitated. "Selene."

She didn't have to see Jac's face to know she was scowling. "Oh, really."

"She wants to talk." Eve bit her lip, committed to keeping her promise about not telling Jac everything. Not yet. "Don't judge me."

"I'm not."

Eve knew that was a lie. Whether or not Jac knew the real reason for Selene's visit, Eve didn't like Jac thinking she was foolish. "You are. And I'm asking you not to."

"Okay," Jac said in a tight voice. "I just care about you. You don't need her bullshit right now."

"I'll be fine. I just wanted to make sure you knew I was expecting her."

"Of course. If you need anything, you know how to call me."

Eve barked out a humorless laugh. "Come on, Jac. Talking to Selene is hardly panic-button material."

"You never know."

Rolling her eyes, Eve said, "I'll see you later, Jac. Enjoy your Saturday."

"You, too."

Eve hung up, tossing her phone aside. She eyed her cereal, but her appetite had vanished. She was going to see Selene again. Groaning, she slumped on the couch and turned up the sound on the television, hoping to drown out her anxious thoughts.

She didn't know what she wanted to have happen. Actually, that was a lie. Though the strictly rational part of her brain rebelled at the girlish, fairy-tale notion, Eve wished for some kind of happily-ever-after, no matter how improbable it seemed.

❖

Less than an hour after Eve hung up with Selene, she heard a knock on her door. She didn't need to look through the peephole to know who it was. She could feel Selene's presence in her belly, a strange curl of electricity that hadn't been there since the night Selene lied about being out of town—the last time they were together. Eve had imagined feeling that same spark of connection numerous times since their breakup, but that had been pathetic yearning. This was the real thing.

Eve walked to the door on rubbery legs, steeling herself for the sight of Selene's face. She knew it would hit her hard, seeing Selene again, and she worried she would lose her head and leap into Selene's waiting arms. Two weeks hadn't been sufficient time to build a wall around her heart strong enough to keep Selene out. Despite the pain Selene had caused, Eve still missed her desperately. It would take everything she had not to surrender her anger to her desire to be wrapped up in Selene's warm embrace.

Calling up an image of the blond woman who had disappeared into Selene's house the night she was supposedly leaving town, Eve took a deep breath and checked the peephole, just in case. Even distorted by the fish-eye lens, Selene looked stunning. Eve's heart thundered as she undid the chain and pulled the door open. The instant Eve's eyes met Selene's, every bit of Eve's willpower dissolved.

"Eve—" Selene stepped forward then jerked to a halt. She fisted her hands at her sides, clearly holding back. "You look beautiful."

Cursing the trembling of her fingers, Eve whispered, "So do you." She stepped aside and gestured for Selene to enter. "Come in."

As Selene walked past her into the living room, Eve inhaled deeply, savoring her scent. She followed Selene inside, working hard to keep her expression neutral. Judging from the rapid rise and fall of Selene's chest, Selene saw the desire in Eve's every movement. To her credit, she didn't seem to take that as an invitation to initiate physical contact.

Eve almost wished she would.

"Sit down." Hurrying to take a seat on the far end of the couch, Eve sighed in relief as soon as she got off her feet. Weak-kneed and dizzy in Selene's presence, she felt like a ridiculous, lovesick schoolgirl. This was what got her into trouble in the first place—letting her emotions overrule a healthy sense of caution. Eve already knew Selene was a liar. She couldn't forget that just because she smelled good.

Selene sank onto the other end of the couch, shooting Eve a nervous look. "I've missed you."

Eve bit back the urge to confess just how much she'd missed Selene, too. "You said you had information about the Golden Gate Park killer."

Swallowing, Selene said, "Yes." She twisted her hands in her lap, looking so anxious that Eve's stomach roiled in sympathy. "I have a lot to tell you, but I don't know where to start."

"Why don't you start from the beginning?"

Selene opened her mouth then shook her head. "I'm sorry. I'm… I'm really nervous."

"Okay." Having Selene so close—and wanting her so badly—was starting to wear on Eve's patience. Especially when it seemed more and more like maybe Selene's involvement in this case went deeper than Eve wanted to believe. "Why don't you just tell me what you know about this guy? We can go from there."

Exhaling, Selene reached into her pocket and withdrew a folded sheet of paper. She passed it to Eve, watching her face for a reaction when Eve unfolded it and read the elegant lettering inside. *Kevin Pike, 106 South Third Street, Apartment 12C, Burlingame.* Eve gasped as the enormity of what Selene had just given her registered. The last thing she'd expected was a name and address.

Eve looked up and met Selene's worried gaze. "What's this?"

"The name of the man who's after you." Selene's accent seemed more pronounced than usual, her words coming out brittle and clipped. "The address is an apartment building in Burlingame, near the airport."

Eve's stomach sank. The man on the phone had said his name was Kev, and now Selene was giving her the name and address of a Kevin. Not one to believe in coincidence, Eve immediately accepted that Selene was telling the truth. Sickened by the thought that Selene had known something that could have led to this man's capture weeks ago, that she'd sat on information that could have saved *lives*, Eve glared at her in anger.

"Jac interviewed you almost two weeks ago. Why didn't you give her this information then?" Unable to tamp down her rage, Eve's voice rose. "Another woman *died,* Selene. If you'd just come clean when you told us you made the phone call, she'd still be alive."

Selene flinched. "I didn't know who he was then."

"Really? What, so this is the result of some detective work on your part? You were able to crack the case the entire San Francisco homicide division hasn't been able to solve?" Aware that she was swiftly losing control of her temper, Eve shouted, "Is that your big secret, Selene? You're a crime-fighting superhero?"

Selene wouldn't meet her eyes. "Maybe I should just go."

"No." Eve fingered the charm she wore around her neck, Jac's panic button. "If you're involved in this mess, you're going to be held accountable. I'm sorry, that's just the way it is."

Finally Selene looked her in the face, eyes blazing. "*Involved*? You think I had something to do with your attack? With those murders?"

"I don't know what to think." Eve waved the piece of paper in the air. "If you're not involved, how in the world did you get this?"

"I followed him."

"Followed him when? How?"

"Last night he came to your apartment about two o'clock in the morning. A dog scared him away from your door." Selene swallowed convulsively. "The detectives didn't see him because he entered the building from the roof, then escaped the same way."

Eve's breath caught. She'd heard a barking dog in the hallway about two in the morning the night before, but she hadn't seen anyone else. When she'd called the detectives who stood guard down in the lobby, they assured her that no one had entered or left the building. A subsequent sweep of the hallways hadn't turned up any sign of the dog, either. Eve didn't understand how Selene could know any of this. More important, she couldn't fathom how Selene could have slipped into the building without alerting anyone to her presence. Or why she would have done so in the first place.

"I wanted to make sure you were safe," Selene said quietly. "When I realized I had the opportunity to follow him and maybe find out where he lived, I had to take it."

Though some aspects of the story rang true, Eve couldn't believe that Selene had been able to not only sneak past her protective detail, but also follow her stalker all the way to Burlingame without being caught. It sounded impossible. Shaking her head, Eve said, "I'm sorry, this just doesn't make any sense. Let's say you managed to get into my building without *any* of the cops on the street or in the lobby noticing. And let's say that this guy broke in via the roof-access door—which is supposed to be locked from the inside, by the way—again, without anybody noticing. Even if I believed all that, I can't imagine how you could have managed to trail him not only across the roof, but then all the way to *Burlingame*? Without him noticing?"

To describe the look on Selene's face as that of a deer in the headlights would be unfair to the deer. Never before had Eve seen such excruciating panic on display. Selene bent at the waist, swaying as though she might be sick, and exhaled shakily. Then she shot to her feet, tugging her shirt over her head and tossing it onto the floor.

Startled, Eve held up her hands. "Whoa. What are you doing?"

Selene walked to the window and drew the blinds, then reached behind her back to unhook her bra. She turned to face Eve, mouth set in a grim line. "I need to show you something. Because if I just tell it to you, you won't believe me."

Eve shielded her eyes, irritated by her body's instant reaction to the sight of Selene's bare breasts. "Is it really necessary to take off your clothes?"

"Well, yes. Kind of." Selene cleared her throat. "Eve. Look at me."

Sighing heavily, Eve lowered her hand and swallowed hard at the sight of Selene's gloriously naked curves. "You'd better not be messing with me, Selene. I mean it."

Selene looked intensely serious. Holding her arms at her sides, she took another deep breath, clearly gathering her courage. "I was able to follow Kevin Pike that night because he never saw me. Well, he did, but he didn't realize it was me."

"I don't understand."

"I know," Selene said quietly. "You will in a moment. Just... promise me one thing?"

"What?"

"Please don't freak out. I swear I'll explain the best I can, but..." Selene shook out her hands. "Just don't panic."

Tired of the dramatics, Eve propped her head on her hand and feigned boredom. "I promise I won't freak out."

And then the impossible happened. Selene simply disappeared as her body seemed to melt into a different shape. One moment she was there, and the next, she wasn't. In her place stood a brown dog with sad, serious eyes.

Eve freaked out. Screaming, she leapt up from the couch and scrambled backward, nearly losing her balance in her haste to put some distance between herself and the dog that used to be Selene. Heart thundering, Eve shook her head in disbelief. That couldn't possibly have just happened.

The dog startled, then smoothly grew upward and morphed into Selene. The process of transformation was so bizarre to witness that Eve's scream died in her throat as her scientific mind took over. How did Selene's skeletal system handle that type of dramatic change? What happened to the extra body mass when she became the dog, which was far smaller than her human form? Was her ability the result of a genetic anomaly or some environmental agent? What the fuck *was* she?

A heavy pounding shook the apartment door on its hinges. "Eve!" Jac's voice boomed out, deep and commanding, but tight with fear. "Open the door or I'll open it myself."

Standing naked in the middle of her living room, Selene appeared terrified. She looked down at her body, then up at Eve, as though imagining exactly what Jac would make of this situation. Torn out of her stupor by the sense that Selene was about to vanish again, maybe for good, Eve picked up Selene's pants and tossed them into her arms.

"I'm fine, Jac! Just give me a moment," Eve shouted toward the door. In a lower voice, she said, "Get dressed. Go in my bedroom and *stay* there. We need to talk, but first let me get rid of Jac."

Fear flashed across Selene's face. "You're not going to tell her?"

The terror in the softly spoken words tugged at Eve's heart. Selene clearly expected Eve's hatred, not loyalty. "I'm not telling her anything until you and I have a chance to discuss this. Now go."

"Eve." Jac banged on the door. "If you don't open this door immediately, I'm using my key."

Flustered by Jac's persistence, Eve gestured at Selene's discarded bra. "Take your clothes."

Selene gathered her clothing and rushed out of the room without speaking, closing Eve's bedroom door behind her. Eve dashed over to the apartment door and opened it, unsurprised to find Jac with key in hand. "I'm sure the neighbors appreciated that," Eve said, managing a tense smile. "What's wrong, Jac?"

"You tell me." Jac shouldered her way past Eve into the apartment. Her visual sweep of the living room was anything but subtle. She walked to the kitchen and glanced inside as Eve closed the door behind them. "Selene gets here and five minutes later you're screaming bloody murder. Where is that bitch?"

"Wait a second, were you standing guard outside my door?"

"Where is she?"

Eve waited until Jac turned to look at her. Then she folded her arms over her chest and tried to act casual yet annoyed. "She's in the bathroom. I screamed because a rat ran across the floor."

"A rat?" Jac gave her a skeptical once-over. "Since when are you the kind of chick who screams about *rats*?"

"When it's in my apartment, I scream. He surprised me."

Jac studied her face carefully. Then she relaxed, even as her gaze kept straying over Eve's shoulder, to the master bedroom. Stepping closer, Jac dropped her voice to a whisper. "Just tell me. Did she hurt you?"

"No." Eve planted her hands on her hips. "Selene and I have stuff to work out, definitely, but she would *never* lay a hand on me." Obviously Eve had a lot to learn about Selene, but she felt confident about that. "Seriously, Jac. I'm fine. And you need to go."

Studying her for a few moments longer, Jac nodded and walked stiffly to the door. "Sorry I bothered you."

"It's fine." Eve forced a light chuckle. "You're right. I'm not really much of a screamer. I'm sure it sounded pretty crazy."

Jac didn't join in her laughter. "It sounded terrifying."

The genuine concern in Jac's voice warmed Eve, gentling her tone. "I'm sorry." Eve patted Jac on the back as she walked out the door. "I do appreciate knowing that you can get to me quickly in case something really happens, though."

Giving her an expression of resigned sorrow, Jac said, "Fine. Use your necklace if you need to."

"I will. Thanks." Eve closed the door behind Jac, then turned around, slumping against the cool wood. She pressed a hand to her forehead, stunned by this sudden turn of events. Knowing that Selene was waiting for a reaction beyond pure, noisy astonishment, Eve walked to the bedroom on shaking legs.

Selene sat on the foot of her bed fully dressed, holding her head in her hands. She glanced up when Eve entered the room, then quickly got to her feet. "I should have prepared you better than I did. I'm so sorry…I never meant to frighten you."

Eve cut Selene off with a shake of her head. "Selene, even if you'd told me, 'I'm going to turn into a dog now,' I still would have screamed. That was…unbelievable."

"I know." The sadness in Selene's voice was palpable.

"Will you do it again?"

Eyes widening, Selene opened and closed her mouth before whispering, "Seriously?"

"I need to see that again." Eve gave Selene a sheepish smile. "For the sake of scientific curiosity."

A single tear rolled down Selene's cheek. "So you're not disgusted?"

"No." Hating that her earlier panic had led to the uncertainty that now racked Selene's tense frame, Eve took a step forward and touched her arm. "I'm surprised. Dumbfounded. Intellectually challenged. But I'm not disgusted. I see horrible things every day, Selene. Man's inhumanity toward man. What you are isn't disgusting. You're amazing."

Selene's lower lip trembled. "Yeah?"

"Absolutely." Eve sat on the bed, focusing on Selene. Now that she knew what to expect, she wanted to pay more attention to exactly how Selene changed shape. "Now do it again."

Blushing, Selene undressed in silence. Despite Eve's attempt at reassurance, she seemed to have trouble making eye contact. "Do you want to see a dog again, or something else?"

A shiver of excitement ran down the length of Eve's spine. "You can…you can change into whatever you want?"

"I guess so." Selene shrugged shyly. "I haven't tried many different things, but I've been able to become whatever I've wanted so far."

"When you…when you change, do you retain your human consciousness and instincts?" Unable to help herself, Eve swept her gaze over Selene's nudity. Now that anticipation had replaced anger, it was hard not to allow her old feelings to take over. She still wanted Selene, badly.

Selene shuddered. "Yes."

"How about a tiger?"

"Okay," Selene said, then smoothly transformed into a large, orange-and-black striped cat. The tiger—Selene—sat on its haunches, staring at Eve expectantly.

Eve bleated out a peal of shocked laughter. Even the second time around, Selene's little trick was astonishing. "Come here."

Tiger-Selene stood and stretched like an overgrown housecat, then sauntered over to Eve. Shaking, Eve reached out and let her hand hover in the air over one of Selene's thick, furry ears. When the ear twitched, Eve gasped and drew back, wary of the power and strength in Selene's massive body. Selene lifted her head and stared into Eve's eyes, as though begging for her trust. Eve exhaled, then sank her fingers into the thick fur covering Selene's skull, closing her eyes when Selene rested her heavy head on Eve's thigh.

"Thank you for showing me," Eve whispered. "We've got a lot to talk about, don't we?"

Selene seemed to ripple beneath Eve's hand. The sight of tiger-orange fur becoming silky black hair between her fingers took Eve's breath away. She watched, rapt, as Selene's transformation completed, leaving a naked Selene resting her face on Eve's clothed thigh. Eve fought against a wave of desire that crashed over her at the realization that things with Selene certainly weren't as they seemed, and perhaps what happened that night with the blonde was similarly complex. Maybe the secrecy had something to do with her ability. That would make sense, as far as Selene not being able to explain. This was a big deal. You wouldn't trust just anyone with a bombshell of this magnitude.

Selene lifted her face and stared up at Eve. Her entire body shook. "We have more to talk about than you even realize."

Caressing Selene's face, Eve said, "Are you okay? You're shaking."

"I just can't believe I told you." Selene stood, swaying slightly as she turned to gather her clothes. "I'm sort of in shock."

Eve caught Selene's arm, stopping her from leaving. She tugged Selene down onto the bed beside her, then gathered her into a tight hug. Though the gentle press of Selene's naked curves sent a shiver of arousal through Eve's frame, the embrace wasn't sexual. She sensed that Selene needed a grounding touch right now. She needed to know that who she was hadn't scared Eve away.

Selene clutched her shoulders, breathing heavily. "You're only the third person I've ever actually told."

"Did the first two times not go well?"

"No, they didn't." Burrowing deeper into the circle of Eve's arms, Selene shivered even more strongly. "I told my girlfriend when we were sixteen. I was in love with her. She wanted to run away with me until I showed her what I was. Then she was terrified. She told me to go. That's why I couldn't tell you, Eve. I already loved you so much and I couldn't bear to go through that again. I didn't want you to look at me like I'm a monster."

Eve drew back so she could stare seriously into Selene's eyes, wanting to soothe her back into calmness. Selene's tumultuous emotion poured over Eve, making it hard to breathe. "Well, you haven't scared me away. I'm still here."

Selene nodded, then pulled away, color rising on her cheeks. "Let me put on my clothes, unless you want to take yours off." She managed a playful wink. "Just feels weird to be the only naked one after two weeks of not speaking."

"Get dressed," Eve said softly. Selene's words hit her low in the belly, the sweet pleasure of being desired. It was a welcome feeling after two weeks of depression and anxiety. Still, they needed to talk before Eve could decide where their romantic relationship stood.

Selene did as she said quickly, glancing every now and then at Eve, who sat on the bed watching. "You can't imagine how grateful I am that you didn't just run away screaming. But you don't know everything yet."

"Everything about you, or everything about how you managed to follow Kevin Pike?" Eve gestured for Selene to come sit beside her. She wanted to keep this conversation in the bedroom, where they had less chance of being overheard if Jac had decided to stick around.

"About me."

Eve wrapped her arm around Selene's waist when she sat down, wanting to stay connected. She meant not only to reassure Selene that she had an open mind about whatever she was about to hear, but also to reassure herself that although she clearly hadn't even begun to discover who Selene was during their month of dating, she had a real connection with this woman. Selene made her feel things that she couldn't deny, and if it was possible to get this relationship back, Eve wanted to try.

Sensing that Selene was having trouble finding the words to start, Eve asked, "The day I was attacked in Golden Gate Park, a wolf saved me, which seemed totally *insane* at the time. I know Jac thought I was mistaken. That wolf was you, wasn't it?"

Selene gave her a sidelong glance. "Yes."

"You saved my life," Eve whispered. Flashing on a memory of Kevin Pike holding her down and threatening her with his knife, Eve quaked with fear that felt every bit as potent as it did that day. Selene clasped her hands, chasing the images away and bringing her back into the present. Without thinking, Eve kissed Selene softly on the mouth. "Thank you."

When Eve pulled back, Selene touched her lips. "You're welcome."

"I'm incredibly lucky that a beautiful shape-shifting superhero just happened to be in the same area of the park I was right when I needed her." The odds of the situation she'd just described even being possible, let alone actually occurring, were infinitesimal. Eve laughed. "That's crazy."

"Yeah."

The sick dread that poured from Selene didn't pass Eve's notice. Obviously there was more to the story than Selene simply being in the right place at the right time. Eve squeezed Selene's hand. "Tell me what happened that morning. Everything."

Selene stared at her feet. "First I need to tell you more about my… ability."

"Okay. Tell me."

Without meeting her eyes, Selene said, "The morning you were attacked, I woke up in Golden Gate Park. That's how I found that woman's body. She wasn't far from where I regained consciousness, and I could smell blood in the air, so I followed her scent." Selene searched Eve's face, as though checking for a reaction. "Even in human form, I have heightened senses. Tracking works better with a canine sense of smell, of course, but that morning the scent of death was strong enough that I could easily pick it up with my human nose."

"What do you mean when you say you 'regained consciousness'

in the park?" Eve sensed that this detail was at the heart of Selene's big revelation. "How did you get there?"

"I don't know if you remember—or were even aware—but you were attacked the morning after the full moon." Selene licked her lips nervously. "The night you came over to my place—when I told you I would be out of town—there was also a full moon."

Remembering Selene's strange behavior, the unrestrained lust and seemingly painful lapses, Eve felt a piece of the puzzle fall into place. "The full moon affects you. What does it do?" At Selene's expression of nervous shame, Eve's heart rate picked up. They were in uncharted territory here—Selene could conceivably tell her anything. Eve desperately hoped it was something she could handle. "Don't tell me you're a werewolf."

The flicker of mortification Selene failed to hide seemed to confirm Eve's worst fear. "I don't know if that's the right word for it. But, yes, the moon forces me to shift. I'm not entirely sure into what, but it's big and stronger than you can imagine. It's probably wolf-like, but I've never seen a picture and I've tried very hard to stay hidden during those times. When I wake up the morning after a full moon, I can't remember anything about what happened the night before."

"Have you ever done anything…bad?" As hard as Eve tried to tiptoe around the topic, it was nearly impossible to sound casual when asking someone whether she was dangerous.

"Yes, the first time it ever happened. When I was sixteen. I wasn't expecting it, but one month the moon just took me over. I woke up outside, covered in the blood and tissue of the sheep we kept on our family farm. Apparently I'd slaughtered them, much like a wolf would—which is why I assume that whatever I become, it's wolf-like." Selene's eyes had gone far away, pain etched across her face as she relived an event that clearly still had the power to hurt her.

Eve threaded her fingers through Selene's, bringing Selene back to the two of them, sitting together on the bed. "So what happened?"

"My parents were the ones who woke me up. My father was screaming, my mother was crying. I tried to explain to them, but telling them what I could do only made it worse. I'd been keeping my ability secret since figuring out I could become the family dog when I was eight years old." A bare smile ghosted across Selene's lips.

"I can't even imagine what it must have felt like to discover that you can do something nobody else can. How exciting."

"It was exciting, at first, but I was afraid to tell anyone. I was in an orphanage until I was four years old and my parents adopted me. Knowing I was different, I was afraid to do anything that might get me sent back. So it was my little secret. I didn't even tell my girlfriend, who I'd been with for about a year when that first full moon got me." Covering her face with her hand, Selene emanated grief. It was as though a dam had burst, and Eve suspected that Selene had just uncorked memories that she had bottled up for years. "My parents disowned me. My father threatened to call the police, actually, so I decided to run away. But I couldn't leave without telling Carla good-bye."

"And that was when she rejected you."

"I couldn't blame her," Selene murmured. "I told her about the sheep. It was the first time I'd ever lost control and I couldn't remember any of it. I was scared out of my mind. She could see that. Who could fault her for not wanting any part of a murderous freak?"

"Well, I can." This new revelation was a game-changer, certainly, but for some reason Eve felt no compulsion to sever ties with Selene. Even if she was some kind of werewolf, Selene had a good heart and a kind nature. How she responded to the lunar cycle was hardly her fault. "You loved her, and you were scared and alone. She should have been there for you when you needed someone. Instead she convinced you that nobody could ever love a freak like you. Didn't she?"

Selene blushed. "I knew you and I couldn't have a real relationship if I was hiding something so big. But I just didn't know how to tell you. I was convinced it would turn out badly. Of course, lying to you didn't exactly work out any better, did it?" Lowering her voice, Selene said, "I tried not to fall in love with you at all, but we have a connection. I couldn't help it."

Eve perked up at the mention of their connection, which had always been so palpable yet improbable to a pragmatist like herself. If a supernatural explanation existed for the instant chemistry and closeness she felt with Selene—not to mention their unmistakable emotional bond—then Eve was happy to hear it. In some insane way, that would allow her to more easily accept it as real.

"Tell me about our connection," Eve said. "I feel it, too, always have. What does it mean?"

"I don't know," Selene said softly, caressing Eve's face with a tentative hand. "I'd never felt it before that morning in the park. That's what drew me to you, how I found you when you were being attacked.

I wasn't even inside the park when I *felt* you cry out for help, Eve. I sprinted for about three minutes to get to you."

Even sitting down, Eve felt her legs weaken at the confession. Were it not for their strange bond, Selene might never have known she was in trouble. Eve was luckier than she wanted to think about. "So tell me more about waking up in the park. Does that happen every full moon?"

"No." Embarrassed, Selene mumbled, "Three nights out of the month, the full moon affects me. The night before and after my forced shift, I have an extremely heightened sex drive, slight loss of self-control, and that's it. On the night when the moon is fullest, I have a standing appointment with a call girl. We don't have sex," Selene said quickly, as though worried Eve would take that as a confession of infidelity. "I ask her to handcuff me to a steel table and tie me down with rope. I play it off like it's some kind of sex game, but really, I just need someone who can restrain me, leave for the night, and release me the next morning. Escort services are kind of known for their discretion."

So that's who the woman at Selene's house was. That Selene had found it impossible to explain—that she'd looked so guilty—made perfect sense. Eve nodded. "I understand."

"The night I escaped I had an appointment with a new girl. The one I'd been using before had graduated from school and wasn't escorting anymore." Now that the truth was out in the open, Selene visibly relaxed. "She didn't want to tie me tight enough. That was the month of the perigee moon—the largest one of the year. I knew I'd escape before she even left my house. But how could I explain why she *had* to tie me tighter, even though she was afraid of hurting me?"

Eve nodded. "When you woke up the next morning and found that body, did you think you'd killed her?"

"Yes," Selene said simply. "I didn't know what to do. I've had more than my share of forgotten, unrestrained shifts, especially when I was younger, but I've *never* hurt a human being." She paused. "Not that I know about, anyway."

Eve touched her forehead. This was information overload. She tried to get a handle on what she'd just learned and what still needed explaining. "So tell me how you found Kevin Pike. I know you were watching over me when he came here last night. But how did you manage to follow him all the way to Burlingame?"

Beneath the faint smile Selene gave her, Eve could see both pride and unease. She was apparently about to hear quite a story. Taking a breath, Selene said, "After I chased him away from your door—"

A thought occurred to Eve. "And barked at me to go back inside."

Selene chuckled. "Yes, and that, I followed him up the stairs to the roof-access door. I had to shift back into human form to get outside, but then I became a bird. That made it really easy to follow him across the roofs of the buildings until he got to the end of the block. After getting away he went to this playground a few blocks away—"

"I know the one you mean."

"He had a little dog tied up there. He untied it and started back to his car. I'm guessing he used the dog to try to look less conspicuous walking around in the middle of the night, because he didn't seem to care for it very much." Selene's mouth set in a grim line. "He was very angry that his plans had been ruined, that much was obvious. I sensed that he would take it out on the dog, and I also started to worry that if he got into a car I might lose him, depending on how far he had to travel. So I saw my opportunity and took it."

Eve held her breath, waiting to hear what happened next. "What did you do?"

"I shifted into a big dog and charged his poor little one. He dropped the leash and I chased his dog out of sight. Then I *became* his dog."

Tensing, Eve realized just how far Selene had gone to protect her. To take that kind of risk for a woman who wasn't even speaking to you showed real character—and proved that Selene's feelings for her were very real. Caught between terror and gratitude, Eve whispered, "You let him take you back to his place."

"It was the best way to find out who he was and where he lived." Selene played with her hair, searching Eve's eyes. "He would have killed his dog if I hadn't switched places with it. I know it."

"How did *you* get away?"

"It was dicey." From the audible waver in Selene's voice, Eve guessed that dicey only scratched the surface of what she'd actually been through. "I found out that my ability has limits. When he came after me, thinking I was his dog, I hid under his bed and tried to become a fly so I could escape. But I was exhausted and had already done seven different shifts over the course of the night, and at first I couldn't. It just…didn't work."

"That's the first time you've ever been unable to change when you wanted to?" Greedy for more detail, Eve wanted to know everything about Selene's gift. It excited her scientific mind more than she ever would have anticipated. "How *do* you change?"

"I just think it and become it." Selene shrugged. "Honestly, up until I met you that morning in Golden Gate Park, I rarely shifted by choice. Too dangerous. Occasionally I'd take trips out to the country so I could indulge my need to go a little wild, but for the most part I was too afraid someone might find out what I was."

"That's a shame."

"I guess so." Exhaling in a rush, Selene collapsed back onto the mattress. She stared at the ceiling as Eve stretched out at her side. "I think that's everything. Now we just need to figure out what to do with that name and address."

That was the real question, wasn't it? Without any evidence or cause to make an arrest, they couldn't take Kevin Pike into custody. The best Jac could do was put a surveillance team on him and watch his movements. If he slipped up, they could question him. Otherwise they had to dig for some way to link the man to his victims or his crime scenes. As meticulous as he'd been so far, that wouldn't be so easy.

But the more immediate issue was how to tell Jac that she now had the name and address of their suspect without raising suspicion that Selene was somehow involved. Obviously Eve couldn't tell Jac exactly how Selene had managed to find such specific information. Given that Jac already suspected that Selene had sinister motives for being involved with Eve, she couldn't easily convince her that Selene had provided good intelligence without knowing more than she'd claimed.

Eve sighed. "I have no idea what to tell Jac. She'll need to get a couple of detectives on Kevin Pike's tail, but it won't be easy to explain how I know who he is."

"She'll know I gave you his name."

It wasn't really a question. More like a statement, laced with defeat. "Yes, she will. Jac isn't stupid."

"But they need to know what I know. It's the only way to keep you safe." Selene's eyelids drooped and she yawned, raising her arms above her head. "Honestly, I can barely think right now. I'm so tired."

Brushing a lock of hair away from Selene's forehead, Eve whispered, "Have you been guarding my apartment every night?"

"Yes."

It occurred to Eve that perhaps the sensation of Selene being close by hadn't been due to her depressed imagination. "You've been keeping watch pretty much all the time, haven't you? I've *felt* you almost every day. I thought it was because I missed you, but that wasn't it, was it? You were here."

Selene gave her a sleepy nod. "I'm sorry. I wasn't trying to spy. I just…needed to know that you were okay."

Eve shook her head. Selene's vigilance didn't feel like an invasion of privacy, but rather a declaration of love. "Why don't you take a nap?" she murmured. "I'll think of what to tell Jac. Whatever I come up with, I promise to protect you."

Eyes drifting closed, Selene mumbled, "I trust you."

Eve leaned close, brushing her lips over Selene's cheek. "I trust you, too."

Selene dropped off to sleep with the barest hint of a smile on her lips. Overcome by the sight, and by the sudden realization that her relationship with Selene wasn't over—not by a long shot—Eve rolled onto her back and put her hand over her heart. It was finally beating again.

CHAPTER THIRTY

Half an hour after Selene fell asleep in her bed, Eve returned to her living room, closing the bedroom door behind her. As much as she wasn't looking forward to calling Jac, the sooner she could pass along Kevin Pike's name and address to the police, the better. Although she still didn't have a solid strategy for introducing the tip—and explaining Selene's part in delivering it—putting off talking to Jac wasn't an option. Every moment she waited gave Kevin Pike the opportunity to hurt another woman.

Eve picked up her phone and dialed Jac's number. Jac answered after the first ring, breathless. "Yes, Eve?"

"Would you mind coming back for a few minutes? I need to talk to you about something."

"Of course." Eve could hear her already walking. "I'm on my way."

When a knock sounded on the door seconds later, Eve rolled her eyes. Apparently Jac had decided to stay close after what happened earlier. Eve opened the door. "That was fast."

Jac smirked. "At your service." She stepped inside, not so subtly looking around. "Where's Selene?"

"Sleeping."

Jac didn't bother to conceal her distaste at Eve's answer. "So does that mean you two worked things out?"

"We didn't have sex, if that's what you're asking."

"Technically it wasn't, but I'm glad to hear that, I guess." Folding her arms over her chest, Jac said, "What did you want to talk about?"

Eve gestured at the couch. "Let's sit down."

"Uh-oh. Something heavy."

"You could say that." When Jac settled at one end of the couch,

Eve withdrew the slip of paper Selene had given her from her pocket. She met Jac's gaze and exhaled. "I have the name and address of the man who I believe is the Golden Gate Park killer."

Jac blinked slowly. Her face betrayed no emotion. "How did you manage that?"

"I can't get into the details with you." Eve crossed the room and sat beside Jac, handing her the paper with Selene's handwriting on it. There was no real point in trying to hide where the information had come from. "Right now I need you to trust me. I know we don't have anything on this guy. Unless he has an outstanding warrant, we can't arrest him. But at least now that we know who he is, we can set up surveillance, watch for him to slip up."

Jac took the paper, scanning the name and address. "You're going to have to tell me how Selene got this information, Eve. First she reports the body of our initial victim, and now she waltzes back into your life with the name and home address of a man who's threatened to kill you. Who's killed at least three other women." Folding the paper in half, Jac slipped it into a pocket inside her jacket. "I can't fathom how Selene would know anything about the guy if she weren't involved somehow."

"I know this is hard to understand, and I get why you're suspicious. I can't explain how this information came to me without betraying Selene's trust, so I'm not even going to try. I'm just asking you to remember who I am and what my values are. Ask yourself whether I'd protect someone who was responsible in any way for the deaths of three women. Not to mention my own stalking." Eve briefly touched Jac's knee. "You know how badly Selene hurt me. Please believe that it would take a genuine, honest explanation about her role in all of this— one that convinced me that she's totally innocent of any wrongdoing— to sway me back to her side."

"Are you back at her side?" Jac asked quietly. It was obvious she knew the answer already and that it disturbed her deeply. "Be honest with me."

Eve wouldn't have considered anything but honesty. "Yes. We talked and I realized we'd had a serious misunderstanding. I think we're planning to work things out."

"You think?"

"She was exhausted. She fell asleep before we came to any real conclusion."

Collapsing against the back of the couch, Jac exhaled harshly.

"I'm not sure I know what to do with this. I mean, even if *I* take you at your word, believe the tip is legit, I don't exactly know what to tell my captain when I'm requesting that resources be allocated to watching some random guy who may or may not be connected to this case."

"He *is* connected." Frustrated but not surprised by Jac's resistance, Eve racked her brain for the best way to act on Selene's tip. "You'll make it sound good, Jac. I know you will." Chancing a playful wink, Eve said, "You *are* the best at what you do, after all."

Jac seemed unmoved. "Flattery won't work this time."

"What will?"

With a low grumble, Jac stood up and walked to Eve's door. Surprised by the abrupt departure, Eve sprang to her feet and followed. Jac put her hand on the doorknob, then faced Eve. "I'll put surveillance on this guy. I can't promise for how long. Obviously if we can catch him in the act of grabbing some woman or harassing you, we're golden. But if not…" Jac shook her head. "Let's just hope he slips up before my captain decides we need to pursue more reliable leads."

"This one is reliable." Eve shrugged helplessly. "I wish I could tell you how I know that. You just have to trust me—this is the guy."

"I do trust you." Her gaze flicking over Eve's shoulder in the direction of her bedroom, Jac curled her lip in disgust. "I just don't trust *her*."

"I know," Eve murmured. "But I do. I hope that counts for something."

Jac stared at her in silence, as though she was trying to decide what to say. Then she opened the door with a shake of her head. "Of course it counts. Just…promise me you'll keep me in the loop as much as you can. Your safety—and the safety of the women in this city—are more important than keeping Selene's confidence."

"If I thought she had additional information material to this case, I'd tell you." At Jac's fleeting expression of skepticism, Eve stiffened. "I swear."

"Okay." Jac patted her pocket. "I'll get to work on this right away."

"Thank you." Relieved that Jac had accepted her lack of explanation so easily, Eve sensed that both she and Selene would need to be cautious around her. Jac was clearly suspicious, and the fact that she held a personal grudge against Selene for having captured Eve's heart didn't exactly help matters. "Let me know what you find out, as far as whether he has any warrants."

"Of course." Tipping her head, Jac slipped out of her apartment then shut the door behind her.

Eve sighed in relief. That hadn't gone nearly as badly as she'd thought. Now that the immediate problem of telling Jac about Kevin Pike was over, Eve dazedly drifted back to all she'd learned over the past hour or so.

It was unbelievable, to say the least. Except she did believe it. She'd seen it with her own eyes. What Selene could do made no sense—hell, it violated the laws of physics and biology—yet it was true. Once again Eve silently thanked her parents for the gift of being able to accept even those things she couldn't explain. Eve wandered back to her bedroom, eager to be close to Selene as she processed the inexplicable truth about her new girlfriend.

She was a shape-shifter—an honest-to-God shape-shifter, with a touch of werewolf thrown in. Opening the bedroom door, Eve stared at Selene's prone form reclining on her bed. She was also gorgeous and still the woman Eve had fallen in love with, albeit far more complicated than Eve had realized. And she hadn't been unfaithful. She hadn't betrayed Eve in any way.

Eve crept to the bed and stood over Selene, watching her sleep. Was Selene even human? Did the answer to that question change anything between them?

Amazingly enough, Eve decided it didn't. What mattered were Selene's actions, her heart. When it came down to it, the question of her DNA—though fascinating to puzzle over—had no bearing on what Eve felt. She was in love.

Yearning to be closer, Eve stripped off her pants and crawled into bed beside Selene. Tentatively, so as not to wake her, Eve laid her head on Selene's chest and curled up against her side. The heat from Selene's body both soothed and inflamed Eve. Selene had always seemed to run hot—now Eve speculated that perhaps a faster metabolism was responsible for the intense warmth that radiated from her lean body. Surely transforming one's entire shape required an extra reserve of energy.

Amused, Eve closed her eyes and forced her analytical mind to power off. Right now she just wanted to enjoy the simple pleasure of being close with Selene again. The science of who she was could wait for another day.

Selene shifted in her sleep, wrapping an arm around Eve's middle and tugging her closer. Content for the first time in weeks, Eve basked in the sense of safety Selene created simply by being there. Eve had no doubt that Selene would do everything possible to protect her if the situation demanded. And if she could become a tiger, Eve doubted Kevin Pike would have an easy time getting past Selene to cause her harm.

Life had just gotten a lot more complicated, but a lot better, too.

CHAPTER THIRTY-ONE

When Selene woke from her deep, dreamless rest, the first thing she saw was the new moon—just beginning to wax—looming outside a curtained window. On instinct she calculated the time until the next full moon—just under two weeks. Always her first thought upon waking, keeping track of her cycle was an unconscious instinct. Being caught unprepared was an irrational worry, but that didn't ease Selene's fear or her distrust of her own body.

Disoriented until she noticed Eve nestled in her arms, Selene remembered what had brought her to Eve's apartment and what had happened between them, and her breathing quickened. Despite Eve's initial knee-jerk reaction, Selene's coming out had gone better than she could have imagined. Eve hadn't rejected her, even knowing the whole truth. Apparently she'd even allowed Selene to fall asleep in her bed, though Selene couldn't remember how she'd gotten there.

"You were exhausted." Eve answered Selene's unspoken question, voice scratchy with sleep. "After we talked, you practically passed out."

Selene had no recollection past shifting into a tiger then giving Eve a long, rambling recap of the past month and a half. That she had woken up with Eve by her side seemed like a good sign. "How long was I out?"

Eve rolled over to check her alarm clock. "About eight hours."

"What?" Selene sat abruptly, shocked and embarrassed that she'd borrowed Eve's bed for almost the entire day. They'd spoken for maybe a half hour before Selene had fallen asleep. After basically being broken up for the past two weeks, that was hardly enough reconciliation to justify treating Eve's place like a hotel. "I'm so sorry. I haven't been sleeping much and I just—"

"Because you've been too busy watching over me." Tugging gently on Selene's wrist, Eve encouraged her to lie back down. "I know. Providing a bed is the least I can do to thank you."

Selene blushed. Protecting Eve wasn't an entirely selfless act. Now that they'd found each other, Eve's safety was the only thing that mattered. Instinctively Selene knew that losing Eve would mean losing a part of herself—the part that made her human. Not only was Eve her most real connection to the human world, but she'd singlehandedly erased Selene's loneliness and convinced her that she could have the same things normal people did. Love. Happiness. A future.

Caressing Eve's face with the back of her hand, Selene murmured, "Until Kevin Pike is in custody, I want to stay with you around the clock. If you don't feel comfortable taking me to work with you, I can keep watch in a different form. I just don't want to leave your side."

"Can you fall asleep when you're shifted without reverting back to human form?"

"No." Selene struggled to put her thoughts into words. Explaining something she barely understood was difficult at best. "My body seems to have a tendency or an impulse to retain its natural form. If I lose consciousness when I'm shifted, I usually wake up myself. Naked. Which is embarrassing." She paused, then laughed shyly. "You know, now that I'm talking about this, I realize that I don't know as much about what I can do as I should. I've never really tested myself. I've mostly just tried to avoid the whole thing."

"No more," Eve murmured. "And as much as I appreciate your protection, if you're going to watch over me during the day, you need to start sleeping at night. If we're locked in my apartment and you're in bed with me, I don't see any reason for you to keep running yourself down like this."

Selene's breath caught at the unspoken implication. "Does this mean we're back together?" Cringing at the quaver in her voice, Selene tensed as she awaited Eve's answer. Since the night of the last full moon, every day she'd dreamed of having Eve back. Until yesterday, she hadn't thought it possible. In a strange way, Selene was almost glad for Kevin Pike. She wasn't sure she would have had the courage to confide in Eve if he hadn't posed such an incredible threat to the person Selene held most dear.

Because of Kevin Pike, she might have a second chance.

"I hope so." Eve closed the distance between them to kiss Selene lightly. "I understand why you didn't feel you could tell me the truth,

Selene. As long as you're willing to be honest from here on out—knowing that I'll *always* keep an open mind—I'd like to try this thing between us again." She deepened the kiss, then pulled back, running her tongue along Selene's lower lip. "Because it was *really, really* good before. And I have a feeling it'll only be better now."

Eve's total lack of uncertainty grabbed Selene's heart and squeezed. She'd expected to see some hint of hesitation or even unease about the prospect of rekindling a romance with someone who wasn't quite human, but Eve didn't look at her any differently than before. Or perhaps she did, but with interest verging on awe, not suspicion or disgust. Selene blinked back tears of relief and silent, unspoken joy.

Eve's hand fluttered to her chest. "Is it my imagination or can I feel that?"

"My happiness?"

Swallowing, Eve whispered, "Yes."

"I think so."

The play of emotions across Eve's face entranced Selene, who tried to untangle the complex rush of feelings that flowed from her lover in a jumble. No doubt the concept of an empathetic bond challenged everything Eve thought she knew, but she seemed excited about it all the same. "I've wondered since we first met, but before it seemed ridiculous to even speculate that I could somehow *experience* your emotions. Now I realize that anything's possible with you."

"It's more than possible." Selene traced the shape of Eve's eyebrows, savoring the freedom to touch her again. The loss of this intimacy had been soul-rending. Not until now had Selene appreciated just how empty Eve's absence had left her. "I feel what you feel. I don't see why it wouldn't work the other way."

"Did you have that with Carla when you were young? That shared empathy?"

"No," Selene said quietly. "I never knew this could happen until you."

"I wonder what it means." Eve searched Selene's eyes.

"I think it means we fit."

"Definitely." Eve gave her a playful pinch on the hip, delivering a burst of warm joy to Selene's core. "That's why the sex is so incredible, isn't it? Being able to feel what the other feels."

"Perhaps. Or maybe I'm just *that* good." Even the mere suggestion of sex set Selene's pulse racing. Unable to keep her hands away, she tickled Eve's side, delighting in the giggle she elicited. "Maybe *you* are."

"Well, that's true." Scooting closer, Eve stilled Selene's fingers by tugging her hand up to cover her breast. Selene sobered at the sensation of cradling Eve's tender flesh in her palm. She watched in wonderment as Eve's eyes darkened, signaling a shift in the mood between them. Eve brought her mouth to Selene's ear and whispered, "But I'm a little out of practice. Maybe you can help me with that."

Selene sucked in a surprised breath when Eve's hand crept between her thighs and skimmed over the inseam of the pants she still wore. The gnawing ache that had been growing deep in her belly over the past two weeks exploded, forcing her hips up to meet Eve's touch. "That would be nice."

Eve kissed her earlobe, then took it gently between her teeth. "I've missed you."

"I've missed you, too." The words triggered a flash of memory of their last time together. Selene stiffened as familiar guilt came to the front. She had been out of her mind with the moon and their sex had been rough. The sight of Eve limping away from her house had haunted her daily, and the idea that she'd crossed a line was almost too much to bear. "I'm sorry about that last time, that I hurt you."

Eve shook her head, brushing dark hair away from Selene's forehead. "It was a good hurt. I wanted that hurt." Chuckling sadly, she said, "If I hadn't had such serious emotional pain afterward, I'd probably consider it some of the best sex I've ever had."

"Masochist," Selene mumbled, kissing Eve's shoulder.

"So?" Eve pushed Selene onto her back and straddled her hips, pinning her down. "But tonight I want us to take our time. Go slow." Sitting up, Eve tugged her shirt over her head unhurriedly, putting on a tantalizing show. "Make love."

Rapt at the sight of bare skin, Selene trailed her hands over Eve's sides. She seemed paler than normal, and thinner. Clearly their time apart had taken its toll, though she was no less beautiful than Selene remembered. "I do love you."

Eve's happiness lit Selene from the inside. "I know. I love you, too."

Selene moved her hands up to cover Eve's breasts. Her nipples hardened against the center of Selene's palms, and she bent forward, brushing her lips over Selene's. Lifting her head, Selene swept her tongue into Eve's mouth as she stroked gentle thumbs along the underside of her breasts. She moaned at the way Eve wiggled against her in an unsubtle search for friction.

Eve pulled back. "We should take off our clothes."

"What happened to taking it slow?"

"We can go slow after you're naked."

Selene laughed as Eve scrambled off and pulled her into a sitting position, getting her out of her shirt and bra with skillful efficiency. She helped Eve unbutton and haul off her pants, then they both worked on stripping Eve of the rest of her clothing. As soon as they were naked, Eve melted into her embrace. Eve echoed Selene's gasp at the electricity of skin on skin, tightening her arms around Selene and holding her close.

"It feels so good to touch you," Eve whispered in a voice full of quiet awe. "I knew we had something special between us, but I never realized how special it really was."

Selene tickled a line down the center of Eve's spine, delighting in the tremor the touch elicited. Eve quaked in her embrace, giving off such an intense jolt of pleasure that Selene's pussy tightened, then contracted, sending an orgasm rolling through her body. Groaning, Selene dragged her fingers down to Eve's bottom, drawing her own orgasm out by scratching Eve lightly with her nails, triggering another rush of sensation that seemed to flow through both of them.

Eve shuddered. "You just came."

"Yes."

"That is *so* cool." Eve dropped a hand between Selene's thighs, sliding into her folds. The soft touch sparked another orgasm, stronger than the last. Selene dropped her head to Eve's shoulder and pressed against her body as she surrendered to her climax. "You make it really easy to feel like some kind of sex goddess," Eve murmured.

Overcome by the continued motion of Eve's hand petting her swollen labia, Selene could only grit her teeth and nod. It would take a lot to wear her out sexually—Selene's stamina always seemed to surpass Eve's—but if Eve's goal was to give Selene a run for her money, she was off to an excellent start.

After coming down from her third orgasm, Selene stilled Eve's hand with a tremulous chuckle. "I need to breathe."

"Breathing is overrated," Eve muttered, but backed out of Selene's arms. Collapsing onto the mattress, Eve beckoned Selene to climb on top. "But I promise to go easy on you."

"I never said you had to go easy." Nudging Eve's legs apart with her knee, Selene settled over her body with her thigh pressed firmly against Eve's slick center. The heat pouring from Eve's pussy scorched Selene, inflaming her lust. Needing more, Selene pressed harder into Eve, grinding the firm length of her thigh against Eve's sensitive clit. "It's just your turn now."

Eve threw her head back and moaned, clutching at Selene's shoulders as she rode Selene's thigh. Planting her hands beside Eve's head, Selene moved against her slowly, setting a steady pace. She stared into Eve's eyes as they rocked together, thrilled by the unself-conscious noises that fell from Eve's lips in a steady stream. There was nothing sexier than how vocal Eve could be when they made love. Selene lived for the opportunity to draw forth those mewling, languid sounds. Knowing that she made Eve feel that good was almost enough to make Selene peak yet again.

But Selene held back, solely focused on Eve's rising ardor. What she wanted more than anything was to feel Eve release beneath her, to experience the psychic aftershocks of Eve's orgasm and hopefully join her in a mutual crescendo of sensation. Coming with Eve in the past had always forged such a powerful, intimate connection, and Selene was desperate to recapture the singular experience of losing herself in their self-contained world of shared ecstasy.

A hot curl of pleasure flared between Selene's legs just as Eve murmured, "I'm going to come."

"Come for me." Selene kissed Eve deeply, lowering one hand to squeeze her hip as she kept up her hard, driving thrusts. Arching her back, Eve cried out and did just that, grabbing Selene's ass in both hands as she jerked helplessly against her thigh. Then all of a sudden Selene was climaxing as well, and she could tell by the way it originated in her belly that what she really felt was all from Eve.

It was breathtaking.

Breaking their kiss, Selene pressed her forehead to Eve's and stopped the motion of her hips when she sensed that they were both on the verge of passing out. Selene slipped her hands beneath Eve's back, gathering her into a tight hug.

"I've missed you so much," Selene mumbled. Now that the sexual tension had eased, turbulent emotion that her release had stirred up threatened to take over. She had come so close to losing Eve—to losing the single most astonishing thing in a life filled with constant surprises. But she hadn't. "I never thought you'd want me like this again."

"You're still the woman I fell in love with." Eve ran her fingertips up and down Selene's spine, but now the touch soothed rather than inflamed. "What you can do doesn't change that. And even though honesty is the most important thing you can give me, I don't blame you for being scared. All that's over now. I know what you are, Selene, and I still want you. I still need you."

Embarrassed by the tears that rose and threatened to drip onto Eve's face, Selene rolled to the side, throwing her arm around Eve's waist to stay close. She didn't want to lose contact for even a moment. "I have no idea what I did to deserve you, but I'm grateful." She glanced out the window again at the new moon, and a niggle of anxiety took root in her belly.

As though sensing where her thoughts had gone, Eve said, "I want to help you this month. On your full-moon night."

Alarmed, Selene regarded Eve's solemn expression. She wasn't kidding. "What?"

"Instead of using a call girl this month, I'd like to do whatever they do for you. Tie you down, whatever you need."

Selene shook her head. "No way. I don't want you near me that night."

Frowning, Eve said, "Listen, I'm not some delicate flower. And even though I know why you've used an escort service in the past—and despite the fact that I *do* trust you to be faithful—I don't exactly love the idea of you continuing to have call girls come to your place once a month."

"And I don't love the idea of you having anything to do with what happens to me during the full moon. If you're there, it'll only arouse me more. Make me crazy."

"How do you know that?" Eve ran her fingers over Selene's jaw, giving her a reassuring peck on the cheek. "Listen, I can do whatever needs to be done. And I already know your secret. I know why it's so important that I tie you tight. Wouldn't you rather have someone you can *really* trust who can help you? Someone who actually cares?"

Selene couldn't argue that the idea had definite appeal. More than once she'd been disappointed by a call girl who hadn't done exactly as she'd asked, partially because they had no way of knowing why it was so important to follow her instructions precisely. Plus, the thought of never again having to see confusion or suspicion in the eyes of a complete stranger exhilarated her.

"If we're going to be together, I'll have to experience the full moon with you eventually. I'm not doing this relationship halfway. This is me telling you that I'm all in, for better or worse." Eve inhaled to continue her speech, but Selene cut her off with a light kiss on the lips.

When Selene drew back, she whispered, "Okay."

"Okay?"

"Yeah, okay. I understand what you're saying, and I appreciate it. Plus, if I have to be super horny around a beautiful woman that night, I'd rather it be *my* beautiful woman."

Eve's eyes sparkled as she gave Selene a playful glare. "Me, too."

"I'm not sure about this month, though." Selene raised a hand when Eve opened her mouth to protest. "Not if Kevin Pike is still on the loose. You've got the cops watching you, Eve. Even if they shift most of their focus to Pike, I suspect they'll keep at least one team on you. I can't have the cops outside my apartment on that night. If something *did* happen, they'd bust me for sure."

"Nothing will happen." Eve caressed Selene's cheek. "Stop worrying."

"I can't, Eve. I can't ever stop worrying. I spend half my life planning for and anticipating the next full moon. Asking me to let you participate is a big deal, but letting you do so when it means the police will be watching is beyond my comfort zone." Hating the disappointment that creased Eve's brow, Selene said, "I'm sorry. I really am."

"Okay, then." Eve exhaled. "I'll sneak away that night. Now that they'll be watching Kevin Pike, it won't be as big a deal for me to slip their protection detail for just one night."

"No." Selene took Eve's hands in her own, kissing her knuckles. "Jac would kill you. Hell, she'd kill *me*, if she figured out where you went. It's too dangerous. I can't let you do it."

"Unfortunately you don't have a choice." From the determined set of Eve's jaw, Selene could see she was speaking the truth. "I'm staying with you that night. Nobody needs to know. I *promise* Jac won't find out."

It was an impossible promise to keep, but Selene knew she wouldn't win this argument. Even without their empathetic link, Selene could hear in Eve's voice just how much this meant to her. She made the offer as a show of trust and commitment, and no matter how nervous Selene was about accepting, she couldn't refuse.

"All right," Selene said quietly. "But promise me one thing?"

"What?"

"I want you to leave after you tie me down. You can do it before dark, then go back to your protective detail. I understand and appreciate what you're trying to show me by staying with me during the full moon, but I won't be able protect you from myself, let alone Kevin Pike." Selene cradled Eve's face in her hands. "I need to know you're safe. Okay?"

"Okay." Eve smiled broadly, closing the discussion with a quick kiss on Selene's chin. "Thank you."

"No, thank you." Selene hauled Eve back on top of her body, ready for another go. "On that note, how would you like me to thank you?"

Eve gave her a wicked smirk, then got onto her knees and turned around to give Selene an enticing view of her slick pussy. "How about we thank each other?" Eve said, just before she lowered her head to swipe the flat of her tongue along Selene's labia.

Groaning, Selene grabbed Eve's hips and pulled her down onto her mouth, sucking languidly. She had a lot of gratitude to express, and they had all night.

CHAPTER THIRTY-TWO

Eve sat at her desk in the lab, trying to distract her wandering mind by working through her never-diminishing mountain of paperwork. Since she'd reconciled with Selene the week before, life had been good. Had Kevin Pike not still been walking free, Eve would even have said she was downright content. The experience of being with Selene in a trusting relationship was more wonderful than she could ever have hoped. And having Selene constantly by her side, poised to come to her defense, eased Eve's mind about the threat that Kevin Pike posed in a way all the police officers in the world couldn't.

A whine drew her attention to the floor, where the large Rottweiler lying next to her chair stared directly into Eve's eyes. Even in canine form, Selene's fierce love for her shone through in her gaze. Sprawled on a dog pillow, hidden in plain sight, she gave Eve quiet support that made her feel like she could conquer any challenge. Dropping her hand to stroke Selene's head, Eve looked down at her but said nothing. With Wayne working at his own desk across the lab, chatting with the dog wouldn't be prudent.

The lab door slid open and Jac strolled inside. She nodded at Wayne without taking her eyes off Eve, mouth set in a grim line. All business, she softened her expression slightly when Eve greeted her with a friendly wave. "Afternoon, Eve."

Selene lifted her head but didn't stand. This wasn't the first time Jac had met Eve's new canine friend, but today she came bearing a gift. Crouching in front of Selene, Jac offered a dog biscuit with a quiet "Here you go, girl."

Eve covered her mouth with her hand, trying not to laugh at the sight of the large Rottweiler taking the biscuit delicately between its teeth. She had no doubt that the last thing Selene wanted was to gobble up a dog treat, but apparently she was committed to staying in character. "Cookies. Perfect."

"Have I mentioned how glad I am that you managed to find such a badass-looking dog?" Jac stroked Selene's chest, triggering Selene's mouth to stretch into unconscious doggy pleasure. "I don't know why I didn't think of this. A dog is an excellent deterrent."

"Well, I'm not convinced a dog will deter Kevin Pike, but I do feel better with Luna around." Eve glanced at Selene, knowing she wasn't a huge fan of the name Eve had given her Rottweiler form. They'd both agreed that it was a nice little inside joke, though. "I'm really grateful that Selene was able to talk her friend into letting me borrow her."

Jac rolled her eyes. "At least Selene's good for something." She startled when Selene growled low in the back of her throat, then pulled her hand away and quickly stood. Glancing at Eve, Jac said, "You train her to do that?"

Eve gave Selene a mock glare that she hoped didn't betray her amusement at the situation. "Maybe Selene did."

"Nice." Jac took a step away, jamming her hands into her pockets. "So Kevin Pike is officially the most boring man on the face of the earth. One week watching his every move and we've got nothing. He likes to go into the city and hang out at coffee shops—one near the morgue, the other relatively close to your apartment. But so far he's done nothing to arouse suspicion. Certainly nothing we can pick him up on."

"You think he's gone dormant, or that he's made his tail?"

Grumbling, Jac said, "My guys aren't complete amateurs. I don't see how he could have made us so quickly."

"He's a smart guy. Meticulous." Eve pushed aside her paperwork, resting her hand on Selene's head. Bolstered by her quiet strength, Eve didn't let herself get swept away by the familiar fear that always rose when she thought back to her encounter with Kevin Pike. Five minutes beneath him hardly made her an expert, but she did feel as though she knew him through the way he left his crime scenes. "He's observant. I don't think it's a stretch to imagine that he might sense he's being watched. Maybe he's just generally paranoid."

"Or maybe he's not our guy." Jac sat on the corner of Eve's desk, eyeing Selene warily. "Look, the chief has given me a lot of leeway on this case. Putting department resources on a guy we *think* might be a serial killer because we got some anonymous tip with no real weight—"

"The tip was good," Eve said. She fingered one of Selene's thick, furry ears, hoping to soothe the frustration she could feel building at Jac's words. "Kevin Pike isn't careless. Building a case against him won't be easy. But nobody's perfect. We just have to wait for him to slip up."

Jac sighed. "Well, I hope we catch a break soon. I can't exactly tie up department resources forever when we have no real evidence pointing to this guy. I've combed through his background and haven't come up with anything suspicious. No criminal record, not even a parking ticket. To the casual observer, the guy looks thoroughly uninteresting. Cleaner than clean."

Eve heard the unspoken subtext in Jac's statement. "Maybe a little *too* clean."

"Maybe." Jac's face softened and she leaned in, lowering her voice. "I watched him the other day for almost ten hours. He didn't do anything suspicious, not one thing. Nothing about him suggests that he's our guy."

"You said he's completely bald, Jac. No eyebrows. Sounds like someone who doesn't want to leave forensic evidence behind."

"Baldness isn't a crime." Despite her attempt to play devil's advocate, the frustration in Jac's eyes signaled that deep down she also believed Kevin Pike was their killer. "Is it a little strange? Sure. Does he have plenty of other reasons to be hairless, besides being a serial killer? Absolutely."

Eve shook her head. "He's our guy. I know it."

"Honestly? I think so, too," Jac said quietly. "He may not have done anything wrong yet, but he *feels* wrong. Unfortunately, my gut isn't exactly admissible in court."

"Shame, that."

"Tell me about it." Jac hesitated, then touched Eve's shoulder. "Trust me, nothing makes me happier than the idea that Kevin Pike's our guy. I'd feel a lot better knowing that we've got eyes on our killer now. If we're watching him, he can't get to you."

Eve agreed, which led to her next request, spurred on by the impending full moon. All week she'd been brainstorming about how to elude her security detail long enough to help Selene through that night—without drawing any attention to her justifiably reclusive lover. "In that case, what do you think about lowering my security detail just a bit? As long as we know where Kevin Pike is, there's really no reason to watch me twenty-four hours a day. I'd rather you take protection off me than surveillance off him, if resources are a problem."

Jac's frown made it clear that the issue wasn't up for discussion. "No way. Your security stays. If he slips our watch, I don't want to have to worry about him getting to you."

Eve knew enough not to push her luck. She didn't want to arouse Jac's suspicion when Selene had such an important secret to keep. Insisting on doing something potentially foolish like shed her police protection when she was under threat of injury or death would almost certainly lead Jac to question her motives. "Okay," Eve said. "Just trying to spare the department's resources."

"I appreciate that, but protecting you is *not* where I choose to cut corners. Understand?"

"Understood."

"Good."

Wayne cleared his throat from across the lab. "I'm due in court in an hour, Dr. Thomas. Need anything from me before I go?"

Eve waved him away. "Nope. Drive safe. And good luck."

"Thanks." He gave her a searching look, as though trying to determine how she felt about him leaving her alone with Jac. Always the protector. "I'll see you later."

"Have fun, geek." Clearly pleased to see him go, Jac grinned and waved. "Try not to gross out the jury too badly."

"Can't make any promises," Wayne said as he walked to the lab door. "Call me if you need anything, Dr. Thomas."

"Thanks, Dr. Black. Bye." Eve turned her attention back to Jac, rolling her eyes at the satisfied expression she wore as Wayne left the room. Tapping Jac on the knee, Eve said, "Got anything else to report?"

"Not really." Jac's entire tone changed now that Wayne was gone. Warmer and more personal, she was being either flirty or simply affectionate. Eve couldn't tell which. "You want to grab some lunch? I'll buy."

Selene didn't have to growl again for Eve to sense her displeasure at the invitation. Apparently Selene had decided that Jac was flirting. Eve put on her best apologetic face. "I'm sorry, I've got so much paperwork to finish today. I was honestly just planning to eat at my desk."

"I could go grab us a couple sandwiches. We could eat at your desk together."

Without allowing her friendly tone to falter, Eve said, "That's really sweet, Jac, but can I take a rain check? Things have been so crazy lately that I've been letting things go here. I promised myself that today I'd play catch-up."

Obviously disappointed, Jac gave her a light pat on the knee. "Sure. I get it." She stood up, running a hand over her kinky hair. "You'll call me if you need anything?"

"Always." Truth was, now that Eve had Selene back—and more important, knew what she was capable of doing—she wasn't depending on Jac for support nearly as much as she had before. Jac cared about her, but when you had a supernatural force by your side, an all-too-human, albeit talented detective just didn't inspire the same confidence. "Thanks for stopping by. I appreciate the update."

"I'm sure you're right. He'll slip up sooner or later." Jac's tone conveyed weary experience. "They always do, right?"

"I hope so."

Jac tipped her head and strolled to the lab door. "I'll let you know as soon as anything changes."

"Thanks." As soon as Jac left the room, Eve glanced down at Selene. "Growling, huh?" Selene gazed at her with sad puppy-dog eyes. Laughing, Eve ruffled the fur on top of her head. "She just cares about me, that's all. She means well."

Selene yawned. She couldn't have looked more disinterested in the idea that Jac meant well if she'd tried.

Eve petted her again. "Hopefully someday you two can get along. Even if I don't trust Jac with my heart, I *do* trust her with my life. So you two have that in common."

Selene flopped back down on the pillow and sighed deeply. Eve exhaled, too, aware that a resolution to Jac and Selene's tensions wouldn't come that easily. Not when Jac badmouthed Selene on a regular basis, totally unaware that Selene was there to hear every harsh word.

"Someday, maybe. Later." At doggy-Selene's skeptical look, Eve said, "Much later."

CHAPTER THIRTY-THREE

Waking up on full-moon mornings was always the same. As soon as Selene came into awareness, a riot of sensation hit her full force, starting between her thighs and exploding outward. What had been merely a heightened libido when she went to sleep had evolved overnight into a painful ache so intense Selene groaned helplessly. All she knew was the need to fuck and be fucked.

On her first full-moon morning with Eve, who knew exactly what to expect and yet still slept beside her in the nude, the presence of a warm body pressed against Selene's introduced brand-new torment into an already-difficult morning ritual. The faint, light scent of Eve's pussy filled Selene's nostrils, so sweetly fragrant it made Selene's mouth water and her blood surge. She fisted her hands at her sides, all too aware that acting on her instincts was not an option.

After their frenzied coupling the last time Selene had been under the sway of the full moon, she'd sworn to herself that she wouldn't allow her need to overwhelm her sense of caution toward Eve. It didn't matter that Eve had gotten pleasure from their rough sex. Selene was stronger than normal on full-moon days and less connected to reality. That was a dangerous combination.

A warm hand landed on Selene's thigh. "Are you all right, darling?"

Selene rolled onto her side away from Eve, drawing her knees close to her chest. She closed her eyes and tried to control the trembling of her hands. Eve's soft touch had very nearly snapped her tenuous hold on her control. "It hurts," Selene moaned. Now that Eve knew everything, Selene didn't see any reason not to be honest. "I'm sorry."

Eve moved closer, making Selene quake at the gentle press of bare breasts against her back. "Let me help you."

"You shouldn't touch me." Selene had trouble forcing the words out. "I don't want to hurt you."

"You won't hurt me," Eve murmured, pulling on Selene's shoulder. "I trust you."

But Selene didn't trust herself. "Maybe I should touch myself first. Take the edge off."

"Don't be ridiculous." Eve tore the comforter off Selene's body, exposing her oversensitized skin to the cool air. "You're in pain. Let me try to ease it."

Selene moaned again and rolled onto her back. Her legs fell open and she dropped her hand to brush against her clit, wincing at pleasure so razor-sharp it hurt. Masturbation usually helped, but right now it was hard to concentrate on what she was doing. Selene gasped when Eve crawled between her legs and pushed her hand out of the way. Then she shouted hoarsely when the soft, wet heat of Eve's mouth covered her throbbing pussy, triggering an orgasm that spread instant relief to the tips of her toes.

"Oh," Selene cried out, tangling her hands in Eve's hair to keep her close. The slow, gentle motion of Eve's tongue against her labia kept her climax going, each contraction and wave of pleasure further lessening the pain of arousal. Staring down the length of her body into Eve's loving gaze, Selene tightened her fingers in Eve's hair, full of gratitude. "Just like that, darling. Don't stop."

Eve's eyes twinkled as she shook her head, swiping her tongue around Selene's clit. She didn't pull her mouth away to answer.

It took almost twenty minutes of Eve's ministrations before Selene felt capable of rational thought. Aware that they both needed a break, Selene tapped Eve on the shoulder. "Come here and kiss me."

Eve surged up the length of Selene's body, a fabulous grin on her face, and kissed her hard on the mouth. Selene wrapped one arm around Eve's back and slipped her other hand between Eve's thighs, pushing her fingers between Eve's slick folds. She angled a single finger inside Eve, then pressed her thumb against Eve's clit, rubbing fast circles. Without breaking their kiss, Selene quickly brought Eve to orgasm with a few practiced strokes of her hand.

Pulling away with a whimper, Eve dropped her forehead onto Selene's shoulder and squeezed her thighs closed. "Good morning."

"Morning." Selene put her arms around Eve, savoring the way their bodies fit together. "Thank you for that."

"Did it help?"

"You have no idea." Selene's desire hadn't disappeared but it had abated, allowing her to focus on the day ahead. This evening would be the ultimate test of their relationship. Selene wanted to be able to face it with as clear a mind as possible. "I could get used to having you around."

"I hope so." Eve lifted her head so she could stare into Selene's eyes. "You shouldn't have to suffer alone anymore."

Selene scratched her fingernails along Eve's bare sides, delighted by the shiver her touch caused. The love that poured from Eve flowed into Selene's chest, filling her up until she thought she might burst. She had never not been alone. The very notion that someone had her back brought tears to her eyes.

"How about I make us breakfast?" Eve murmured, stroking her knuckles over Selene's cheek. "We can talk about how we're going to sneak me past the detectives outside tonight."

Selene frowned. As much as she appreciated that Eve wanted to help her through the full moon, she didn't love the idea of helping Eve intentionally elude her protective detail while Kevin Pike was still walking around free. But she'd already agreed to let Eve tie her down— all she could do now was make tonight as safe as possible for Eve.

"Okay." Shifting beneath Eve's weight, Selene could already feel her ardor rising again. "Let me take a quick shower and I'll join you."

A cold shower and one self-induced orgasm later, Selene wrapped a robe around herself and shuffled to Eve's dining room. Until tonight's transformation, the effects of the moon would only get stronger. Last month she'd managed to stay away from Eve for most of the day, so this was the first time Eve would really see the extent of the moon's influence on her behavior. Embarrassed by the way it seemed to dumb her down and reduce her to base instinct, Selene avoided Eve's eyes as she sat at the table and tried not to squirm against the chair.

Eve set a plate of pancakes on the table in front of Selene, then handed her a bottle of syrup. "Are you hungry?"

Selene nodded vigorously. She picked up the bottle and squirted a large pool on her plate, then grabbed her fork and sawed at the stack of pancakes with its edge. Shoving a forkful into her mouth, she tried hard not to look as ravenous as she felt.

"Yummy?" Eve swallowed her own dainty bite, watching Selene shovel down her breakfast with obvious good humor. "Should I make more?"

Selene shook her head and swallowed her last bite. She could eat another stack, no doubt, but her real hunger took over at the sight of Eve's amusement. Her fork clanged against her plate as she set it down, clumsy with desire. Less than an hour had passed and already she wanted Eve again.

"I'm sorry," Selene whimpered, but Eve had already scooted her chair closer, undoing the sash of Selene's robe with a firm tug. Eve ran her hand over the hardened peak of Selene's naked breast, then lowered it between Selene's thighs.

"Spread your legs." Eve gave her a sympathetic kiss on the cheek.

"You don't have to do this again."

Eve laughed. "It's hardly a sacrifice. Now spread them."

Selene obeyed and Eve immediately rewarded her with the delicious sensation of two fingers sliding deep inside her pussy. Leaning back in the chair, Selene moved her hands to her own breasts, pinching and twisting her erect nipples as Eve set a fast, hard pace. The torrent of pleasure began almost instantly, building to a crescendo over the span of breathless minutes. Eve fucked her energetically, fingering her pussy in exactly the way Selene loved best. Selene contracted around Eve, coming again and again, until the dull roar inside her head had quieted to a manageable hum.

Wrapping her fingers around Eve's wrist, Selene stilled her with a quiet plea. Eve withdrew slowly, searching Selene's face. "Better?"

"Yeah." Sheepish, Selene brushed a lock of sweat-dampened hair from her face. "Sorry."

"No more apologies." Eve stood and gathered their plates, taking them into the kitchen. She raised her voice so Selene could hear her from the other room. "I love making you come, especially when I know it's literally bringing you relief."

Selene retied her robe. "That it is."

Eve returned to the dining room wearing a sexy expression. "There are worse gigs than being your full-time sex machine, trust me."

Snorting, Selene said, "If you say so."

"I do." Eve sat down at the table and exhaled. "So about tonight… if I want to leave my apartment without the detectives knowing, we'll need a distraction."

Clear-headed for the moment, Selene beamed as the perfect plan occurred to her. Since meeting Eve, she had been forced to start thinking about her unique skills in creative ways. It was so satisfying to solve problems that relied upon using her ability to hide in plain sight. After years of fearing her own nature, she finally saw its potential when it came to getting out of impossible situations.

"I know exactly how we can do it." Selene grabbed Eve's hand, appreciating the tether to her human concerns. "We just need to get the timing right. If we do, we're golden."

"Tell me more."

❖

They agreed that it was best to wait as long as they possibly could before escaping to Selene's house. The longer Eve was gone, the more likely someone would notice. Wanting to give Eve enough time to return to her apartment before dark, Selene planned for them to depart at six in the evening. That would let them sneak away from Eve's apartment unnoticed, travel to Selene's place, then go over the details of her monthly ritual. Selene didn't want Eve to linger outside of police protection any longer than necessary on the one night she couldn't protect her.

By a quarter to six, Selene had once again descended into the throes of agonizing, moon-induced desire. It seemed to peak every hour or so, and each time it did Eve sated her need passionately and without hesitation, conveying pure, unconditional love in every stroke of her fingers and tongue. The longer the day went on, the more primal their connection began to feel. In her lucid moments Selene was embarrassed by the instinctive, wholly physical state the moon had reduced her to, but she was also in awe of how Eve handled the situation. Instead of feeling reduced to some kind of sexual servant, Eve seemed to relish the opportunity to give Selene something no one ever had before.

That's why when Eve got on her knees in front of the couch and pushed Selene's thighs apart fifteen minutes before they had to walk out the door, Selene didn't tell Eve not to help or apologize for her body's betrayal. Instead she cradled the back of Eve's head and moaned as her hot tongue slid over Selene's puffy, hypersensitive labia. Eve's touch was the only thing that had ever eased the pain of the moon, and Selene surrendered to it with gratitude.

Eve lifted her face and stared at Selene's pussy, obviously entranced by its permanent state of wet, swollen arousal. "Oh, sweetheart, that does look painful."

Selene tightened her fingers in Eve's hair, moving her mouth back to where Selene needed it most. "Not when you suck it, darling." She shuddered as the first wave of pleasure rolled through her body, relaxing her muscles. Wrapping soft lips around Selene's impossibly distended clit, Eve milked her length with deliberate care. Grunting her approval, Selene pushed her hips into Eve's mouth greedily. "Good girl. That's so good."

Eve was beaming by the time Selene pushed her away. "It's probably best this only happens once a month, for both our sakes, but I'd be lying if I said I wasn't enjoying every second of it."

Laughing weakly, Selene struggled to her feet. This was the best full-moon day she'd ever had. "We'll see how you feel in a year or so."

Eve's bright giggle preceded a burst of warm happiness that hit Selene in the center of her chest. "Crazy, supernatural sex once a month? With orgasms we can both feel? I'm pretty sure that'll take more than a year to get old."

"That's a relief." Selene gave Eve a quick kiss. It was time to put their plan into action. This was as clear-headed as she would feel for the rest of the night, so they needed to move fast. "Ready to go?"

"Absolutely."

Selene handed Eve the backpack that held her clothing, as well as her keys and wallet. They'd decided that Selene would create a diversion, but that meant she needed to leave Eve's apartment naked. They would meet after Eve slipped away and made it around the block, then walk to Selene's car, which she'd parked out of sight nearly three blocks away. If all went as planned, they'd get to Selene's house with over an hour to spare before she changed. The cops watching Eve's apartment wouldn't even realize she'd left until she returned in Selene's car.

Selene had come up with this plan because she knew that Kevin Pike was being watched. If he did anything suspicious, if he approached Eve in any way, the police would arrest him. Allowing Eve to sneak away tonight was a risk, but a calculated one. And it was clearly important for reasons neither of them needed to vocalize.

Selene walked to the window that faced the street and opened it, glancing down at the black sedan parked at the curb. She couldn't see the detectives from this floor, so it was impossible to know how closely they were observing the situation. Playing it safe, Selene stepped away from the window and met Eve's excited gaze. "Okay. As soon as I fly out the window, I want you to leave your apartment. Don't forget to lock up. Go downstairs to the lobby but *don't* go outside until my signal."

"Which will be?"

"You'll know. My goal is to get the detectives looking at me so you can slip out the door and reach the end of the block without them noticing. Leave when you're confident that they're not paying attention to the front door."

"Okay." Eve nodded determinedly, tugging a dark hooded sweatshirt over her head. She completed her outfit by tucking her hair under a Giants baseball cap. The uncharacteristic clothing did the trick; at a glance, she looked nothing like her normal, immaculate self. "I'll meet you there."

"Yes." Selene pulled Eve into a quick hug, moaning helplessly at how good it felt to have her close. "I'll see you in a few minutes. Be careful."

Selene hated to let Eve out of her sight and only did so because she'd sense if Eve got into trouble. As long as she had her human consciousness, Selene was tuned in to Eve on a cosmic frequency. That would have to be enough.

Making sure she was out of the line of sight of the open window, Selene shifted into a small sparrow. She wouldn't be able to create much of a distraction in this form, but it was the best and sneakiest way to get down to street level. Glancing at Eve, Selene felt pleased rather than insecure at the slack-jawed look of wonder on Eve's face.

Eve had tried to explain just how mind-bending Selene's ability was, from a scientific standpoint—something to do with mass and the laws of physics—but Selene hadn't understood half of what she was saying. All Selene cared about was that Eve seemed genuinely excited about what she was. After both her parents and Carla accused her of being a monster, Eve's enthusiastic acceptance was beyond her wildest hopes and dreams.

Selene chirped at Eve, then flapped her wings to take off, soaring out the window to dive to the ground below. She tried to imagine Eve's movements inside the apartment building, desperate to get the timing right. Flying over to land on the banister outside the front entrance, Selene watched and waited for Eve's arrival in the lobby. They were lucky that Jac had agreed to remove the officers stationed inside now that the cops were watching Kevin Pike. Jac had made it clear that the officers would return if they lost track of Pike, but the slight loosening of security definitely made tonight easier to pull off.

Eve stepped off the elevator and walked to the front door. She stood beside the window, out of sight of the detectives on the street.

Satisfied by Eve's position, Selene flew across the street into an alley, landing behind a Dumpster so she could move to part two of her plan. She wanted to get the attention of the police officers without causing a panic, so doing something like unleashing a tiger in the middle of the city street was out. Likewise, she didn't want to become a creature they were likely to open fire on if they feared for their safety.

That's what made a bald eagle the perfect choice. Unusual enough that people didn't see them every day, such a spectacular bird was sure to capture the detectives' attention. And they sure as hell wouldn't decide to shoot at her even if she did startle them. Her second shift—from sparrow to eagle—required more effort than the first, and took her a little further away from her human self. But it was exhilarating to occupy the large body of the majestic bird.

Selene flapped her wings and rose into the air, swooping out of the alley and across the street to land on the hood of the black sedan. She watched the detective in the driver's seat spill his coffee on his lap, while his partner grabbed at his chest, going round-eyed with surprise. Extending her wings to their full width, Selene tipped back her head and cried out three times. It was her signal to Eve and also a wild, triumphant sound of unrestrained joy.

Never before had she voluntarily shifted on a full-moon day, and it was glorious. Nearly as good as sex. Hopping around on the hood of the car, Selene flapped her wings and jumped from side to side, glancing at the front of Eve's building. Now was the time for Eve to make her escape—her performance had completely enthralled the detectives. Eve could probably tap-dance down the street without them seeing.

When Eve slipped out the front door and skulked down the block, Selene launched into her grand finale. She lifted herself into the air, then came down hard on their windshield, drawing shouts from inside the car. The detective on the driver's side laid on the horn, startling Selene backward. She glanced down the block just in time to see Eve round the corner and disappear from sight.

Satisfied that she'd accomplished her mission, and wary of the attention she was drawing from onlookers gathered on the street, Selene pumped her wings and took off. She coasted over Eve's building to the place they'd agreed to meet. Landing in the narrow passage between two buildings, she pulled off yet another shift—this time into Luna the Rottweiler, Eve's canine protector. Selene trotted out onto the sidewalk, zeroing in on Eve's location immediately. Drawn to her partner's side, Selene tore down the street to meet her.

Eve greeted her with a gentle pat on the chest. "Good girl."

Selene walked close to Eve's side, hoping not to attract any attention with their failure to adhere to the leash law. Eve rested her hand on Selene's head, sending a wave of contented pleasure through her entire body.

"That was pretty impressive stuff back there," Eve murmured under her breath. She ruffled Selene's fur. "There's no way they saw me leave. Not with the show you put on."

Eve's cell phone buzzed inside her pocket. She pulled it out and glanced at the display. "Well, I guess we're about to find out." She answered with a casual, "This is Eve." Selene listened to the detective check in while attempting to explain the very unusual thing that had just happened. Eve did a perfect job of playing up fake surprise. "You're kidding me. I thought I heard a commotion down there, but I never would have guessed that." She listened, then laughed. "Well, good luck with that. Glad I'm safe up here and not at the mercy of a crazy bird. Okay. Bye."

Clicking off the phone, Eve murmured under her breath, "Don't you love it when a plan comes together?"

Selene whined in agreement. Her skin tingled with excitement and her animal brain threatened to take over as she struggled to pay attention to their surroundings. As difficult as it was to concentrate, she was now the last line of defense between Eve and Kevin Pike. Without the cops as backup, she needed to be at the top of her game.

Eve unlocked Selene's car as they approached, opening the driver's side door to allow Selene to jump inside first. They'd decided that Selene wouldn't change back into her human self until they reached her apartment—cutting down her risk of exposure as much as possible. Selene curled up on the passenger seat and exhaled deeply, trying to relax. Three shifts had her adrenaline pumping. She wanted to go home, get strapped down, and ride out the rest of the night in the safety of her apartment.

Clearly sensing Selene's unspoken urgency, Eve broke the speed limit on the drive back to Selene's house. As soon as they pulled up to the curb Eve threw the car into park, then opened the driver's side door quickly and let Selene jump out of the car behind her. They jogged across the street together, Eve leading the way. Selene circled Eve's feet excitedly as she unlocked the door, then dashed inside, shifting back into her human self as soon as Eve shut the door behind them.

The moment Selene returned to her body, hot lust surged through her veins. Thinking became impossible as the air molecules surrounding her tickled her skin like a thousand tongues lapping at her clit. Selene groaned in agony, zeroing in on the beautiful, fragrant form of her lover standing not five feet away.

Eve must have seen the struggle in her eyes. "It's okay, darling," she said, taking a step closer. "Do what you need to do."

Selene closed the distance between them and grabbed Eve's shoulders, walking her backward into the living room. One desperate, recurrent thought cut through the noise in her head. *Don't hurt her.* Frightened by her single-minded need, Selene spun Eve around, then bent her over the arm of the couch. Hands shaking, Selene unbuttoned and unzipped Eve's jeans, yanking them down around her ankles. Then she grasped the waist of Eve's panties in both hands and lowered the silky material to expose the firm, bare flesh of her ass.

Eve glanced back over her shoulder, meeting Selene's eyes. "I want you, Selene. Take me."

Emboldened by Eve's words, Selene used both hands to spread her open, whimpering at the sight of her slick pink pussy, the delicate pucker of her anus. Stepping forward, Selene pressed her center against Eve's soft warmth. She used her fingers to expose her distended clit, grunting as she rubbed and thrust herself against Eve in a mindless, animalistic pantomime of rear-entry sex. Once she settled into a satisfying rhythm, clit perfectly positioned against Eve's wetness, Selene reached beneath Eve's sweatshirt and cradled a hard-nippled breast in each hand.

"Pinch them," Eve gasped. Despite the lack of clitoral and internal stimulation from Selene's attentions, she sounded as though she was building toward a crescendo. "Twist my nipples. Don't be afraid to get rough."

Selene obeyed Eve on instinct, tugging and squeezing her nipples as she continued to drive her hips into Eve's bare bottom. Arching her back, Eve moaned loudly, then shook as an unmistakable orgasm tore through her body. Eve's climax sent Selene into screaming release, delivering white-hot pleasure to the tips of her toes. The more she came, the easier it became to think, until finally Selene collapsed onto Eve's back, exhausted but blessedly lucid.

Eve chuckled weakly, patting Selene's thigh. "Well, that was a new experience for me."

Embarrassed, Selene stood on shaky legs. "I'm sorry. I didn't mean to…" Selene cleared her throat, unsure how to label what she'd just done. Eve might have been willing to service her for the sake of keeping her comfortable and focused, but Selene worried that she'd crossed a line. Allowing Eve to use her fingers and tongue was one thing—degrading her was something else entirely. "Shifting got me really worked up. But I shouldn't have done that."

Eve rose to her feet, giving Selene a dazed laugh. "Are you kidding me? I just came from having my *nipples* touched."

"Yeah, well…" Selene pulled up Eve's pants, buttoning them clumsily. "I could have probably made that more comfortable for you."

"That was incredibly hot, Selene." Eve touched her face. "I'm pretty sure I had a fantasy along those lines once."

Selene managed a smile that felt a lot like a grimace. She could feel the late hour in her bones—soon she would be totally unsafe for Eve to be around. "It's getting close, darling. We need to go over the instructions now."

"Okay." Eve casually arranged her clothing as though she hadn't just been ridden senseless. "You seriously never fucked those call girls? I'm asking without judgment. It's just that I can't imagine how you could have held back when you felt like this."

"Honestly, you might be intensifying those feelings just a bit."

"Really?" Eve looked strangely flattered.

"Absolutely. And no, I never did anything with the escorts. Didn't want to get attached. But, believe me, it required a lot of willpower." Selene grabbed Eve's hand and led her to the guest bedroom, where her trusty steel table sat waiting. "Which is something I seem to lose when you're around."

"I'll take that as a compliment." Eve stroked her thumb over the side of Selene's hand, sending another orgasm rolling through Selene's body. At Selene's tormented groan, Eve murmured, "Sorry."

Shaking her head, Selene hopped up onto the steel table and lay down in the center. "I'm guessing I've got just over an hour before I change. We need to get started if you're going to be able to leave before dark."

Eve nodded solemnly. "Tell me what to do."

Having someone who knew the stakes was an entirely new experience. For the first time, Selene faced the prospect of her full-moon transformation with a sense of comfort. She had someone looking out for her interests. Someone she could trust. Someone who didn't want her to escape and would do whatever it took to ensure she wouldn't.

Selene had a partner in the truest sense of the word.

Nostrils flaring as her emotion rose, Selene gave Eve a tender, lingering kiss on the lips. It took everything she had not to deepen it. Drawing away, Selene whispered, "Just don't be afraid of hurting me, okay? You won't. I promise."

"I'm not afraid," Eve said bravely. And, indeed, she had no fear in her eyes. "*I* promise."

Selene wished she could say the same.

CHAPTER THIRTY-FOUR

The cops had been watching him for at least eleven days now, maybe longer. Kevin noticed them first while sitting at the coffee shop near Eve Thomas's apartment, two men in the dark sedan who sat parked nearby. They watched him without watching, obvious in the way law-enforcement types always seemed to be. They clearly underestimated his intelligence, because after he picked them out the first time, they were consistently easy to spot.

Kevin didn't let on that he knew. Since they'd already seen him visit the coffee shop, he continued his daily trips. He stuck to the habits that wouldn't incriminate him, not wanting a change in behavior to raise any alarm. It was better for him if they didn't know he realized they were watching. He figured if they thought he was ignorantly doing nothing wrong, maybe they would look elsewhere.

They had to have a reason for placing him under surveillance. But no matter how many times he retraced his movements and actions over the past couple of months, he couldn't figure out how they knew who he was. He'd given Eve his first name, but he couldn't imagine that would be enough to find him. He wasn't on anyone's radar. No criminal record, nothing to suggest anything off about him.

The timing was suspicious—he'd spotted his surveillance detail not long after that damn dog had chased him away from Eve's apartment. He hadn't left any evidence behind. He hadn't spotted any potential witnesses during his escape. Despite his failure to get to Eve, the mission hadn't been a total disaster. He'd gotten away without being seen.

But his head hadn't been right since that night, and he was starting to second-guess his instincts, maybe even his sanity. Because as angry as he was, he still didn't understand where his little dog had gone.

He remembered being enraged, knowing he would take it out on the dog, who ran under the bed and hid. And then the dog was gone. Disappeared.

Now the cops were tailing him. That meant he'd done *something* wrong, even if he couldn't figure out what. Maybe he was losing it— maybe he'd made a mistake with one of the bodies, or with that phone call to Eve Thomas. His present. The clue. He'd gotten cocky. Over-confident. Most regretfully, he'd become obsessed.

He was positive he wasn't leaving behind any usable evidence at his scenes or on his victims. His biggest risks were when he attempted contact with Eve. That's when he bent his self-imposed rules, the basic tenets to which he'd sworn to adhere lest he be caught. Be smart about forensic science. Don't make hair evidence available, so shave your head, eyebrows, and body. Don't take trophies. Don't stash evidence. Use a new weapon every time. Above all else, don't do anything stupid. Act from the brain and not the heart.

With Eve he'd thrown not being stupid out the window. When he'd imagined this game before it started, he fantasized about leaving a trail of victims behind him, perpetually unknown, slipping out of the shadows only to kill before disappearing into them once again. As soon as he attacked Eve the morning of his first kill, he'd changed the game. He'd allowed his desire to inflict fear and pain on Dr. Eve Thomas to overwhelm his sense of caution and his intelligence.

Not anymore.

Kevin didn't plan on getting caught. Tonight two detectives were parked outside his apartment building, but tomorrow was a new day. He'd leave tonight, go somewhere else. Do what he loved to do but make it about himself next time—not about some goddamn best-selling author/forensic pathologist. Just about him and the women he chose, the ritual, the pleasure it gave him.

He'd get back to the basics.

Just as soon as he finished here.

Kevin couldn't just leave Eve Thomas without some kind of closure. He wasn't suicidal—going after Eve directly was no longer an option. It was too dangerous when the cops had their eye on both of them. So his original endgame was, tragically, aborted.

But that didn't mean he couldn't still pull off a closing move with a flourish.

A couple of days before he discovered the cops' presence, Kevin had been doing his own surveillance of Eve's block, noting the comings and goings at her apartment. To his surprise, her old friend showed up. Selene, according to the mail he'd intercepted one day at her house. Kevin had written off their relationship as over after their shouting match a couple of weeks prior, but it appeared that they'd rekindled something. Selene had entered the apartment in the morning and still hadn't emerged by the time he packed in his surveillance.

Unfortunately Kevin hadn't been able to monitor Eve at all since making his tail, but he suspected that Selene was still important enough to Eve that her murder would be devastating. If he was lucky, Selene might be home alone in her apartment tonight. Even if she wasn't, he should be able to break in and lie in wait. When Eve went to work tomorrow morning and Selene returned home, Kevin would deliver his parting shot. He'd give Eve something to remember him by.

Then he would disappear. He would win.

This Plan was even better than his original—this way he wouldn't kill Eve. He would destroy her spirit, but let her body live. A new concept for him, admittedly, but he appreciated the poetic nature of this ending. Never-ending torment for Eve Thomas. Because of him.

And who knew? Maybe he'd come back for her someday.

CHAPTER THIRTY-FIVE

All day Eve told herself she'd keep her promise and leave Selene before dark. She wanted to prove that she was worthy of Selene's trust. The best way to do that was to follow Selene's instructions exactly. This monthly ritual was something Selene had perfected over time. Years of experience had taught her what needed to happen to keep everyone safe. Yet when the moment came and Selene told her to go home, Eve couldn't.

Seeing Selene strapped down, writhing in pain as nightfall approached, made walking away easier to say than to do. She understood why Selene didn't want her to witness the transformation, but after the day they'd just spent—building a primal connection Eve could feel in her bones—she couldn't bear to abandon Selene to the torment of the moon.

She wanted to stay. To help, somehow.

"No. You agreed to go." The panic in Selene's voice tore at her heart. "It's time. Go!"

Tears welled in Eve's eyes and she didn't try to hide them. She knew Selene could feel her anguish. "I hate seeing you like this. I don't want to leave you alone."

Selene gritted her teeth and her face turned red. "Listen to me. In about fifteen minutes, I won't know who you are. You won't be safe around me."

"You won't hurt me." Eve had no idea where she got her confidence as far as that statement went, but she believed it to the bottom of her soul. Especially after today, having shared what felt at times like some kind of primitive mating and bonding ritual, Eve just couldn't imagine Selene causing her harm. "Maybe my presence will help with the transformation, too. Like it did today, with the arousal."

Shaking her head furiously, Selene squeezed her eyes shut against the tears that had started to fall. "You promised me, Eve. Don't break your promise."

"But I just—"

"We can talk about it tomorrow." Selene opened her eyes, which were so haunted Eve shivered as soon as they fixed upon her own. "I can't protect you tonight—not even from myself. And I need to know you're safe. This will be so much easier for me if I know you're out of danger."

It was clear she wouldn't be able to talk Selene into letting her stay. Going back on her promise could damage their relationship irreparably. No matter how intensely they connected, their relationship was still new. Eve expected Selene to be honest with her, so she needed to demonstrate loyalty and honesty in return.

"Okay," Eve said. She swiped the tears from her face quickly, putting on a brave front. "I'm sorry. I just love you. This is so…hard."

Selene's eyes had gone wild. She was slipping further and further away. "Love you. Now go."

With a teary nod, Eve bent and kissed Selene on her damp cheek, then turned and walked swiftly out of the guest room. She shut the door behind her, then put the key to the cuffs in her pocket as Selene had instructed. She walked to Selene's living room, glancing out the window at the darkening sky. According to Selene, the transformation would happen any minute now. Eve hoped tonight would go as planned, and that Selene would be safe until she returned in the morning.

Eve's cell phone rang inside her backpack, which still sat where she'd dropped it just inside the front door. Heart pounding, she rushed across the room to unzip the bag and dig the phone out. Praying she wouldn't see Jac's name on her caller ID, Eve feared someone had discovered her absence. When she checked her phone and confirmed that Jac was calling, she exhaled and answered the phone in as casual a voice as she could manage.

"Hey, Jac. What's up?"

"You're not home. That's what's up." Jac sounded like she was trying hard to keep her tone neutral, which meant she was very angry. Eve wouldn't have expected anything less. "I'm standing in your living room and you're not here. So where the hell are you?"

"I'm coming home now."

"That's not what I asked. What possessed you to sneak away from your protective detail?"

An agonized, guttural shriek rattled the walls around Eve, cutting off her reply. Eve whipped around, zeroing in on the closed guest room door. Her stomach flip-flopped uneasily—Selene's transformation must be under way.

"Eve! Are you okay?"

The alarm in Jac's voice brought Eve back to their conversation. "I'm fine." The growing commotion within the guest room sent Eve scurrying to the front door, afraid that Jac would overhear the growling, groaning, and plaintive, agonized wail. Each sound of distress unleashed an answering wave of pain within her own body. "I'm sorry, it's just the television."

"Are you at Selene's house? Tell me and I'll send someone to get you."

Eve's stomach leapt into her throat. "That won't be necessary. I told you, I'm coming home right now. I'll be there in fifteen minutes. There's no reason to worry."

"Did Selene convince you to do this? What reason did she give you for why you should put yourself at risk?" Jac no longer tried to hide her fury. "Doesn't she care about you at *all*?"

"Hey," Eve said sharply. "It's not like that. Stop making assumptions, calm down, and we'll talk about this when I get back. It's not a big deal. Unless you've neglected to tell me that Kevin Pike is in the wind."

Jac grumbled under her breath. "According to my guys, he went up to his apartment two hours ago and turned out the lights. No movement since then."

"Taking a nap, maybe?" Despite her rattled nerves, Eve forced a light chuckle. "Explain to me why you're so freaked out again?"

"Because I don't want anything to happen to you. Because it's not like you to do something this stupid."

Eve realized that the noise from the guest room had suddenly ceased, leaving Selene's house almost unnaturally quiet. Just as she wondered whether she should be worried, a piercing howl arose from behind the door, so mournful it sent chills down Eve's spine.

"Television again?" There was no humor in Jac's voice.

Eve snatched up her backpack, zipping it closed, then slinging it over her shoulder. She needed to leave now. Jac knew where she was, and Eve had already overstayed her welcome. She was skating dangerously close to exposing Selene's secret, which was a risk she couldn't take. Eve was pretty sure Jac didn't believe in the supernatural, and if she was confronted by evidence of its existence, her reaction would *not* be good.

"It may not be like me to do stupid things, but *I* did this. Me. I decided to get away for an hour because I wanted some privacy. It is what it is, and I'm sorry. We'll talk about it when I get home. Okay?"

Sighing, Jac said, "Fine."

Eve picked up Selene's house keys and threw open the front door. Her terse good-bye to Jac died in her throat. Standing on the porch was a man whose face she'd never seen before, yet she recognized him immediately.

Kevin Pike.

Eve quickly stepped back and moved to close the door, but he shouldered his way inside, shoving her backward hard enough to knock her to the floor. Her cell phone clattered out of her hands and skidded across the hallway, coming to rest beneath a small end table.

For a terrifying instant she couldn't breathe. Couldn't open her mouth, couldn't force out sound. Then her lungs started working and she screamed, "Jac!"

Kevin kicked the door shut and launched himself on top of her, hitting her hard across the face with his fist. Stunned into momentary silence, she moaned in pain as he scrambled over to the cell phone and disconnected it. He shoved it into his pants pocket and clambered back onto her body, pinning her down before she could gather her wits and try to escape.

"I wasn't expecting to find you here." His pupils were so dilated they made his eyes look black. Sweat beaded on his forehead. The expression on his face was a curious mix of fear and arousal. "I came for your girlfriend. She was going to be my final gift to you."

"She's not here," Eve said. Even as the lie rolled off her tongue, a growl from the guest room raised the hairs on the back of Eve's neck.

Kevin glanced sharply at the closed door, then back at Eve. "Is that your new dog? I saw you walking her right before I discovered the police watching me."

"Yes, that's my dog." Eve's heart hammered in her chest. It would take Jac at least fifteen minutes to get here, assuming traffic was moving. Kevin Pike might not keep her alive that long, especially when he knew someone had heard his entrance. "Please don't hurt her."

"What good is having a protection dog if you're just going to leave it locked in a room?" Amusement transformed his face into something almost human. "I mean, it's a little tragic to be murdered right after you've put away your only weapon. Stupid bitch."

Kevin's words sparked Eve's memory. She'd shoved the gun Jac had insisted she carry into her backpack before she left her apartment. Though she hadn't honestly imagined that Kevin would escape his surveillance detail and come after her on the one night she was unprotected, Eve had liked the reassurance the gun provided. Not that it was doing her much good, hidden in a backpack that lay facing away from her, just out of reach.

A vicious snarl erupted from the guest room, then a series of increasingly frustrated howls. Selene could sense she was in danger. Even now, with Selene's mind completely divorced from its human sensibilities, their connection remained. The emotion coming from Selene was raw and disjointed, difficult to discern. But Eve knew that she was enraged. As Eve's terror grew, the noises from the guest room rose in volume.

"What the hell's wrong with your dog?" Confusion passed across Kevin's face and he met her eyes for the first time, really studying her. "What *is* it with you and dogs? Every time I get close to you there's some fucking dog to chase me away."

"I like dogs." Eve fought not to let her gaze stray to her backpack, not wanting Kevin to anticipate her next move. "The police are on their way. You should leave now if you don't want to get caught."

Kevin laughed. "Stick to forensic pathology, Doc. Your psychology needs a bit of refinement." Sitting up slightly, Kevin reached behind his back and withdrew a large, wickedly sharp-looking knife. "I wasn't expecting to get close to you again. I'm not losing this opportunity. Not after everything we've been through."

Eve's stomach churned. He spoke of her almost fondly, as though they had a relationship he truly valued. "You're going to kill me? Is *that* your endgame? I thought this was about getting the better of me."

"Oh, I'll get the better of you." Kevin stroked the back of his hand across her cheek, tenderly. "Trust me, when the cops find you, they'll know who won our little game." He dropped his hand to her throat, paralyzing her with the fear that he would cut off her air supply, then touched her breast through her shirt. "When I came to see you last time, I'd intended to rape you and cut your face up. Pity I don't have the time or the prophylactic to do that tonight."

Eve's stomach dropped into her feet when he raised the knife, positioning the edge of the blade against her cheek. "Please," she whispered.

"Well, the raping part at least." He drew the blade down her cheek in a quick, brutal slice, splitting open her skin with searing precision. Eve winced as hot blood oozed from the wound and ran down her face. That would leave a scar.

An absolutely savage roar shook the walls around them, pulling Kevin's attention away just long enough for Eve to drive her fist into his neck. Choking, he brought his hands reflexively to his throat. Eve shoved against his chest as hard as she could, scrambling out from beneath him as he fell to the side.

She crawled to her backpack and unzipped it, thrusting her hand into the bottom in a mad search for the gun. Just as her fingers brushed against the cool metal, Kevin grabbed her legs and yanked her toward him. She lost her grip on the gun with a defeated whimper, swearing in frustration when Kevin surged up over her to shove the backpack farther away.

Rolling over beneath him, Eve kicked out wildly, first striking his shin, then landing a solid blow between his legs. He gasped and rolled away, holding himself protectively. Taking advantage of his momentary lapse, Eve leapt to her feet and ran toward the guest room. Going for the gun hadn't worked the first time, so Eve abandoned that plan in favor of going straight to her most deadly weapon—a pissed-off, fiercely protective werewolf.

Or at least that's what Eve hoped she'd find behind that door. Deep in her heart she believed that Selene would recognize her even in her changed state, but that didn't stop a slight trill of apprehension from crawling down Eve's spine. Selene was making noises unlike anything Eve had ever heard before. Vicious, throaty growls of murderous intent.

Still, Eve would rather take her chances with full-moon Selene than with Kevin Pike.

Taking a deep breath, Eve opened the guest room door, then quickly closed it behind her. The door didn't lock from the inside—Selene probably figured there wasn't much use for that—so shutting it could only slow down Kevin briefly. But every second counted, especially when Eve thought about just how tightly she'd tied Selene.

At the sound of her entrance, the hulking creature strapped to the table lifted its head and stared at her with malevolent green eyes. Eve's hands went numb at the sight of her lover, now wholly unrecognizable—larger than any wolf on earth, but distinctly canid and devoid of any humanity. Her silver fur caught the low light, gleaming, as she bared her impossibly sharp fangs in a classic aggressive snarl.

There was no sign of recognition in Selene's eyes, yet Eve still felt their connection in her gut. Selene was reacting to Eve's fear and pain—even if Eve couldn't *see* Selene in there, she could feel her. Running to the table, Eve looked deeply into cold green eyes as she dug the keys to Selene's cuffs out of her pocket.

"I know you're in there, Selene," Eve murmured. "I trust you. You will *not* hurt me, okay? I'm going to untie you, because I need you right now—"

The guest room door banged open and Eve jumped, nearly dropping the keys to Selene's cuffs. Refusing to get distracted, she fumbled to unlock the first cuff around Selene's wrist. Already she knew she would never have time to unlock the other three, let alone untie the rope that held Selene down, but she refused to give up until the last possible second.

"What the *fuck* is that?"

Eve glanced up at the terror in Kevin's voice, just in time to watch him bring her gun up and aim at Selene. Releasing her wrist, Eve jumped out of the way when Selene swung her massive arm through the air, trying to use her new leverage to break free. The loud crack of gunfire pulled a scream from Eve's throat, which turned into a sob when she saw a vivid bloom of red stain the silver fur on Selene's chest.

"No!" Unconcerned with her own safety, Eve ran at Kevin Pike and tackled him around the middle. They fell backward into the hallway even as another shot rang out. Eve drew back her fist and threw a punch at Kevin's throat, but narrowly missed when he moved his head to the side. Her hand slammed uselessly against the hard tile floor, sending breathtaking agony rocketing through her body. He took advantage of her pain by rolling them over so he was on top.

"You're one crazy fucking bitch." Kevin wrapped his hands around her throat, squeezing hard. Apparently he was done messing around—no more toying with her, no more drawing things out. The end was here. "I don't know what the fuck is up with you and your freaky animal friends, but I'm done. *You're* done."

Eve opened her mouth to call out to Selene, but couldn't draw in enough air to do more than whimper. She kicked out a foot, knocking weakly against the guest room door frame. It was getting more difficult to fight back without oxygen—her perception became distorted in the strangest way. A terrible groan filled her ears, then a blood-chilling howl of rage from Selene.

At last, all of the pressure around her throat eased and Eve could breathe again. Drawing in a lungful of cool, sweet air, Eve sat up clumsily, ready to move. She scanned her surroundings, assessing the situation, then went still when she spotted Kevin's body just inside the guest room. He stared sightlessly at the ceiling, body convulsing as blood poured from the savage gouge in his throat. An impossibly large wolf loomed over him on all fours, its silver fur standing on end in a line down its back.

"Selene!"

At Eve's exclamation the wolf turned its head and fixed its stare on her face. Selene, Eve reminded herself. That wolf is *Selene*. Forcing her way past her instinctive caution, Eve extended her hand to the wolf and met her eyes. "Selene, I'm safe now. Everything is okay."

Lips still drawn back in a snarl, Selene took a step away from Kevin's dead body. Then she slowly relaxed her face, transforming from ferocious beast to majestic creature in a heartbeat. Lowering her head and gazing up into Eve's eyes, looking almost submissive, Selene trotted over to Eve and bumped her head against Eve's chest.

Eve inhaled sharply at the unmistakably affectionate gesture. "You saved my life." She lifted a careful hand, running her fingers through the thick fur covering Selene's broad skull. "Thank you. I love you."

Selene lifted her head and brushed her face against Eve's. Then a large, warm tongue lapped gently at the blood that covered Eve's face from the slice Kevin had made. Eve could feel Selene's concern and lingering anger, even in this primal state.

"Jac will be here any second," Eve said softly. "We need to hide you until after I deal with the police. Do you understand? The body is in the guest room, so I'll need you to stay in the bedroom." Eve had no idea how she'd explain the rope and the table to Jac, but knew that moving the body somewhere else wasn't a good idea. It would be obvious if she tried to cover anything up, and Eve knew Jac's suspicion would fall on Selene.

Selene whined and rested a large paw on Eve's thigh. It was obvious she wanted to stay close.

"I know, darling. As soon as I can get Jac to leave, I need to look at your wound." She touched the bullet hole in Selene's chest, wincing at the blood that oozed from the opening onto her fingers. "I'll try to make it quick."

As though triggered by her words, Selene's front door crashed open. The sound of rapidly approaching footsteps raised Selene's hackles and she leapt in front of Eve, assuming a protective stance. Eve got to her knees and called out, "Jac? Stay where you are."

She didn't really expect Jac to do as she asked, so it wasn't a surprise when Jac careened around the corner into the hallway. Her gun was in her hands and instantly she had it trained on Selene. "Eve, get away from it. I'll handle this."

Selene exposed her fangs and grumbled low in her throat. She took a step closer to Jac, clearly unafraid of the gun. Eve could see Jac's fingers tighten on the gun and her stomach bottomed out at the imminent violence that threatened to explode between the two people she cared about most. "Jac, put your gun down. Just give me a few minutes to get her into the bedroom and we can talk. Kevin Pike is dead. The wolf saved me."

Jac's eyes narrowed and she licked her lips, adjusting her aim. "That's not a wolf. It's a goddamn monster."

Selene crouched and went still, ears held back against her head. She was getting ready to pounce, which would almost certainly draw gunfire. Terrified that the situation could turn deadly at any moment, Eve's mouth went dry when Selene crept slightly closer to Jac. She could see the instant Jac decided to fire her weapon and immediately opened her mouth. "Selene, no! She came to help." Frantic, she met Jac's eyes. "That's Selene, Jac. I promise to explain, but just don't shoot her. She saved my life."

Darting her gaze between Eve and Selene, Jac hesitated, then lowered her gun. Selene didn't back down, drawing another step closer. Jac took a nervous step backward. "Call it off, Eve. You don't want me to shoot it, it needs to back the fuck up."

"Selene!" Eve spoke in a firm tone. "Come here *now*."

Selene froze in place, then turned around, dropping her head as she trotted back to Eve. When she got there she sat at Eve's side, tall enough that her head easily came even with Eve's shoulder. At the end of the hallway, Jac's mouth was agape.

"You can't be serious," Jac said. "About that thing being Selene."

"I'm dead serious." Eve rested her hand on Selene's back, stroking her fur gently. Selene leaned against her, nearly causing her to lose her balance. "Tonight is the full moon."

"You've got to be shitting me."

Eve shook her head then gestured at the massive creature at her side. "Do you have a more reasonable explanation for this?"

Jac swallowed. "You're bleeding pretty badly. Who cut you?"

"Kevin Pike. Selene killed him to protect me." Eve pointed at the room behind them. "He's in there."

Exhaling, Jac waved Eve away. "Go. They're sending cars here right now. Get her hidden before this place is crawling with cops. And make sure she *stays* hidden." Jac lifted a trembling hand, patting her hair nervously. "Once they're gone, you and I are going to have a long, serious talk."

"Okay." Despite her obvious unease about Selene, Eve knew Jac would do everything she could to protect her secret tonight, if only because she could see how important it was to Eve. "Thank you, Jac."

"Don't thank me yet. Just go."

"Come on, Selene." Eve turned and jogged down the hallway, relieved when Selene followed without paying further attention to Jac. She led Selene to the master bedroom, ushering her inside as the sound of police sirens rose from outside. Then Eve shut the door behind them, completely and utterly exhausted. Selene stalked around the room, sniffing a trail along the floor. "You need to be very quiet, understand me?"

Selene cocked her head to the side, then took a running leap and jumped onto the bed, which creaked under her weight. Fat droplets of blood splashed onto the comforter, compelling Eve forward to snap her fingers and point to the floor. "Off."

Obeying immediately, Selene crossed the room to sit attentively on the rug at her feet. Eve had to laugh. After all Selene's concern that her full-moon wolf incarnation was a murderous, bloodthirsty beast, she really seemed quite docile. When she wasn't in protection mode, at least. Eve theorized that her sheep-slaying had been the hard-wired instinct of a wild, juvenile wolf and not an indicator of purely evil intent.

"I need to look at your wound," Eve said, getting on her knees in front of Selene's massive body. Confident now, she felt around in Selene's thick fur, only slightly tentative about how she might react to pain. Despite Selene's size and obvious disconnect from humanity, Eve felt as safe as ever in her presence. Moving around Selene to inspect her back, she exhaled in relief. "There's an exit wound. It went clean through."

That was a good sign—so was the fact that Selene didn't act like she was in pain. Also that the bleeding had already slowed to a trickle. Eve sensed that she would recover from her wound without issue, but she needed to clean the area to make sure it didn't get infected. Dressing it properly would be a challenge.

Eve went into the bathroom to find clean towels and disinfectant. She also found some gauze pads and tape, which would have to do. Shaking her head as she started cleaning Selene's blood-soaked fur with a wet washcloth, Eve murmured, "You're never going to believe this when you wake up tomorrow, darling. But if you're in there right now, then listen to me—you are *not* a monster. You're my hero. Okay?"

Selene flinched as Eve dabbed disinfectant on her wound, growling low in the back of her throat. But she stayed perfectly still, lowering her head in submission.

Overcome with warm affection, Eve threw her arms around the wolf's neck and buried her face in silky silver fur. "I love you, Selene."

There was no response, of course—at least not in words.

CHAPTER THIRTY-SIX

Eve stayed in Selene's bedroom for at least an hour and a half, listening to the sounds of police officers and technicians wandering through the house. It felt strange to hide away while the scene was documented and the body prepared for transport to the morgue, but Eve was confident that Jac had offered a reasonable explanation for her absence. Probably trauma, of which she'd suffered plenty.

Selene snored loudly next to her. She'd fallen asleep at the foot of the mattress almost immediately after Eve bandaged her wound. Curled into a tight ball, her massive body still took up most of the bed. Eve stroked her absentmindedly, grateful for her presence. Despite seeing Kevin Pike's corpse with her own eyes, Eve remained on edge, as though he might burst through the bedroom door at any moment.

When Jac finally knocked on the door shortly after the house went quiet, the sudden noise made her jerk in surprise. Selene picked her head up and blinked sleepily at the door, but when Jac said, "It's me. Jac," Selene sighed and fell back against the bed, already closing her eyes again.

"I'll be right there." Eve untangled herself from Selene, lifting an enormous paw from her thigh and gently laying it on the mattress. Selene cracked open her eyes and Eve flashed her palm, hoping she would understand. "Stay here, Selene. I'm just going to talk to Jac for a few minutes."

But when Eve walked to the door, Selene jumped off the bed and followed close behind. Eve raised an eyebrow at her but didn't say anything. She had a feeling this was an argument she couldn't win.

Jac took an instinctive step back when Eve opened the door with Selene at her side. She lifted her hand, stopping short of touching Eve's cheek. "Evie, your face."

"Oh." Eve brought her fingertips to her jawline, wincing at the tacky, drying blood that she'd forgotten to wash away. Now that she'd had time to catch her breath, her injured hand was beginning to throb as well. She had been so concerned with Selene's injury—and so worried about what Jac would do with Selene's secret—that her own aches and pains had taken a backseat, until now. "I was so busy tending to Selene's bullet wound that I forgot all about it."

Reluctantly dropping her gaze to Selene for the first time, Jac said, "Is she all right?"

"She will be. The bullet went through her."

"She doesn't need to go to the hospital?"

"I don't think so." Eve touched Selene's back, careful to avoid the newly cleaned exit wound. "We'll see what happens when she becomes human again, but she seems really strong."

"That's good." Jac cleared her throat and gestured at Eve's face. "I think you'll need stitches. Why don't you leave Selene here and I'll take you to the hospital?"

No way was she leaving Selene tonight—Eve sensed she was the only thing keeping Selene inside the house. Even with her injured hand, she should be able to handle her own care. "That won't be necessary. I'll just find a needle and thread and sew it up myself."

Jac gave her a familiar look of uneasy admiration, something she usually reserved for when Eve made incredible forensic leaps based on evidence Jac found disgusting. "You're hardcore, Eve Thomas. Don't ever let anyone tell you otherwise."

"I'm not feeling all that hardcore at the moment. Just tired."

Glancing quickly at Selene, Jac slowly reached out to take Eve's hand. "Let me help you clean up your face. Then you can play Frankenstein with yourself."

Pleased that Selene accepted Jac's friendly contact without even a growl, Eve let Jac pull her into the guest bathroom. She settled against the counter as Jac wet a washcloth with warm water, then gently dabbed at her face. Tensing when Eve hissed in discomfort, Jac said, "He really did a number on you."

"He hit me a few times, cut me, then finally tried to choke me. That's when Selene got loose."

Snorting, Jac said, "Bet he never knew what hit him."

Warmed at the reluctant affection in Jac's voice, Eve said, "Timing is everything. I can't believe he came after Selene tonight, of all nights. How did he slip past the detectives, anyway?"

Jac tightened her jaw, clearly upset. "Pike must have known they were watching him. I guess he went upstairs to his apartment, turned out the lights, and the detectives assumed he went to sleep. Instead he broke into a neighboring apartment and climbed down a rope at the back of the building. We're assuming he took a cab into the city."

Eve had no idea what had compelled Kevin Pike to choose tonight to make such a bold move, but the consequences of his decision were staggering. Not only did he sign his own death warrant, but he had enabled Eve to discover that Selene wasn't half the mindless, murderous beast she thought she was. And, of course, he'd exposed Selene to Jac, at the very least.

Shaking her head, Eve murmured, "I guess he tried to get into my apartment two weeks ago. Said he'd planned to rape me and cut my face. Apparently he came here tonight looking for Selene, but when he found me instead—" Eve waved a hand at her cheek. "I guess I'm lucky he didn't bring a condom this time."

Jac's face darkened as she continued to wipe away the dried blood. "If Selene hadn't killed him, I would have."

Pushing back a wave of revulsion at the thought of all the ways the night could have ended badly, Eve took a deep breath and focused on the fact that she was safe. "So that night two weeks ago, that was when I called down after two in the morning to tell your detectives there was a barking dog in my hallway."

"Yeah, I remember."

"Well, turns out that was Selene. She'd been sneaking into my building to guard my door and just happened to be there when he broke in that night—using the roof-access door. After she chased him away, she was able to follow him home. That's how she knew who he was."

Jac's hand slowed as comprehension spread across her face. "So this isn't strictly a full-moon thing?"

"She…" Eve glanced at Selene, wishing she had her permission to share her secrets. Not that it mattered much in this instance—Jac already knew the worst of it, and if Eve was going to ask her to keep it a secret, she figured Jac deserved the truth. "She's a shape-shifter, I guess. She can become whatever animal she wants. Normally she retains her human consciousness no matter what form she takes, but not when the moon's full. It forces her to transform into this wolf, and she doesn't remember anything the next day. She's convinced that she's a killer on these nights, so she's always spent them strapped to a steel table."

Jac chuckled. "Well, that explains the setup in the guest room." Raising an eyebrow, she pulled the bloodstained washcloth away from Eve's face. "I told the responding officers that Selene's probably into kinky sex."

Blushing, Eve checked her face in the mirror. She definitely needed stitches, and antiseptic. "Last month, when I thought she was cheating on me? She had a standing appointment with an escort service to have someone come out on the evening of the full moon and tie her down. Then they'd leave and come back in the morning to release her. That's why she lied to me about being out of town. That's who the blonde at her door was."

"So it was all just a big misunderstanding."

"She didn't feel she could tell me the truth." Eve turned to Jac, aware that Selene sat in the bathroom doorway listening. She knew Selene wouldn't remember any of this conversation tomorrow, but it was still strange to have this discussion in front of her. "Believe it or not, her first couple of experiences with having people find out what she is didn't go well."

"Not surprising." Jac tossed the washcloth aside, glancing back to regard Selene, who watched her with intense green eyes. "Well, the hardest part about covering this up will be trying to explain what exactly killed Kevin Pike. Call me crazy, but I don't think Wayne—or whoever examines his body—will believe you used a knife to make the wound that killed him. Seemed pretty obvious to me that his throat had been torn out."

Eve shivered. She had no idea how Selene would react to the news that she had finally done what she most dreaded. Whether or not she'd been acting in self-defense—to protect Eve—Selene had killed a human being. And she'd never remember doing it. "I'll say that I had Luna the Rottweiler here with me. She came to my defense when Kevin broke in." A trained forensic pathologist would no doubt determine that the creature that had caused Kevin Pike's wounds was larger than a Rottweiler, but no one would assume she was covering something up. Hopefully the medical examiner would accept her story and not probe too deeply. "That's the best I have to offer. Hopefully it'll be accepted without too much scrutiny."

"Luna the—" Jac laughed and shook her head. "Oh, no. That was Selene, too, wasn't it?"

"Yup."

"Dude, she ate *dog biscuits*. I fed her dog biscuits!"

"She didn't want to be rude and not accept them."

This set Jac off on a long, loud fit of laughter. Eve joined in, grateful for the moment of levity. Jac's ability to find humor in the situation reassured her that everything would be okay. Finally sobering, Jac said, "Damn, I sure wasn't shy about talking smack to her face, was I?"

"It's not like you knew she could hear what you were saying."

Jac sighed deeply, running her hand over her hair. She regarded Selene, who lay stretched out in front of the door, with wary eyes. "How long will she stay like that?"

"Until tomorrow morning, I guess. Probably sunrise?" Eve stepped out of the bathroom and led Jac to the living room. Selene followed. "I'll sew up my face in a few minutes. Why don't we sit down?"

As soon as Eve entered the living room she drew the blinds, ensuring that nobody would be able to see inside. More than twice the size of a normal wolf, Selene wouldn't be mistaken for a family pet. It was bad enough that Jac knew the truth—Eve wanted to contain the night's damage as much as possible.

Jac slowly lowered herself onto a high-backed leather chair, while Eve sat at one end of the couch. Selene jumped up to stretch out along the rest of it, laying her head on Eve's lap.

Seemingly unable to tear her eyes away from wolf-Selene, Jac said, "You really want to let it get on the furniture?"

"Considering that *she's* the one who paid for the furniture, I'm not sure it's my place to tell her no." Eve sighed and collapsed against the cushions. "You can't tell anyone about this, Jac. Seriously. She's spent her whole life hiding and finally trusted me enough to share this secret. If I end up being responsible for her loss of freedom and anonymity, I'll never forgive myself."

Jac shook her head, searching Eve's face. "Tell me the truth. Do you think she's dangerous?"

Selene chose that moment to stretch out her front paws and yawn loudly, then she released a contented sigh and nuzzled farther into Eve's lap. Snorting, Eve said, "Do *you*?"

"Maybe not now, but when I first got here—"

"She had *just* stopped Kevin Pike from choking me to death. Adrenaline was flowing, for everyone." Eve gave Jac a pointed look. "You *were* aiming a gun at her, remember?"

"Fair enough." Sniffing, Jac looked around Selene's living room as though she could no longer sustain eye contact. "You know Selene isn't my favorite person, but she did save your life tonight. And your feelings for her—well, let's just say it's pretty obvious that I won't exactly win you back by doing something to hurt Selene. So…"

"Thank you, Jac." After the night she'd had, Eve couldn't stop the tears from spilling onto her cheeks at Jac's reassurance. Selene picked up her head and stared into Eve's face, and if Eve didn't know better, she'd think Selene was experiencing a lucid moment. Stroking Selene's head, Eve said, "I know Selene will be grateful, too."

"That doesn't mean I won't be keeping my eye on her." Clearing her throat, Jac stood up and straightened her clothing. "I know this relationship matters to you, so I promise to try and get to know Selene better, but I'm telling you right now…if she hurts you, she's answering to me."

"I wouldn't expect anything less."

"Okay." With a determined nod, Jac approached the couch and held out her arms. "Now stand up and give me a hug. If you don't think Fido will mind."

Eve maneuvered her way from beneath Selene's body and got to her feet, moving into Jac's embrace with a grateful sigh. "You're a good friend." She could feel Jac's sadness at the statement—not literally, but she knew Jac well enough to know that the sentiment triggered genuine regret.

"Go sew up your face. I'll check in with you two tomorrow and get your official statement."

"Sounds good." Eve brushed her lips against Jac's cheek before withdrawing. "I owe you one."

Jac shook her head. "Nah. *Selene* owes me." When Eve cocked her head curiously, Jac said, "Obviously we could put her special talents to good use in certain investigative situations. If something comes up—"

"Well, that's between you and Selene." After spending a lifetime denying her gift, Selene might not be ready to use it for solving crimes on a regular basis. Then again, she *did* seem to have a natural talent for surveillance and tracking. "Give her some time to adjust to the fact that somebody else knows, especially somebody she isn't acquainted with all that well."

"Sure." Jac gave her a toothy grin. "I'll see you two tomorrow."

Eve saw her out, sighing in relief when she and Selene were alone again. After she addressed her wounds, Eve planned to get some rest. Tomorrow would be an interesting day.

CHAPTER THIRTY-SEVEN

Selene startled awake, opening her eyes to stare at a painted white ceiling. Eve's familiar warmth at her side provided a strange juxtaposition with the moon hangover that left her feeling slightly disconnected from reality. Her whole body ached. She was naked. Turning her head to the side, she exhaled shakily as she processed what it meant that she was in bed with Eve and not lashed to the steel table in her guest room. Confusion turned to horror when Eve rolled over to reveal a battered face and bruised neck. Selene gasped out loud at the long, ugly slice across Eve's cheek held together by small, neat stitches.

Sitting up quickly, Selene threw the covers off Eve's pajama-clad body and scanned her for further injuries. Last night she would have been capable of tremendous violence. If Eve had gotten away with only a few cuts and bruises, they were both lucky. But why Eve had stayed after being attacked was beyond Selene's comprehension.

"You didn't do this." Suddenly wide-awake, Eve sat and grasped Selene's arm, staring into her eyes. "Don't panic. This wasn't you."

That didn't exactly make Selene feel better. But it did stop her hyperventilation, which had threatened to send her into an emotional tailspin that would no doubt end in an uncontrolled shift. That was the last thing she wanted after the night she imagined they'd just had. "What happened? Did I get loose?"

"In a manner of speaking." Eve patted the mattress beside her, projecting a calm strength that brought Selene's tumultuous mood further under control. "Kevin Pike came here looking for you right as I was getting ready to leave. He…had intended to murder you, to punish me, I guess. He pushed his way inside and we struggled, and at one point I managed to break free and run into the guest room. I started to undo your cuffs but could only release one of your arms before he shot you. So then I tackled him and he started choking me. That's when you broke free. Right in time to save me."

Selene swallowed hard. On the one hand she was thrilled that her beast-self had acted instinctively to protect Eve, especially when Eve had trusted her enough to intentionally try to set her free. But on the other, she had a sense that Eve had witnessed unchecked brutality last night. It must have been a horrific sight, what she had undoubtedly done to the man who was hurting the woman she loved. Yet Eve still slept beside her, perhaps even when she'd been her beast-self. "Did I kill him?"

"Yes," Eve said plainly. "I don't think you had much choice. He was about to kill me. He'd already shot you. You acted in self-defense, to protect me, and you have no reason to feel ashamed about any of it."

Truthfully, Selene didn't feel half as guilty as she'd have expected. Maybe it'd hit her later. Right now she was just relieved that her beast-self had been cognizant enough of their connection to protect Eve—not harm her. Selene scanned Eve's body again, less frantically this time. Besides the wicked cut on her cheek, her throat was covered with finger-shaped bruises, the skin below one eye was swollen and purple, and her right hand was bandaged.

"I didn't do *any* of that?" Selene met Eve's eyes. "You swear?"

"That was all Kevin, trust me." A small smile broke across Eve's battered face, seemingly genuine. "Darling, you've seriously misjudged yourself. Last night you were a giant, fiercely protective wolf-puppy who followed me everywhere I went."

Selene blushed at the characterization, strangely embarrassed that what she'd always assumed to be a ferocious, murderous creature was really so docile. It seemed too good to be true. "I don't believe you."

"Well…" Eve's good humor faltered and she exhaled, clearly nervous about what she was about to say. "Ask Jac. She can confirm that the only time you were anything close to threatening was when you thought I was in danger."

Selene's knees buckled at Eve's comment and she finally accepted the unspoken invitation to get back in bed. Dropping her head into her hands, Selene closed her eyes, wishing she could remember what exactly had happened. "Jac saw me?"

"She realized I wasn't at my apartment and called to check on me just as I was leaving. We were actually on the phone when I opened the door and found Kevin Pike on your front porch. She heard him attack me and rushed right over, naturally. By the time she got here you'd already taken care of Pike, but I hadn't gotten the chance to hide you yet. So she walked in and found us in the hallway outside the guest room."

It was a good thing Selene was already sitting down. "She's lucky I didn't kill her. To walk in right after something like that—"

Eve wrapped an arm around Selene's middle, pulling her close. "We had a bit of a standoff when Jac pointed her gun at you and you felt threatened, but I was able to de-escalate things. Unfortunately, that required telling Jac that the giant wolf was actually you. And that you'd saved my life."

Burying her face in Eve's neck, Selene closed her eyes. The idea that Jac knew her secret—Jac, who flatly didn't like her and who had every reason in the world to want her out of Eve's life—made Selene's stomach churn. Already she was mentally packing her bags, picking up and leaving San Francisco behind. Maybe Eve would come with her. She didn't know how she could go otherwise.

Eve pressed her uninjured hand between Selene's shoulders, holding her close. "Stop panicking. Jac won't tell anyone. She and I had a serious talk, and I can promise you that. Your secret is safe."

"Why? Jac hates me. Why would she agree to cover up something like this?"

"Because she knows that telling anyone would end our friendship." Drawing back, Eve caressed Selene's face tenderly. "She knows what you mean to me, and that you're the only reason I'm alive right now."

Selene blinked away the emotion that rose at Eve's solemn words. Never had she imagined her beast-self doing something heroic. In the past twenty-four hours her worldview had changed completely. After years of honoring the same paranoid routine, terrified of what might happen if she made even one mistake, now Selene no longer had to fear the worst. And she didn't have to face the future alone.

"I don't know what to say," Selene said quietly. "I'm in uncharted territory now."

"Isn't it wonderful?"

She didn't have to think about that one. "Yes."

Eve pressed a soft kiss to her temple. "Let me check your wounds. I tried to clean them and dress them as much as possible last night, but the fur complicated things."

Chuckling, Selene pulled back and glanced down at her chest. "I'll bet." The gauze and tape that covered a small area right above her breast was clearly the result of a makeshift patch job. She peeled away the dressing, curious what she would find beneath. The wound had nearly healed over, leaving only a small, angry pink mark. "Oh, that doesn't look too bad."

Eve's jaw dropped open. She grabbed Selene's shoulder and tugged her forward, then peeled another bandage away from her back. "That's unbelievable," Eve murmured. "You were *shot* last night. Entry and exit wound. Today it looks like you got a couple of severe paper cuts, maybe."

Selene shrugged, both sheepish and proud of Eve's awestruck reaction. "I heal fast."

"That's an understatement." Touching her face, clearly self-conscious, Eve said, "Wish I could say the same. I'm pretty sure he left me with a nice scar."

"Doesn't make you any less beautiful."

Eve raised her injured hand, frowning at the bandages. "And unfortunately, my dominant hand is out of commission for a while."

"Shame. We'll work around that, I promise." Selene very carefully put her arms around Eve and hugged her as tight as she dared. "But otherwise you're okay?"

"I'm okay. Kevin Pike is dead, our Golden Gate Park killer case is closed, and I'm lying in bed with the woman I love." Eve gave Selene a playful pinch on the hip, guiding them back against the pillows and pulling the comforter over their entwined bodies. "I've got to be honest, I'm *more* than okay."

"And we're okay?"

"We're perfect." Licking gently at Selene's lower lip, Eve said, "Well, except for the fact that I'm too beat up to make love to you this morning."

Selene shook her head. "Honestly, there's nothing I'd rather do right now than this right here. Just holding you, loving you."

"Good. Me, too." After a brief hesitation, Eve said, "I should warn you that Jac is coming over later. She needs to get my statement about last night, about how Luna the Rottweiler attacked Kevin Pike after he broke into my girlfriend's house."

"Jac, huh?" Selene could think of better ways to spend her afternoon, but she supposed that she couldn't possibly avoid Jac for the rest of her life. Now that their relationship had just become immeasurably more intimate, she would probably be wise to get off on a better foot sooner rather than later. "Super."

"Who knows? Maybe one day you two will be friends. Heck, maybe even work together."

Selene could tell from the buoyant lilt of Eve's voice, as well as the cautious, nervous energy spilling from her every pore, that her curious desire was more than just idle hope. Clearly Jac had her own ideas about where this circle of trust left them. "We'll see."

"In the meantime, you've got all morning to kiss my bumps and bruises away." Eve wiggled out of her T-shirt and tossed it onto the floor. She pointed at the smooth slope of her bare breast with a shy smile. "You can start right here."

Obedient and eager, Selene didn't waste any time doing exactly as Eve asked. "Yes, ma'am."

About the Author

Born in a suburb of Detroit, Michigan, Meghan O'Brien relocated to a small town about an hour north of San Francisco in 2005. As a relatively recent transplant, she's enjoying the moderate weather and gorgeous scenery of the Bay Area. Meghan lives with her partner Angie, their young son, three cats, and two dogs. Yes, it can be just as chaotic as it sounds. In her free time (HA!), she enjoys playing video games, spending time with friends, and exploring the beautiful place where she lives.

Meghan works as a Web developer by day, but her real passion is writing.

Books Available From Bold Strokes Books

Wild by Meghan O'Brien. Shapeshifter Selene Rhodes dreads the full moon and the loss of control it brings, but when she rescues forensic pathologist Eve Thomas from a vicious attack by a masked man, she discovers she isn't the scariest monster in San Francisco. (978-1-60282-227-6)

Reluctant Hope by Erin Dutton. Cancer survivor Addison Hunt knows she can't offer any guarantees, in love or in life, and after experiencing a loss of her own, Brooke Donahue isn't willing to risk her heart. (978-1-60282-228-3)

Conquest by Ronica Black. When Mary Brunelle stumbles into the arms of Jude Jaeger, a gorgeous dominatrix at a private nightclub, she is smitten, but she soon finds out Jude is her professor, and Professor Jaeger doesn't date her students...or her conquests. (978-1-60282-229-0)

The Affair of the Porcelain Dog by Jess Faraday. What darkness stalks the London streets at night? Ira Adler, present plaything of crime lord Cain Goddard, will soon find out. (978-1-60282-230-6)

365 Days by K.E. Payne. Life sucks when you're seventeen years old and confused about your sexuality, and the girl of your dreams doesn't even know you exist. Then in walks sexy new emo girl, Hannah Harrison. Clemmie Atkins has exactly 365 days to discover herself, and she's going to have a blast doing it! (978-1-60282-540-6)

Darkness Embraced by Winter Pennington. Surrounded by harsh vampire politics and secret ambitions, Epiphany learns that an old enemy is plotting treason against the woman she once loved, and to save all she holds dear, she must embrace and form an alliance with the dark. (978-1-60282-221-4)

78 Keys by Kristin Marra. When the cosmic powers choose Devorah Rosten to be their next gladiator, she must use her unique skills to try to save her lover, herself, and even humankind. (978-1-60282-222-1)

Playing Passion's Game by Lesley Davis. Trent Williams's only passion in life is gaming—until Juliet Sullivan makes her realize that love can be a whole different game to play. (978-1-60282-223-8)

Retirement Plan by Martha Miller. A modern morality tale of justice, retribution, and women who refuse to be politely invisible. (978-1-60282-224-5)

Who Dat Whodunnit by Greg Herren. Popular New Orleans detective Scotty Bradley investigates the murder of a dethroned beauty queen to clear the name of his pro football–playing cousin. (978-1-60282-225-2)

The Company He Keeps by Dale Chase. A riotously erotic collection of stories set in the sexually repressed and therefore sexually rampant Victorian era. (978-1-60282-226-9)

Cursebusters! by Julie Smith. Budding-psychic Reeno is the most accomplished teenage burglar in California, but one tiny screw-up and poof!—she's sentenced to Bad Girl School. And that isn't even her worst problem. Her sister Haley's dying of an illness no one can diagnose, and now she can't even help. (978-1-60282-559-8)

True Confessions by PJ Trebelhorn. Lynn Patrick finally has a chance with the only woman she's ever loved, her lifelong friend Jessica Greenfield, but Jessie is still tormented by an abusive past. (978-1-60282-216-0)

Ghosts of Winter by Rebecca S. Buck. Can Ros Wynne, who has lost everything she thought defined her, find her true life—and her true love—surrounded by the lingering history of the once-grand Winter Manor? (978-1-60282-219-1)

Blood Hunt by L.L. Raand. In the second Midnight Hunters Novel, Detective Jody Gates, heir to a powerful Vampire clan, forges an uneasy alliance with Sylvan, the Wolf Were Alpha, to battle a shadow army of humans and rogue Weres, while fighting her growing hunger for human reporter Becca Land. (978-1-60282-209-2)